ASK ME
NO
QUESTIONS

ASK ME
NO
QUESTIONS

Patricia Veryan

ST. MARTIN'S PRESS • NEW YORK

ASK ME NO QUESTIONS. Copyright © 1993 by Patricia Veryan. All rights reserved. Printed in the United States of America. No part of this book may be used or reproduced in any manner whatsoever without written permission except in the case of brief quotations embodied in critical articles or reviews. For information, address St. Martin's Press, 175 Fifth Avenue, New York, N.Y. 10010.

Design by Judith A. Stagnitto

Library of Congress Cataloging-in-Publication Data

Veryan, Patricia.
    Ask me no questions / Patricia Veryan.
        p.   cm.
    ISBN 0-312-08699-7
    I. Title.
PS3572.E766A94   1993
813'.54—dc20   92-41836
                                                    CIP

First Edition: April 1993

10 9 8 7 6 5 4 3 2 1

Ask me no questions,
and I'll tell you no fibs.

—Oliver Goldsmith
"She Stoops to Conquer"

ASK ME
NO
QUESTIONS

ENGLAND, 1748

PROLOGUE

INCIDENT IN LONDON

ne o'the clock of a fine Friday morning! And all—ll's well!"

The watchman's singsong proclamation went largely unheard, and at this point in his rounds he had little need of his lantern. Tonight, my lord Geoffrey Boudreaux gave a ball to celebrate the christening of his infant great-grandnephew, Master Trevelyan Jonathan Boothe, and Boudreaux House on Grosvenor Square was ablaze with light. The flambeaux on each side of the entrance cast their flickering brilliance on the eager faces of the small crowd that lingered to see the late arrivals and a few early departures. And, because of the warmth of this July night, many windows were open, allowing the pleasant sounds of music, talk, and laughter to be heard.

Special constables kept the common folk clear of the red carpet that led from the kennel to the steps of the mansion while, in a steady stream, luxurious coaches came and went, receiving or disgorging the noble and the famous, and a few of the infamous, of London's Society.

Preparing to step into the street so as to pass by, the watchman slowed his stride and for a moment joined those gazing into the windows. He could catch glimpses of the immaculately bewigged heads and rich coats of the gentlemen, the colourful silks and satins of the ladies' wide-hooped skirts; of feathers tossing in high-piled coiffures, jewels sparkling, and fans being plied vigorously. "Ain't no wonder!" he muttered. "Must be fair sweltering in there."

"Wish you was sweltering with 'em, don'tcha, mate?" enquired a voice in his ear, and a fat man with a perspiring face leered at him mockingly.

"No, I don't, if you wants ter know it," he answered. "Ain't me place, nor I wouldn't—"

From one of the upper windows a piercing shriek rang out so charged with terror that the watching crowd was struck dumb.

"Hey!" interrupted the fat man, pressing closer against the railing of the area-way. "Hey! What's afoot?"

Even as the watchman jerked his head around, he was conscious of a difference in the festive sounds. The music had stopped. The laughter was dying away and the chatter took on a note of alarm.

A youthfully ambitious special constable started up the steps. Making a recovery the watchman cried, "Stand aside for the Watch! Move aside there!"

Abashed, the young constable stepped back, but brightened when the watchman thrust out his lantern together with an admonition to "Hold this here!"

The watchman was admitted to the mansion by a scared-looking lackey. It was very apparent that consternation reigned inside, and the curiosity of those outside increased when a lackey and a footman emerged and went off at the run.

"Gorn ter fetch a Runner from Bow Street," said the special constable knowledgeably.

The fat man nodded. "Must be bad, then. Here," he added, his voice eager, "you don't never think there's been a murder done?"

Several of those listening uttered shocked gasps at this

remark, but the constable put an end to such gruesome suppositions. Murders, he said, did not take place at the homes of fine gentlemen such as Lord Boudreaux.

In less than half an hour a coach clattered up the street and the footman alighted. He was accompanied by a tall, sombrely clad man with a solemn expression who carried a short baton surmounted by a crown. This symbol of Bow Street confirmed the opinion expressed by the young constable and earned him several admiring glances, bringing a gratified smile to his face.

The footman and the man from Bow Street went swiftly into the mansion and the doors were closed, leaving the titillated crowd to engage in ever more lurid conjecture as to the nature of the crime the officer of the law would discover.

That gentleman, who made himself known as Mr. Warkin, was conducted to a luxurious second-floor bedchamber and presented to the occupants. Mrs. Letitia Boothe, a slender young matron, was seated on a chaise longue, weeping softly and being comforted by her husband, Mr. Snowden Boothe. The watchman was talking earnestly with Lord Geoffrey Boudreaux. The elderly aristocrat's fine-boned scholarly face was pale and ravaged by the shock of what had taken place in his home, but he greeted the Runner with quiet courtesy. On the floor, a sheet had been spread over a human form, and Mr. Warkin went in grave silence to remove the sheet and stare grimly at the lifeless woman it had covered.

"A proper bit of the devil's work," he muttered. "Shocking that such things should happen in England. Shocking! I'll own, melord, as I'd hoped your footman was mistook and that the unfortunate female had survived." He drew out notebook and pencil. "With all respect, I shall have to take down statements, sirs and ma'am." He glanced to the watchman who was waiting in wide-eyed silence. "I hope you've made sure that nobody won't leave these premises?"

Lord Boudreaux interpolated, "I have requested that my guests remain for a while. As for questions, the watchman has already taken statements from us all. This dreadful brutality has come as a great shock to Mrs. Boothe, and she is in no state to endure more questions tonight. Mr. Boothe and I will be only too glad to cooperate with you, however."

There could be no doubt that Mrs. Boothe was deeply grieved. Her gentle face was streaked with tears, and as she went out on her husband's arm she told the Runner in a broken voice that the dead girl had been her abigail for several years and that she had been very fond of "dear Meg."

Mr. Warkin prowled about the room, read the watchman's notes, and questioned Lord Boudreaux briefly. He then left the watchman to guard the dead woman, and accompanied his lordship to a ground floor study. When Snowden Boothe joined them there he found the Runner seated at the desk writing busily in his notebook, and Boudreaux, looking rather weary, watching him from the sofa.

"I'm glad as you could come, Mr. Boothe," said the Bow Street Runner. "I've writ down details as given, and will now read them aloud. If you can add to 'em, I'll be grateful."

Boothe nodded and crossed to stand beside the sofa.

Mr. Warkin coughed behind his hand and began:

"Victim of murder most foul: Margaret Potter, spinster, aged six and thirty, personal maid or abigail to Mrs. Snowden Boothe. No known enemies or unsavoury acquaintances. On evening of Friday, July 12th, a ball was given at Boudreaux House, Grosvenor Square, in honour of birth of son to Mr. and Mrs. Snowden Boothe, the lady being grandniece of Lord Geoffrey Boudreaux. Victim, or murderee, was in employer's bedchamber. She failed to go downstairs for supper, and upon being sought for was found shortly after one o'clock in the morning in a expired condition, having been struck on head with great force. Murder weapon, some heavy object, not found on premises." He looked up. "Correct up to now, gentlemen?"

"So it would appear." His lordship frowned and remarked heavily, "Jove, but it fairly chills the blood to think that even the lowest criminal could do so cruel and pointless a thing!"

"It does indeed," said Boothe. "And how strangers could have got in here, with the house full of people, baffles me."

"Very right, sir," the Runner agreed approvingly. "Unless they was—(a) admitted by someone, possibly Miss Potter. Or—(b)—" he paused, leaned forward and uttered in a dramatic fashion, "—they were *not* strangers!"

Boothe stared at him.

Lord Boudreaux said coldly, "I am perfectly sure that poor Meg Potter had nothing to do with such rogues. She was a most superior woman."

"As for the guests," put in Boothe, "one or two of 'em have been knocked into horse-nails from time to time, I grant you. But there was no one here tonight so purse-pinched as to have robbed his host and carelessly murdered an innocent servant. I think it more likely that the thieves were alarmed when Meg surprised them, and struck harder than they intended."

Mr. Warkin pursed his lips. "Possible, sir. But it's also possible as they done *just* what they intended. The rewards they thought was worth the risks, and—"

Leaning forward, Lord Boudreaux interrupted intensely, "And now you have come to the most puzzling aspect of this horrible business. Their reward was trivial!"

Boothe said, "Well you may look surprised, Mr. Warkin! But it is so. My wife's jewel case contained among other articles a very fine diamond necklace, a superb ruby brooch, and a large emerald pendant. All of which were left. The thieves took instead a single strand of pearls, a gold bangle, and an antique ring."

"Curious, melord," the Runner acknowledged. "Most extreme curious. Unless . . . What about that housemaid who screamed? Might she perhaps have driven 'em off before they had the chance to take the lot?"

Boothe said, "The girl who found Meg fainted. We were attempting to revive the housemaid when she came to her senses and screamed."

"Then they'd already made off. Clear and no hindrance," muttered the Runner thoughtfully. "With a small haul when they'd had time and opportunity to snatch a big'un."

"Which makes the taking of an innocent life seem even more savage and pointless," said Boothe in disgust.

"I doubt they considered it pointless," said Lord Boudreaux. "They wanted no witness left to describe them to the authorities."

Boothe argued, "Yet it seems such a fearful risk to take, sir. Had they committed the robbery alone they'd have had a chance of transportation were they caught. But why invite the hue and cry that will result from so brutal a murder? And certain execution? They'd have done better to have gambled that Meg wouldn't be able to describe them accurately."

"Ah, but she might have," said Mr. Warkin. " 'Specially if they was known to her. This way, they'd be sure. Still, I'm bound to agree that having brought the stain of murder to blacken their immortal souls, you'd think as they'd have took enough to justify such wickedness. The question being—why didn't they?" He chewed on the end of his pencil for a minute, then said, "No answer popping into me nob, or tibby, I must ask another question of you gents. Which is, was there anything unusual about the items or objects took? Any carvings or precious gems on that bangle, for instance, as might make it easier to trace?"

Lord Boudreaux said rather testily, "The watchman asked that same question. According to my grandniece the bangle was of good quality, but not remarkable in any way."

With a despondent look the Runner said, "Unfortunate. Most unfortunate. "You said there was a old ring took, I think? A family heirloom, Mr. Boothe?"

"Possibly. But not of our family. A friend of my wife wore the ring to a ball a year or two ago. My wife admired it, and her friend made her a present of it. I'll own that I wasn't much taken with the ring myself, but I understand it is of great antiquity."

"Hmmn. I expect Mrs. Boothe can give me a description of it."

"That won't be necessary," said Boothe. "I can tell you. The ring is of gold, fashioned in the shape of a dragon with rubies for eyes."

This piece of information dispelled the gloom from Mr. Warkin's countenance. He licked the end of his pencil and had recourse to his notebook once more. "Very interesting," he muttered. "*Very.* Also stole, one . . . old . . . dragon ring. With red . . . eyes."

Lord Boudreaux's lip curled. "Solved the case for you, has it?"

The Runner gave him a reproving look. "That there ring will be the undoing of them vicious murderers. Mark my words, gentlemen. A pearl necklace is like any other pearl necklace. And gold bangles—well, they ain't so rare. But a dragon ring! No one what sees that ain't going to ferget it! We've got 'em now! When that there ring is fenced—we've got 'em!"

"Provided," said Snowden Boothe dubiously, "they intend to fence it."

"God bless my soul, sir," exclaimed the Runner, opening his eyes very wide. "Them murdering villins mean to get rich by their crimes, I promise you. What other reason would they have for taking Mrs. Boothe's valuables?"

His face sombre, Lord Boudreaux muttered, "What, indeed?"

INCIDENT IN SUSSEX

Few people were abroad at this hour, especially on the rutted and pot-holed lane that wound through the Ashdown Forest. There was no moon, and a change in the weather had brought a chill wind that moaned fitfully, sometimes flailing the branches and awakening a mighty chattering of leaves, and sometimes fading to so hushed a stillness that it was as if the forest held its breath. It was a night to make a man hold his breath also, and listen for something, though he knew not what. A night fit only for ghosts and goblins, whereby honest men scurried for home and set a good solid bar across the door.

And it was just the kind of night Bill Wiggins liked. Taking care not to crush the two pheasants securely tied under his coat, he scaled the manor wall and plunged into the forest with not a qualm for ghost nor goblin. A sturdy and practical man, with little interest in matters of the occult, his every thought was for how pleased Mattie would be, and the children. The birds were plump and would feed them for a week, maybe.

Something wet and cold was carried on a powerful gust to splash onto his cheek, and he grinned up into the impenetrable blackness and started to hum to himself. Better and better. No keepers would brave the gloom of the forest in wind and rain, and in a half hour or less he'd be home and safe from the threat of capture, prison, and the hangman's rope, or maybe the doubtful mercy of transportation. "No conies tonight, Mattie me love," he muttered exultantly. *"Pheasant, old lady!"*

The wind slept again, the immediate smothering silence having such an uncanny quality that, despite his confidence, Bill paused, then moved to the side of the rutted lane. Just in case.

His heart gave a lurch when he saw a faint glow off to his right. There wasn't no cottage over that way. Shouldn't oughta be no light, neither. He stood very still, staring, then crept closer. If it was a trap, if they was laying for him, better to know, 'fore he blundered into something.

The wind roared in renewed blusterings, and the light came and went with the tossing of branches and shrubs. He was close enough now to hear the stamp and snorting of nervous horses. The source of the glow became visible. "Cor," whispered Bill.

He had come upon a clearing wherein a fine carriage stood. The four spirited horses were fretful because of the storm, and a coachman at the heads of the leaders was trying to calm them. If there was a footman behind, or on the box, he was out of sight. And if there wasn't no footman . . . 'Aha! A woman's in this, I shouldn't wonder,' thought Bill, who harboured a streak of romance under his phlegmatic exterior. 'Some young Buck's come to meet his light o' love on the sly, and she's—'

Hooves were coming up behind him. With a gasp of fright he leapt for the screen of a holly bush and crouched low, praying he'd not been silhouetted against the glow of the waiting carriage's lamps.

A moment later wheels rumbled within a yard of him and went on past to pull up closer to Bill than to the other carriage. The coachman swung down from the box to open the door, and a gentleman descended: a tall man, his cape drawn tightly about him and his tricorne pulled low.

"Put out the lamps, fool," he growled, and stamped over to climb inside the first carriage.

From within, another voice, sharp and harsh, commanded, "Coachman, wait by my friend's carriage. And do not come back until he leaves me."

The door slammed shut. The lamps on both vehicles were extinguished.

Bill heard heavy footsteps drawing near, and a man grunted, "Perishing night."

"Makes yer wonder," said the other coachman, keeping his voice low, "what could be so blistering important as to bring them two fine gents into this 'ere godforsaken wood."

"Don't make *me* wonder, mate. I don't *see* nuthink, I don't 'ear nuthink, and I don't never *wonder* 'bout nuthink. Them as wonders, mate, them's dead 'fore they've time ter spit. So me, mate, I don't.''

'Cor!' thought Bill Wiggins again, and with the next gust of wind prudent poacher and plump pheasants melted into the night.

Unlike the sagacious coachman, however, Bill did wonder. He had evidently stumbled upon a secret meeting. They'd been gents, no doubt of that, and from what the coachman had said, mighty dangerous gents. 'Up to no good,' thought Bill. Lucky for him he hadn't been a few minutes earlier, else he might've been caught when the first coach arrived, and likely he wouldn't be here now, with his two fine pheasants. It was a rum business. He decided not to tell Mattie about it. A good soul was Mattie, but she was a woman, and he'd never met a woman yet who could hold her tongue. He hastened his steps. She'd had a long wait, and Mattie fair hated waiting.

In the clearing he had just left, one of the gentleman in the darkened coach was of a similar frame of mind. "You must know, Emerald," said he in a cold and authoritative voice, "that I do not care to be kept waiting."

The big man seated opposite responded curtly, "Nor do I care for clandestine rendezvous."

"Do you not? You would have preferred perchance that we chat over a card table? At Brookses? Or the Cocoa Tree? Don't be foolish, Rudi!"

"No names, damme!"

"I'faith, but one might suppose your nerve to be failing. And so early in the game. Calm yourself, dear boy. Who can overhear in this desolation?"

"Never make the mistake of doubting my nerve, Squire." There was a note of menace to the deep voice. "Nor of becoming complacent. The slightest relaxation of vigilance could become habit. It needs but one slip, and we all would wear a hempen cravat."

A soft laugh. "Very true, my dear. I accept the reproof. Still, we have made excellent progress, you must allow. We hold all but three of our—er, prizes. The training program goes well, and our cargoes have been most gratifying." Waiting for a comment, he received none and frowned slightly into the darkness. "Well? You signalled for a meeting. I'll have your report, an you please." A pause, and he said sharply, "For God's sake speak up, man! There are only owls to spy on us."

"I could wish that were so. I fear, however, that I am spied upon by more than owls."

"The devil! Do you say you have allowed yourself to be identified as a member of our League?"

The response was immediate and angry. "That would be counted a major error, eh, Squire? And we are permitted but one. Think well before you condemn me. I'll not suffer the punishment you mete out to others, and so I warn you."

The Squire's voice now was very gentle. "But warnings are such pointless indulgences, do you not think, my Emerald? Tell me instead who spies upon you. Gideon Rossiter and his little band of misguided patriots?"

"You must surely have expected it when you ordered me to buy his father's estate."

"I don't see that. Poor dear Sir Mark Rossiter was ruined and disgraced. What more praiseworthy gesture than for his staunch friend and neighbour to buy Promontory Point and—er, hold it till the old fool is able to buy it back?"

"We may have succeeded in toppling the Rossiters, but a man don't become the head of a great financial empire by being a fool. And his son is far from one. Sir Mark's cries of 'conspiracy' were ignored until Gideon came home from the war. I make no doubt that he and his friends have taken note of the—er, untimely death of Lord Merriam; the disgrace and imprisonment of Admiral Albertson, and—"

"Even so, the useful properties of those unfortunates were not gathered in by *you*, Emerald."

"They were gathered in by *us*. And furthermore, young Rossiter cries friends with Lord Horatio Glendenning."

The Squire grunted, and said angrily, "Who eluded our net, the traitorous hound!"

"It was a close-run thing. Almost we had my lord's worthless head on the block, and his whole family with him."

"Almost . . . Such a sad word. Especially does one consider how very gratifying it *could* have been. Instead, 'twas a deplorable failure, for which a useful member of our League paid the price. But how should that sorry fiasco have turned Rossiter's eyes to you?"

There was the suggestion of a shrug. The man called Emerald said thoughtfully, "If he has detected a pattern to our successes 'twould explain why I am followed. And you may believe that I am. The unspeakable Falcon one day, Morris another. Yesterday I fancy 'twas Owen Furlong."

"Furlong! Enrolled him, have they? Hmm. He'd have a score to settle at that, if he suspects we were behind the Albertson business. Furlong and Miss Albertson were betrothed, did you know it?"

"I thought she drowned?"

"So she did, poor lady. Her brother sent her to Italy to recuperate from the shock of her papa's disgraceful descent into Newgate. What a pity that her ship went down with no survivors."

Genuinely shocked, Emerald exclaimed, "My God! I hope we had nought to do with that!"

"Do you? But how admirably gallant. Now, to revert to more immediate problems, whatever Rossiter may suspect, I think he cannot prove you linked to us only because you purchased his sire's estate."

"Which the old man now wishes to buy back."

"Egad! Has he regrouped so soon? My compliments to him. You must hedge, Emerald."

"That will properly rouse their suspicions. I promised Sir Mark I did but buy it to hold in trust for him."

"Hmm. Very well, then agree to sell it, but institute delays. Within three months we will be ready. You can hold

Rossiter off till then, by one means or another. 'Tis as well we purchased the other estates through intermediaries." The Squire was briefly silent, then murmured, "Even so, Gideon Rossiter and his friends are tiresome creatures. We really must deal with them."

"Aha!" Emerald's tone brightened. "Who shall it be this time? Falcon, I hope?"

Amused, the Squire drawled, "You really do not care for the deadly August, do you?"

"In company with most of the men in London, I detest the scurvy damned half-breed."

"Such vehemence! Truly, it grieves me to disappoint you, but our next acquisition must be near Dover."

"Lac Brillant? Ah! Then you know!"

"Know what?"

"Why, this was my prime reason for signalling a meeting. Young Chandler—Gordon, I mean—was prowling about Larchwoods."

"*What?*" The Squire snarled furiously, "It *cannot* be! 'Tis a relatively small estate and we acquired it with no great drama to draw attention. "No, it *must* be coincidence, only. What transpired?"

"Chandler claimed to be calling on Trevor Shipley. He was denied admission, of course, but ten minutes later was caught climbing over the north fence."

"Pox on the cur! How much did he see, I wonder? Our vigilant guards let him slip through their fingers, no doubt?"

"I am told he led them quite a chase. But he got clear."

"Bastard! May he rot in hell!"

"By all means. I take it then that your move on Dover was not inspired by his snooping."

"No. I knew, of course, that he was one of Rossiter's revolting friends, but our web was fashioned about Lac Brillant some time ago. I'd no notion that the heir to it had ranged himself 'gainst us."

"Perhaps he has not. Perhaps 'tis as you said, merest coincidence. But tell me of your plan, Squire. Did Sapphire design it? He has no love for the Chandlers."

"He has no love for anyone, save that wanton he married. In truth he's an unpleasant creature, and vindictive in the extreme, but he has his uses. No, this time our plan was devised by Topaz. 'Tis somewhat oblique and much hangs on chance, but if it works it holds a double trap that should serve us well." He said musingly, "Lac Brillant . . . a prize worth the having, eh?"

"It meets many of our requirements certainly, and is of a rare beauty besides."

"Just so. I've had little to do with the family. How do you judge them?"

"I've only seen Sir Brian a time or two. He's seldom in Town and at all events," bitterness crept into the deep voice, "likely considers me *nouveau riche* and beneath his touch. I believe it's a close-knit group. Quentin inherited his sire's good looks but is a reckless fool and a fugitive, conveniently obliged to languish in France, as you know. The heir's a haughty young buck and holds himself aloof."

"Like Falcon?"

"No. A very different article. There is no malice in Gordon Chandler, I give him that. But his nature is cold and proud, and his temper hasty. I think he loves the estate though. He'll fight to save it."

"If all goes well," purred the Squire, "he'll not have the chance."

CHAPTER I

t. James' Park, always a peaceful oasis in the heart of the bustling city, was a riot of colour on this pleasant afternoon, for the warmth of the sun had lured much of fashionable London out of doors to see and be seen. The white gowns of shy and jealously chaperoned damsels not yet presented provided a demure contrast to the vibrant scarlets of military coats. Gentlemen in wigs or powder escorted their fair charges gallantly, or joined friends to share such fascinating topics as the latest Toast, horses, sports, or the more ponderous matters of politics and diplomacy. Young ladies with their first Season behind them paraded in great-skirted gowns of pastel silks and satins; and the greys and purples affected by the dowagers mingled with the brighter hues that might safely be worn by young matrons.

Seemingly out of place among this bright and merry throng, a slight lady clad in deep mourning strolled towards the area reserved for the dairy cows. Her black veil was sufficiently sheer to allow a glimpse of delicate features framed by hair of pale gold. She was accompanied by a small boy and a woman whose neat but plain garb marked her for a superior servant, perhaps a companion or the child's governess.

"Poor creature. How sad she looks," murmured a young lady of small stature, whose awkward steps were steadied by the use of a cane. "And no older than me."

Despite her infirmity and the fact that she fell short of being designated a beauty, Miss Gwendolyn Rossiter was escorted by two decidedly dashing gentlemen. One was a military man of about five and twenty, with a fair-skinned cherubic countenance lit by merry green eyes. The other, a few years his senior, was very dark, his neatly tied-back hair jet black, his lean and superbly clad figure marked by the grace of the born athlete, and his countenance so extraordinarily handsome as to win admiring glances from every lady they encountered, and as many frowns from the gentlemen. Despite his good looks, under their flaring brows August Falcon's midnight blue eyes had a faintly Oriental slant that betrayed his mixed blood. He held his head high and proud, but there was no warmth in his eyes, and his lips, although shapely, were down-trending and disdainful. "With but one glance," he drawled, "you have penetrated her veil to discover that the lady is poor, sad, and youthful. *Incroyable.*"

Lieutenant James Morris asked, "Have you her acquaintance, ma'am?"

Gwendolyn's brown curls bobbed as she shook her head. "Only I *looked* at her, whereas August did not deign to notice her. Besides, I cannot but feel sorry for any widow. How dreadful it must be to lose the one you cherish."

"Always supposing—(a) that she *is* a widow and, (b) that she cherished her defunct mate," qualified Falcon. "But so long as this is merest speculation, what if yon dainty relict loathed her lord and master and, as Tummet would say, 'done him in'?"

Miss Rossiter uttered an indignant exclamation and informed him that he was a horrid cynic.

"Yes, well we all know that," agreed the lieutenant. "Poor Falcon cannot help but judge everyone by himself. As always, he is 'the pot that calls the kettle black.'"

"I am neither a pot," retorted Falcon witheringly, "nor have I murdered anyone. Though"—he slanted a thoughtful glance at Morris—"with luck, any day now . . ."

Accustomed to this bickering, Gwendolyn's attention had returned to the widow. "At least," she murmured, "she has her little boy, and her woman looks kind."

"Her maid, if such she is, may be kind," allowed Falcon, "but the brat is ready to explode. Only see how he tries not to skip. What is he? Ten, perhaps?"

Falcon's parents had been blessed with only two children. Morris, who came from a large and boisterous family, jeered, "Ten! Good God! Much you know of children!"

"One must give thanks for small mercies. How old, then?"

"I would guess five. Six perhaps. What d'you say, ma'am?"

Gwendolyn's limp was becoming a little more noticeable, and she said apologetically, "That I would like to sit down, an you do not object. But to answer your question, I agree with you, August, that the child's energy cannot for much longer be suppressed; and with you, Jamie, that he is likely five, or thereabouts." Ushered to a vacant bench, she sat down gratefully and remarked that were she the little boy's mama, mourning or not, she would send him off to see the cows.

The object of their interest had also taken a seat. She said in a soft cultured voice, "Poor Thorpe. Were your brother here you could play, my love."

"Jacob was silly to catch a cold." The small boy gave a hop and, his blue eyes alight, added, "I never get colds might I go and see who that man is the one they're all bowing to might I please Aunty Ruth?"

"Mercy on us," exclaimed the woman who accompanied them. "Three sentences with not a single breath 'twixt 'em! And 'tis rude to point! For shame, Master Thorpe!"

The widow's gaze had turned to the wide grassy area the boy indicated, where stood a splendid gentleman surrounded by a small and fashionable group. His habit was rich, orders flashed on his breast, and, although they were a merry company, those about him treated him with deference, while passers-by bowed respectfully.

"Why, I believe 'tis Prince Frederick," said the widow. "And see, Grace, over there, by the trees, is that not the King?"

Grace Milford had been five and twenty when she'd been hired to serve as abigail to fourteen-year-old Miss Ruth Armitage. Three years later, Miss Armitage had become Mrs. Thomas Allington, and Grace had accompanied her into her new life. Now thirty-five, she was a combination of governess, companion, confidante, maid, and housekeeper. She had never lost the rosy cheeks and buxom figure of the country-woman, but the hazel eyes she turned upon the royal group were shrewd. "Aye, that's the Prince of Wales," she said. "And the King only yards distant, but pretending not to see him! A fine pair! Will I take the boy over, Mrs. A.?"

The widow hesitated.

"Please, let me go and see him!" Master Thorpe jumped up and down vigorously. "Please, Aunty! An' then the cows?"

Mrs. Allington smiled at him. "Very well. But—not too near the royal parties, Grace."

She watched fondly as they left her, the woman walking sedately, the child leaping and hopping along. They were soon lost amongst the crowd and the widow's gaze wandered. She loved the park, but this would be her last visit here, for the house on Mount Street was no longer her own, and she must go down to Lingways and see that things there were set to rights. After that— She forced away any thought of "after that" and concentrated on the beauties of dancing sunlit leaves and air spiced with the scents of blossoms and newly scythed grass. Soft talk and lilting laughter drifted to her and her gaze turned to the other occupants of the park. How gay they were; how happy and free from care. And how cut off she felt. Banished from them and the way of life she had always known and that had slipped away so gradually yet so inexorably, like a satin rope that had frayed even as she clung to it until the last fine threads were now sliding through her fingers. Within a few days it would vanish altogether and be as lost to her as were her dear father, her beloved brother, her gentle husband. And whatever was to become of—

At this point she was startled by the discovery that a young lady and two gentlemen seated nearby were watching her. The lady and the military gentleman looked away at once, but the second gentleman continued to stare at her, his brows haughtily arched, his dark eyes bold. Lud, but he was a handsome creature. And very aware of it to judge by that arrogant manner. But perhaps, even with the veil, they had recognized her. Perhaps they knew about her brother's shameful death; and about poor Papa's ruinous attempts to prove his son's innocence. She turned her head away in time to see Thorpe galloping towards her, laughing, and calling over his shoulder that Miss Grace must make haste to see the cows.

"Oh, do take care!" cried Mrs. Allington, coming to her feet hurriedly.

She was too late. The tall, gaunt, but extremely elegant matron who had just passed by was proceeding towards the Prince and her attention was no more on the boy than his was on her. Her footman, whose eyes had lingered upon a pretty nursemaid, gave a shout, but he also was too late.

A violent collision. A shriek. A small, frightened face turned to the widow. A torrent of infuriated accusation capped by a sharp box on the ear.

Mrs. Allington hastened to the debacle, and slipped an arm about the boy. Thorpe shrank against her skirts, one hand pressed to his reddened cheek.

"I apologize for the accident, ma'am," said the widow angrily. "But you had no right to—"

"*Right?*" screamed the victim, turning a rageful countenance. "So you are the little monster's mama, are you? I do not scruple to tell you that he should be—"

"He did not mean to run into you." The widow raised her voice a trifle. "And there was no—"

"Do not dare to interrupt, you impertinent creature! I will say again that this vicious young ruffian—"

"He is not a ruffian, but—"

"—all but knocked me down!" Inspecting the rich green silk of her wide-hooped skirts even as she spoke, she uttered another shriek. "Ah! He has muddied my gown! *Insufferable* little beast!"

"If you would but moderate your tone, madam, I—"

"*Moderate* my *tone*, is it! That you dare say such a thing to me is a fair indication of your lack of manners and breeding! And only *look* at my reticule! Hackham, fetch the Park Keeper! People like these should not be allowed . . ."

On and on she went, her harsh tones attracting attention so that every head was turned their way.

Her warm heart touched, Gwendolyn Rossiter said, "Oh, how awful for her! August, do go and see if you cannot calm that dreadful woman!"

With an incredulous stare, Falcon enquired, "Are you run mad? Even were I so inclined, which I am not, I've no least intent to come within range of *that* female!"

Lieutenant Morris asked curiously, "A formidable lady? Should I know her?"

"Not if you can help it," said Gwendolyn with her customary bluntness. " 'Tis Lady Clara Buttershaw. An odious woman. August, you know very well she fairly hangs on your lips. One word from you and she would cease persecuting that poor widow. Have you no compassion for your fellow man?"

"Precisely as much as my fellow man has for me. And as for allowing that skirted adder to flirt with me—I thank you, no! Let the widow fend for herself." He stood, and bowed with easy grace. "In point of fact, I refuse to share the same park with her noble ladyship. Adieu."

"Heartless coward!" hissed Gwendolyn as he strolled off.

Falcon laughed and waved airily, but continued on his way.

Turning to the apprehensive lieutenant, Gwendolyn pleaded, "Jamie—you are so kind. Only listen how she screeches, the wretch! And she has sent her footman to fetch the Keeper. You *cannot* allow that poor widow to be so publicly humiliated."

The lieutenant whimpered and quailed. And, of course, a minute later, was asking Lady Buttershaw in a scared voice if he could "be of some assistance?"

The widow, very pale, threw him a grateful glance.

Lady Buttershaw rounded on him, flushed and raging. "I think we have not been introduced, young man. Mind your business!"

'Jove, what a dragon!' thought Morris, and drew back, but there were tears on the boy's white face and his scared eyes pleaded. Wherefore, "By your leave, ma'am," he persevered bravely, "I am Lieutenant James Morris. I was presented to you at—"

"You have *not* my leave! And I will tell you, because I am honest in all things, that did I know a gentleman cursed with freckles and sandy hair, I would assuredly remember him, since I despise both. At all events, I number no junior officers among my acquaintance, so—" Her ladyship checked, and her hard dark eyes narrowed. "Morris? Of the Cornwall Morrises?"

"Lord Kenneth is my father's cousin, ma'am."

"Which lends *you* little consequence," she observed with a sniff. "Indeed, one can but wonder that you've the gall to boast of such a distant connection." She brought her guns to bear upon the widow once more. "I shall charge you and your brat with assault upon my person, and destruction of my—"

"Mr. Falcon asked me to—" began Morris in desperation.

He had come upon the secret formula. My lady's tirade ceased, and she whipped around, a sugary smile affixed to her sharp features, and her eyes scanning the park eagerly. "Do you refer to my dear friend *August* Falcon? Where is he?"

"He was obliged to leave, but desired that I do whatever I might to assist you and this lady. I—er, think his father is acquainted with hers."

"Such a *kind* creature," purred Lady Buttershaw, and with an arch giggle that appalled Morris, enquired, "And did August charge you with a message for me?"

"Only that I do what I might to mend matters between you and Mrs.— Oh, egad! My apologies, ma'am, but—I've forgot . . ." He looked hopefully at the widow.

"I am Mrs. Thomas Allington," said Ruth, her voice trembling a little. Lady Buttershaw's basilisk gaze darted to her and she added defiantly, "Of Lingways, in Essex."

My lady stared at her in silence, then said in a markedly less strident tone, "You may present Mrs. Allington, Lieutenant."

Breathing an inward sigh of relief, Morris said, "Lady Clara Buttershaw—Mrs. Thomas Allington."

Ruth also had detected a thaw. The encounter had left her already worn nerves even more strained, and the thought that this horrid woman might indeed bring charges against them was terrifying. She said, "I am indeed sorry if your gown was muddied, my lady, and—"

"I think you are not blind, and can see that it is. And my reticule is quite ruined," grumbled Lady Clara, flourishing that article.

There did indeed appear to be a tear beside the handle. "My companion is an excellent needlewoman, ma'am," said Ruth, spurred by a sight of the footman returning, with a burly man in uniform beside him. "An you permit that I have it repaired, 'twould be my pleasure to return it to you."

"Handsomely said," remarked Morris, beaming. "All's well that—"

Lady Clara's fan rapped upon his arm. "Be off with you, Lieutenant! And tell that rascal August Falcon that I expect him to call upon me within the week. Run along, now. We ladies can handle these little fusses very well without the aid of clumsy gentlemen, can we not, my dear?"

'My *dear* . . . ?' thought Ruth, dazed.

'Allelulia!' thought Morris, and bowed himself away.

The green saloon was very like its mistress, Ruth decided. Large, intimidating, and rather too busy. She had come to the luxurious neighbourhood lying east of Hyde Park with considerable reluctance, but had not dared send Grace to return the repaired reticule, guessing that Lady Buttershaw would be offended. My lady moved in the very circles in which an impecunious widow might be obliged to seek employment, and it would be the height of folly to further antagonize so powerful a member of the *ton*. The size and magnificence of the mansion had deepened her unease, however, and she'd cherished the hope that her ladyship would be from home this morning, so that she might leave the reticule and a note of apology, and make her escape. Her heart had sunk when the butler, a majestic individual, had looked at her calling card and advised that she was expected. He had conducted her across a richly appointed entrance hall, up a staircase overshadowed by portraits of contemptuous and (presumably) ancestral Buttershaws, and into this ornate chamber.

It was very quiet, and a rather musty odour hung upon the air. Looking about curiously, Ruth thought that Lady Buttershaw and her husband must have a deep interest in things past, for everywhere were antique objects, many with framed informational texts beside them. A gloomy tapestry hung upon one wall. She was unable to determine what it represented and, as the minutes slid silently past, curiosity got the better of discretion, and she crept over to peer at it. The faded forms remained indeterminate, and she had decided it was some kind of coronation ceremony until she read the accompanying text and discovered it to be "The Execution of the Martyr King." She suppressed a giggle, whispered her apologies to the shadowy Charles Stuart, and moved to the next curiosity. This was a glass case containing objects ranging from a lock of hair purporting to have been taken from the severed head of Guy Fawkes, to a faded and tiny slipper worn by the mighty Queen Elizabeth. An impressively framed document caught her attention, and she found it to be a letter from King Charles I to a Colonel Montmorency Yerville. The spidery handwriting was difficult to decipher, but it was evidently a commendation for valour and there was no doubt of the signature, and the date, "This fifteenth daye of December, in the Year of Grace 1647."

Starting back to her chair, the widow hoped her ladyship would come soon. There was very little time left in which to complete the closure of the London house, and the sooner she reached Lingways and disposed of whichever furnishings might fetch a decent price, the— Sensing that she was no longer alone, she glanced up.

A slight lady watched her from the open doorway. Of early middle age, she wore unrelieved white, the bodice of her gown buttoned high to the throat, and the long sleeves having falls of lace at the wrists. Her wig was neat but not of the latest style, and her countenance, although pleasant, was fine-boned and pale, adding to an impression of fragility. Coming swiftly into the room, she said in a soft rather breathless voice, "I think you are Mrs. Thomas Allington. Allow me to introduce myself; I am Lady Julia Yerville."

Ruth curtsied respectfully, but before she could respond, Lady Julia's timid glance had darted to the open door and she was saying in the same hurried fashion, "Do sit down, my dear. No not there. On the sofa, beside me. I should not be here, but I did so very much want to speak with you before..." She gave a vague gesture and left the sentence unfinished.

Obediently, Ruth sat beside her and was at once enveloped in a faint air of lavender.

"I know why you are come," Lady Julia went on. "My sister, Lady Clara, has told me of your—er, meeting in the park." Another nervous glance to the door, then a rush of half-whispered words. "I was distressed to hear that a young widow—especially one in your circumstances— Does it surprise you that I know your sad tale? I do. Long and long ago, you see, I knew your papa." Her eyes, which were a very light blue, were large and luminous, and sorrow came into them as she added with a sigh, "Poor Greville. So handsome and charming, yet with so great a talent. I have often thought he might be delighting us with his paintings to this day, had it not been for Jonathan."

Ruth stiffened. "My brother was innocent, ma'am! No matter what his men said, he was a splendid sailor and would never have left the bridge while his vessel was at such risk! And as for being intoxi—"

"I do not doubt you for an instant, dear Mrs. Allington." Lady Julia leaned forward to take her hand. "I met Jonathan once, after he grew up. Such a fine fellow. As handsome as his dear papa, almost. I never believed he was addicted to strong spirits. *Never!* But—alas, I do think Greville was deeply grieved when he was accused. No?"

Ruth looked steadily at the small fingers closed over her own, the all too familiar pang striking hard as it always did when she thought of that dreadful time. Even now, two years after that ghastly morning when first the news of her brother's death had come, she could almost see the newspapers. "East Indiaman sinks off Cornwall with heavy loss of life! . . . Captain of doomed ship accused of gross negligence! . . . Renowned artist's sea-captain son drunk in cabin as his ship runs onto rocks!"

She muttered, "Papa was heart-broken. But he never believed it of Johnny."

"Of course. For that was not Greville Armitage's way. I admired him even more for his staunch efforts to clear Jonathan's name. Although—it broke him, alas, both physically and financially. And now you are to lose even the country estate, I hear. My poor, poor child! It must be five years since your husband went to his reward, but I had thought him very well to pass. Did he make no provision for you?"

Torn between pride and the need to unburden herself, Ruth hesitated. Since poor Johnny's death and subsequent disgrace so many of their erstwhile friends had ceased to acknowledge them, and when, a scant year later, Papa had followed the son he adored to the grave, she had felt so lost. So alone and in need of a friend. Grace had stood by them, God bless her. But—

She glanced up. The gentle eyes watched her anxiously. A sympathetic smile curved the pale lips, and Ruth's defenses crumbled.

"Mr. Allington left me well provided for, my lady. But— but Papa was never very— That is to say, he was of an artistic temperament and had no head for business."

"So when he over-extended himself in striving to defend your late brother's good name you rallied to help him. As any dutiful daughter would do. I should have guessed it. But— forgive me, surely your father's paintings must be of extreme value?"

"Yes. And we lived off them this past year, my lady. Until the robbery." Ruth sighed helplessly. "So many of his best works were taken. I had sold a few, mostly to pay debts. But—now . . ." Tears stung her eyes, and suddenly the feeling of helplessness was crushing.

Soft arms were around her. A scented kiss was pressed on her cheek. "There, there, my dear. We must find a way. There is always a way, you know."

Drying her eyes, Ruth said threadily, "Oh, that was . . . very bad. I do beg your p-pardon, but you are so very kind. Whatever must you think of me?"

"Why, that you are extreme brave and resourceful, to have survived so much tragedy. Thomas Allington was a good many years your senior, of course, but devoted to you. We all knew it. And then, to lose your brother under *such* circumstances! And within a year, your poor papa! My dear, you cannot know how I admire you. I myself am such a frightful coward and weakling."

Struggling to control her emotions, Ruth looked into the pale face, and said, "I cannot believe th-that, my lady."

"Oh, but it is perfectly true." Lady Yerville glanced to the door, leaned closer, and whispered confidingly, "I wish I had just a teensy particle of your courage. But I am very silly, and am easily frightened. To hear the gentlemen discussing the Uprising . . . The least hint of violence . . ." Her voice fluttered, but she went on, with her timid smile. "Things of that nature make me tremble rather. How wonderful it must be for a lady to have a husband to take care of her. To protect her from . . ." The softly uttered words ceased.

Recalling Lady Clara Buttershaw's strident voice in the park, Ruth could well imagine how this gentle creature would be cowed by her bullying sister. Her own troubles momentarily forgotten, she said, "Forgive my impertinence, ma'am, but I would think if you were wishful to be married— Well, you are so dainty and pretty, I fancy many gentlemen would be—"

"Would be willing to offer for me?" The great eyes were wistful. "A gentleman did offer once. A very dear gentleman. We were to be married, but you see—"

"I see that you have been chattering about family matters again, Julia!"

The resonant voice startled both women, and they turned with varying degrees of alarm as Lady Clara Buttershaw rustled into the room.

Today, her gown was of magenta satin, cut very low at the bosom, the stomacher tight about her thin waist, the great hooped skirts billowing out below, so that, irreverently, Ruth was put in mind of a dust mop on a stick. "I cannot believe," Lady Clara went on, "that I have kept Mrs. Allington for so long, Julia, as to require that you provide her with entertainment."

Her sister had come to her feet. Wringing her hands, she pleaded, "But I *knew* Greville Armitage, Clara. You will remember that we were acquainted, and—"

"What has that to say to the point? I apologize for Lady Julia, Mrs. Allington. You will be thinking that she is, as the gentlemen would say, very rag-mannered. She has never learned, alas, that 'tis in the poorest taste to regale strangers with personal details in which they very properly have no least interest. My callers are too often embarrassed by such misplaced confidences. I wonder she has not told her life history to the dustman!"

The target of these waspish remarks hung her head and shivered.

Longing to say much that would have been considered a good deal more than rag-mannered, Ruth bit her tongue and said nothing.

With a tight smile that barely broadened her lips, Lady Clara swept on, "I see you have returned my reticule. Let me see it, if you please."

Ruth made haste to pass her the reticule. "Lady Julia was so kind as to—"

"As to try for your sympathy by complaining how I am hard and overbearing and have taken over her house—though who would keep this great place in order were I not here, I wish someone might tell me!"

Ruth's wish was to be anywhere but between these most odd sisters, but before she could voice a denial, Lady Julia stammered, "Indeed, I did not say such things, Clara. And you know how grateful I— But—but Mrs. Allington is poor Greville's child, and I did so want to see her. She is in most trying circumstances, and I had hoped we might be able to—"

Lady Clara rolled her eyes heavenward and interrupted impatiently. "Sit down, both of you. I have something to say." She then positioned herself on the sofa, her great skirts taking up so much of it that the other two ladies were obliged to occupy the chairs to which she waved them.

"I have made it my business," she announced regally, "to discover Mrs. Allington's circumstances, and I have given a good deal of thought as to how we might assist her. In spite of what you may have been told, Mrs. Allington, my heart is kind, and my nature generous. Furthermore, being an earl's daughter and the widow of a statesman, I have a wide acquaintanceship among the *haut ton*. Indeed, one might say without fear of contradiction there is *no* body who is *any* body that I do *not* know. I cannot abide missish airs and false modesty, and do not scruple to assert that everywhere I am held in high regard. It is thanks to my position in Society, that I believe I may have found a solution for you. But I must know of your accomplishments, if any, before I commit myself."

Despite her initial inclination to wrap Lady Clara Buttershaw's head in the faded tapestry and knot it tightly about her throat, Ruth was beginning to be amused. The woman was so outrageous she was downright laughable. But there was no doubt that she could be an invaluable ally, mindful of which Ruth lowered her eyes and said meekly, "You are all consideration, ma'am. I believe myself well qualified to fill the position of a governess, perhaps, or—"

"Or a scullery maid? Or a shop assistant?"

At this, Ruth's amusement vanished and she was rendered so speechless with indignation that my lady was off again before she could recover her voice.

"Nonsense! As a last resort perhaps, but I think we are not brought to that pass as yet. Nor do I require an inventory of your commonplace accomplishments, for I am sure that however much of a flibbertigibbet he may have been—and all artists I will tell you are flibbertigibbets—Mr. Greville Armitage was also a gentleman and had sufficient sense to see that his daughter was provided with an education befitting her station in life. Now, what I *do* wish to know is—are you at all proficient in your father's field of endeavour?"

This most unexpected question brought a quickening of hope, and Ruth rallied her wits sufficiently to assert that she had some artistic skills. "Papa said I showed promise. Sometimes he allowed me to prepare his canvasses, and I took care of his brushes and colours and, very occasionally, he permitted that I paint the backgrounds for his pastorals."

"Excellent. Now—and this is a more difficult question for you—are you in the slightest familiar with the work of restoration?"

Almost stammering in her eagerness, Ruth said, "It chances that I am, ma'am. When I was sixteen my father was commissioned to restore some fine old frescoes in an Italian villa, and he took me with him to Milan. I was most pleased to be able to assist him. Much of the work was rather tedious, and he—"

"Aha! I do believe it may serve!" Lady Clara clapped her hands, then frowned at the tapestry through a taut silence during which neither of her companions dared utter a word. " 'Twill be tricky," she murmured thoughtfully. "He would likely pay no heed to anything I might write in your behalf . . . But— Of course!" She looked from her sister to the widow as though she had discovered some great truth. "Falcon!"

Bewildered, Lady Julia said, "Mr. Falcon has a situation for Mrs. Allington?"

"No, you silly creature! Sir Brian Chandler has. And since dear August is a friend of Mrs. Allington's he should be only too willing to write a letter for her. Is that not right, ma'am?"

"W-well," said Ruth uneasily. "I scarcely—I mean . . . Do you really think Sir Brian would hire me? Surely, he will want—"

"A male. Of course! So we must proceed with cunning and caution. But if he will only grant you an interview . . . Stand up, if you please."

Too excited to resent the autocratic command, Ruth stood.

Lady Clara walked around her, eyeing her critically. "Hum. You are not unattractive. The blacks must go, of course."

"But, my lady—'tis only ten months since Papa—"

"Quite long enough. Mr. Greville Armitage was not so blockheaded as to wish that strict observance of the proprieties should stand in the way of gainful employment. You will wear sensible garments, mind. No bows, frills, or laces, and absolutely no jewellery. Instruct your woman to cut your hair, or at least arrange it in a plain, no-nonsense style. You must not mention your maiden name, or Sir Brian will likely have none of you, for he is prodigious strait-laced and abhors scandal. But conduct yourself with meekness and humility, and the battle will be half won! You will have to place your son with relatives, of course, for Sir Brian would not tolerate a small boy about the estate, but that should present no difficulty."

"Well, I— The fact is—"

"Good! Run along then, and I shall at once write a note to dear August Falcon." Her ladyship smiled with anticipation. "I may even deliver it myself."

Ruth said earnestly, "Lady Buttershaw, I do not know how to thank you, but—"

"You may thank me when we have done the thing. Is a chancy business at best, and you shall have to use all your woman's wiles—I hope you have some!—to win Sir Brian's acceptance. Keep in mind that tears may serve if all else fails, for they frighten the gentlemen to death. A sensible female can usually achieve her goals does she resort to tears!"

Miss Gwendolyn Rossiter's disposition was amiable and, despite the affliction of a knee damaged at birth and unimproved by a painful operation, a smile was seldom far from her blue eyes. On this windy morning, those eyes were vexed however, and as she limped down the majestic staircase of Falcon House, she demanded sharply, "What is the meaning of all this uproar? Tummet! Stop playing with Apollo this instant! You know perfectly well that Mr. Neville Falcon and Miss Katrina are ill."

The two lackeys and the footman at once ceased plunging about the entrance hall in nervous pursuit of the black hound whose name might more aptly have been Monster than Apollo.

Panting heavily, Enoch Tummet looked up. He was a square, powerfully built man, not above average height, and although his well-cut habit proclaimed him for a gentleman's gentleman his appearance seemed to deny such a genteel calling. His features, which might charitably be described as rough-hewn, held no trace of the disdainful superiority that so often marked the valets of wealthy aristocrats. His brow was low and heavy, his nose looked to have been broken several times, and the neat wig rested lopsidedly upon his bullet head.

"Playing!" he echoed, that one word betraying his cockney origins. "Cor, luvaduck, Miss Gwen! D'ye think as I'd *play* wiv that there perishing 'ound?" He groaned despairingly. "Only look at 'im shake of it! Tear it ter shreds 'e will, and that'll give Mr. August the excuse 'e wants—which is to do nought. You know who'll be blamed. Orf-on-a-spree!" He glanced at Miss Rossiter and translated, "Me!"

Gwendolyn had acquired some proficiency in his rhyming slang, and said with faint indignation, "I *knew!*" Wisely settling then for the small part of the rest of his utterance that she could comprehend, and having arrived at the ground floor, she took up the riding crop that lay on a cabinet, said briskly, "Apollo! Fetch!" and sent the crop flying down the corridor.

Apollo, who had come to associate this young woman's visits with games, at once dropped his lesser prize and went with ungainly enthusiasm after the larger one.

At once, Tummet pounced on the wreckage of the letter, and attempted to restore it. "'Ave me ears, she will," he moaned. "Look at it! Couldn't read it if 'e wanted to. Which 'e don't!"

The floor shook. Apollo was returning at speed. Gwendolyn told the trembling lackeys to throw the crop outside for him, and led Tummet into the book room.

"Let me try if I can come at the root of this," she said. "A letter was delivered for Mr. August, only Apollo seized it from you, and the lady who left it will hold you to blame—is that right?"

"Yus. And—no. Lady Buttershaw 'ad writ out what she wants Mr. August to copy dahn and send orf. Like 'e writ it 'isself. Only when Mr. August see'd milady tripping up the steps, 'e said she was a—" He checked, leering. "Never mind what. But 'e up and climbed out the winder, and sent me to make 'is excuses. Course, 'e wouldn't of done nuthink anyway. But you think *she'll* believe that? Not blooming likely! It'll be Enoch Tummet what spoiled it, sure as green apples."

Gwendolyn stretched out a small but imperative hand and, peering at the tattered sheet that was obediently placed in it, said, "Goodness me! How ever could you decipher this?"

Tummet sighed. "Didn't need to, Miss. I already knowed all abaht it." In response to the curious glance she slanted at him, he explained, "Fact is, I bin . . ." His craggy face reddened, and he directed his eyes at the empty fireplace and said gruffly, "I bin walking out wiv a superior female woman."

"Why, Tummet! How very nice! And your friend is employed by Lady Buttershaw?"

"No, mate— I mean, Miss. Me lady friend works fer Mrs. Allington what's up to 'er pretty nose 'oles in trouble. On top of which, she runs afoul of 'er ladyship!"

"Yes, poor thing. We were in the park and saw it. Oh, 'twas dreadful! Lieutenant Morris was so kind as to try to placate the odi— I mean, Lady Clara Buttershaw."

"Right y'are. But—may I kiss a newt if the lieutenant

could get 'er ladyship to listen. Not till 'e tells 'er that Mr. August 'ad sent 'im over."

"So *that's* how he managed it!" Gwendolyn's eyes began to sparkle. "Everybody knows that Lady Clara has a—er, fondness for Mr. August. Never say she now means to offer assistance to poor Mrs. Allington?"

"In a way, yus. She winkled out that Sir Brian Chandler's looking fer someone to mess about wiv some paintings what 'e found dahn at Lake Brill—whatever it's called."

"You mean Lac Brillant, Sir Brian Chandler's country seat. I heard he had uncovered an old fresco in his chapel. So now he wants it restored, is that it? Oh, how perfect that would be! Mrs. Allington's papa was Mr. Greville Armitage, the great artist, and she doubtless would know exactly—" Gwendolyn's expressive little face darkened. She said dubiously, "But—would Sir Brian hire a lady to do such work?"

"There you got it, mate, in a flea's back tooth! Lady Buttershaw, she knows as Sir Brian wouldn't so much as listen to a female widow if she went toddling dahn there. Never mind 'ow clever she was."

"True. So Lady Buttershaw wants August Falcon to write a letter to Sir Brian in Mrs. Allington's behalf?" Gwendolyn looked even more dubious. "Is a kind thought, but I doubt 'twould be of much use."

"No use at all, Miss Gwen, if that was what she wanted. Ain't. What she *wants* is fer me guv'nor to write to Sir Brian about a extry clever artist 'e knows of, by name of R. Allington, and—"

"And when R. Allington arrives, and turns out to be *Mrs.* R. Allington, she will at least be *there* and have a chance to persuade Sir Brian to hire her for the task!" Gwendolyn clapped her hands delightedly. "Oh, how very naughty!"

"She wants Mr. August to send the letter dahn to Dover right away." Tummet looked glum. " 'E won't do it, mate. I told and told Miss Milford—me lady friend—that Mr. August would 'ave no part of it. But she'll blame me, just the same." Struck by a new thought, he said craftily, "Unless p'raps *you'd* be willing to . . . ?"

"To forge a letter? Indeed I would! 'Tis time August Falcon began to put something back into the world to make up for all his silly duelling." Her enthusiasm faded. "But alas, I could never imitate his writing."

Through the brief following silence came the sound of wheels outside. Tummet crossed to the windows. "It's Lieutenant Morris come with flowers. Fer poor Miss Katrina, I 'spect. I 'opes as she's feeling better terday, Miss Gwen? A real lovely lady she is, and don't deserve to 'ave caught that 'orrid influenzy what her pa brung 'ome."

"She has only a mild case, thank heaven, but I'm glad Lieutenant Morris has called. He always can cheer her up and is so devoted and . . ." Her blue eyes became very round. Gripping her hands together, she breathed, "Tummet! *Lieutenant Morris!*"

"Cor!" he exclaimed. "You don't never think as you could persuade 'im?"

"Perhaps not," admitted Gwendolyn. "But were Miss Katrina to ask . . ."

"Cor!" he said again. "The lieutenant fair worships the ground she walks on."

Gwendolyn giggled mischievously. "Doesn't he just!"

CHAPTER 11

uth was nervous when she boarded the stage-coach at the Blue Boar posting house in Holborn. Never in her life had she travelled alone, much less on a public conveyance, but Grace's pleas to be allowed to accompany her as far as Dover at least, had been rejected. They could not all go, Ruth had pointed out, and the boys were much too young to be left alone. Every penny must be guarded now, and an extra fare would be expensive. Besides, while she was away, Grace could finish packing. In her heart Ruth acknowledged that this was the start of a new way of life. However much she dreaded it, she must meet the challenge bravely, not cling to old habits nor lean on the support of others. She, alone, must somehow provide for Thorpe, Jacob, and Grace, and Resolution must be her watchword.

Despite this firm little self-lecture, having worn blacks for so long, she felt oddly vulnerable in her grey gown and neat cap. When she'd finished dressing this morning, with her long hair tightly plaited and coiled behind her ears, and the absence of even the few cosmetics she had been used to wear, her reflection in the mirror had seemed that of a stranger, and her altered appearance had drawn a wail of dismay from Grace. To face the uproar and confusion in the mist-draped yard of the old posting house without the protection of a gentleman was terrifying, but she managed to hide that weakness and bade Grace farewell with a smile, then waved cheerily from the window-seat the kindly guard had procured for her.

The coach was soon filled. A thin little woman sat beside her, and murmured an apology when Ruth's shawl became caught up on her large basket. A very bulky man Ruth judged to be a prosperous farmer took up much too much of the remaining space, ignored the woman's attempt to occupy her own share of it, and looked blandly out of the window, as though he had been stone deaf while she wriggled and protested. A worried-looking man climbed in next, accompanied by a youth with pimples and a sullen face. The only space left was opposite Ruth, and she hoped it would be taken by another small female, for there was little knee room. The coachman bellowed to the ticket agent to stand away. Ruth's sigh of relief was cut off however, when the closing door was wrenched open again. A gentleman sprang inside. Before she lowered her eyes, she noted that he was of early middle age, neatly dressed, and seemed well bred. A moment later, the carriage lurched forward, and the gentleman staggered. Ruth clutched her reticule and gave a startled cry as the late arrival trod on her toe.

"My deepest apologies, ma'am," he said, regaining his balance, and taking his seat. He raised his tricorne and smiled pleasantly. "I trust I did not hurt you?"

The farmer sniggered. Righting her basket, which had been almost knocked to the floor, the thin woman muttered indignantly. Ignoring her, the newcomer watched Ruth. He seemed genuinely concerned, and his voice was cultured. She thought that he should have apologized to the woman with the basket, but she thanked him, and said quietly that she was unhurt, then turned her attention to the window and forgot him.

How little she had suspected during that terrible encounter in St. James' Park that Lady Clara Buttershaw would become her benefactor. She had been little short of astounded yesterday morning when a footman had delivered a letter in which my lady advised that she had been able to secure an interview for Mrs. Allington with regard to a position at Lac Brillant, near Dover. The instructions were involved and were, her ladyship wrote, to be followed exactly. The cautions about dress and her "son" were repeated. She was not to mention Lady Buttershaw's part in this, "for Sir Brian Chandler will be far more likely to be influenced by dear Mr. Falcon's kind recommendation than by my own efforts in your behalf." Miss Allington was to proceed to Dover the very next day, for time was of the essence. Sir Brian's carriage would be waiting for "R. Allington" at the Ship Inn, and from there, Miss Allington (not Mrs. or he would want to know her maiden name and that would never do!) must fight her own battles. As to remuneration (was she hired) she must ask at least five guineas a month, or Sir Brian would think she had little confidence in her own artistic abilities.

Ruth gripped the handle of her reticule tightly. If Lady Clara dreamed how little confidence her protégée had of securing this post, she would throw up her hands in disgust. But five guineas a month would allow Ruth to put a little away, besides paying for food and shelter for Grace and the boys—hopefully, in rooms somewhere nearby, so that she could visit them on her day off. It would be the answer to a prayer and, if she should please Sir Brian, might lead to other commissions when the work was completed. She *must* be confident! 'Resolution!' she told herself sternly and, realizing that she had given a small involuntary nod of her head, glanced up in embarrassment.

The gentleman opposite was still watching her and he smiled sympathetically. He was clearly eager to strike up an acquaintance. Ruth could not help but be pleased to find that she was not as unattractive now as she had supposed, but she looked away, annoyed by the awareness that she was blushing.

Next to her admirer, the man and the sullen boy were arguing in low but vehement tones. They had done so, Ruth now realized, ever since they'd entered the coach. A father and son, she decided, and felt sorry for the father because he seemed so careworn.

"Ask me, that there boy's a thorn in his flesh." The thin woman put one hand over her lips as she turned to murmur the remark. "I knows, Miss," she went on. "Bred up six boys, did me and Mr. Y. and every one of 'em was a thorn!"

"My goodness," said Ruth. "How dreadful for you. Did none of your sons turn out well?"

" 'Course they did! Turned out very nice. All married. All kind t'me, now that Mr. Y's gone to his reward. Good boys, they is. Now. But—then? Cor!" A sudden beaming smile illumined the peaked features. An elbow dug into Ruth's ribs. "That's lads for you, though, ain't it? Young or old. Thorns. The whole blessed lot!"

Amused, Ruth said, "Had you to do it over. I doubt you'd wish a day different. You must be a wonderful mother, ma'am."

Her new acquaintance wriggled with pleasure. "A grandmother now, dearie. Off t'see me youngest and his little girl. Brung her a present." She gave a conspiratorial wink. "In me basket. Wanta see?" She released the catch and opened the lid. At once, a small striped head lifted and two green eyes blinked sleepily.

"Oh, how sweet!" exclaimed Ruth. "Your granddaughter will love it!"

"Have you a cat in there?" The gentleman opposite was leaning forward. His knee, which had repeatedly brushed her own, ostensibly due to the motion of the carriage, now maintained a steady pressure. Annoyed, she drew back as far as she was able, and made a deliberate rearrangement of her skirts. A glance she could only judge as being slyly amused was slanted at her from under his heavy lids, but he made neither comment nor apology. He had a youthfully pink and white complexion that did not seem to equate with his years, or so thought Ruth, for she judged him to be at least forty. His eyes she found rather unpleasant, for they had a hooded appearance and despite his smile, which never seemed to waver, were cold. His voice however, was mild, and he peered at the kitten with interest.

"He won't be no trouble, sir," said the thin woman anxiously. "He's just a slip of a kitten."

"What a pretty fellow." The gentleman reached out. "May I stroke him? I am very fond of cats."

It was the start of a long exchange into which the worried man and his son entered. The kitten was made much of and, as is the way with small creatures, was the catalyst that drew the passengers into friendly conversation. Ruth listened, fascinated. She was glad to see that the sullen look had vanished from the youth's face, and his father seemed less troubled. She found herself imagining the scene when grandmama opened the basket and gave the kitten to the little girl. Jacob and Thorpe had so wanted a puppy, but it had become all too apparent that their future was uncertain, and she'd not dared— Sighing, she glanced up. Opposite, the gentleman's smile was ready, managing to impart such mocking familiarity that her aversion deepened, and for the rest of that long journey she contrived to avoid meeting his eyes.

They reached Dover at a quarter past three o'clock, having been delayed in Maidstone by a splitting wheel which had to be replaced. The farmer, who had snored through the last hour of the journey, woke up and made it clear to everyone within three hundred yards that he meant to lodge a complaint with the ticket agent. The door was swung open and Ruth smelled the fresh tang of the sea. She had hoped to be assisted by the guard, but the smiling gentleman forestalled him, springing nimbly from the coach so as to help her down. His hand was gloved and didn't linger, but she was not reassured and having murmured her thanks she went at once to the rear to find her valise.

The yard was almost as busy as had been the one at the Blue Boar. The air was chill and a light drizzle had made the cobblestones slippery. Shouting to one another, ostlers shot and skidded about at reckless speed, unpoling tired teams and poling up fresh ones. A loud dispute added to the din as the coachman and the ticket agent responded with vigour and volume to the continuing bellows of the displeased farmer.

Serene amid the uproar, the old inn soared above them in all its Tudor dignity, lamplight glowing from some casements despite the early hour, and smoke rising languidly from its many chimneys. A door was opened, and the tantalizing smell of hot food drifted out. Ruth had boarded the stagecoach at eight o'clock that morning, and the stops had been too brief to allow her to buy luncheon, besides which she'd shrunk from the prospect of the smiling man's assistance, which she was sure would be offered. Yearning to delay long enough to at least purchase a cold pastie, she dared not. Lady Buttershaw had said she would be met, but of course, Sir Brian Chandler's servants would be looking for a male passenger and she must be vigilant lest they leave without her.

There were several vehicles standing about, obviously waiting for travellers. The thin little grandmother called her good-byes and waved as she made her way to a waggon where a small girl was jumping up and down on the seat, squealing excitedly. A donkey cart was drawn up at one side, but Sir Brian would not have sent such a vehicle, surely, even for a prospective employee? Ruth eyed a light travelling coach hopefully until a dowager with enormous hoops left the inn and was ushered to it by two servants. The luxurious carriage waiting near the entrance Ruth judged unlikely, but she watched as a footman clad in cream and brown livery left it and approached the stagecoach.

Someone touched her elbow. The smiling gentleman offered her valise and lifted his tricorne respectfully. Quite proper. Perfectly polite. Yet her dislike suddenly became fear. Poor Thomas had been wont to state that she was beautiful, but in her candid way Ruth knew that although she was attractive, hers was not the kind of beauty to dazzle strange gentlemen. She had consistently snubbed this man. He could not fail to be aware of her reaction, yet he persisted. He must see that she was a respectable lady. What did he want of her? Was he—horrors!—a superior type of bailiff? Or a special constable? She had tried so hard to pay all the bills, but there had been so many. Were some still outstanding? Did he mean to serve a summons upon her, or have her arrested for debt? A mental picture of being weighed down with heavy shackles and hauled away before everyone caused her to feel faint for a moment.

"Beg pardon, sir. Would you by any chance be Mr. R. Allington?"

The footman had come up and was addressing the smiling man, who shook his head and then turned aside to collect his luggage.

'Resolution!' Ruth reminded herself. The footman was looking about. She tried to sound firm. "I believe you are looking for me."

The man appraised her in one swift and supercilious glance. "Thank you, madam, but I am to meet a gentleman."

"My name is Miss Allington. I have an appointment with Sir Brian Chandler, and was told I would be called for."

The man's jaw dropped. "But," he gasped, scandalized, "you're a—*lady!*"

"Quite true." She smiled and handed him her valise. "Is that your coach?"

"Yes. But— I do not— Miss—"

She paid no attention to his spluttering bewilderment and despite shaking knees walked to the waiting coach, the footman trailing after her.

The coachman, a powerful-looking man with powdered hair and greying bushy eyebrows, leaned from the box, grinning broadly. "Hey! Mackey!" he called. "You ain't brung the proper party."

Ruth looked up at him. "To the contrary, he has indeed brought the proper party."

His pale blue eyes became very round and he gawked at her speechlessly.

The footman stammered, "Lady says she's M-Miss Allington, Dutch. What you think—?"

Ruth turned and stared at him until he gave a gulp and sprang to open the door and hand her inside. When the door was slammed, shutting out his aghast countenance, Ruth sank back against the squabs feeling limp with relief.

There came the muttering of voices, capped by an irked, "All right then. But what the master's goin' ter say, I dunno. I just dunno!"

The carriage jolted and began to roll out of the yard. The persistent stagecoach passenger stood in the drizzle and watched their departure. Smiling. Then they were out on the street and in bustling traffic.

Ruth closed her eyes and gave a shuddering sigh. The first hurdle was past!

Unlike the stagecoach, Sir Brian Chandler's carriage was well sprung and luxuriously appointed. It moved smoothly and rapidly and the picturesque old town was soon left behind. They followed a north-easterly route along the top of the cliffs. Through the right-hand windows Ruth could see the Strait and two ships, their sails hanging motionless in the still air. After a while the carriage turned inland. The road narrowed into a lane, edged with trees. Even in this grey misting drizzle it was beautiful country, with lush well-kept fields and occasional little clumps of thatched and whitewashed cottages. Soon, the cottages dwindled and were gone and the carriage bowled along through open country.

In spite of her dread of the coming interview, Ruth was warm and comfortable, and her head began to nod. She jumped when the footman blew up a hail on the yard of tin.

They were slowing. Shouts were exchanged. Then, they went on again through wide iron gates, passing the gatekeeper's lodge and a tall man in dark green livery who stood holding the gate open and craning his neck to peer into the carriage.

The drivepath seemed to go on for miles. They traversed a strip of woodland, then a wilderness area, followed by a spacious park, its neatly scythed lawns dotted with great trees. The drivepath curved into a loop, and Ruth gave a gasp as she saw Lac Brillant for the first time.

A large lake spread in a sheet of silver at the foot of a low broad-shouldered hill. Near the top, was the house. It was unlike any great house she had ever seen, for, instead of a massive and dignified mansion, three semi-circular white buildings with red tile roofs were spaced in a wide crescent shape and separated from one another by flower gardens. A short distance away the tower of a small and apparently ancient chapel peeped from a grove of beeches. Little pools and streams were everywhere, and in the centre of the crescent a winged horse reared from a great fountain, which sent feathery sprays high into the air. Except that the central structure was larger, the houses were identical and looked, thought Ruth, more like a collection of Italian villas than the country seat of an English aristocrat. Fascinated, she forgot her problems as she gazed at low yew trees, neat box hedges, colourful flowerbeds threaded by meandering pathways. Urns, benches, and statuary added their charm to the scene, as did the rock gardens and enchanting topiary. Quaintly balustraded little stone bridges crossed the streams and miniature waterfalls, while rising behind house and gardens like a verdant frame, loomed tall graceful trees.

The carriage pulled up outside the central building. Ruth gathered her courage again. His eyes as disapproving as ever, the footman swung open the door and followed her up the steps, carrying her valise. She hesitated, wondering whether she should go to the servants' entrance, but the panelled front doors were already opening.

The butler, a rather stout but dignified individual in a pigeon-wing wig and a black habit, directed a startled glance from Ruth to the footman.

Ruth said quickly, "I have an appointment with Sir Brian Chandler. My name is Miss Ruth Allington."

The butler's dark eyes returned to her. They were without expression now, but for a moment he was motionless. Then, he gestured to a lackey to take Ruth's valise, sent the footman off with a nod, and murmured, "This way, if you please, miss."

They crossed a superb great hall with beautifully carved ceilings, floors of gleaming marble, and a graceful curving staircase. The butler turned into a wide corridor where thick rugs were spread on parquet floors. He opened a door, ushered Ruth into a spacious room whose high windows overlooked the fountain court, murmured a polite request that she wait, and sailed off.

Her palms wet with nervousness, Ruth looked about her. There were bookcases on the panelled walls, and a large mahogany desk stood at the centre of the room, a leather chair behind it. Above a charming marble fireplace in the right-hand wall hung a portrait of two young men, somewhere in the early twenties, she thought. Neither wore a wig or powder, and the firm chins, well-shaped lips, and lean features were sufficiently alike that she guessed them to be brothers, but that they were very different men was obvious. The taller of the pair was extremely good looking, with thick auburn hair rather carelessly tied back, and a winning smile. One slim hand rested gracefully on the parapet beside them, and Ruth's trained eye admired the detailing of a dragon's head ring he wore, and the way the artist had captured a gleam of mischief in his brilliant green eyes. There was something in the look that reminded her of Jonathan. 'A dashing rascal,' she thought wistfully. Although a comely man, his brother, whom she judged to be the eldest, was darker, his hair more severely dressed; there was no smile on the lips, which were set in a stern line, and the grey eyes reflected a trace of impatience, as though he had resented the time spent in posing for the portrait. Always interested in others, Ruth decided they must be Sir Brian Chandler's sons, and she wondered if they lived here, and if they were friends.

A door slammed somewhere, and she sat down hurriedly on a straight-backed chair facing the desk.

The door was flung open. A deep voice said irritably, "Papa, an I do not leave now, I—"

Ruth jerked around as the elder of the men in the portrait strode into the room. He was clad in riding dress, and he paused, one gauntletted hand on the latch as he stared at her.

"Oh," he said. "Your pardon, ma'am. I had thought Sir Brian was in here."

She started to tell him that Sir Brian was on his way, but the door was already closing.

"Most ill-mannered," she advised it. The portrait, she thought, must have been painted about a decade since, for he looked closer to thirty than twenty. He also looked even more unamiable, and one could but hope he was visiting merely, and did *not* dwell here.

She turned the chair slightly, so that she would be prepared next time the door opened. The minutes slid past and her nerves tightened again. Suppose Sir Brian did not mean to come? It would be simple for him to refuse to see her, and if his health was poor, as she'd heard, that would be the logical thing for him to do. Especially if his nature was as forbidding as that of his son. She sent up a quick prayer. 'Dear God— *please* . . .'

"Miss Allington?"

She pulled her head up. A tall thin gentleman watched her from the doorway. Suddenly, her knees were weak; they shook as she stood and made her curtsy.

He came into the room and offered a slight but polite bow. Ruth scanned a careworn face and weary green eyes that also reflected incredulity. He looked far from hearty, but he was not as elderly as she had supposed; certainly not much above sixty. He must, she thought inconsequently, have been an exceeding handsome man in his youth. And there followed another thought. 'He is sad, poor old gentleman. I wonder why.'

In a kindly and concerned tone he said, "I am Sir Brian Chandler, and my dear lady, I fear there has been a dreadful misunderstanding. Indeed, I do not know what Mr. Falcon can have been thinking of when he wrote to me in your behalf. The position I have to offer requires an experienced artist. A *male* artist. I am sorrier than I can say, but—"

Ruth gripped her hands together and interrupted desperately, "I beg of you, sir. Do not set your mind 'gainst me. I *am* an experienced artist. I worked closely with my father, whose work is greatly admired in—in Europe."

The poor girl looked distraught, he thought uneasily. And how pale she was. "Pray be seated," he said, and walked around the desk to occupy the big chair. "I am unaware of an artist by that name, but you must understand, Miss Allington, that were your father to have been a great man with the skill of—of a Greville Armitage, for instance, I could not hire you."

Ruth crossed the fingers that were hidden by the folds of her gown and slid deeper into deception. "My Papa worked with Greville Armitage, Sir Brian. 'Twas Mr. Armitage taught me all I know of art." (That, at least, was no lie!) She saw that he was impressed, and hurried on. "I helped him often. In fact, Papa and I worked with him on the restoration of frescoes in the Villa Albertini, outside Milan."

His tired eyes brightened. "Did you, indeed? I have seen the Albertini frescoes. They are magnificent! But I'd no idea—" He broke off and regrouped hurriedly. "I cannot but be impressed, ma'am. But nothing could sway my decision. This, you see, is a bachelor establishment. My eldest son resides here, for the present at least. And it would be considered quite shocking were I to allow an unmarried lady to share our roof."

"But, sir, might I not take rooms nearby? I would never expect to be allowed to live on your beautiful estate, but surely there is a farmhouse where I might find accommodation? Oh, Sir Brian, if you would just give me a chance. I do not ask for charity. I promise you I can work as hard and as long as any man. Only give me a chance to prove my ability. I have brought some of my work, if you would but look at it."

She was, he thought, a pretty creature, in spite of her severely dressed hair and rumpled gown. And she appeared so desperate, poor thing. Deeply troubled, he took up Falcon's letter and made a mental note to have a few words with that young madman in the very near future. For the present, however, he must be firm. He said, "Alas, 'twould be pointless, Miss Allington. However, I shall set my steward to try and find a suitable—ah, post for you. Though I'll confess myself astonished that the daughter of a fine artist must be reduced to earning her own livelihood. You have family, surely?"

"My brother was lost at sea," she said truthfully. "And Mama went to her reward years since. Papa was all I had. He was successful, as you say, and had an adequate fortune, but he was of the artistic temperament. Which is to say," she added, feeling shockingly disloyal, "that he was a brilliant man, but with no least concept of business matters. His investments proved to have been poor, and he borrowed unwisely. Indeed, I believe 'twas worry over what should become of us that—that brought about his death." The memory of her beloved father overcame her at this point, and she pressed her handkerchief to her lips.

Sir Brian squirmed in his chair and prepared to end this unfortunate interview at once, but Ruth recovered herself and swept on before he could administer the *coup de grace*.

"I am not a foolish woman, sir, and I was sure I could manage quite well when we were left all alone, but—"

"We?" he intervened keenly.

'Bother!' thought Ruth. "My—cousin. I have always cared for her because she is a— Well, she is not quick-witted."

'Good God!' thought Sir Brian.

"But," she went on hurriedly, "I have had all I could do to pay our creditors. I knew that my dear father would want that. He was always so—so moral a man, you see. And now, the house has been swallowed up, and—" She bit her lip and for a moment her voice was suspended.

Sir Brian rushed into the breach. "My poor child," he said, standing. "Rest assured I shall do whatever—" He blinked, shattered by the tragic despair in two lovely grey eyes framed by tear-wet black lashes. "Truly," he faltered, feeling the ultimate villain, "I wish I could—"

The door opened and the man who had looked in earlier started to enter, then hesitated. "Your pardon, sir," he said, eyeing Ruth curiously. "I had thought you were talking to the applicant for the restoration."

"Quite correct." Sir Brian gave an inward sigh of relief. "Miss Allington, allow me to present my son, Mr. Gordon Chandler."

Even as Ruth stood to make her curtsy, her heart sank. There was a kindness in Sir Brian. She had sensed it, and sensed also that he had been touched by her plight and that with a little more time she might have persuaded him. But now he was all cool control again.

Gordon Chandler's bow was perfunctory. He said in faintly incredulous amusement, "A *female* applicant? No, really, sir, I think you quiz me."

'Brute!' thought Ruth, and sinking into the chair again tore open her valise and thrust her sketchbook across the desk. "If you would but look at some of my work, Sir Brian."

"Oh, come now, Miss Allington." Chandler's grey eyes were suddenly alight with mirth. "This task will be arduous and is not for a lady. You cannot really expect that my father would consider such an arrangement."

"Surely, Mr. Chandler," she persisted, her soft voice at

odds with her murderous thoughts, "Sir Brian will want to engage a person of skill and experience? I can offer him both."

His lips twitched. Clearly, he was struggling not to laugh out loud. In the manner of one addressing a tiresome child he said, "Yes, I've no doubt you can, but—"

Sir Brian, who had been sorting through the sketchbook exclaimed, "By Jove, but these *are* good! Gordie, only see how—"

The smile in his son's eyes faded. He said austerely, "If ever I heard of such a thing! 'Tis not to be thought of, Papa, and we must not be so unkind as to raise the lady's hopes. Now, if you've a moment I'd like your decision about the new steward."

Sir Brian said with a trace of petulance, "I was not displeased with Durwood."

"But—sir, I told you how his books were—"

"Yes, yes. I know you never liked the man."

"I'll own it. But that has nought to do with—"

"I am engaged at the moment, Gordon. We will discuss the other matter when I am free. You know, I believe that 'tis *never* my wish to be unkind."

Sir Brian's voice was silken, but suddenly the air was full of tension and Ruth held her breath. For a moment the two men looked at each other, then Chandler's eyes fell. "Of course, sir. My apologies."

"Very good. Now, spare me a moment from your busy schedule and look at this extraordinarily fine sketch. 'Tis of the Villa Albertini in Milan, as you can see. We were there in . . . forty-three, was it?"

"I have never been to Milan, sir."

Sir Brian's head jerked up.

His son said expressionlessly, "You took Quentin."

A look of infinite sadness chased the frown from the handsome features. There was the impression of a sigh restrained, then he nodded. "Ah, yes. Memory plays me false at times." He returned his attention to the sketch, but the enthusiasm had gone from his voice when he said, "Still, you must agree this shows a marked degree of skill."

Chandler glanced at the sketch. "Charming. Papa, it grows late. If Miss Allington is to catch the afternoon stagecoach . . ."

Sir Brian stood and began to gather the sketches together. "Quite so."

Ruth said imploringly, "But, sir. You like my work, and—"

"My father is tired, ma'am," said Chandler, the frigid tone forbidding further discussion.

"And so is the lady," said Sir Brian gently. "I'faith, but you look much too wearied to travel back to Town tonight, Miss Allington. My son will arrange for you to be conveyed to Dover and obtain rooms for you, and a ticket on the morning stagecoach. Truly, I am sorrier than I can say to be obliged to . . ."

He went on speaking in his kind courtly voice while he came to offer her her sketchbook.

Ruth scarcely heard him. She had failed. Despite all her lies and prayers and pleadings, she had failed. The abominable Gordon Chandler had seen to that. Whatever would become of Thorpe and Jacob now? Would they all be thrust into debtor's prison? The thought of those two dear little boys in such a ghastly place as Newgate made her knees grow weak. She'd had too many worries and not enough sleep and it was many hours since she had eaten. The room began to grow dim . . .

From a long way off, she heard Sir Brian's voice raised in a near scream . . .

Only a moment must have passed when she opened her eyes. She was in the big chair behind the desk. Sir Brian was bending over her, slapping at her hand gently, his face white as death and his eyes terrified.

She put up a hand and touched her brow dazedly.

"Oh . . . my dear sir . . . I am so sorry! Whatever must you . . . think."

Inexpressibly relieved, he drew a trembling breath. "That you are worn out, poor child. And have not eaten since— when?"

"I . . . do not recall . . . That is— Oh, I feel so stupid . . ."

"You are not in the least stupid. I should say rather that you are very brave. Your situation must be desperate indeed. If I cannot offer you employment, I can at least see to it that you have a good meal before sending you off."

She could hear Mr. Chandler's voice, upraised and wrathful, in the distance, and she sat up, trying vaguely to tidy her hair. "No, no. I thank you sir, but—" She glanced fearfully to the door. "I quite understand why you must refuse me. Pray believe that not for the world would I bring your son's anger down upon you."

He stiffened. "Nor will you do so, I promise you! There is but one master in this house, ma'am."

'Hah!' thought Ruth. But she peered at the portrait on the wall and enquired timidly, "Is the other gentleman your son also, sir? He looks very like you. Such a handsome man."

He glanced at the portrait and said rather heavily, "Yes. That is Quentin, my younger son."

Quick to note the wistfulness that again came into his eyes, she murmured, "He does not much resemble his brother. Is he— I mean, does he have the—er, same temperament as Mr. Gordon Chandler?"

Sir Brian laughed. "Oh, no. Quentin is a most amiable young fellow."

"Well, well." His face a thundercloud, and having obviously heard his father's comment, Chandler was coming back into the room. He was accompanied by a middle-aged lady carrying a glass of water, whom he introduced as the housekeeper, Mrs. Tate. "What a remarkable recovery, Miss Allington," he went on. "I trust my return was not too prompt for you?"

Yearning to rap the tray over his dark head, Ruth reached for the glass with a hand that shook, and whispered, "Thank you, ma'am."

"I think there is no cause for such a remark, Gordon," said Sir Brian sharply. "Mrs. Tate, pray ask Chef to prepare a warm meal for Miss Allington."

"You are too kind, sir," said Ruth, keeping her eyes, suitably awed, upon Chandler. "But—but I think it best—"

"Nonsense. Now you must not be frightened by my son. He has a sharp tongue at times, but I promise you his heart is kind. Ain't that so, Mrs. Tate?"

From under her lashes Ruth saw a muscle ripple beside Chandler's jaw, and could all but hear his teeth grinding.

The housekeeper, a poised woman with grey-streaked auburn hair under her neat cap, said in a beautifully modulated voice, "Very true, sir. Perhaps the young lady would be the better for a short rest while Chef prepares her meal."

"By all means." Chandler added sarcastically, "I'd not be at all surprised does Miss Allington find herself too weak to return to Dover tonight, eh ma'am?"

Ruth said nothing, but shrank a little closer to Sir Brian.

"I thought so," said Chandler. "You must let her stay here, sir. I feel sure you can arrange suitable accommodations, eh, Mrs. Tate?"

The housekeeper looked quickly from Sir Brian's tight lips to his son's angry eyes. "I think 'twould be improper, sir."

Gordon Chandler had suffered a frustrating day on several counts. He was quite aware that his sire was displeased with him, but his temper overbore his customary good judgment. "How so?" he demanded. "Why, 'twould take no more than three or four hours to open, clean, and prepare one of the cottages so as to show our hospitality to so—ah, talented a lady."

"That will not be necessary." Sir Brian turned to Ruth, and added smilingly, "However, I have reached a decision, ma'am, and you may thank my son that I am enabled to accept your application. Had it not been for his quick wits I'd not have thought of it, but he is quite correct. While you work here the blue cottage will both provide you with comfortable accommodation and protect your reputation. Especially, if you bring your cousin to serve as chaperone."

Momentarily overwhelmed, Ruth was too choked with emotion to thank him, and tears slipped down her cheeks.

"There, there," said Sir Brian. "Never upset yourself, little lady." He smiled at his housekeeper. "I leave her in your care, Mrs. Tate."

His face grim, Gordon Chandler stalked over to open the door. He bowed as the housekeeper guided Ruth from the room, and through his teeth murmured, "One can but hope, madam, that you ply your brushes as well as you play your cards!"

CHAPTER III

hree days later Ruth stood very still in the centre of the withdrawing room at Lingways, listening to the tall case clock strike eleven, and savouring the delights of this loved and lovely old house. The scent of woodsmoke that still faintly permeated the air; the thick carpets and tasteful furnishings; the heavy maroon velvet of the draperies; the pale gold bar of sunlight that slanted through the mullioned windows to accent the brass peacock in the hearth. It had been sad to say good-bye to the house on Mount Street. It was wrenching to have to leave Lingways. She sometimes thought she cared more for the Essex estate than had Thomas, though it had been in his family for almost two centuries. Thomas, bless his gentle soul, had not been a man to concern himself with belongings; nor indeed with anything save the ancient Greeks and their writings, which had, he believed, been so erroneously translated.

She could almost see him, half-buried behind piles of mouldering volumes, blinking at her over his spectacles, and murmuring absently, "You must do whatever you wish, my dear. Whatever will make you happy." Always, he had wanted only to make her happy, but it had never seemed to occur to him that a bride so much younger than himself might have wished him to share in that happiness. Proud of her, never belittling her accomplishments, delighting to see her clad in the latest fashions and enjoying her friends, he had denied her nothing—except himself. For, dwelling so much in his own world, he had kept the door to it firmly closed, and all her attempts to lure him into walks or conversation, or into accompanying her to social functions had been not so much refused, as simply not noted.

She smiled faintly. In his way, he had loved her dearly. And she had loved him. He had left Lingways to her when he died, and after a while Johnny had come with the twins, and Lingways had become home to them all, until—

"Dear Mrs. A. This must be so hard for you."

Holding some squares of paper and a pencil, Grace Milford had come into the room and stood watching her sympathetically.

"Only think how much harder 'twould be had I not secured the post in Kent," said Ruth, summoning a bright smile. "I was thinking, Grace, that we might bring the price down to fifteen guineas for the drum table. Would you change it, please? And there's Mr. Allington's desk. I was sure it would sell to that farmer yesterday. I suppose that must be reduced, too." And she thought that if only it had not rained so, they could have done much better.

Grace Milford wrote a painstaking "15 gns." on one of her paper squares and went to put it on the drum table and remove the sign that read "28 gns." "Be lucky to get ten guineas for the master's desk, I think, ma'am," she said.

Ruth nodded reluctantly. "But the big desk and the reference table in the book room are both fine antiques. They should surely fetch a hundred guineas if—"

"If we'd time to wait for better weather *and* the proper buyer, maybe. But we've only today! And by the time we reach the farm— Is it far from Lac Brillant?"

Ruth said absently, "Farm . . . ?"

"Aye. The farm where the boys are to stay. Proper excited they be. You *did* say 'twas a farm?"

Looking anywhere but into those honest eyes, Ruth felt her face getting hot. "Er—did I? What I meant to say was I had found a place for them near Lac Brillant where they'd be properly cared for, but—" She was grateful to be rescued by the sound of hoofbeats and the grind of wheels. "A coach!" She flew to the windows. "It *is!* We've a *customer!* Oh, my! A most elegant lady—no, two ladies! Pray, dear Grace! You have such power in prayer. Pray they will buy *lots* of our lovely things!"

The prospective buyers were elegant indeed. The younger of the pair was about her own age, Ruth judged, and of a rare beauty with great dusky eyes, high cheekbones, and a full-lipped rather wilful mouth. Tall and blessed with a generous bosom and a tiny waist, she moved with assured grace. Her dark curls were quite short under a ruffled cap threaded with a scarlet riband. Matching ribands were tied about the falls of lace on the sleeves of her pink muslin morning gown, and she carried a pink reticule richly embroidered with red and gold silks. Her companion was younger, shorter, and rather plump, with a round face, big blue eyes, and a giggle. Her green gown was sadly over-embellished with bows and rosettes, and not improved by the elaborate blue and white shawl draped around her shoulders.

"We are come," said the dark lady as Grace showed them into the withdrawing room, "in response to the sign in the lane. I trust," she added, her glance flickering over the upholstered furniture and lingering briefly on the drum table, "that these are not the only articles you mean to sell?"

Her tone was disdainful, her manner haughty, and she did not give her name. Her friend appeared to find the situation hilarious, and whispered and giggled as Ruth led the way into the book room.

The plump girl's eyes shot to the desk, and she interrupted

her own amusement to squeak, "Only look, Lady Dee! Just what you wanted!"

The dark lady gave her an irked glance and said disparagingly, "It might serve, but—dear me! Not at that price! Fifty guineas, indeed!"

Her heart sinking, Ruth pointed out that the desk was an antique piece and beautifully made. "As is the reference table, ma'am."

The plump girl said, "Oh, that is lovely. See the carving, Dee."

"Lady Dee" sniffed. "I see that 'tis prodigious over-priced. If this is all you have, Mrs. Lingways, I fear 'twas a waste of my time to stop here."

Ruth began, "My name, ma'am, is—"

Ignoring her, Lady Dee observed that the rug by the fireplace was fair, and that she might take it if the asking price was "not absurd."

Ruth gritted her teeth. The rug had been brought home by Jonathan after one of his voyages, and was a thing of beauty. " 'Tis from Persia," she said, "and—"

"I will give you ten guineas for it," said Lady Dee. Oblivious to Grace Milford's outraged gasp, she sailed into the hall, proceeding at speed through the dining room with its handsome mahogany furnishings, and into the study. Thomas Allington's desk she dismissed with a shudder, the bishop's chair in the corner received a thoughtful look, and she walked on.

A quarter of an hour later, Ruth was seething, Grace was red-faced and bristling with indignation, and Lady Dee's friend had ceased to giggle and was casting longing backward glances at the book room.

My lady swept towards the entrance hall, and Grace hurried past and reached for the front door handle.

Lady Dee paused, and regarded Ruth in a considering fashion. "I collect that you need the money, poor thing," she said loftily. "So despite my better judgment I will do what I can for you. You may have fifty pounds for the reference table, desk, and Persian rug in the book room, the drum table in the withdrawing room, and the display cabinet in the dining room."

Ruth stared at her.

Grace tugged at her sleeve. "But, ma'am," she hissed audibly. "The other gentleman said he would come back, surely."

Lady Dee favoured Grace with a look of loathing. "Come, Hetty," she ordered.

Grace opened the front door.

Ruth thought achingly, 'Fifty pounds! Not even fifty guineas! And they are worth at least three hundred guineas!'

The two prospective customers went onto the front steps.

The plump girl muttered, "Dee, if you do not want—"

My lady swung around. "Very well, Mrs. Lingways. You drive a hard bargain, but clearly my friend is taken with that foolish rug, and I will be generous in the name of Christian charity. One hundred pounds for all the items I named, plus the brass bird in the withdrawing room fireplace."

It was an improvement certainly, but still Ruth hesitated. Perchance someone else *would* come. This unpleasant young woman shouldn't have all those beautiful things for such a niggardly price. But—there was so little time left. Perhaps no one else would come. And a hundred pounds would enable her to give Samuel Coachman and William their back wages, and pay Grace for the first time in many months. She would even be able to repay their kindly benefactor, Dr. Osbrink, and Grace could settle the grocer's bill in Shoeburyness, and arrange for the hire of a coach to take them as far as Croydon. She stifled a sigh. "Very well, I accept."

Grace hissed, "But—ma'am! The *other* gent!"

Lady Dee snapped, "I shall take the rug, the drum table, and the brass bird with me. Hetty, go and call my footman. The rest," she went on as her friend trotted dutifully away, "I will send my people to collect later this afternoon. I will pay you now, however, so that you cannot dicker for a better offer once my back is turned."

Ruth flushed. "As if I would do such a—"

"Here." A fumbling in the pretty reticule and a fat purse was extracted from which my lady removed two banknotes already written in the amount of fifty pounds each. "Take them, do," she said impatiently, "before I repent of my poor bargain. Good God! *Now* why must you look displeased? You have seen banknotes before, surely?"

Troubled, Ruth said, "My late husband would never accept paper money."

"What nonsense! This is 1748, not 1478! Should you expect that I would carry such a sum in gold pieces?" She gave a scornful titter. " 'Faith, but I would need a coal scuttle!"

With quiet persistence, Ruth said, "Perhaps your ladyship could pay for the articles when you come back to—"

"Whilst you haggle with your other buyer and then claim the sale was not final, eh?" With the words it was as if a blight fell upon Lady Dee's beauty. The lovely eyes narrowed and became hard, her chin jutted, and the line of her mouth thinned so that suddenly Ruth felt sorry for her husband. "I have already wasted too much time," my lady declared. "Make up your mind, madam, or I'm done with you."

Humbling her pride, Ruth accepted the notes.

With no more of a farewell than a derisive, "I should think so!" Lady Dee turned to give instructions to the waiting footman, then hurried to her carriage.

Once inside, she turned to embrace her friend with a squeal of excitement. "*What* a bargain!" she trilled. "Those articles are splendid, and worth closer to four hundred guineas than a paltry one hundred! That stupid woman could have no notion of their true value! Only think, Hetty! I am finished with searching for something to please my tiresome papa-in-law. He will love that desk and fancy I paid a great sum for it."

"Perhaps Mrs. Lingways was desperate," Hetty murmured. "I could not but feel sorry for her. She seems so young to be a widow. And very pretty did not you think?"

"La, but how silly you are! Why should you feel sorry for such an insolent woman? As for looks, I thought her plain as any pikestaff. Really, Hetty! Sometimes I think you need spectacles, like your mama!"

Hetty stammered and giggled, and not until they were well on their way did she venture to point out that dear Lady Dee had not obtained a written receipt for her one hundred pounds.

This very sensible reminder startled her ladyship, but only for a moment. "Pish," she said. "The widow Lingways would not dare to cheat a lady of Quality. And even if she should, she would catch cold at that, for we know where she is to be found, and I would have her clapped into Newgate before she could wink her eye!"

The grocer in Shoeburyness was overjoyed when his bill was paid in full, and Grace Milford went back onto the street torn between relief at having been spared the embarrassment that usually attended her visits to the aromatic little shop, and regret that dear Mrs. A. had been obliged to sacrifice her belongings. Momentarily dazzled by the bright spring sunlight, she was pleasantly surprised when a familiar voice spoke in her ear.

" 'ullo, 'ullo, 'ullo! This is my lucky day! Just who I 'oped ter find."

With a tricorne under his arm and a broad smile on his square countenance, Enoch Tummet made an awkward but energetic bow.

"Well, I never did!" said Grace, blushing, and fluttering her lashes coyly. "Mr. Tummet, as ever was! What brings you all the way up here?"

He proceeded to escort her along the street. "Told you as

I'd come 'fore you runned orf. Gotta keep me ogles on a pretty girl like you, Miss Grace, or some young and 'andsome Buck will snatch you away."

Far from displeased, Grace giggled and said, "How clever of you to find me. Did you call in at Lingways first?"

He admitted this, then added with a rather odd note to his voice, "Good thing, too. Not that I dared to say nuthink to yer lady. But I see that there sign you got stuck out on the lane, and I says ter meself, 'E. Tummet,' I says. 'This 'ere must be looked inter. Quick-like.' So I ups and asks your Sam Coachman where I might 'ope ter find a certain 'andsome young female." He winked and gave Grace a nudge with his elbow. "Meaning you, ma'am. And being a downy file, Sam Coachman told me. So—gooseberry-jam, 'ere I am!"

With a coquettish smile, Grace turned into the yard of the livery stable.

Tummet seized her arm and drew her into the shade of a laburnum tree. "Sam says as you're orf terday, Miss Grace. That right?"

She nodded. "The greatest piece of luck, Mr. Tummet. That letter your Mr. August writ done the trick proper! I'm to hire a coach this very minute. Mrs. Allington's been give a pretty cottage to live in, and the exact wages she was asking! And *I'm* allowed to go down and look after her!"

"Very 'appy fer the lady, I'm sure. All packed up, is you?"

"Yes." Touched because of his mournful expression, she said, "We ain't going to the end o' the world, y'know, Mr. Tummet. Leastways, I hopes you don't find it so."

"Even if it was, I'd find it," he declared. He still looked sombre however, and he said with rare gravity, "Not to stick me nose in where it ain't wanted, but—why don't yer lady 'ave Sam Coachman drive you dahn?"

"Well, Lady Buttershaw arranged it all, as you know. And she thought it best that Sir Brian Chandler didn't find out Mrs. Thomas Allington was used to be Miss Ruth Armitage.

So our coachman is to bring us only this far. Then we'll travel by a *hired* carriage to Croydon, and—"

"*Croydon!* Cor, luv a duck! She really reckons on being follered, does she?"

Grace said uneasily, "Not followed, exactly. But Sir Brian Chandler's heir was proper put out when Mrs. A. was hired. Very rude, he was."

Tummet nodded. "That'd be Mr. Gordon Chandler. A bit stiff-rumped sometimes, but—"

"Mr. Tummet!" exclaimed Grace, scandalized.

"Whoops!" he exclaimed. "I'm a commoner and no mistaking!" His impenitent grin won her to a smile again, and he went on, "So Mrs. Allington don't want Mr. Gordon Chandler follering Sam Coachman back 'ere and asking all manner o' questions and finding out about Captain Armitage, is that it?"

"Lady Buttershaw says there was so many wicked things said about the poor Captain, and Sir Brian won't bear with any least sniff o'scandal . . ." Grace shrugged. "My dear Mrs. A. fought so hard to win the old gentleman over, Mr. Tummet. It'd be cruel hard if she was to lose the commission now."

"Then you better tell yer lady to take that there sign dahn, mate. 'Fore she sells something! Else there'll be another scandal, quick-like!"

Frightened by his stern manner, Grace cried, "Why? 'Sides, she already sold some things."

"Oh, Lor'! She shouldn't oughter 'ave done that, Miss Grace."

"Why ever not, I should like to know? They was all her own things, what Mr. Allington had give her, and what belonged to her and her papa, rest his soul. Now why must you shake your head and look so glum as any goblin?"

"Because them things *wasn't* hers, Miss Grace! Not 'cording to law, they wasn't. And afore you starting snipping orf me poor nose, I'll remind you, marm, as I were once a bailiff, and I knows. Fact is, I'm surprised there ain't been a execution at Lingways."

"If you means a man sent to guard the house, there—"

"Not just the 'ouse, marm. *All* the property's been took over by the Court, so as to pay back the creditors."

"And very cruel, I calls it! Besides, Mrs. A. knows about it. They've got their money. Or will have, when it's sold."

He said patiently, "But what that means, Miss Grace, is that *everything* was confiscated. All what's *inside*, as well as buildings and grounds. Furniture and all, marm. Not *none* of it can't be sold by your lady!"

"Oh!" gasped Grace, clutching his sleeve in her dismay. "Oh, dearie, dearie me! There *is* a bailiff s'posed to come today. But I thought— Mrs. A. thought 'twas to take care of the place lest thieves break in and— Oh! My Lor'! Is it very bad that she sold some things?"

He thought, 'Not if you don't mind being transported—or worse!' But his admired lady was pale and trembling, and a gent didn't frighten persons of the female persuasion, so he asked, "Can she buy 'em back?"

Grace pressed a hand to her lips and shook her head. "She hardly got a quarter of what they was worth. And she's spent what little she did get on paying off the servants and me, and making good on bills and loans. She can have back what she give me, of course. But—"

Tummet shook his head ponderously. "That won't do no good, mate."

With a stifled sob Grace again seized his arm. "Mr. Tummet, they—they wouldn't never accuse her of— I mean—they wouldn't put her . . . in *gaol?*" Distracted, she moaned, "Oh, *crumbs!* The poor soul's had so much grief, and been so brave. *Whatever* are we to do?"

Enoch Tummet had survived a somewhat checkered career and was nothing if not resourceful. After a moment's frowning introspection he said briskly, "Right y'are, mate. We'll 'ave to cook-a-tart— I mean, look smart. But if you do what E. Tummet says—*eggsack*, mind!—we might just get yer lady safe outta this bog!"

"Oh, I will, Mr. Tummet," said Grace, gazing up at him with tearful but grateful eyes. "I'll do *exactly* what you say!"

It was five and twenty minutes past two o'clock when Grace hurried up the kitchen steps of Lingways. William, the footman, was seated in one chair, his feet on another, a mug of ale in his hand. Fully expecting a rebuke, he sprang up guiltily, his youthful face scarlet as he stammered apologies.

"Never mind that," hissed Grace. "Did anyone call whilst I was gone?"

"A farmer and his wife. They bought the case clock, ma'am. Took it with 'em."

Grace moaned. "What about the two ladies who was here this morning? Did their servants come for the things they bought?"

"Not yet, Miss Grace."

'They better make haste!' she thought. "Where's the missus?"

"In the master's study. Fell sound asleep in his chair, she done. Master Thorpe and Master Jacob wanted to talk to her, but I sent them out to play, so she could get a bit of a kip, poor lady."

She told him he'd done just right, and gave him certain instructions that sent him scurrying off, his eyes round with curiosity.

Grace bustled along the silent hall. The case clock was gone, then. One less. But there was still the marble one on the mantelpiece in the book room, and the little china one in Mrs. A's bedchamber . . .

The marble clock struck the half-hour as she opened the book room door, causing her to jump and swing the door shut quickly. She ran to the hearth and stood on tiptoe.

"What you doin', Miss Grace?"

With a yelp she whipped around, her heart thundering.

One of the twins stood watching her, his grey eyes too solemn for a five-year-old.

"How you frightened me!" panted Grace, a hand to her chest. "You shouldn't creep up on folk that way, Master Jacob!"

"I din't creep. An' I'm Thorpe. What you doin' to—"

"It was—it was running down and the time was wrong, so I'm putting it right again."

"Oh." He walked out with her, and followed her to the stairs.

At the top she said, "Go and put on your coat and hat, dear. And tell Jacob to get ready."

"All right." But instead he stayed with her as she hurried to Ruth's bedchamber. Grace paused and looked down at him. Poor mite, he still had that solemn look. She put a hand on his fair curls. "What is it, Master Thorpe?"

"Aunty Ruth says we're goin' away." The tone of his voice remained the same, but he took her hand in both of his and clung to it tightly while his big eyes searched her face. "Are we all goin' . . . to the same place?"

She suffered a pang. "What did your aunty say?"

"She says we are. But she looks funny with her hair all squashed like that. An' she was too tired to talk, she said."

"Well, I expect she was. She'll tell you all about it soon, dear. Now run along and do as I told you."

He relinquished her hand reluctantly, and turned away. As she opened Ruth's door, he said with a gulp, "If they're goin' to send us all different places, Jacob and me—we'll run away. To be pirates!"

He galloped off then, but she had seen the glint of tears, and her heart was wrung.

Half an hour later, sitting beside Grace in the rocking coach, and with Jacob and Thorpe craning their necks to watch the afternoon countryside race past, Ruth said, "I cannot believe I slept for such a time. Thank goodness you woke me, Grace, else we'd never have reached Croydon before dark."

"I thought I'd best, Mrs. A. Being as the other carriage will be waiting for us in Shoeburyness."

"Yes, indeed. Still, I wish that unpleasant woman had come to collect her things before we left. You did tell William which items are hers?"

"I told him," said Grace woodenly.

"He's such a good man. 'Twas kind of him to offer to stay and help Samuel move the rest of our furnishings into the cellar. I don't think the new owners will object, do you? 'Twill only be for a few months. When I finish Sir Brian's fresco I should have sufficient put by that we'll be able to rent a little house, perhaps, and can try to sell some more of our things for—" She broke off with a gasp as the carriage swerved and Samuel Coachman shouted something uncomplimentary.

A stagecoach thundered past from the opposite direction, having all but forced them into the ditch.

"Wheee!" hooted Thorpe. "I wish I might go by a Portsmouth Machine!"

"Not me," said Jacob. "The people were all squashed together, an' that big outside passenger looked jus' like a rank rider. 'Sides, they're called stagecoaches now."

His more adventurously inclined brother scoffed, "Highwaymen don't *ride* on stagecoaches, stupid. They *rob* 'em!"

"Even so, you should not make such unkind judgments," said Ruth. "People are seldom what they look to be. The gentleman might very well be a—a parson. Or perhaps a dancing master."

As she had hoped, this sally relieved the shadow of anxiety on two small faces and awoke shrieks of laughter.

Grace did not join in the merriment. In her view, the outside passenger had looked to be just what she was sure he was: a bailiff. She thought with deep thankfulness, 'In the nick of time! Thank God, and Mr. Tummet!'

Very soon, Samuel Coachman set them down outside the stagecoach station on the southern edge of Shoeburyness. Their parting was painful, for the man had been employed by Thomas Allington since his youth. Loathing the deceit she must practice, Ruth refused to allow him to wait with them until the London coach he believed they were to travel on was ready to leave, though her heart was touched when he insisted he must stay to protect his "family."

"You are so good, so loyal, dear Sam," she said, her voice breaking. "But you must get back to Lingways and help William store my furniture. Besides," she added, seeing tears glittering in Thorpe's blue eyes, "Miss Grace and I have two fine young gentlemen to protect us."

Jacob's troubled face brightened a little, and Thorpe, at once the more mischievous and tender-hearted of the pair, sniffed, and said in his best "manly" voice that Samuel need not be worried. "Jake an' me would die a awful death 'fore we'd let anyone hurt my Aunty, or Miss Grace," he growled. And in the next instant he had hurled himself into the coachman's ready arms, and was sobbing out how much he would miss him.

They all watched sadly as the familiar coach rattled around the corner and out of sight. Nobody spoke. Scared and bewildered as this last link with the life they'd known vanished, the boys pressed closer to Ruth. She hugged them and fought tears as she said huskily that they were not to worry; they were going to a very beautiful place in the country. And with an inner prayer that she spoke truth, she promised that everything was going to be all right.

A quarter hour after Samuel's departure the shabby coach and pair Grace had hired pulled into the kennel, and the coachman scrambled down and began to load their luggage into the boot.

Puzzled, Jacob said, "But I thought we was to go on the London *stagecoach*, Aunty?"

"Mrs. Allington was obliged to change her mind," said Grace. "But this will be much nicer."

It was a small change perhaps, but the twins were deeply afraid and after an exchanged glance, as if by mutual consent, once again they clung desperately to their aunt's skirts.

How helpless they were, poor little boys, thought Ruth; their young lives already sadly mauled by Fate, and now quite at the mercy of the decisions she made—or that the authorities forced upon her. She relaxed an earlier edict and said they might ride on the box beside the coachman for the first stage at least, so long as they obeyed him with no arguing. Even this glorious prospect failed to cheer them, and not until they had made sure that she and Grace were indeed inside and the coachman had closed the door did they tussle to be first one on the box.

The carriage pulled into traffic and turned to the west and Tilbury, where they would be conveyed by ferryboat across the Thames to Gravesend. The clear voices of the twins could be heard upraised in eager questioning, but inside it was quiet, neither woman speaking for a few minutes, both plagued by similar thoughts.

"Poor wee lads," sighed Grace then. "So fearful, they are. But the farm will cheer them, surely. What is it like, Mrs. A.?"

Ruth took a deep breath. 'Now!' she thought, and admitted, "There is no farm."

"But—but—you said—"

" 'Twas what I thought at the time. Now—the boys come with us."

" 'Pon my word!" exclaimed Grace, her eyes big with astonishment. "Sir Brian Chandler must be a saint to have agreed to . . ." Something in Ruth's tight-lipped silence alerting her, she interrupted herself. "He *did* agree they could come?"

Ruth turned her head and looked at her squarely.

With a moan, Grace clapped both hands to her paling cheeks. "You've tricked him in some way, that's what it is!

Mercy me! I knew it! Oh, Mrs. A., 'tis tempting Providence to tell falsehoods!"

Perhaps because of her own feelings of guilt, Ruth was infuriated. "Foolish creature! Why must you at once assume I told falsehoods? I did not speak of the boys at all. And if you look at me as if I was Delilah, or—or Jezebel, I promise you Grace Milford I will box your silly ears!"

Grace looked cowed, but since her ears had never been boxed in all the years she had served Ruth, her dismay was momentary. "Then, if you didn't speak of them, why did he give you leave to—"

"He did not," said Ruth through her teeth. "There! So you have it! I mean to smuggle them there, and keep them hid! Well? Say it! Name me a shameless sinner and a wicked woman, and have done!"

Grace was pale, but armed with the convictions of her strict Methodist upbringing, she said, "You are not a Jezebel, nor yet a Delilah, ma'am. But the gentleman was so kind as to offer you a position 'gainst his own wishes, and in return you have told untruths, and mean to deceive—"

"Aye, I mean to deceive," Ruth confirmed fiercely. "And I would resort to more lies and deception to keep those two dear orphans by me! Their mama was taken 'ere they knew her; the father they worshipped is gone, leaving a shamed and dishonoured name behind him; and my papa, who adored them and whom they adored, is now lost to them also. I am all they have left. Do you think I'd abandon them now?"

"There is no need to abandon them. We could take a room like you'd planned, and I would care for—"

"You would, I know. But . . ." Ruth crumpled suddenly, and sat huddled against the squabs. "Oh, Grace, I've seen such terror in their eyes. The poor mites dread lest we be separated forever—as well we may be, Lord help us! When I tried to explain that we would have to live apart, but for no more than a few weeks, I could see they did not believe. Can I keep us all together for just a *little* while longer, perhaps they will be less frightened. Besides, this will save the expense of a room and food." She sank her head into her hands, her voice shaking. "I know 'twas wicked, and—and that I do indeed deceive Sir Brian. But—if the worst happened and the twins should have to be split up— Oh, Lord! They are *inseparable*! 'Twould break their dear hearts! *Truly*, I am . . . at my wits' end!"

"There, there now." Grace discarded scruples and hugged her mistress fondly. "You meant only for the best, and you may be sure as the Good Lord will forgive, for He ever loved little children. We'll have to try to make the boys understand, though. And how we'll keep 'em safe hid is more than I can see."

Ruth sniffed, and dried her tears. "You will see when we reach Lac Brillant tomorrow. The cottage is far removed from the main house and surrounded by trees, and there are woods behind. The boys will have to be careful, for there are many gardeners, but they will do *anything* if it means we can keep together. Faith, but they're more than like to fancy it a fine game." She sighed and said wryly, "I do regret telling fibs, for Sir Brian is such a good, kind gentleman."

"*He* is, perhaps. But what of his son?"

"Mr. Chandler is a very different kettle of fish; the type of man who likes a woman to be soft and timid. I expect he has chosen a meek lady for his bride, and after the poor creature is wed, he will demand that she walk several paces behind him. Well, I shall be all humility and meekness myself, and defer to him in all things. Can I just win over Mr. Grimly Gordon, I may be able to tell the truth to his papa, and then we shall go along splendidly."

Heartened by this prospect, she smiled, and thought 'Resolution!' But in the back of her mind a small mean voice awoke and gibbered, 'For a few short weeks, mayhap. And after Lac Brillant? What then? . . . What then?'

CHAPTER IV

he following day's approach to sunset was glorious, the sky a blaze of colour and a warm breeze
carrying the smell of the sea to mingle with the
scents of blossoms. But riding at a leisurely pace
through the Lac Brillant woods, Gordon Chandler was too
lost in thought to admire the gold, scarlet, and amethyst of the
heavens or notice the fragrance of the air. His journey to
Canterbury had been disappointing. Gatewell, their man of
the law, had heard none of the rumours about a Jacobite
amnesty and had said in his gruff way that he did not expect
the King to grant an amnesty for a long time to come. "Your
brother," he'd added with a stern glance from under his heavy
eyebrows, "should count himself fortunate to be alive at all,
even if he has to live outside England." Chandler frowned.
He'd not relay that news to Papa. Since he had to be in Town
tomorrow, he would see what he could learn there. He must
seek out Gideon Rossiter as well, and ask him about the
peculiar affair at Larchwoods. There was something dashed
havey-cavey going on out there, and he'd have investigated
before this save that Nadia had been in such a taking.

He seldom followed the estate road when riding in from

the north, preferring to travel cross-country over Peggoty Hill. From there one was afforded an exquisite view of the house and grounds, all the way down to the blue glitter of the Strait and their little cove with its guardian offshore rocks and the crumbling and no longer used old lighthouse. Today had been no exception. He'd let Carefree have her head after they crested the hill and had ridden with slack rein through the woods. His thoughts turned to Quentin, wondering what he was doing on this sunny afternoon, missing the wild scatter-wit, recalling some of their childhood escapades, and sighing over the final deadly escapade that had robbed him of his brother, and driven Quentin, a hunted fugitive, out of England.

Carefree's meandering route now brought them out onto the side of the hill just behind the blue guest cottage, and the pretty piebald mare slowed, her ears pricking forward. Chandler looked up. Against all reason a shabby coach stood half on, half off the narrow rear footpath, and a coachman, equally shabby, was staggering towards the open rear door of the cottage with a large portmanteaux on his back.

Noting that the ill-matched pair was contentedly devouring what had once been a neatly trimmed shrub, and that the coach wheels had dug deep grooves into the velvety lawn, Chandler thought numbly, 'Swinton will turn inside out!'

Recovering, he attempted an enquiry. "What—the—DEVIL—are—"

However justified, his question was poorly couched. His roar, shattering the drowsy silence of late afternoon, sent Carefree hurtling straight into the air, drew frenzied neighs from the startled pair, caused the coachman to drop the portmanteaux scattering its contents, and awoke a screech from a plump little female who had apparently been carrying a cup of tea to the coachman. Her reaction was not limited to the screech, for she flung up her arms, at the same time essaying a spirited leap. The cup shot from the saucer and deposited its contents on the back of Chandler's neck as he made an abrupt descent into the flower bed.

The lady artist, coming rather belatedly onto the scene, said in surprised accents, "*Whatever* are you doing, Mr. Chandler?"

Gordon Chandler was widely held to be a rather stern young man, with a reputation for shrewd common sense and a temper that was usually held in check. Mr. Chandler's temper however had, for several reasons, been somewhat frayed of late. One of those reasons stood before him now, and the knowledge that he had stupidly allowed himself to be thrown into a flower bed, that his hair was in his eyes, his new riding coat torn, and that he must look a proper fool, did nothing to improve his mood.

"I might well ask the same of you, madam," he snarled, coming swiftly to his feet. "Who the deuce gave you leave to use this garden as a shortcut? It escaped your notice, I gather, that this is a footpath! *A footpath*, Miss Arlington!" Clutching the back of his neck, which smarted considerably, he glared at her.

"Allington," she corrected involuntarily. "I am so sorry if we have come the wrong way. We were lost, you see, and arrived on this side of the grounds, so— Oh, my! You have tea leaves in your cravat, sir." She snatched a small handkerchief from the bosom of her gown. "Allow me to—"

"Thank you—no." He stepped back and brushed at his cravat. His hand, being muddy, did not help matters. He saw Miss Allington's lips twitch and, lightning fast, a dimple came and went. Glancing down, he swore under his breath.

From the cottage behind her came a squeak of mirth. Aghast, Ruth retained sufficient presence of mind to clap a hand over her mouth as though trying to muffle the sound.

Her apparent amusement did not please. "Allow me to inform you," he raged, shaking his riding crop for emphasis, "that this lawn—" The riding crop, broken in the fall, sagged ludicrously.

The dimple in Miss Allington's cheek struggled against suppression.

Gritting his teeth, Chandler hurled the crop from him. With fiendish perversity it flapped through the air to drape itself over the nose of the coachman's tall bay horse. The bay took violent exception to such treatment and made a determined effort to jump backwards over the coach. His cohort, jerked back willy-nilly, became equally alarmed and succeeded in getting a leg over the pole. The coach veered crazily, creating havoc in the flower bed.

Alarmed by the murderous expression on the face of this crusty young gent, the coachman ran to seize the harness and shouted threats at his animals.

Chandler moved quickly to tear the leathers from his hand. "Gently, you fool," he growled, reaching up to stroke the sweating neck of the big bay. "Easy now, poor fellow. Easy."

Ungently, the bay bit him.

Ten minutes later, the uproar having quieted, the coachman followed Mr. Chandler's piebald mare and strove to obey the gentleman's terse orders to keep to the disastrous tracks he'd wrought in his initial journey.

Watching Chandler's rigid back with no small apprehension, Ruth called, "I am truly sorry, sir."

He turned in the saddle. "Your arrival, madam," he advised pithily, "has not been propitious."

The two women looked at each other.

"Oh, dear," sighed Ruth.

The blue cottage was a delight; a fairy tale house much larger than Ruth's perception of a cottage, with the same red-tiled roof as the main buildings. On the ground floor were a small entry hall, a cozy sunken parlour, a dining room, kitchen, and a small bedroom. The charming spiral staircase led up to two larger bedchambers, each with dressing room; and there was also a study equipped with well-stocked bookshelves and a writing desk. The furnishings were tasteful, the walls were hung with fine old prints and watercolours, and, much to Ruth's relief, each of the casement windows was provided with heavy draperies calculated to keep out the cold winter winds. These were pulled back at present but when closed would keep out prying eyes.

They were all pleased with their new home, and it was swiftly decided that the boys would share one of the upstairs bedchambers, Ruth taking the other, and Grace occupying the smaller downstairs room. The twins rushed about exploring every nook and cranny, and discovering such wonders as a tiny bedroom cupboard evidently intended for shoes, a frigid little pantry off the kitchen, and some deliciously creaking floorboards. Even the fastidious Grace was satisfied that the wardrobes, drawers, kitchen cupboards, and shelves were immaculate, and she at once went to work to unpack and put away their belongings.

After a preliminary and pleased inspection of the rooms, Ruth washed, tidied her hair, and changed her dress as quickly as possible, but the shadows were long across the gardens when she hurried down the path to the main house. The sun was going down in a blaze of crimson and purple, the fiery glow painting the exterior walls pink. Candles had already been lit inside, and the windows glowed a mellow amber. The air of early evening was mild, birds were sharing the day's news as they settled into the trees, and the stream gurgled and chattered over its stony bed. Beset as she was by anxieties, Ruth could not fail to be struck by the beauty all about her, and when she came around to the front of the building her steps slowed and she paused briefly, looking out over the charming prospect.

"So here you are, Miss Allington. Sir Brian wondered when you were going to come."

The housekeeper stood at an open casement. She was

bathed in the warm light, but her tone was cold and she did not return Ruth's smile. It was not to be wondered at, Ruth acknowledged glumly. Mr. Chandler had undoubtedly relayed the news of her disastrous arrival, and during her first visit here she had gained the impression that Mrs. Tate was devoted to him.

She hurried to the door, which was already being held open by a liveried footman. Mrs. Tate glided across the hall to meet her, the dark grey bombasine of her gown whispering.

"I was not quite sure," said Ruth, "whether I should use the back door."

"But you came to the front." Mrs. Tate's dark eyes were expressionless. "Sir Brian is waiting. He desired that you join the family for dinner. We shall send a tray down to your cousin."

"Oh, but—"

"This way, if you please."

Ruth followed, willy-nilly. If Sir Brian had invited her to dine with the family he must not consider her hopelessly far beneath them, nor could he be too angry over her unfortunate arrival.

Mrs. Tate led her across the great hall, past the graceful sweep of the fine old staircase, and opened one of double doors into a wide and wainscoted withdrawing room.

"Miss Allington," she announced, and went away.

Sir Brian rose from a sofa and turned, smiling. With him was a clerical gentleman of about forty, with a high forehead, the gentle eyes of a dreamer, and beautifully chiselled features. Advancing to shake Ruth's hand, Sir Brian presented his chaplain, the Reverend Mr. Nathaniel Aymer, who was, he added, "a most distinguished scholar."

Mr. Aymer's rather grave smile told Ruth that he did not approve of lady restorers, but she betrayed no awareness of his reaction. Sir Brian drew up a chair for her, and she answered his polite enquiries by saying that their journey had been pleasant and the cottage was a joy. Her cautious attempts to refuse the dinner invitation were brushed aside. She must not deny three lonely gentlemen the pleasure of a lady's company for once, and Sir Brian promised faithfully that he did not mean to "talk business."

At this point, Gordon Chandler arrived. He had changed his clothes and looked quite well, thought Ruth, trying to be fair, in a plum-coloured coat, the great cuffs rich with silver braid. A diamond sparkled amid the laces at his throat. His hair was powdered and drawn back severely, and the glance he rested on Ruth as he made his bow was also severe.

"Here you are at last, my dear boy," said Sir Brian. "You see, you were not 'the last act to crown the play,' Miss Allington, though crown it you do. Perhaps, Gordon, you will be so good as to offer the lady a glass of ratafia."

Chandler went over to a credenza and filled two glasses, one of cognac.

"Now, you must give me your opinion, ma'am," said Sir Brian, with a twinkling glance at his son's broad shoulders. "What do you think of this room?"

"I think that, like the rest of your estate, sir, 'tis very beautiful."

The lace at Mr. Chandler's wrist shifted as he offered the glass of ratafia and Ruth gave a shocked gasp.

"You do not think all this panelling a touch gloomy, perhaps?" prompted Sir Brian.

Appalled by the lurid bruise on his son's wrist, Ruth stammered, "Sir Brian—I must apologize for—"

"My father asked your opinion of this room." Chandler's dark face was forbidding. Strolling to take a deep chair near Sir Brian, he raised his glass in salute to him and said with fond mockery, "I am very sure he awaits your verdict with bated breath, ma'am."

Mr. Aymer chuckled. "You place the lady in a most difficult situation, Mr. Gordon," he remarked in an unexpectedly high-pitched tenor voice. "She is scarcely able to be anything but complimentary."

"No, no, that will never do," protested Sir Brian. "When I ask a question, Miss Allington, I want only the truth. However unpalatable it may be."

There was clearly more here than met the eye. Ruth wrenched her mind from its preoccupation with Mr. Chandler's damaged wrist, and glanced around the room. It was spacious, richly furnished, and panelled throughout in oak, and she said with genuine admiration that she could find nothing to dislike. "Truly, I have never seen such superb carvings as those on the heads of the panels."

Chandler laughed softly and again raised his glass to his sire.

'He manages to look human when he laughs,' thought Ruth.

"Alas, we are outnumbered, Sir Brian," said Mr. Aymer with a rueful smile.

"Oh dear," said Ruth. "Never say I have committed another faux pas?"

"To the contrary." For once the ice in Mr. Chandler's grey eyes had been replaced by a look of approval. "Your judgment must only be excellent, ma'am, since my brother and I share it."

Sir Brian smiled. "You agree with me, at least, Nathaniel. And you should, Miss Allington, for had I not stripped all the gloomy wood from the chapel walls, our fresco might have stayed unrecovered for another two centuries."

"Instead of which, we have a mouldering fresco and a cold chapel," his son murmured into his wineglass.

Mr. Aymer explained, "Mr. Gordon holds that walls covered with plaster and paper admit draughts, ma'am. And that panelling keeps a room snug."

"With all your many virtues, Gordon, you have been denied an appreciation of art." Sir Brian gave a start as his son waved a gesture of acknowledgment. " 'Pon my soul! What a'plague have you done to your hand?"

Chandler looked vexed and shook down the laces at his wrist. "A small accident, merely. 'Tis of no consequence."

"Of no consequence!" Mr. Aymer sprang to his feet and seized Chandler's arm. "What a frightful bruise! There may be bones broke, which can be deadly dangerous, and I'd not be surprised—"

Watching his father's alarmed face, Chandler jerked his arm away. "Such a pother you make, Aymer. You will have my father thinking me a block because I took a simple toss."

Still uneasy, Sir Brian exclaimed, "You were unhorsed? Which animal scored that rare victory? When did it happen?"

Darting a stern glance at Ruth, Chandler answered, "My piebald mare was the culprit. In the woods this afternoon. Something spooked her and I was woolgathering." He shrugged. "That'll teach me."

"Mr. Chandler is not being entirely honest, I fear," said Ruth.

Sir Brian and the chaplain jerked around to face her.

Chandler said irritably, "Oh, let us have done with this! There's no cause to make so much of a stupid—"

"Be still!" Sir Brian raised one hand autocratically. "Pray go on, Miss Allington."

" 'Twas entirely my fault, sir," she said, as she had re-hearsed. "I did not properly recall the way, and we followed the back road onto your lands. In my confusion I failed to correct my hired coachman when he mistakenly turned onto a footpath."

"A—*what?*" Sir Brian's face darkened. "Do you say that you brought a carriage up *behind* the blue cottage? Not across my lawns, I trust?"

"The coachman was a fool," said Chandler. "I was a—er, trifle short with him, which frightened my mare into a buck that caught me by surprise. No harm done."

"Except to my lawn," grumbled Sir Brian.

Ruth said humbly, "I am truly sorry."

Sir Brian was not appeased, and his tone was chill when he said that he trusted his gardeners could rectify matters.

Feeling a depraved criminal, Ruth lowered her eyes to the hands folded in her lap and kept silent.

"The gardens of Lac Brillant are famous, Miss Allington," said Mr. Aymer reprovingly. "We all treat them with the greatest care and are exceeding proud of them."

"And I am exceeding ravenous," said Chandler. "Has that fool of a chef expired?"

Almost as he spoke a gong somewhere sent out a sonorous peal. Sir Brian offered Ruth his arm. As she rested her hand on it, he said, "If that wrist starts to swell, Gordon, we must have Keasden out to look at it."

Chandler muttered something about an "old curmudgeon," and Sir Brian led Ruth into what he told her was the breakfast parlour, used for dinner when they did not set out very many covers.

It was a good-sized room wherein a long table was spread with snowy linen. Candlelight awoke answering gleams from silver and crystal. Lackeys stood ready to pull back chairs. The casements were open to the balmy evening air, the food was delicious, and to add what should have been the final touch of delight, a harpsichordist in an adjacent room began to play familiar old airs.

At any other time, Ruth would have been enchanted, but although Mr. Aymer kept up a stream of obviously well-meant but rather inane chatter in which Mr. Chandler occasionally joined, Sir Brian's countenance was austere and he scarcely spoke. Ruth sensed that she was in disgrace, and her heart sank.

The meal seemed interminable, and when it was over she declined Sir Brian's polite offer to take tea in the withdrawing room, and begged to be excused.

"Of course. You will be tired," he said. "My son will see you back to the cottage."

They all stood. Ruth offered her thanks and said her good

nights, and was soon very gratefully walking across the lawns with Chandler pacing beside her. She made a few nervous attempts at conversation, but his replies were curt and monosyllabic.

Most of the curtains were drawn when they reached the cottage, but a lighted lamp brightened the parlour windows. Ruth turned on the top step and said firmly, "I know you do not wish to speak of it, sir. But I must thank you for trying to shield me. I fear Sir Brian was very provoked."

"Had you not persisted in talking out of turn, Miss Allington, he would have had no cause to be provoked. An I attempted to shield anyone, it was him. My father is not a well man. We all of us do everything in our power to spare him distress. Pray bear that in mind. For the short time that you are with us." And with a brief inclination of the head, he was striding off again.

Mortified, Ruth watched his tall figure blend into the night. "Horrid . . . brute!" she hissed, and went inside.

At the darkened upper window two fair heads turned, two small boys exchanged looks of outrage.

"You were right, Jake," whispered Thorpe. "He's a bad 'un."

"Awful bad! Did you hear the way he spoke to Aunty?"

"I think she was piping of her eye."

"If I was a man I'd—I'd grass him!"

"I wouldn't," said Thorpe with ferocity. "I'd say—'confound you, sir!' An' I'd jolly well call him out!"

Jacob looked around uneasily, and with the authority of being thirty minutes his twin's senior said, "That's swearing! You shouldn't say swearings."

"I'll do more'n that if he's rude to Aunty Ruth again! I'll cut out his heart an' feed it to the frogs! Like the pirates do."

Jacob sighed. "I wish we *was* pirates," he said, the notion of murder and mutilation apparently less offensive than an oath. "But we're not, so I 'spect he'll keep on being bad. Unless . . ."

"Unless—what?" Eagerly, Thorpe accused, "You're brewing, Jake!"

"Well, if you or me was t' speak to a lady like he did, we'd be punished. An' *I* think that if Mr. Chandler don't mend his ways, *he* oughta be punished."

"Oooh," said Thorpe, titillated. "Could we?"

"Aunty Ruth says you c'n do anythin' if you try hard 'nuff."

As they climbed into the canopied bed, Thorpe enquired, "D'you think frogs really eat hearts, Jake? Has they got teeth? You'd have to have teeth to eat a heart, wouldn't you?"

" 'Course, silly. We'll catch a frog an' see."

A short silence, then Thorpe murmured sleepily, "Still, this is not so bad for a little house. An' I'm glad we c'n all stay together."

"So'm I. But it wasn't *him* what 'ranged it. I heard Aunty Ruth tell Miss Grace *he* tried to stop it. The old gentleman 'ranged it."

"Oh." Thorpe yawned. "Then it's not un-hon'rable if we have to punish him."

"No. Hon'rable, in fact. A man's s'posed to take care of his ladies. That's what Papa said."

"Oh." Another yawn. "Jake, d'you 'member Papa?"

"Not much. But that's what Grandpapa said he said. An' he said Papa was a fine gentleman 'cause it was in the blood. So that's what we'll be, Thorpe. Fine gentlemen."

"Righto. We better catch a frog t'morrow . . ."

The next morning Ruth resisted Grace's attempts to dress her hair less severely, insisting the tight plaits be wound behind her ears, with no curling tendrils allowed to escape.

Grace sighed. "Your beautiful hair! All scrinched flat. How can you hope to win the old gentleman over when you look such a dowd? And that plain old brown dress . . ."

"Let him once suspect I am an Armitage, and we're finished. Goodness knows, he may send us packing as it is, for he was most huffy with me about the lawn we spoilt. I mean to try very hard to please him, you may be assured. Now, all my tools and paints are in this box. Sir Brian will send a footman to carry it to the chapel, so when he comes, be sure to behave as if you're exceeding nervous. And for heaven's sake, keep the boys hid! I've told them they've to pretend the grounds are full of spies searching for them. Keep the doors locked and the curtains drawn, and if the windows are open, they must speak very quietly, just in case there are busybodies about."

"But if anyone should come they'll think it monstrous strange, Mrs. A. Nobody locks doors, or closes curtains in the summer time."

"Which is why we're so fortunate that you are of a—er, retiring disposition."

"You mean ripe for Bedlam," sighed Grace.

At the main house a footman directed Ruth to the chapel, where Sir Brian had attended early morning service. Her enquiry elicited the information that Mrs. Tate also attended service when she was able to get away, and Mr. Gordon sometimes did so, but not today since he was gone up to Town "for a indefinite time." This news lightened Ruth's spirits considerably, and the sun seemed brighter when she went outside again.

It was cooler today, and seagulls were wheeling overhead, uttering their piercing calls. She paused for an instant, looking up at them.

"Good morning, Miss Allington." The housekeeper approached, a crochetted shawl drawn close about her shoulders. "I trust you slept well."

The words were polite, but her eyes reflected no more

interest than if she had addressed the stone bench set in a recess of the path beside them.

"Very well, I thank you," replied Ruth.

"Have you an interest in birds, ma'am?" There was just a hint of mockery in the question. Ruth was tempted to give the woman a set-down and had to remind herself that she was not the mistress here, but only a hired worker, and one regarded with disapproval. She said, "My late brother believed that seagulls go inland when a storm is coming. You've an interest in music, I believe. I heard you playing last evening, and you have a lovely speaking voice. Are you Welsh, perhaps? If so, I fancy you sing—no?"

Briefly, surprise flickered across the impassive features. "I am from Aber Tawy, madam, which you would call Swansea. My singing is unremarkable, but I am so fortunate as to sometimes play for Mr. Chandler's affianced when she is here. Lady Nadia has an exquisite soprano voice." Unsmiling still, she went on past.

It was such a pity, thought Ruth, that the people here must be so unfriendly, when the estate was so beautiful. Still, it was early days, and at least the individual who most resented her would not be a problem for a while. So his bride-to-be was called Lady Nadia, and was "an exquisite soprano." The ethereal type, no doubt, who sang in the church choir and was a model of gentle kindliness. Poor girl.

Just before she had left Lac Brillant on her first visit, Sir Brian had delegated to his son the task of conducting her to the chapel. Chandler had left what sounded to have been a contentious meeting with the steward, and had begged the patience of the half-dozen men waiting to see him. Obviously seething with impatience, he had rushed Ruth across to the chapel, jabbed a finger at the dingy fresco, and barely allowed her to take three steps towards it before remarking that the carriage waited to convey her to Dover.

This morning, the ancient little structure was chill but bright. The deep, richly carven rafters imparted a medieval elegance to the chapel and the rose window high in the east wall gleamed like a multi-coloured jewel in the early sunlight. Sir Brian was seated in a rear pew, deep in converse with Mr. Aymer. They ceased their discussion at once, and rose to greet Ruth. The clergyman's manner had thawed considerably, and she was glad to see that Sir Brian's distinguished face wore a good-humoured expression. 'Is a gentleman of moods,' she decided.

The chaplain left them alone, and Sir Brian led Ruth to the fresco, which was situated between two more stained-glass windows on the south wall. It was not a work of great size, being roughly six feet wide and four feet high with the lower edge approximately six feet above the floor. A sturdy platform had been erected before it for her use, and Sir Brian assisted her up the steps to this edifice.

After only a brief inspection she realized that the work must be much older than she had at first thought. The surface was dark and cracked. It appeared to be a landscape, but it was difficult to make out details, and there was no apparent signature nor any indication as to who the artist might have been.

Watching her, Sir Brian said, "I brought an alleged expert down from London. He said it was the work of a nobody, and not worth the expense of restoring. Do you agree?"

"The gentleman must possess much keener eyesight than I do," she replied carefully. "He might very well be correct, but at this stage 'tis practically impossible to tell either who painted it, or what its intrinsic value might be. Is very old, certainly, and were this my home, I would value it excessively as part of my family history."

Obviously pleased, he said, "My own thought, exactly. My son disagrees with me. My heir, I should say. Although my younger son was much excited when I wrote to him of the discovery, and urges me to proceed with the restoration. You think it can be saved?"

"I think it well worth the attempt. It would be much more

badly damaged had it not been covered by panelling for—how long a time, sir?"

He pursed his lips dubiously. "So far as I can determine, about two hundred years. One of my ancestors evidently took a dislike to it. Or perhaps, as Gordon says, sought to shut out the draughts by having the panelling installed. You think the wood protected it?"

"Not from damp, sir. But 'gainst the smoke from candles and braziers. Have you any idea of when it was painted, or what is the subject of the work?"

"This chapel is all that remains of the original pile, and was erected in the early thirteenth century. Perhaps the fresco dates back to that time. It may very well be a Biblical study. There is a hill there, do you see? And in the foreground, some figures. Many early family records were lost when Puritans stormed and burned much of the original house during the civil war, else we might have more knowledge of the work." He leaned closer, and peered up at the fresco. "I am forced to agree with Gordon that it shows little of either colour or promise."

"Take heart, sir," said Ruth with a smile. "In a few weeks you might be pleasantly surprised."

"Jupiter! Do you say you'll complete the work in so short a time?"

"That will depend on how you wish to proceed, Sir Brian. Also, if your fresco should begin to appear to be of great importance, you might be advised to call in experts from Italy. There is an exceptionally gifted gilder in Florence who would—"

He laughed. "Who would cost me a fortune, I've no doubt! No, no, my dear lady. This painting is of personal value to my family, but I doubt would warrant a major outlay of funds. Certainly, Gordon, who has a good business head on his shoulders, would put up a great to-do if I proposed such a course." He drew back, gripping his hands together, his eyes glinting. "Bless my soul! I begin to be excited. But what did you mean when you said your progress would depend on how I wanted to proceed? You are here, and ready to begin—no?"

"Assuredly, sir. If you wish the fresco to remain here."

His jaw dropped slightly. "Do you say it could be moved into the main house? How, Miss Allington? By witchcraft?"

With a smile she admitted she lacked such powers, and seizing this opportunity to impress him, went on, "Still, there are several possibilities. The *a massello* method, for instance, is simply to cut out the entire section of wall and move it to the desired location. There is also a process called stripping, which is rather more chancy. Alternatively, just a thin layer of the wall could be removed, rather than cutting out the entire piece, but again, 'tis chancy, with more risk of disintegration."

"Stap me, but you are prodigious knowledgeable," he exclaimed. "Were I to choose one of the methods you spoke of, could you do the work?"

Her heart sank, and she wished belatedly she had not been so generous with her information. "If you decided to remove the entire section of the wall, I could guide and oversee the stonemasons you would have to employ, and afterwards I could proceed with the restoration. The other techniques I spoke of are too difficult for most restorers, and the masters who developed them guarded their secrets. You would really have to import an expert, sir."

"I admire your honesty," he said with a smile. "I shall tell my son he was quite mist— Er, that is to say, I am more certain than ever that my confidence in you is well justified." He patted her hand. "Now never look so apprehensive. 'Twould be impressive in the house, I grant you, but my fresco shall stay here, where it was intended. And you must commence your work as soon as your tools have been brought to you. Meanwhile, I beg you will come and take a dish of tea with me. You can tell me how you like the cottage."

As she was handed down the steps, Ruth's triumph was shadowed by resentment. Sir Brian's hurriedly cut-off remark made it clear that Mr. Chandler had spoken unkindly of her. What did the nasty creature suspect? That she had inveigled her way into Lac Brillant with some nefarious scheme in mind? Well, it no longer mattered what evil thoughts lurked in the mind of Mr. Gordon Chandler. Sir Brian had forgiven her for the ravaging of his beloved lawn and had given her permission to start work. By the time Mr. Chandler returned, the restoration would be well under way, and even so suspicious a man might have to admit that Mrs.—whoops! That *Miss* Allington knew what she was about!

CHAPTER V

"I can but hope your sire will not hold me to have set a bad example, Jamie." Gideon Rossiter carried a glass of cognac to the chair occupied by Lieutenant Morris and handed it to his friend. A tall young man, and still too thin, although he was almost recovered from the wounds that had kept him in hospital for a year after the Battle of Lauffeld, Rossiter had been given no choice in the matter of selling out of the army. That Morris now meant to do so, came as a surprise. Returning to his own chair in the sunny withdrawing room of the narrow little London house he shared with his bride, he added, "Or is it that the doctors have certified you unfit?"

The words were teasingly uttered, but Rossiter's grey eyes were keen, aware of which Morris laughed and said, "Never judge me by yourself, my tulip. The great ones at the Horse Guards fairly begged me not to sell out. Truth is . . ." He hesitated. "I'll own you've set me an example in one way. I'd give a deal to be snug in a cozy little place like this, with—with Katrina Falcon."

Rossiter swirled the brandy in his glass and was silent. He'd begun to hope that Naomi was mistaken and that Morris was over his *tendre* for August Falcon's bewitchingly lovely sister. His bride, it seemed, was right as usual.

Morris shot a sideways glance at him. "I collect you think it a forlorn hope. Well, it ain't. Miss Katrina has become quite fond of me." Rossiter met his eyes gravely and, flushing, he added, "I dare to hope."

"Then I wish you all the luck in the world, old fellow."

"And think I'll need it." Morris sighed. "If only I hadn't put that ball through her miserable brother."

"August rode straight at us with a pistol in his hand. How were we to know he wasn't one of the highwaymen who'd stopped Naomi's coach?"

"Absolutely! Any reasonable man would accept that. Trouble is, Falcon's about as reasonable as Mount Vesuvius. I'll not fight him, Ross. However many times he arranges the damned meeting."

Rossiter said thoughtfully. "You could delope, you know."

"You're mad!" declared Morris, shocked and indignant. "Fire in the air while facing that maniac? What it is, you're eager to attend my last rites!"

"No, really Jamie, it might be better to get it over with. Falcon don't mean to put a period to you, and with the duel behind you, 'twould clear the air and he might look upon you with less—"

' "Loathing? Not likely. And despite your generous advice, I ain't eager to let him put a hole in me! If I chose swords, I'd blasted well have to—"

A discreet knock at the door, and Rossiter's new man minced in to offer a silver salver. Rossiter glanced at the card on it. "Show him up, if you please," he said, and after the door closed muttered, "I now have a pompous idiot for my valet!"

"Who has come? Must I take myself off?"

"Gordon Chandler. As if he needed to send in his card.

Jupiter, but sometimes I feel like telling Falcon I want Tummet back!"

Morris said with a grin, "I never thought to see the day you'd welcome that uncouth lout."

"That uncouth lout saved Naomi's life, and mine belike."

"Very true." Sobering, Morris nodded. "Then have him back."

"The silly clunch has some notion that now I'm a benedick his rough ways won't do for me. At least, that's what he says. But my sister has the notion that Tummet thinks Falcon needs him."

Morris all but gawked his astonishment. "My apologies to Miss Gwendolyn, but that maniac don't need anyone in this entire world save for Katrina and his father. And he guards the pair of 'em like some savage ogre who—"

"Aha! Caught you talking about me, I see!"

Both men stood to welcome Gordon Chandler. When the greetings were done and he was installed in a comfortable chair with an appropriately filled glass in his hand, he glanced around approvingly. "Nice lodgings, Ross. I didn't know you and Naomi had settled in Bond Street. Thought for sure you'd have moved in with the earl. Especially since that great house of his sits empty while Collington jaunters about—Spain, is it?"

Rossiter and Morris exchanged a swift glance.

Morris said, "This ain't Ross's place, Gordie. Belongs to Owen Furlong. He's letting them stay here."

"Till Emerald Farm is ready for us," said Rossiter. "But how is it that you're back in Town? I thought you intended to rusticate in Kent for a while?"

"I did." Chandler frowned. "I am obliged to hire a new steward. I was at last able to persuade my father to send Durwood packing."

"You've my sympathy," said Rossiter. "Couldn't the registry office send applicants down to you?"

"They could, of course. But—" Chandler's lips tightened.

"Oh, I had to be in Town at all events, and I wanted to have a word with you."

Rossiter asked shrewdly, "Nothing wrong, I hope?"

"Several things. But the one that brings me here is a peculiar affair, and I hoped you might be able to enlighten me."

"We are experts in peculiar affairs," said Morris. "Never hesitate, dear boy! Who is she?"

Chandler laughed. "Nothing of that nature, 'pon my word. Have either of you the acquaintance of Trevor Shipley?"

"Heard of the family," said Morris. "Forget what."

"I met him here and there, before I bought my commission," said Rossiter. "Nice fellow. Why?"

Chandler set his glass down. "Trevor and I are friends of long standing, but from one cause or another we've not met this year and more. Last week I chanced to be near their country seat, so I decided to pay a call. It's a fine old place. Larchwoods."

"That strikes a chord," said Morris thoughtfully. "I seem to recall my father mentioning something . . . Some trouble—no?"

"Would that I knew. I got no farther than the lane. A group of insolent louts crowded me into the ditch, upset my mare, and rode past, howling." Chandler's chin jutted. Frowning at the memory, he went on, "When I reached the lodge, the gates were closed and the same louts were ranged across the drivepath, leering at me like so many filthy Mohocks."

Rossiter asked, "Is that what they were?"

"If so, they're in residence! I was denied admission, told the Shipleys no longer own the estate, and as good as run off!"

"Be damned!" said Morris.

Chandler jerked out of his chair and stamped over to the windows. "You know I am not usually quick to take umbrage."

"Placid as a parson," agreed Rossiter, a smile coming into his eyes. "Until you are provoked. Went back, did you?"

"Yes. I was afraid old Trevor might—" Chandler paused and said awkwardly, "Well, we were school chums, you know. At all events, I rode clear to the north end of the estate and climbed a tree so as to come over the fence. There never used to be one, but there is now. Damned great thing above six feet high, with broken glass on the top."

"Is that what happened to your hand?" asked Morris.

Chandler scowled down at the greenish bruise and said shortly, "No. But—"

He was interrupted by a sudden cacophany of deep-throated barking mingled with shrill shouts, a man's deep laughter, and a slamming door.

"That'll be Falcon," said Rossiter, with a wry look at Morris.

Arming himself with a heavy vase, Morris said, "He's brought that blasted hound!"

"Well, well, well," drawled August Falcon, opening the door and checking on the threshold to survey them languidly. "A distinguished gathering, indeed. Is this why your blockish servant wanted me to send up a card? I'll go away if I'm *de trop.*"

Rossiter went over to shake his hand. "Have you murdered the poor fellow?"

"Probably has," said Morris, still clutching the vase.

"No need. Apollo barked at him and he decamped. At speed. If you've decided to fight me at long last, Morris, I care not for your choice of weapons."

Morris put down the vase. "And I care not for your confounded brute."

Falcon acknowledged Chandler's polite greeting with a careless nod and wandered to a chair. "Tremble not, Sir Galahad. Apollo is taking Miss Rossiter for a walk."

"My sister came with you?" asked Rossiter, handing Falcon a glass of cognac.

"We met on your steps and having done his duty by your man, Apollo commandeered her. Which she quite deserves, since she chose to ruin his character by teaching him how to play. Marriage agrees with you, Ross. Almost, you begin to resemble a living being."

Rossiter grinned and bowed low.

Resorting to his quizzing glass, Falcon aimed it at Chandler. "Who convinced you to powder your curly locks? Do I detect the fine hand of a lady? Truly, you must be enchanted, but capitulation before wedlock is fatal, I warn you."

His face a little red, Chandler returned to his chair. "Much you know of it. For all your *affaires de coeur* I've yet to hear of your becoming so much as mildly interested in a lady."

"An I am only mildly interested, *mon ami*, I do not enter into an *affaire*. And 'tis *because* of my—er, excursions into the realm of *l'amour* that I avoid marriage like the plague." Falcon sipped his cognac and added airily, "Which it is, and I would expound on the subject save that you're likely too besotted to heed the voice of wisdom."

"The only exposition I require from you, Falcon," snapped Chandler, "is on quite another subject."

"But—how intriguing," said Falcon with a chuckle. "Our pedantic peer presumptive hath a touch of choler. What ails you, my Buck? Love? Or liver?"

"Since my father is a baronet, I am never likely to become a peer. As I'd think even you would know!"

"*Even* me . . ." Falcon watched the lazy swing of his quizzing glass and said with his cynical half-smile, "Even—the Mandarin. Is that what you mean?" His beauteous grandmother had been the product of a marriage between a Russian princess and a Chinese mandarin and, knowing how deeply he was despised by London's *haut ton* because of his mixed blood, Falcon knew also that this was the name that was applied to him behind his back.

Rossiter's amusement faded. "Oh, have done, man! Gordie meant nothing of the kind."

Chandler said stiffly, "He knows that perfectly well. He seeks to pinch at me as he does poor Morris. But you'll not turn me aside, Falcon. I'll have an accounting, or—"

"That's the ticket," said Morris enthusiastically. "Give him one of your famous set-downs."

"Do not interrupt the adults," said Falcon, brightening as he always did when arranging a fight. "I do believe Chandler means to call me out. I will oblige you with all the goodwill in the world, my poor fool. Swords, or pistols?"

"Best have both, Chandler," advised Morris.

Rossiter laughed.

Falcon said agreeably, "By all means. Sword in one fist, pistol in t'other, and a dagger 'twixt your teeth, an you desire. Is all one to me. Though I must attend to Morris first, to which end—"

"Well, 'tis not all one to me," interposed Rossiter. "What a fellow you are, August, to come roaring in and spoil our civilised discussion with your ferocities. Chandler was telling us of an odd affair at Trevor Shipley's country seat." He gave a brief recounting of the episode, at the end of which Falcon murmured, "Pray do not leave me in suspense. Surely the intrepid Chandler was not daunted by a mere fence? Having scaled it, I hope he taught them a lesson?"

Chandler fixed him with a level stare.

"Pay him no heed, Gordie," advised Morris. "His tongue is so sour he takes very little coffee with his sugar."

"Peace, children," said Rossiter, with a touch of asperity. "Will you tell us what did happen, Gordon?"

Chandler did not at once answer. Then, reverting to his usual cool manner, he said, "I think I am neither a bravo nor a fool. I will not run from reasonable odds, but seventy to one—no."

Startled, Rossiter leaned forward in his chair. "Do you say there were *seventy* gentlemen wandering about your friend's preserves?"

"I do not. There were seventy, perhaps more, *men* in there.

They were neither wandering, nor were they gentlemen." He paused, frowning. "It sounds absurd, but were I to hazard a guess I'd say they were—playing charades." He met their astonished stares and added defiantly, "They were a decidedly rum lot."

"Charades," murmured Falcon. "What kind? Did you discover the solution?"

"I discovered how fast I could run."

Rossiter said sharply, "You were seen?"

"Seen and marked for slaughter! My God! How they came at me! One might suppose I had spied upon a sultan's ladies at their bath! I mounted up barely ahead of the first lot, but they were after me like so many madmen. How I came through that hail of shot unscathed, I do not know."

Incredulous, Morris said, "You were *fired* upon?"

"Aye. For a mile and more. Till I gave the damned hounds the slip!"

Falcon breathed a soft "Aha!" put down his glass, sprawled lower in his chair, and over loosely interlocked fingers watched Rossiter intently.

Meeting that brilliant stare, Rossiter muttered, "Larchwoods. It lies somewhere near Bosham on the south coast, I think. You're a Sussex man, August. What d'you know of it?"

"Now what should a humble social outcast know of such high-in-the-instep members of the *haut ton*? Never been invited to place my sullied boot across the threshold."

Chandler pointed out dryly, "Had you not deliberately enticed Trevor's last bird of paradise away and then laughed at him, you might have been."

Falcon chuckled and bowed his head in unrepentant acknowledgment.

" 'Tis a splendid estate, Ross," Chandler went on. "A fine park, ringed in on all sides by woodland. The house is rather in need of repair, but it has been in their family for centuries. I cannot conceive why the old man should have sold up."

" 'Twas not entailed, then?"

"Not to my knowledge. But it might as well have been—or so I thought—for Trevor and his papa regarded it almost as hallowed ground."

Falcon murmured, "Is there not an elder brother? Robert . . . ? Roderick . . . ? or some such name? Of decidedly murky repute, if memory serves. Oh, never look so damned prim, Chandler. If only half the scandals laid at that lad's door are truth, it must have cost Sir Bertram Shipley a considerable fortune to buy off his victims and avoid disgracing their name."

Morris looked solemn. "He'd be stuck fast, like a cow in wet clay."

Chandler stared at him.

Between his teeth, Falcon said, "Don't ask him, Chandler. Do not! An we ignore the gudgeon, with luck he'll content himself with just one of his revolting homilies."

Rossiter muttered, "That's how they did it, then. The poor old man was blackmailed till he had to sacrifice his estates."

"They?" echoed Chandler, bewildered. "Who?"

Rossiter stood and refilled glasses. His voice ringing with suppressed excitement, he said, " 'Twould fit! By God but it would! Another of the League's devilish tricks! And this estate they've filled with rascals to do their murderous—" Struck by an afterthought, he exclaimed, "Jove, Gordie! Were you recognized?"

"Perhaps. What the devil difference would it make? And what a'plague are you jabbering at? What League?"

"It might make a difference to your continued existence," said Falcon. "He should be warned, Ross. An you think he deserves it."

"My *existence?*" echoed Chandler incredulously. "What in Hades have I come upon?"

Looking grave, Morris said, "Something we are sworn not to speak of. Though that don't weigh with old August."

"Certainly not," agreed Falcon, "since we've reason to

question the integrity of the man who swore us to secrecy. We may have a likely recruit here, eh, Gideon?"

Rossiter frowned, but after a moment's consideration said, "Falcon's right, Jamie. I'll accept the responsibility." He turned to Chandler. "It began whilst I was in the Low Countries, Gordie. I came home to find my family ruined, our shipyards and estates lost to us, our name a by-word for dishonest dealings, and my father raving of some malignant and powerful conspiracy 'gainst him."

"Yes. I recall. 'Twas a beastly home-coming for you, Lord knows. You did damned well to bring your sire clear of that bog. I fancy 'twas easy enough for him to imagine a conspiracy under the circum—"

"Fool," put in Falcon contemptuously. "He did not imagine."

Chandler stared at him, then glanced to Rossiter, who nodded in sombre verification. " 'Twas indeed a conspiracy, perpetrated by a secret and most malevolent group of aristocratic gentlemen calling themselves the League of Jewelled Men." He sat beside his astounded friend and said earnestly, "Allow me to explain . . ."

Ten minutes later, Gordon Chandler broke a long silence to say in a dazed voice, "Let me see if I have the right of it. You suspect that this League of Jewelled Men hatches some dastardly plot 'gainst England. Their leader is someone calling himself the Squire, but their true identities are unknown, even to one another. You believe they carry jewelled figures as a means of identification at their secret meetings; that they contrive to discredit, disgrace, and destroy highly regarded and highly placed gentlemen for some unknown purpose. And that they may have schemed to acquire several large estates."

"Not *may* have," exploded Falcon impatiently. "*Have!*"

"They succeeded in wresting away my father's country seat," said Rossiter. "We suspect they are responsible for the ruination and imprisonment of Admiral Albertson, and for the death of Lord Harlow Merriam—"

Chandler interrupted, "But—Merriam was a suicide!"

"Because he was caught cheating at cards?" Falcon gave a derisive snort.

Rossiter said, "You knew Merriam, Gordie. Did ever you know a more upright, honourable gentleman?"

Chandler looked troubled. "Never," he admitted, trying to grasp all this.

"Furthermore," went on Rossiter, his face stern, "their connivings came damnably close to causing the death of my dear wife, and only a few weeks back they came within a hair's breadth of sending Tio Glendenning and all his family to the block for high treason."

"Good God!" gasped Chandler.

Morris put in, "And we are perfectly sure that Glendenning Abbey was their target."

"But you are quite at liberty to question that conclusion," said Falcon, bored. "As you very obviously question all the rest."

Chandler frowned. "If you are right, then you also hold this pack of noble wolves responsible for the death of Lord Norberly—"

"Who was a member of the League," nodded Rossiter. "As was—or perhaps *is*—my father-in-law, I regret to say."

Chandler's jaw sagged. "The Earl of *Collington?* Naomi's father?"

"Had she another?" enquired Falcon sweetly.

Staring at him unseeingly, Chandler muttered, "Lord above, what a coil! 'Tis so hard to believe that—"

"That—what?" demanded Rossiter. "That villainy exists? That there are those who so hate our Hanoverian King they would conspire to destroy him? Cast your mind back a year or two, Gordie."

"Yes. But Charles Stuart was a Scot and fought openly for what he considered, with some justification, to be his birthright. And—"

"And lost. So perchance this little covey of maniacs fancy they'll succeed by following a more devious route."

Awed by the enormity of it, Chandler shook his head. "If you're right, what d'you mean to do?"

Morris said, "We've come at the identities of a few members of the League."

"But unhappily, most of 'em died—from one cause or another," put in Falcon.

"Not our doing—directly, that is," said Rossiter. "The man who leads the League is called the Squire. He don't permit failures."

"So now we attempt to discover who buys up forfeited estates," said Falcon.

Morris grinned. "And then we follow 'em."

"Jolly good!" exclaimed Chandler. "That should surely—" He interrupted himself. "But 'twas Bracksby bought Promontory Point! Oh, Gad! You never believe *Rudi* could be a member of this league?"

"Don't we just," drawled Falcon.

Rossiter stood. "Gordie, there's much you don't yet know, and we could spend all night in explanations. You have enough, I think, to make a judgment. Either we are ripe for Bedlam, or we are uncovering a threat of such magnitude that it would spell sure execution for all those concerned."

"Whereby we are each of *us* marked for execution," said Morris.

Despite that terrible assertion, Falcon laughed softly. "Look at him. He don't believe a word of it!"

Standing also, Chandler looked from Rossiter's clean-cut face and steady eyes, to Morris' earnestness, to Falcon, all lazy insolence. He drew a deep breath. "I wish to heaven I did not believe it. But I cannot doubt the word of such men as yourselves."

"Good," said Rossiter, smiling. "Then—will you join us, Gordie?"

A faint flush lit Chandler's cheeks and his cool grey eyes

were suddenly ablaze with excitement. "Yes, by God! I shall be proud to—" He broke off abruptly, and for a moment stood very still, his eyes remote, as though they scanned a scene only he could see. The animation died from his face, and when he spoke again his voice was cool, and the grey eyes were veiled. "No. My regrets, but I cannot."

Falcon gave a muffled but contemptuous exclamation, and lay back in his chair.

Chandler resumed: "We are already under a cloud. My father's health is uncertain, and were I to become involved in anything that might—er, bring us into the public eye once more, the strain upon him . . ." His jaw tightened. "No. I am sorrier than I can say, but I must stay clear of this. Besides, I am soon to be married." He hesitated, clearly mortified, then said, "You will, I hope . . . understand?"

Morris said kindly, "Only a fool turns a waggon in a narrow lane."

"A predictable idiocy," snorted Falcon.

"Of course we understand," said Rossiter. "But I'll ask that you keep all this to yourself, Gordie."

Chandler nodded. "You have my word. Now, I must be off. I can only wish you well, with all my heart." He shook hands with Rossiter and Morris, then turned to Falcon.

Still lounging in his chair, Falcon stared fixedly at the ceiling.

Flushing, and still numbed by the shocking disclosures he'd just heard, Chandler walked to the door. With his hand on the latch he turned back. "If you want to know something, August," he said angrily, "that was a damned stupid letter!"

Falcon jerked upright. "Eh? What a'plague—"

A look of guilt overspreading his suddenly scarlet countenance, Morris gabbled, "I'm coming, too! Wait up, Gordie!"

"Hey!" cried Falcon to the closing door.

There came the sound of galloping steps on the stairs. Misinterpreting Morris' abrupt departure, Falcon settled back again. "He wastes his time, the block. Katrina didn't come with me. She and my father are still recuperating from the influenza."

Rossiter, who was fond of Morris, said nothing, and there was a short silence. Then, Falcon asked idly, "When does Chandler wed?"

"In the autumn, I believe."

Falcon's lip curled. "How fortunate for him."

Irritated, Rossiter said defensively, "A man about to be wed has a right to steer clear of this ugly business."

"You did not steer clear."

"I had no choice."

Falcon smiled his cynical smile. "If Chandler was recognized down at the Shipley estate, he may find he also has no choice."

"The Prince of Wales," observed Lady Nadia de Brette, smiling, and bowing her lovely head as an acquaintance passed by, "is a very great rascal, and will do anything to annoy his father."

The afternoon was warm, and Covent Garden Market was well patronized. My lady was enjoying this stroll with her fiancé. Her new gown of gold and white brocade with the flattened panniers, which had become so popular, was not perhaps the best choice for a stroll through the market, but she was fully aware that it set off her dark beauty to admiration. She was aware also of the envy in the eyes of the ladies, and could not fail to be pleased. The man on whose arm her hand rested lacked the heart-stopping good looks or the devilish allure of August Falcon; nor could one enjoy a delicious gossip with him, as one could with dear Reggie Smythe. But he was heir to a great fortune and a splendid country seat, and was considered one of the finest catches in the matrimonial stakes. All of which my lady found satisfactory.

"Papa," she went on, "says that Lord Hervey's dislike of the Prince is absurd. Pitt likes him very much, of course."

Gordon Chandler forced his mind from its preoccupation with the appalling business of the League of Jewelled Men, and his uneasy feeling that, in some inexplicable fashion, his life had been changed by his awareness of it. He said unequivocally, "Pitt is a lunatic. Shall you come down to Lac Brillant with me?"

Dismayed, she wailed, "Oh, Lud! You're never going back there? I thought you surely meant to attend the Fowles' boat party. No, really! 'Tis prodigious tiresome of you, Chandler!"

"I expect it is, but I do not enjoy Town even during the Season, and in the summer time I find it unbearable. Furthermore, now that we are officially betrothed, I think you might sometimes address me by my Christian name."

With a pretty moue, my lady said, "You are cruel, Ch— Gordon. La, but I vow you care nothing for what *I* enjoy! Truly, you think more of your silly old farms, and tenants, and—and gardens than you do of poor me!"

She looked young and wistfully beautiful, and he laughed and patted her dainty fingers. But instead of assuring her that she was the centre of his world, as many of her admirers would have done, he said lightly, "You love Lac Brillant, or so you have always told me. Though we seldom see you there."

"How can you say such things, sir? Why, only a month or so ago I spent a—a week at the dear old place."

"You came down to see the shipwreck, an I recall."

"Yes, yes! Oh, how frightening it was to see the poor broken thing tossing about on your rocks, and to know how many lives were lost! Everyone was agog in Town when I described it, for there have been so very many. And I actually saw one!"

"A rock?" he said innocently.

"Wicked tease! The shipwreck. Papa says 'tis a veritable epidemic."

"Yes, well our wreck took place in February, m'dear—considerably more than a 'month or so ago!' And as I recall you stayed for three days only. Did I not know better, my lady, I'd think you dislike Lac Brillant."

"Well, you *do* know better, Mr. Chandler! I adore it. But I'd not want to live there."   .

He slanted a startled glance at her, and she retrenched swiftly. "All the time, I mean. I enjoy to visit your dear papa, and I know you do not like to leave him, now that Quentin is gone." She sighed. " 'Tis so very sad."

Her sorrow was genuine, if fleeting. It had once seemed to her a pity that Quentin had not been the heir. He was the dashing one; the one always with a laugh on his lips and some outrageous escapade either in hand or in mind. She glanced up at Gordon. His face was stern again. He did not like to be reminded of his brother. Beyond doubting, he must envy Quentin his good looks, his popularity, and the fact that he was Sir Brian's favourite. Such emotions she found perfectly understandable. When, at seventeen, she had made her come-out, she had also made a private vow to ensnare Quentin Chandler. But although she had flirted with him determinedly, and although she had swiftly become a reigning Toast, Quentin, while always ready to flirt, had never succumbed to the point of becoming a member of her court. Eventually, he had vanished from the London scene without so much as a farewell. Not for one second had she entertained the notion of marrying anyone but the heir to the Chandler fortunes, of course, but she had been piqued. If handsome Quentin Chandler was ever able to return to England, he would find her the mistress at Lac Brillant, and she would see to it that he received short shrift for his folly.

Gordon had not responded to her remarks, and she tightened her clasp on his arm. "Do not be grumpy, dear sir. Stay for the boat party. Gilbert offers a fine breakfast on the barge, strolling minstrels, and a cruise down to Hampton Court."

She saw his lips parting, and said cajolingly, "You would not say no without so much as considering my feelings?"

Repentant, he said, "Of course I consider your feelings, Nadia. But I do not see—"

"You never see! You are a young man, Chandler! Not a hoary old sage!"

"Well, yes, but I do have obligations at home, and—"

"Oh, pish! Do not be so adamantly set 'gainst a merry, frolicsome party. The best of the *ton* will be there. Fowles, of course, and Samantha Golightly, and my dearest friend, Lady Melissa Coombs, and her silly husband. And Reggie Smythe—such a droll gentleman! And Albert Harrier, and Duke, and . . ."

'Oh, Lord!' thought Chandler as she rattled on, not once naming anyone with whom he cried friends.

"And you need not be anxious for dear Sir Brian," she finished at length, "for you told me he is happily involved with that grubby old fresco he unearthed. Only look at those cherry ribbons! Such a delicious shade! Pray be sweet and buy me some."

Obediently, he detoured to a stall and made the transaction, and my lady went on as though there had been no interruption. "Besides which, now he has found a restorer, you are free of that charge 'pon your time." Intrigued by his scowl, she asked, "Why so murderous a look? Do you not like the man he hired?"

"If 'twas a man, I might," he grumbled.

Lady Nadia's mouth fell into a very pretty O of surprise. "You never mean— Oh, you quiz me, you naughty thing!"

"Would that I did. No, I am perfectly serious. My father has taken on a female artist."

"If—*ever* I heard of such a thing!" she gasped, scandalized. "Why, 'tis . . . 'tis *monstrous!* Did you not protest?"

"You may believe I did, but—" Her sudden faint scream interrupted him, and he bent to chase away the emaciated little dog that had cringed with a pleading whimper about her skirts. "Poor fellow," he said, looking after the animal. "He is starving by the look of—"

"Oh! How dirty he is! And he touched my gown! You never think there are fleas?" Lady Nadia shook her voluminous skirts anxiously. "Do look, Chandler! I vow I cannot *abide* creatures!"

Irritated, he said, "A fine figure I should cut, shaking out your skirts in public! How many would believe 'twas fleas I sought?"

"Chandler!" But she had seen his vexation and knew he was not in sympathy with her dislike of livestock—as though a lady of fashion could have anything but abhorrence for filthy little mongrels! "I am sorry I am not brave," she said meekly. "But I count on you to protect me, and—" It was apparent that her effort to please had not succeeded. Moving closer to smile her enchanting smile into his frowning eyes, she said, "I cannot blame you for being impatient with me, when I am so silly . . . Gordon."

In that moment she was all clinging and coquettish femininity, and very beautiful indeed, so that he relented and said warmly, "How could a man be cross with so lovely a creature?"

"La, la! I am forgiven!" Her merry little laugh rang out. "Now, do pray tell me of this female. What like is she? Old, and one of those dreadfully strange artist types?"

"She is about five and twenty, I suppose, and—"

"*Five . . . and . . . twenty?* Why—why 'tis *immoral!*"

" 'Tis nothing of the kind! An you fancy my father would bring his lightskirt to Lac Brillant, ma'am, disabuse your mind of such nonsense! The woman is not particularly attractive, and is besides installed in the most distant guest cottage, with—"

"My God in heaven! Why ever would Sir Brian permit the woman to dwell on the estate?"

Through his teeth he said, "I do not scruple to say, ma'am, that I mislike the inference."

He was far from having a silver tongue, but in spite of his often brusque ways had never used such a tone to her.

"But my dear Gordon," she said earnestly. " 'Tis not your kind papa whose motives I question, but hers! You may depend upon it that anyone so bold as to insinuate herself into a post which should have been given to some worthy male can only be an adventuress! What it is, she means to become your step-mama, and—"

Halting, Chandler threw back his head and laughed so heartily that several heads turned, the shivering little mongrel crept closer again, and a vendor with a tray of lace-trimmed caps and fichus hurried up to suggest that "the happy milor' " might like to buy some for his lady.

Lady Nadia said huffily, "You may laugh, sir! But the day will dawn when I'll remind you of your gullibility!"

CHAPTER VI

uth awoke to the sound of birdsongs and the smell of coffee brewing. She yawned and stretched luxuriantly before pulling back the bed-curtains. Sunshine flooded the room and the air was already warm. She got up and went over to open the casements wider. The weeping willow tree that trailed its long green fingers in the stream was full of birds and each one had its own branch that must be hopped on, and its own hymn to the sun that must be rendered before the business of the day began.

Drinking in the beauties of this breezy morning, Ruth suddenly recollected that today was the first anniversary of their arrival. One week since their hired coach had crept in the back way and violated Sir Brian's velvet lawns. She smiled reminiscently. How very angry Mr. Chandler had been. When Sir Brian had viewed the damage later, he'd also been angry, but by that time Grace had busied herself with some improvised garden tools so that the wheel ruts had not been quite so raw and glaring, and the flower bed less flattened. The head gardener, Mr. Swinton, had caught Grace at work and had all but danced his rage. It had been necessary, she'd said with a tilt of her chin, to speak sharply to him. That intelligence had rather worried Ruth, but so far as she knew there had been no further incidents.

There were no stirrings as yet from the boys' room. They slept so much more soundly here. And, bless them, they were happy, although they were obliged to spend so many hours indoors. After the first few days she had made them take a nap in the afternoons, and when dinner was over they were allowed to slip outside to play in the woods behind the cottage. They went armed with strict instructions that they must be very quiet, and at once return when she lit the lamp in their bedchamber, or if they saw or heard anyone. They seemed to have turned the situation into a game in which they were Chivalrous Knights, with gardeners, grooms, or gamekeepers designated variously as Enemies of the King, Outlaw Knaves, or Dragons. Gordon Chandler was inflexible in demanding a good day's work from those who served his father, but in return they were well paid, comfortably housed, and never required to labour outside after the evening meal. As a result the twins had not yet been obliged to hurry home, and they very obviously counted the hours until their early evening forays.

Two days after their arrival here, there had been a close call. While Ruth was at work in the chapel, Mrs. Tate had suddenly appeared at the cottage door and had been irked to find it locked and all the curtains tightly closed. Grace, loyally fulfilling her role as the feeble-minded chaperone, had evidently been convincing, for that afternoon the housekeeper had so far unbent as to tell Ruth she had met her "cousin" and had added with a shake of the head, "poor creature."

It was all going so well, Ruth thought gratefully. The work was slow and taxing, and at first she had been very tired, her back and arms one large ache. She had experienced the same difficulties in Italy, but Papa had taught her how to pace her initial efforts and gradually she was able to work a little longer before being obliged to rest.

Sir Brian came often to the chapel. Initially, he had commenced his visits with a concerned question as to whether such labour was not too hard for a lady. No matter how exhausted she felt she'd always found a bright smile for him and denied being in the least tired. She'd been afraid that she must certainly look tired and feared he would question her further, but he instead had passed at once to other subjects, and she had realized that although he was not unkind, he was not one to be deeply interested in the affairs of others. He neither enquired into her family background, nor invited her opinion on anything save the estate or the fresco. Often, when he wandered in to view the progress of the work, he would bring his chaplain with him, and the Reverend Mr. Aymer was unfailingly gentle, grave, and in complete agreement with whatever Sir Brian chanced to remark. Amused by these traits, Ruth was not at all offended by them. She had, in fact, been relieved that Sir Brian did not complain over the slow progress of the work, but was instead almost childishly delighted by the brighter colours that were beginning to appear from under the mantle of grime that had for so long concealed them.

Had Mr. Gordon—as everyone seemed to call him—been present, she was sure he would have found fault with her painstaking methods, but heaven was kind; he was still away, doubtless paying court to his betrothed who was, so Mr. Aymer had imparted, the most beautiful lady in London Town. If that were so, Ruth had said rather tartly to Grace Milford, it was unfortunate, for very beautiful ladies were often extreme spoiled, and Mr. Gordon's disposition would not be improved did he marry someone as ill-tempered as himself.

She experienced a twinge of guilt for that unkind judgment, but at this point her introspection was cut off abruptly as a shriek, followed by hysterical outcries, broke the stillness. Snatching up her wrapper she ran downstairs, her heart hammering with dread. In the kitchen, Grace stood on a stool, her skirts tight clasped about her knees as she sobbed and pleaded to be forgiven and protested herself "innocent of all but steadfastness and loyalty to my poor Mrs. A.!"

Her apprehensive gaze having swept the room and found nothing to cause such behaviour, Ruth said sharply, "Have done, or you will frighten the twins! To whom are you talking?"

"S-Saint Paul," sobbed Grace. "He w-was a sinner afore he came to be a saint . . . so he'll be more like to understand and s-speak up for . . . a good and honest woman. I *knowed* we shouldn't have done it! I *knowed* as we'd be punished!" Her voice rose to a wail. "Oh, Lord save us all! 'Tis—'tis retribution!"

"Good gracious, what a state you've come to! Get down from there at once. At *once*, you silly creature! Now, sit here and calm yourself." Ruth patted the trembling hand she held, and when Grace was breathing more evenly and some colour had returned to her pale cheeks, demanded, "Whatever upset you so? Was it a mouse?"

"Oh, how I wish it had been, Mrs. A.!" Her eyes still haunted with terror, Grace said, " 'Twas a great hugeous . . . *d-daemon!*"

"Nonsense!" declared Ruth, after a surreptitious re-checking of the sunny kitchen. "If truth be told, you saw but the shadow of—"

"That's *just* what I see! And heaven grant I *n-never* see no more'n its shadow, for it was a foul fright, Mrs. A." She lowered her voice to a half-whisper, clutching at Ruth's arm with her cold hands, and staring apprehensively into the corners. "A most *drefful* thing! A great wild boar . . . with its fur all sticking up round its shoulders like any mane! And—a long pointy snout! Oh!" Poor Grace threw her apron up to her face and wept again. " 'Tis all them wicked lies we told! The devil hisself is coming after us, sure as sure!"

There was no doubt but that the poor woman was terror-stricken, and Ruth's conscience was made no easier by the knowledge that she really had, as dear Jonathan would have said, told some raspers. "But we have done nothing so evil as to bring daemons after us," she asserted with as much confidence as she could muster. "We have heard no complaints from Chef about the amount of supplies he sends us. The boys have been so good. And Sir Brian is getting full value for the wages he pays me, for truly, Grace, I work very hard. Surely, the Lord would not punish me only for trying to keep us together?"

Grace was in reluctant agreement with this summation, but she had been badly shaken, and Ruth was obliged to spend the next half hour in trying to calm her. There was no time left for breakfast. She dressed, and plaited her hair in a scramble, but when she hurried across the dew-spangled gardens she took with her the comforting knowledge of having convinced Grace that her "daemon" had been no more than the shadow of the hollyhocks by the kitchen window. Even so, long after she was busily working the matter still preyed on her mind and she was so deep in thought that she did not hear someone come into the chapel, and gave a little jump of fright when Sir Brian spoke just behind her.

"Oh!" she gasped, jerking around to face him, one hand pressed to her galloping heart. "How you startled me, sir!"

He smiled up at her. "So I perceive. You are white as a sheet. I had but come to persuade you to share a cup of coffee with me, never dreaming I might sound as if I'd been a fearsome ghost!"

"You are very far from that, sir," she said, laughing as she took the hands he reached up to help her down. "I must have been extreme deep in concentration."

It was this scene that met Gordon Chandler's eyes as he strolled into the chapel. He halted and stood very still. The sun was slanting a bright beam onto Miss Allington's face and awakening her hair to a pale gold. It was less severely dressed this morning, several tendrils having escaped the tight plaits to curl down beside her ears. Her eyes were sparkling mirthfully, and with that winning smile curving her lips she did not look nearly so plain as he remembered. Were she to be clad in a fashionable gown and her hair more attractively styled, she might even be judged pretty. With a stirring of unease he heard his father's answering laugh, and noted the way he held the woman's hands—*both* of 'em! Was it possible Nadia was in the right of it? But that was fustian. Were Papa in the petticoat line he could have his pick of the eligible ladies in the south country.

He said heartily, "So I have found you, sir."

Looking pleased, his father swung around. "Come home at last, have you Gordon? Welcome!"

Chandler threw a searching glance at Miss Allington. The laughter had died from her face. She looked vexed. Most definitely, she looked vexed. He thought, 'Why, the jade is annoyed because I disturbed them! I think I owe Lady Nadia my apologies!' He returned his attention to his father. Was it his imagination, or was the dear old fellow less downcast? He said, "You're looking very fit, sir."

"That is Miss Allington's doing," said Sir Brian with a mischievous wink. "We enjoy such pleasant chats together. I'd quite forgot how much a house is brightened by the presence of a lady. Speaking of which, did you see your lovely bride to be?"

"I did, and she sends you her affectionate regards, sir. I'd hoped to bring her here but, alas, she was unable to accompany me. I have instead brought a likely seeming man for you to interview. He's waiting in your study. I think he'd make you a good steward."

He declined Sir Brian's invitation to walk back to the main house with him, saying that he wanted a word with Miss Allington. When his father was gone, he moved nearer to the resident restorer. She was at work again, presenting her back to him as she scrubbed away at the painting with some sort of cloth or brush. Running lightly up the steps, he said, "By your leave, ma'am, I should like to see what you've accomplished."

Ruth stepped back. She had been quick to note the annoyance on his face when he'd first come in. Likely he thought it improper for his noble sire to talk to the hirelings. She was quite sure how he would react to the results of her back-breaking labours.

She was perfectly correct.

"Jupiter!" said Chandler, staring with a frown at the small area where colour was flowering from grime. "Is that all you've done in an entire week?"

She had to bite back a comment that she'd really finished, but had put the grime back so as to still be here to see his charming scowl again. Instead, bowing to Resolution, she said humbly, "I have to make haste slowly, sir. 'Tis delicate work."

"Evidently. At this rate, we'll have you here for Christmas, ma'am."

'Would that we might use you for the Yule log,' she thought savagely, and with a demure smile murmured, "You are very kind, Mr. Chandler."

He was a head taller than she, but his look of disdain seemed to be levelled from a great height. In a voice of ice, he said, "Were I you, madam, I would not count on that."

Her chin jerked up. For just an instant, he thought to see a flash in the eyes, which were a much lighter grey than his own. Then, she resumed her efforts. Given pause by that glimpse of fire, he watched her speculatively for a few minutes, noticing that she was using some mixture that constantly fell onto the platform. "I'd think you could achieve more with some honest soap and water, instead of whatever that stuff is," he offered.

Ruth closed her eyes and counted to ten. "Would you, sir?"

"Decidedly. I shall have a couple of the lackeys come over to assist you."

"You are all consideration. I rather doubt Sir Brian would be pleased, however."

"My father would be *pleased*," he snapped, "to view the fresco sometime in this decade!"

"An this work is hurried, or the wrong materials used, Sir Brian will view a bare wall."

'A likely tale,' thought Chandler, and said derisively, "So you have convinced him that your material contains—what? Some magical qualities?"

Yearning to scratch him, she faced him again. "But of course. We restorers guard our secrets, and—"

"Aye! I'm aware of that!"

"—and Sir Brian has had the courtesy not to require me to divulge them," she finished.

Her cheeks were flushed now, and the sparkle in her eyes was plain to see. Irritated by the fact that she looked even more attractive when she was angry, he growled, "Has he so? Then I shall be courteous also, and give you fair warning, Miss Allington, that whilst you are guarding your, er—secrets, I shall be on guard also!" Satisfied with this Parthian shot, he turned on his heel and stalked off.

Ruth spent the rest of the morning composing crushing set-downs to be hurled at the Grimly Gordon, and was so preoccupied that she was able to forget the fact that she'd had no breakfast. Hurrying to the cottage for luncheon, she swept, seething, through the door Grace held open for her.

"Gordon Chandler," she said through gnashing teeth, "is a monster *véritable!* Oh, but that smells delicious, and I am *starved!*" She threw her shawl over a chair, caught sight of her reflection in the glass of a picture, and wailed, "Lud! My hair!"

Carrying plates from the kitchen, Grace asked anxiously, "Whatever did the gentleman do to—"

"*Gentleman!* Crudity, rather! A viper! He stuck his proud nose in the air, sneered at me from under his horrid eyelids, and implied—he *dared* to imply—that I— Oh! That he must *guard* his papa from me! Jezebel that I am!"

Grace uttered a shocked squeal and, encouraged, Ruth

raged on, thoroughly blackening Gordon Chandler's character, and feeling much better for it when she was done.

At the top of the stairs, Thorpe and Jacob looked at each other.

"He went an' did it again," whispered Thorpe.

Jacob nodded solemnly. "We gave him a chance, too."

"We shouldn't of."

"No. We better brew our campaign."

Unaware of the plot that thickened abovestairs, Ruth interrupted her luncheon to say repentantly, "How unkind I am become not to have mentioned that lovely vase of flowers. You know I love peonies. But you must not indulge me, my dear, lest we offend the mighty Mr. Swinton."

"The mighty foolish Mr. Swinton." Grace hurried in with a succulent slice of apple pie to put before her mistress. "He told me as peonies come from Chiney if you please, when I know for a fact as my grandfather used peonies for medicine! Nor he didn't send to Chiney for 'em!" She gave a derogatory snort. "A fine head gardener Swinton is!"

Ruth was remembering the affection in Mr. Gordon's eyes when he'd told Sir Brian he looked "very fit." If anything good could be said of the man, it was that he was devoted to his sire . . . She said absently, "In all fairness, I think he may be right, you know. I seem to recall Mr. Allington mentioning that the Chinese had found peonies to have medicinal qualities long before we—" She broke off abruptly. "Mr. Swinton *talks* to you? You never said aught of it."

"Why—er . . ." Her cheeks suddenly ablaze, Grace stammered, "He didn't exactly— I mean— That is, at *first* he—"

"Grace Milford! I know that look! Have you been flirting with Sir Brian's stern head gardener?"

"As if I would do so bold a thing!" Despite this denial, Grace found it necessary to dash back into the kitchen to fetch the milk jug.

Ruth looked after her uneasily. Grace had never betrayed the least inclination to matrimony, but her bright eyes and generously molded figure had won her several admirers. It had seemed to Ruth that she favoured the burly man who rather incongruously filled the post of valet to Mr. August Falcon, and she had prepared herself to receive notice that Miss Grace Milford had accepted an offer to become Mrs. Enoch Tummet. Perhaps she had attached too much importance to that friendship . . .

"Besides," said Grace airily, returning to fill Ruth's glass with milk, "Mr. Swinton ain't so very stern. He forbade me to dig in the garden, but when he come upon me, I teased him a bit, and next time he come he said he had to admit as I'd a way with plants. And he let me have them peonies, Mrs. A., with not a murmur. Cut 'em for me with his own hands, he did. 'Course," she directed a twinkling glance at Ruth, "that were after I'd given him a slice of our apple pie."

Her unease having become dismay, Ruth said, "But you must *not* encourage his attentions! If he should take to lingering about here, he might see one of the boys, or begin to suspect—"

"Now don't you never worry, dear soul. I'm careful as a clam, and let him know as I don't allow no gents in my kitchen, being a good church goer and bred up to what's right and proper."

"But you are supposed to be simple-minded! Surely, he must know that you are far from being so?"

Grace giggled. "He thinks I'm a half-wit. I told him about my fancying them shadows was a daemon boar, and he laughed and laughed, and went off shaking his head and saying as I be a silly little gal!"

Unconvinced, Ruth insisted that Grace must under no circumstances encourage Mr. Swinton's attentions. Grace promised to be very careful, but as Ruth was going out of the door, she added an unsettling, "On the other hand, Mrs. A., it don't do no harm to find out as much as we can. You never know when a pinch o' gossip might fend off a peck o' trouble."

Ruth had told Sir Brian she must go into the village for more supplies, and it had been arranged that Dutch Coachman should drive Miss Allington and her cousin into the old town, attend to some errands for Sir Brian, then call for the two ladies at Brodie's Lending Library in the High Street. Fortunately, there was no one about when Ruth walked into the stableyard. She told Dutch Coachman that her cousin had not felt up to the drive and, although he protested against her going into town alone, she managed to convince him that she only meant to place her orders and was not likely to encounter any ravening beasts in the High Street. The big man grinned and capitulated, and soon the coach was rolling down the drivepath.

Dover was full of activity this afternoon, the narrow streets crowded with coaches and waggons, horsemen and sedan chairs, and with seafaring men everywhere. Ruth was set down outside a bakery shop where she astonished the proprietor by her exacting requirements, and left him beaming with delight at the order she placed. From there she made her way to a far from fashionable bazaar where she was able to find the type of cotton goods she required and arrange for a bolt to be delivered to Lac Brillant the following day.

The transactions took less time than she had expected, and she strolled happily along the High Street, looking into shop windows and enjoying being surrounded by the bustle of town life once again. Eventually reaching the well-patronized lending library, she browsed among the books for a while. She was examining a new volume of poetry when she experienced the sensation that she was being watched. She looked up quickly. There was a blank space on the shelf and through it she could see into the next aisle. A gentleman stood there. Today, his coat was dark blue, but he was as neat, his smile as blandly ingratiating as ever. He raised his tricorne to her and inclined his head respectfully.

Nothing alarming in that, surely? Yet there was about this man an air of the relentless. The sense of being hunted was strong. She told herself it was illogical, but suddenly Ruth was so frightened that her hands became icy and she had to battle the impulse to run away. Somehow, she managed an answering nod, though a smile was beyond her. He replaced a book he'd been holding. She was sure he meant to approach her and, not waiting to find out, she walked rapidly to the door. If Dutch Coachman had not come yet she would go into another shop, or call a chair. Anything to get away from that persistent creature with his sly eyes and perpetual grin.

Outside, the breeze was becoming blustery and the temperature had dropped noticeably. The sky was more white than blue, the sudden glare dazzling. She hurried along the flagway, heard a startled exclamation as she almost collided with someone, and threw up a hand to shield her eyes. Dreading lest the smiling man had come up with her, she said "Your pardon, sir," her own voice shrill and strange in her ears.

There came a deep and familiar, "I should think so! You dashed near ran into me, madam! Where the deuce are you off to at such—" Gordon Chandler paused and took the hand she was lowering from her eyes. "Here—what is it?"

Never would Ruth have dreamed she would experience such a rush of relief at the sight of him. His brusque tones were so welcome, his grip on her hand so strongly comforting that instinctively she shrank against him.

He pulled her hand through his arm, holding her firmly. "I forbid you to swoon, Miss Allington! Someone been annoying you?"

"Yes— No— I never swoon! But— Oh, do not regard it. Is—"

"I *shall* regard it—whatever—or more to the point, *whom*ever it was." He relinquished her hand for an instant as he turned to the library. "Some Buck in here? Which one?"

She caught his arm as he flung the door open. "No—please! Do not!"

"The devil I won't! My father's people are not molested when they come into Dover, madam. I give you my word!" He stalked inside, grasping her hand again so that she had no choice but to follow. "Well?" he said, not troubling to lower his voice. "Point him out, if you please."

Heads turned. The proprietor looked alarmed and hurried to them.

Ruth caught a glimpse of a dark blue coat making for the rear door. "I cannot. He—he did nothing really. Said nothing. Mr. Gordon—*please!*"

The proprietor asked anxiously, "Is there some difficulty, Mr. Chandler? Is the young lady unwell?"

Chandler said curtly, "You should be more careful whom you let in here, Brodie. One might suppose a lady could venture onto your premises in broad daylight without being annoyed by some would-be Ranelagh rake!"

Unhappily aware of the battery of eyes now fixed upon her, Ruth flushed scarlet and murmured, "It is quite all right, Mr. Brodie. I thought I saw a—a rather tiresome acquaintance. I must have been mistaken. I am indeed sorry to have caused such a commotion."

"Nonsense!" barked Chandler. "Is the fellow here? Look about you, ma'am."

She hissed, "*Will* you let be! He is gone."

He took her arm, said a terse, "Good day" to the proprietor, and propelled Ruth outside again just as Dutch Coachman brought the carriage deftly into the kennel. The footman sprang down to open the door and hand Ruth up the step. Chandler sent him off to collect his mount from the livery stable and ride her home, then climbed in after Ruth.

"And now," he said, sitting beside her as the carriage started off, "we will have the truth of it, an you please Miss Allington. You were annoyed, I am perfectly sure. By whom?"

"I have not the remotest notion," she said, mortified, yet rather touched by his concern. Her response brought an angry snort from him, but before he could rail at her she went on, "I first saw him on the accommodation coach when I came to be interviewed by your papa." The memory of the smiling man's knee pressing against her own made her skin creep. If she told Chandler of such a personal matter he would likely think she was just exaggerating an incident caused only by the rocking of the carriage. She added rather lamely, "Even then, he really did nothing. Save to stare at me."

Chandler frowned. She was very pale again, and her hands were gripped tightly. He said, "Not such unusual behaviour, I think. An attractive young lady, travelling unescorted. A gentleman should not persist, of course. Assuming that he was rebuffed."

"I did rebuff him," she said indignantly. "At least, I tried. But he smiled and smiled, so that I was obliged always to avoid his glance. Why must you always—" She stopped then, for she saw a quirk tug at his lips and a twinkle come into his eyes. "Oh," she said with a rather shaken laugh. "You are teasing I see, and likely think me making a mountain out of a molehill. But—truly, there was something about his eyes . . . The *way* he looked at me. And that horrid, unending smile. Even after I had changed into your carriage, he still stood there in the rain. Smiling after me. To suddenly see him in the library . . ."

"Hmm. What did he look like? Was he a gentleman?"

"He was dressed like one, and spoke in cultured accents. I would guess him to be about forty, not tall, but quite well formed, and very neat. His complexion was light, rather too pink and white, in fact. And—those hooded eyes . . . !" She shivered.

Chandler reached over and placed a strong tanned hand over both of hers. "He sounds a slippery article, I grant you. You may be at ease, ma'am, for you're safe away from him now. But I'll thank you not to go out alone in future."

"Why ever not? I am far past the age of being a school-room miss! When a lady is left alone in the world, sir, she has no choice but to—"

"You are not alone in the world! You are, for the time at least, a member of my father's household, and as such entitled to our protection. And you'll have it, Miss Independence, in despite yourself!"

It occurred to Ruth that she could easily come to like this high-handed interference, and that Mr. Gordon's affianced bride might be obliged to struggle 'gainst his masterful ways, but she was unlikely to be neglected.

As if he suddenly realized that he was still holding her hands, he drew back and changed the subject. "I had thought you were coming into town for supplies. Are we to stop somewhere?"

"No, I thank you. The articles will be delivered tomorrow."

He smiled faintly. "Still guarding your secrets, eh, Miss Allington?"

She smiled also. "But, of course."

And she thought, 'You little know how many!'

When Grace opened the back door both boys were hiding behind her, and they sprang out to greet Ruth with such exuberance that she had to caution them lest they were overheard. Jacob drew back at once, but Thorpe clung to her skirts while she walked across the kitchen, telling her in a stage whisper that they had finished their lessons and reminding her of her promise to read to them after dinner.

"Of course I will." She sank onto the settee in the parlour and smiled at Jacob, who stood regarding her in his grave way. "Now what is in that busy head of yours, dearest?" she asked.

"Wonderings."

"What kind of wonderings?"

"Whether you're happy here, Aunty."

"Very happy."

"You don't sometimes look happy," said Jacob.

"An' you have to work awful hard," said Thorpe. "My papa would not like it."

The thought of Johnny brought a pang, but Ruth managed to keep her smile intact. "Hard work is good for people."

Jacob said, "An' that Chandler man is unkind to you."

"We *know*," said Thorpe reinforcingly.

She thought, 'Oh dear! They must have heard me ranting and raving at luncheon!' Choosing her words with care, she explained, "Mr. Chandler is a rather—er, stern gentleman. But he could be a deal worse." And that was perfectly true, she realized. He could be the kind of man who thought any female on his staff must submit to pinches and fondlings, or a beast upon whom her efforts to make herself unattractive would make no impression since he would view her as a faceless creature he could force to satisfy his lustful cravings. She'd heard tales of such satyrs. She shivered instinctively. Instead of which, this afternoon Gordon Chandler had been someone to whom she had turned without question, and who had been quick to spring to her defense.

Her thoughts were not apparent but, unfortunately, her shiver was, and the twins exchanged a grim look.

"And what about you young gentlemen?" asked Ruth in a lighter tone. "You are being very good to stay in the house whilst the gardeners are about. Is it better now that you're able to go out for a little while in the evenings? You've not been seen?"

Thorpe said stoutly, "Pooh! He never even knows we're there!"

Ruth's heart gave a leap of fright.

Grace demanded sharply, "Who doesn't?"

"Mr. Chandler. He creeps about in the trees." Thorpe crouched dramatically. "An' he talks to 'em!"

"Talks to—who?" asked Ruth, so dismayed that she forgot her grammar.

"I told you. The trees," said Thorpe. "When he's not whistling."

"That wasn't him," argued Jacob.

Thorpe said defiantly, "It was him what I heard talking."

"Mercy me!" exclaimed Grace, paling. "Is he spying on us, then?"

"We're much better spies than he is," Jacob said. "We hear him long afore he gets a chance to hear us."

Thorpe grinned. "That's 'cause of the whistling. He does it sort of under his breath. Like he was thinkin' 'bout something else, and didn't know he was doing it."

The notion of someone creeping about at dusk, softly whistling, sent cold fingers down Ruth's spine. "What does he whistle? A song?"

Jacob nodded. "Always the same one. I 'spect it's all he knows."

"Lawks, Mrs. A.," said Grace nervously. "The twins had best not go out no more."

There was immediate consternation. From dauntless spy trackers, they became small boys, tearful at the prospect of being denied their brief daily escape into the glorious outdoors.

"But my darlings," said Ruth, taking their hands and drawing them closer. "You know how afraid we are of being separated. We daren't risk being discovered, and that's just what would happen if you were seen."

"But we won't be seen, Aunty." Thorpe's lower lip trembled betrayingly. "We're awful careful, and don't make any noise, almost."

"An' there's no one about after dinner—usually," said Jacob. "P'raps if we was to go out a bit later, Mr. Chandler wouldn't be there then."

Ruth said emphatically, "If you mean after dark, certainly not!" But they looked so devastated that she hugged them, and said, "My poor dears. What can I do to make it better?"

"You could let us have a—a pet," said Thorpe, sniffing.

"How I wish you could. But 'tis not possible. I am so sorry."

Jacob dragged a hand across his eyes and said gruffly, "Thass all right, Aunty. We'll pretend one."

"Please let us go in the woods," begged Thorpe. "Please, Aunty. Jus' for a little while. We'll swear a pirate's oath to be more carefuller!"

She had to take exception to 'carefuller,' but looking into their tearful faces she thought, 'They are just babes. How can they be expected to really understand?' So much had been taken from them; so much sorrow might lie ahead. And the end of it was, of course, that she gave in and said they might still play in the woods after dinner, but she would light the upstairs lamp in exactly half an hour, and they must come home at once. Even more important, they must tell her if the man who whistled ever came near to them. And especially they must let her know if it was indeed Mr. Chandler.

Sleep was long in coming that night. She could not banish the memory of the smiling man in the library. Nor of Gordon Chandler's brusque kindness to her. And now it seemed he prowled the woods at night . . . Why? Did he really suspect that she had secrets? If Jacob was right, he talked to someone. If he was not the person who whistled so constantly, was it possible that he had hired someone to watch her? Was that the man he met so secretively . . . ? Oh, *why* must everything seem so much worse during the hours of darkness?

She tossed and turned restlessly. Her last coherent thought before she at length drifted into an uneasy sleep was that she had quite forgotten to discover why the twins had not come downstairs this morning when Grace had started screaming . . .

CHAPTER VII

uth was early on her platform next morning in spite of a dull and persistent headache, probably the result of her broken slumbers. She stood back for a moment, admiring her progress. In the small section she had cleared, the fresco was beginning to take form. At the top was a sunny sky, then a narrow body of water as seen from a distance with a single-masted sailing ship barely visible, and nearer at hand the beginnings of what might be cliffs and a hill. It was still too early to evaluate the work, but the colours did not appear to be irrevocably damaged, and even if the level of skill was not outstanding, the fresco would certainly be a worthy addition to Sir Brian's chapel.

She resumed her careful cleaning. Her arms were becoming inured to the constant effort and she went along smoothly, her mind almost at once reverting to the extremely troubling possibility that Gordon Chandler might prowl the woods at night.

Mr. Aymer came in after a little while. With the exception of Sundays, morning services had been moved to the music room of the main house until work on the fresco was completed, and the handsome cleric scolded Ruth in his gentle fashion because she had not attended the service today. Her explanation that she'd been unable to do so without making herself late to start work did not satisfy him, and he embarked upon a long monologue that began with the sins of omission and rambled about until it became inextricably tangled with self-sacrifice and Sir Brian's expectations of his employees. The reverend gentleman's demeanour towards Ruth had changed of late: At first she'd attributed this to Sir Brian's kindlier attitude, but once or twice she had surprised a look in Mr. Aymer's eyes that had been warmer than simple kindness. He had begun to drop in several times each day and make anxious enquiries as to whether she was not becoming weary. Her slightest comment would send him off on one of his discourses; she had once made the error of showing an interest in his remarks on the Holy Land, and he'd plunged into a lecture that lasted the better part of an hour. He was well travelled and learned, and under other circumstances she would have enjoyed his company while she worked. She had not the least desire to engage his interest however, and in an effort to spare them both embarrassment kept her responses monosyllabic.

Today, it seemed to her that his smile was warmer than ever. This made her so uneasy that she scarcely responded to his chatter, and when he enquired if she had enjoyed her "jaunt into Dover yesterday afternoon," she did not reply at all, pretending to be deep in concentration. He tried a few more times, then said with a sigh that he would not hinder her, and went away.

She watched his rather disconsolate departure feeling a proper flint-heart, but could only hope he would take the hint and not become a problem. It was really a great pity. He was charming, agreeable, and certainly a fine figure of a man. But with no least intention to criticise, she found him dull and rather pompous, and could not think of him in a romantic light. That judgment was of itself ridiculous, she told herself sternly. She was in no position to reject an offer that might provide her with a kind and worthy husband. One moreover, who could offer security and a comfortable home for them all on this estate that had become so dear to her heart. She giggled softly. Poor Mr. Aymer! Little did he know that an offer to Miss Allington would involve three other dependents! Somehow, the very thought of so proper a gentleman having to cope with her two mischievous nephews was hilarious. And what Jacob and Thorpe would think of—

" 'Pon my soul!" exclaimed an indignant voice behind her. " 'Tis nothing more than bread!"

She whirled around. Gordon Chandler must have come in very quietly, and he'd gathered a handful of fallen crumbs and was scowling up at her as though she'd committed a heinous crime.

"What a take-in," he said, tossing the crumbs down again. "And you'd have had me believe 'twas some magical mixture!"

She was annoyed, partly because she'd been quite foolishly glad to see him, and partly because he must immediately place her at fault.

"I'd have had you believe nothing of the kind," she responded, too indignant to remember her position in this household. "And if your papa had hired an Italian restorer you would not dare interfere with him whilst he worked!"

That did not seem to come out exactly as she'd intended, and she saw by Chandler's lowering brows that it had not pleased him.

He said tartly, "I have not—interfered—with you, Miss Allington! Nor have I the least interest in doing so!"

Perversely stung by this declaration, which was scarcely less foolish than her own had been, she remarked, "I'faith, but I rejoice to hear it! Perhaps you will be so good as to allow me to continue with my work and earn the wages Sir Brian pays me."

"What—with a piece of bread and a rag? Any fool—I mean, anyone could do that!"

" 'Tis but one step in the process, sir. And any *fool* would likely ruin the fresco, as I have told you before. By all means, prove my point." She gathered her skirts, and stepped aside.

Chandler scowled up at her. How haughty she looked with her little nose stuck up in the air. Anger fairly radiated from her. Suddenly, he was amused and a lurking smile eased the stern line of his mouth. "What a splendid set-down, ma'am! And likely I deserved it."

At once remorseful, Ruth said, "No, for you are the employer and may say what you will. As a hireling I have no right to—"

"To defend the secrets of your trade? Or to submit to tyranny? A fine rogue you think me!"

"Were I you, Miss Ruth," said Sir Brian, strolling into the chapel at that moment, "I'd refrain from commenting upon that remark. I apologize for my son. He lacks finesse at times."

She saw Chandler's face redden, and in an attempt to mend matters she said with a smile, "I think Mr. Gordon does not always mean what he says."

"I have sometimes reached that same conclusion," murmured Sir Brian, who had an axe of his own to grind.

"You are mistaken, sir," said Chandler, irritated. "I dislike deception."

Sir Brian chose to misinterpret. "Why, Miss Allington," he said chidingly. "Have you been deceiving me?"

It was a home question and for an instant Ruth was so guilt-ridden that she could not find an answer.

She was quite pale and looked stricken. Chandler could not but feel sorry for the poor creature; she must really be in desperate need of this commission. He said, "I was teasing the lady, sir, because she sought to protect her methods. I believe all restorers guard their secrets. Miss Allington"—he offered a small bow—"I promise not to pry. In fact, I shall take my father away and leave you in peace."

"You will do no such thing," said Sir Brian indignantly. "This is taxing work for so slender a young lady. Miss Allington shall have a rest and accompany me on a stroll in the garden. Besides, 'tis Saturday you know, ma'am, and I do not expect you to labour all day long."

Pleased, she felt obliged to say, "But 'tis slow work, sir, for I am often obliged to pause. I would not wish you to fear you'll not see the fresco in—this decade." She glanced obliquely at Gordon, who grinned in acknowledgment of the hit.

Unaware of the double entendre, Sir Brian laughed. "I have no such fears, dear lady. It goes along very well, I think. And how magical to see the colours appear from under that pall of dirt. I thought at first it might be a Biblical scene, Gordon. But the grass is too green for the desert, do you not think?"

"It looks to me," said Gordon, narrowing his eyes, "as though it might be some historical depiction. If that ship were more visible it would help us place the period."

"At all events, I am far from dissatisfied." Sir Brian took Ruth's hand as she came down the steps. "Your immediate duties, Miss Allington, are to brighten my walk."

Chandler's lips tightened. He said nothing, but followed them to the door.

Sir Brian paused, and looked at him with brows upraised.

"By your leave, sir," said Chandler, "I shall accompany you."

"You have not my leave, you rogue! Do you think me so old as to be willing to share a lovely young woman with another gentleman? You have your own lady. Be off with you!"

Chandler smiled, and halted, but Ruth saw that his eyes were bleak. His father's words, she thought, had undoubtedly reinforced his conviction that she had designs upon the old gentleman.

The sun was pleasantly warm today, the sky blue and clear, and the flower beds a blaze of colour. Strolling beside

Sir Brian along the meandering little paths, Ruth said impulsively, "How you must love this beautiful estate, sir."

"I do. And your admiration of it is heart-warming. Are you country bred, Miss Ruth?"

Here was dangerous ground. "My father had a nice home, but it was lost with all the rest, alas. Your sons are very fortunate to have grown up in such idyllic surroundings."

"So I think. And they are fully appreciative of it, I promise you. If he had his way, Gordon would live here the year round. As for my other son . . ." Sir Brian sighed. "Quentin was always dashing off somewhere, following the lure of adventure and excitement. Much good it did him."

"He was in great trouble, I heard. That must have been monstrous worrying for you."

"It was, and is. I'd give all I have to see the boy safe back in England." He looked so sad that she was moved to squeeze his arm sympathetically. He smiled at once, and patted her hand. "But there, I must not repine. Quentin is alive and well, and Gordon also, though I came perilously close to losing them both."

Shocked, she exclaimed, "How dreadful! I'd no idea Mr. Gordon was of the Jacobite persuasion."

"Nor is he! He's too long-headed for that. But he is devoted to his brother and was willing to put his life on the line for him. Had it not been for Gordon, Quentin might not now be safe and happily wed, and soon to make a grandpapa of me."

So she had been wrong and, far from resenting his brother, Gordon had saved his life. She felt inordinately pleased and experienced also a stirring of pride, which puzzled her. Probably, she thought, it was because she placed a very high value on family loyalties and affection, and her own family had been so sadly broken. Sir Brian glanced at her curiously, and she made haste to offer congratulations on the coming blessed event.

"Shall you journey to France to see the babe, sir?"

"I hope to do so. If my health permits." He halted, looking down the hill towards the sea and the distant shadow along the horizon that was France. "Faith," he muttered, "but I miss the boy . . ."

She said bracingly, "You are soon to gain a daughter, I hear. Are you fond of Mr. Gordon's bride, Sir Brian?"

"More than fond!" He brightened. "Her father was my dearest friend, and we arranged the match years since. The lady is a delight. Her nature as sweet as her beauty is striking."

"Your son must count himself fortunate to have won such a lovely bride."

His lips pursed and he said a rather dubious, "Hmm . . . Now, tell me what you think of our chapel."

"That it is wondrously well preserved considering its age. Have there been many renovations?"

"From time to time, down through the years. It was much damaged by gunfire when Puritans destroyed the main building, and eight or nine years ago the tower was blown down by high winds. When those repairs were effected I also had the rose window installed there." He chuckled suddenly. "Within a month, 'twas shattered."

"Was it poor workmanship, sir?"

"Tomfoolery, rather. Quentin and a friend decided to climb the tower. Quentin slipped and would have been killed, save that his friend was able to break his fall, whereupon both young scamps crashed through my beautiful new window!"

He was off again, reminiscing about his younger son while Ruth listened and made the comments he obviously wanted to hear. They came at length to a little summer house offering a fine view of the Strait, very blue and calm this morning. Here, Sir Brian decided to stay, saying he liked to sit and watch the ships go by. Ruth offered to keep him company, but was given strict instructions to go back and pack up her tools and stop work for the day. "You will join us for morning service tomorrow, I trust," he said. "At eleven o'clock, my dear. And by all means bring your poor cousin."

Ruth thanked him, and walked back to the chapel deep in thought. It was quite clear that Sir Brian was breaking his heart for the son so far away. Knowing men, she suspected that he was proud of Gordon and at once pleased and a trifle irritated by his shrewd handling of the business of the estate. But it was the reckless firebrand who had barely escaped the executioner's axe who held the greater share of his love. Heaven knows, it was a very human failing to have favourites among one's children, but it said much for Gordon's character that such partiality had not soured him, and that his love for his father was—

She had entered the cool dimness of the chapel and now gave a gasp of indignation. "Whatever are you about, sir?" she demanded.

Before the second word of her question rang out, Chandler had uttered a shocked cry and whipped around. The cloth fell from his hand, scattering bread crumbs. "I just—" he gasped, "I didn't think— I mean—"

His grey eyes, usually so enigmatic, were wide with fright; he had actually paled, and looked so much like a small boy caught red-handed in a prank that Ruth had to fight back a chuckle.

"You have interfered with my work," she accused. "And have likely ruined everything!"

"No, no! I promise you, ma'am." He hurried to the steps as she came up them and declared with almost frantic earnestness, "Truly, I have not hurt a thing, and was but— I—er thought I'd just try a little work myself. To—er, to help you."

"I think it more likely, Mr. Chandler, that you were curious, and could scarce wait till my back was turned so as to try the game yourself. 'Tis despicable to be so sly!"

He watched anxiously as she moved closer to inspect the fresco.

She said in her sternest voice, "This is *not* a game, sir. This work of art is my responsibility."

"I know 'tis not a game. And I did not mean to be sly,

but—" He broke off, then admitted with a wry grin, "Well—yes, I suppose I did. But truly, I shall take the blame if any harm has been done. It hasn't—has it?"

Relenting, she smiled. "No, sir. But you really were very naughty."

"Mea culpa. I could not resist. Do you see, ma'am? I've uncovered a little patch of blue. Down here. It cannot be the sky, so I think it must be part of a gown—no?"

"Very likely. 'Tis fascinating work, do you agree?"

"Fascinating, but tiring. I did but work for a short while, and my arm aches. Surely, this is too taxing for you?"

She began to gather her tools together. "Not so taxing now. I am become used to it. The first few days!" She made a face.

He frowned and offered to carry the basket back to the cottage for her. As they walked out into the sunshine, he said, "It seems wrong that a well-bred lady should be reduced to performing such labour."

"These are not easy times for a woman alone, sir. Many ladies in reduced circumstances are obliged to accept positions as governesses or companions, or some such thing. Often with people who treat them unkindly."

He thought with a twinge of guilt, 'As I have done,' and glanced with new curiosity at the young woman who walked beside him. She seemed so slight and delicate, but her chin was firm and there was determination in the tilt of her fair head.

She turned to look at him smilingly, and he said, "Forgive. I do not mean to pry, but—have you no family at all?"

Her smile died. "There is an uncle. But he lives in the north, and his wife, who might take me in, will have nothing of poor Grace." She added a mental, 'Or the boys.'

"And you will not abandon her."

"Grace would never abandon me, were our situations reversed. From what Sir Brian said, you stood by your brother when he was in a fix."

He grunted disparagingly. "I suspect my intellect of tottering at times. Certainly, there is no reason why I should support that ruffian, for he has caused me nothing but trouble since I was in short coats."

"Oh, yes," she said, amused. "I am very sure that the next time he gets into a fix, you will abandon him to it."

His eyes became grim. "If there is a next time I'm more like to break his neck."

"Because of your father?"

"Why do you say that?"

" 'Tis very clear that Sir Brian is dear to your heart, sir. And that you worry for him."

He did not at once respond, continuing to watch her. Then, he said, "My father was very ill a few years ago. It has left him frail. But I think he would be much better physically was he not constantly bedevilled by anxiety. And he misses my brother a good deal. Quentin is a fine conversationalist and he and papa used to talk about anything and everything for hours. I—" He shrugged ruefully. "I've not the gift of a silver tongue."

"I see. And Mr. Quentin cannot come home, of course."

He frowned. "My father has told you a good deal, I see."

"And you are thinking I've been prying into your private affairs?" She turned her head to look up at him. "I have not, Mr. Chandler."

"No! I did not mean— Egad, madam, but you take one up so!"

Ruth chuckled.

He said, "Since you are evidently aware of my brother's unfortunate political persuasions, you likely know also that he is devilish reckless. The bond between him and my father is strong. My fear is . . ." He paused, looking sombre.

"Your fear is that if your papa should become ill again, Mr. Quentin would dare to come home, however great the risk."

He nodded.

"That would be dreadful, indeed. Cannot Sir Brian live in France for a while? Certainly, he knows that his estates and tenants will be well cared for by you."

"Thank you for that, ma'am. However, Papa is not a good sailor, and his doctors frown upon such a journey. Were it once undertaken, it would be expedient that he remain for several months before attempting the return voyage, and much as my father longs to see Quentin, he cannot bear to be long away from Lac Brillant." He shrugged. "Point Non-Plus."

"Oh, dear. What a fine pickle."

They were approaching the cottage now, having slowed almost to a halt, and Ruth reached for the basket.

Chandler swung it away. "You are extreme deft at turning a conversation, Miss Allington. I had wanted to learn more of your circumstances, and you have instead manipulated me into talking about my family affairs, which I am persuaded can hold little real interest for you."

"They hold interest for me, Mr. Chandler, because I have become fond of Sir Brian." She saw the wary light that at once came into his eyes, and her own twinkled. "No, but you really must not think I am setting my cap for him."

Again caught offstride, he said, "What next will you say! As if I would think such a thing!"

"Stuff! You have been thinking it since first you laid eyes on me. Never deny your guilt, sir."

The boyish grin that she found quite astonishingly attractive overspread his bronzed countenance, and he bowed theatrically.

"Such a Jezebel you think me," she teased.

"No, no! But I was foolish past permission. I should have realized that so lovely a lady must have admirers. Are you by chance betrothed, ma'am?"

Ruth blinked. What a satisfactory way to assuage his suspicions, and how generous of him to provide it. "I have accepted an offer of marriage," she said with considerably oblique truthfulness.

"Ah, then I need not be anxious for your future. Are you soon to be wed?"

That would never do! "Not for a year. Or two," she said, quickly distancing this threat to her continued employment. "He is—er, in the military, you see. In—India at present."

"Is that so? What rank, ma'am?"

"A—major."

"Splendid! And shall you be going abroad after your marriage?"

"I rather expect I will, for a wife's place is beside her husband." She took her basket. "Only think, Mr. Chandler. A year from today I may very well be en route to a new life halfway around the world, while you and your bride will be happily settled into this beautiful home." Saddened by the reality her words concealed, she looked around the gardens wistfully.

Chandler said a rather clipped, "Yes. Just so. Well, ma'am, whatever the future holds, for this afternoon you can enjoy some peace and quiet without having to scrub away at our chapel wall."

"Thank you. I'll own 'twill be lovely to be lazy. And what of you, sir? Shall you work as usual, or do you dare to be lazy also on this lovely afternoon?"

It really was a lovely afternoon. Tempted, he said, "By Jove, but I shall! I've not gone fishing in an age!"

"C'est bon!" She turned back from the front door and called, "Save one for me, sir!"

Over his shoulder he said, "With luck, I'll bring one for each of you."

Ruth scarcely heard Grace's whispered words of astonishment at her new rapport with Mr. Chandler. She was thinking, 'So in spite of my present appearance, he judges that I am a lovely lady . . .'

It was peaceful in the shade of the elm tree, and Chandler propped his back against the trunk and watched the drift of the stream. It was not the best time of day to fish, especially with the afternoon having become so warm, but half the pleasure of fishing lies in the quiet beauty of the countryside, and the opportunity to do very little but enjoy one's thoughts and surroundings.

He'd have been here sooner save that he'd been obliged to spend some time at Swinton's cottage. Yesterday, the gardener had seemed rather taken aback by the new responsibilities placed upon him, but he'd followed instructions, and if he was resentful there'd been no trace of it. He was concerned for his garden, of course, though there was small need. A bit of a fanatic was Swinton. Chandler grinned as he recalled the head gardener's amusement about Miss Milford's "daemon." Despite her foolishness, one gained the impression that Swinton was rather taken with Miss Allington's reclusive cousin. From what he'd said she had a lush shape, and for many men, of course, intelligence in a female was the least of their requirements. Even so—daemons, indeed!

The branches of the elm tree whispered in the soft breeze; the air was fragrant with the scents of damp earth and wild flowers; the stream slapped lazily at the bank, and the surface was broken occasionally by the swoop of a bird as it snatched up some insect. Chandler felt drowsily content, a feeling he'd not known for some months. He had Miss Ruth to thank for that. He saw in his mind's eye her teasing smile. So she was betrothed. It was a relief to know that her major would take care of her. Poor lady, she'd had a heavy burden to bear. In all probability, her fiancé would allow her cousin to stay with her after they married. They'd be setting up their nursery, and Miss Milford would likely be of great assistance when the babes arrived.

Inexplicably irritated, he heard that clear voice again. "You and your bride will be happily settled into this beautiful home . . ." One hoped they would. Nadia was all fondness for and admiration of Lac Brillant when she was here, but her unguarded remark at Covent Garden had reinforced his suspicion that my lady really preferred the excitements of London's social whirl. Logical enough. Nadia was young and so very beautiful, and it was but natural that she should enjoy being petted and made much of. Certainly, she had many admirers. He wondered suddenly, and for the first time, if she cared for him. And with a frown he wondered also if he really cared for her. It had been such a long-accepted thing. He'd never thought of love in connection with his marriage. Matter of fact, he'd never thought of it at all. At school he'd had pretty Sylvia to warm his bed and lighten his pockets, but he'd been under no illusions that she nourished a real *tendre* for him, any more than he had done for her.

He watched a dragonfly hovering over the water, the sun drawing flashes of purple from its delicate wings. He'd have to talk to Nadia and see if—

A jerk on his line startled him into tightening his hold on the pole. "Zounds," he muttered. "I've got a bite!" He sat up straight, then stood, playing the line carefully. In a few minutes he dropped a fine trout into his basket. Surprised to have caught anything at this hour, he was also mindful of his promise to Miss Allington. He selected a worm and made another cast.

Twenty minutes later he was flushed and jubilant, and two more trout of a very respectable size had been added to his catch. It was foolish to cast again, but he did, and was little short of astounded to almost immediately feel a strong tug. It was clear at once that this was no trout. He'd hooked a big one. With a whoop he entered the fray. And wishing with all his heart that Quentin was here to see such a run of luck, he didn't dream that two others were.

When he pulled his catch in he gave another involuntary

shout. It was a perch, one of the biggest he'd ever seen. Holding it up, he gasped, "Jupiter! It must be a six-pounder, at the least! Papa must see this!" He added the giant to his basket, and was preparing to leave when he heard a loud splash behind him. Half expecting to see a sturgeon break water, he jerked around.

In that instant a very young gentleman darted from concealment, snatched up the perch, and galloped madly for safety. Unfortunately, Chandler's efforts had resulted in a considerable dampening of the grassy bank. Thorpe's feet shot from under him. Instinctively, his arms flung upward. The perch sailed into the air.

Chandler, scanning the surface eagerly, was petrified with astonishment when his prize perch suddenly leapt high above him and splashed down far out in the stream. His jaw dropping, he stared, glassy-eyed and briefly too stunned to move. Recovering his wits he sent a narrowed gaze all around. There was no sign of life. He snatched up his basket. The three trout were still there, showing no tendencies towards athletic prowess. Of a practical nature, Chandler was inclined to dismiss such commonly accepted phenomena as miracles and witchcraft. But it went against Nature for a landed fish to suddenly essay a leap of such Herculean proportions. His jaw jutted angrily. Snarling profane assessments of village pranksters, and appending his intention to apply a cane vigorously to the seat of the culprit's breeches, he plunged into the adjacent trees and shrubs.

His search was thorough and lasted for some ten minutes, but since it did not occur to him to look up as well as down, he found no sign of another presence. At least, not of a human presence. When he finished, the uneasy whispering at the edges of his mind had grown louder. That blasted fish *had* sailed through the air, yet there was not a trace of anyone who might have perpetrated such a dastardly deed. Swinton's tale of Miss Milford's daemon began to seem less ridiculous.

Heated, disgruntled, and bewildered, he gave up at last

and, having lost all interest in fishing, departed at a rather brisk pace.

He left behind him two small boys, who clung to each other on their leafy branch, trying to stifle their sobbing hilarity.

A short while later, the head gardener looked up as Chandler marched from the woods. "Any luck, sir?"

"Not too bad. Three nice trout."

Swinton left his flower bed and came at once to peer into the basket. "Nice indeed." He grinned. "Not so nice as the one what got away, eh?"

Chandler started and looked at him fixedly for a minute. But it wasn't possible. Had a man of Swinton's size crept up and heaved his superb fish back into the stream he couldn't possibly have then vanished so quickly and completely.

Curious, Swinton asked, "Bean't nought wrong, be there, Mr. Gordon?"

For an instant Chandler considered revealing that he'd caught a giant perch and that the minute his back was turned the creature had vaulted twenty feet into the air to return to the stream some twelve feet from the bank. He thought bitterly, 'They'd have me clapped up!' There was a slight motive here, however, so he said experimentally, "It occurs to me that the task I inflicted upon you yesterday may be an annoyance, Swinton."

"Lord, sir," said the gardener, shaking his head. "A little thing like that? Never. Not my place to be annoyed by anything you or Sir Brian ask of me."

Searching the broad, honest features, Chandler found only respect and an affection that made him ashamed of his doubts. He said, with the smile that endeared him to his dependents, "Thank you. That's a nice bouquet you've gathered. For the house, is it?"

Swinton reddened, and his eyes fell. "Er, well, as a matter of fact, Mr. Gordon, I was going to take the flowers over to the blue cottage. It's like I told you. I were a bit sharp-like with the little lady when the coach tore up my—your lawns, sir. And—well, I thought her and Mrs. Allington . . . er . . . you know."

"A peace offering, eh? You sly dog!"

"I wouldn't have ye think as I was stepping outside o' me station, sir. Nothing hanky-panky, I promise you. I reckon as I knows a proper lady when I see one."

"Had words with her often, have you?"

"Not to say often, sir." Swinton turned the bouquet in his work-roughened hands. "Mrs. A. be very strict, y'see. Miss Grace told me right off as I wasn't welcome in her kitchen. But I don't mind that. It's easy to see she's had a few of the lads come flirting round her."

"Who? Miss Allington?"

Swinton let out a guffaw. "That's a good one, Mr. Gordon! Not likely! She's a proper high-bred lady is Mrs. A., and—"

"Hold up!" Chandler intervened sharply. "Why do you keep saying *Mrs. A.?*"

Dismayed, Swinton stammered, "Sorry, Mr. Chandler. I—I meant no disrespect. 'Tis what Miss Grace calls the widow. Mrs. Allington, I should rightly say."

His eyes suddenly as dark as storm clouds and as threatening, Chandler thrust his fishing rod at the gardener. "Take this back to the house, if you please. And be so good as to delay offering your bouquet to Miss Milford for half an hour."

Without another word, Swinton hurried off. When he was safely out of earshot, "Cor," he muttered to his carefully gathered bouquet, "you're going to Mrs. Tate, me pretties! I ain't running up agin Mr. Gordon no more today. Not while he's got that black scowl on his phiz!"

There was a wooden chaise longue beside the cottage, set in the shade of the acacia tree. Ruth carried some cushions out to the chaise and settled down to enjoy the peaceful warmth of the afternoon, insofar as was possible. Grace had gone to try and find the twins. Convinced they would not have ventured far, Ruth was nonetheless put out as she waited for them to come creeping home. The fact that she would have to discipline them cast a shadow over the balmy afternoon. So many times she had warned that they must not be seen. They were only five, true, but they were such bright little boys, and should be aware of what a blessing this situation was, for them all. Whatever could have possessed them to disobey her and go out so early in the afternoon? With Gordon Chandler off at his fishing, he might very well run right into them! She uttered a faint moan of frustration. But she wouldn't dwell upon it. If she did, she'd only become more and more apprehensive.

Her thoughts somehow found their way back to Mr. Gordon. She had been shown a very different side of him this morning. A nice side. And a charming smile that lightened his grave grey eyes. He really was most attractive; thrown into the shade by his brother's exceptional looks, perhaps, but having his own appeal nonetheless. It must not have been easy for him, she realized, managing this great estate, steering troublesome matters away from his sire, and keeping his firebrand of a brother from getting himself killed. She smiled faintly. She admired steadiness in a man, and when Mr. Gordon had been shocked into displaying that engaging grin, she'd realized that warmth and humour lurked behind the stern face he showed to the world.

She wondered drowsily what his chosen lady was like . . . Mr. Aymer admired her . . . but . . .

"I have brought your fish, Mrs. Allington."

She jerked awake, holding up one hand against the bright glare of the sky. She must have dozed off, and here was Mr. Gordon looming over her; a dark silhouette, holding out a basket.

"Why, how very good of you." Sitting up and lowering her feet to the ground she reached out for the basket.

Her hand, the left one, was caught in a grip of iron and wrenched upward. Chandler's head bowed above it. For a heart-stopping minute she thought he was going to kiss her fingers. Then, he all but flung her hand down.

"So it *is* Mrs.," he snarled. "Another deception, eh, ma'am?"

She felt cold with fear and, standing to face him, demanded feebly, "Whatever do you mean by that?"

"You know perfectly well! You deceived my father into thinking you a male when first you applied for this position. Now, 'twould appear you also lied about being unmarried." He gestured impatiently as she attempted to speak. "No, never deny it. The mark of your ring is plain enough, though I fancy you tried to conceal it with powder and paint. Why, madam? Was your husband of so lurid a reputation that—"

"How dare you imply such a thing?" she said hotly. "He was—" She broke off abruptly. Tears stung her eyes. Turning away, she said low voiced, "Well, you may be proud, sir. You trapped me into—"

"Into the truth for once?" He seized her shoulders and wrenched her around. "I'll have the rest, if you please. What is it? Some scheme to discredit my father?"

"Good heavens! Why ever would I wish to do so? Let me go at once."

He released her, but because he was so deeply disappointed said harshly, "I think such a thing because from the start I misliked this arrangement. Clearly, you are an adventuress, and . . . and—" The expression on her flushed face cut off his angry words.

"Oh, never stop, sir," said Ruth fiercely. "First I was a wanton. Now I am become an adventuress. What next will you name me? Thief? Murderess?"

"Do not take such a high and mighty tone with me,

madam. I have found you out, and you'd as well admit what you hoped to gain by all your lies."

"Why—Lac Brillant, of course! Had you any doubt? Good God, but you've an evil mind! Is that why you and your friend creep about after dark, watching the cottage?"

"The devil! I do no such—"

"In truth, you make a poor spy, sir! An you want to slither through the woods unobserved like some—some night crawler—"

"*Night crawler?*"

"—you had best learn not to whistle while you are about it."

"What a'plague are you babbling at?" He caught her wrist. "And where are you going?"

"To find Sir Brian." She tried unsuccessfully to free herself.

"You will do no such thing! Sit down!"

He stepped closer. Of necessity, Ruth drew back and all but tumbled onto the chaise. Behind Chandler then, she saw Thorpe and Jacob standing as if frozen, rage on their small faces. Desperate, she wailed, "Oh! You have hurt me! Look at my poor wrist!"

Chandler released her as though he held a hot coal, and looked down at her hand. Ruth directed a taut glare at the twins, and jerked her head to the cottage, and they ran inside.

"My apologies." Chandler sat on the end of the chaise. "But now I want the truth, if you please."

The truth . . . Dear God! How much of it dare she give him? She gripped her hands tightly. "I am very sure," she began, her mind racing, "that *you* can have no conception of what it means to be utterly desperate. To face the possibility of being thrown into Newgate, or—"

"My God, what dramatics! What crimes should lead you to Newgate, Mrs. Allington?"

"Debt," she said quietly. "I explained my circumstances to Sir Brian."

"You explained *some* of your circumstances to him. I thought it unfortunate that your father saddled himself with a mountain of debt. But your husband must have been a regular slowtop to allow himself to also be pauperized by it."

Seething, Ruth said, "My husband died *before* Papa's—difficulties."

"I see. So 'twas *your* decision to compound folly by throwing good money after bad."

"Oooh!" She sprang to her feet, glaring at him. "Have you *no* compassion? No understanding at all? How could I watch and do nothing to help?"

Standing also, Chandler said scornfully, " 'Twould appear, madam, that you make a habit of helping lame dogs over stiles. Continue on that road and you will most assuredly land in Newgate. Or—worse."

"*Lame . . . dogs?*" Ruth crouched slightly, her hands clenching. "Is that how you thought of *your* brother, when you aided him to escape execution? Is that how you think of *your* father, now that—"

"Different matters entirely," he interrupted hurriedly. And because she looked so furious, he lied, "Allow me to warn you, *Mrs.* Allington, that I know how to deal with females who so far forget themselves as to resort to violence."

"I can well believe you've had experience with such women!" She inspected her wrist and added in a forlorn way, "I suppose that explains why you think it justifiable to treat a lady with brutality, when she attempts to defend herself."

Red to the roots of his hair, Chandler all but cringed, and mumbled that he had certainly not intended to hurt her. To his great relief, she sighed and sat down again. He remained standing, and resumed the attack, but with considerably less force. "The fact remains that none of what you have seen fit to divulge explains why you failed to admit at the beginning that you are a widow."

'*Admit!*' she thought, but she felt drained now and without hope, and answered wearily, "I was desperate to find a situation. When a friend told me of this opportunity, it sounded like the answer to a dream, but—I have heard men say that widows are—are predatory, or of easy virtue. It appeared safer not to mention my marriage."

"Safer, indeed! A charming parcel of rogues you think us!"

"No, but—" Looking up at him pleadingly, she said, " 'Twas very obvious you thought me to be setting my cap for your papa. Had you known I was a widow, *would* you have hired me?"

He thought, 'By God, but I would not!' But to admit that would strengthen her position, so he counter-attacked. "Instead of seeking employment that must only be demeaning to a lady, one might suppose you would instead have turned to the major for help."

Puzzled, Ruth almost asked "Major who?" and in the nick of time remembered her gallant "fiancé." "W-well, I have, of course," she gabbled. "But letters to India take months and it will be the better part of a year before I can expect a reply from him."

This was true, but she seemed inordinately flustered. He said, "I fancy that Major— I have not his name, ma'am."

Her chin lifted in the proud defiance he could not help but admire. "Leonard has sufficient difficulties to overcome without being distracted by a letter from you informing him of my—'demeaning' situation."

A letter was not quite what he'd had in mind, although he intended to make enquiries. He said loftily, "You credit me with more interest in your affairs than I possess."

"Yet you declared that you were anxious for my future."

He had said that. In a moment of weakness. Irritated with himself, but more irritated with her, he muttered, "I suppose I am as capable of nonsense as the next man." He snatched up his basket which, at some time during their quarrel, he had allowed to fall onto the grass, and began to stride off. Pausing, he turned back and in his gruffest voice demanded, "Do you want your fish?"

A sudden bubble of mirth lightened Ruth's heavy heart. She said meekly, "Yes, if you please."

He stamped back and thrust the basket at her; glowering.

"Oh, how lovely! You *did* bring me two!"

"I brought you three!" Peering into the basket, he muttered, "The devil! There *were* three! I'll swear I've not dropped any . . ." He began to look about the lawn, but there was no sign of the missing trout.

With a tentative smile, Ruth asked, "Did one get away, Mr. Gordon?"

"No. Two." Bemused, he shook his head, and her thanks came to him as from a distance.

Walking back to the main house, his mind fairly whirled and he checked at one point to feel his brow. There was nothing to indicate a fever, but between bounding perch, deceitful widows, and disappearing trout, a man could not fail to wonder if his intellect was becoming disordered.

From the upstairs window Jacob and Thorpe watched the retreat.

"He's worse'n I thought," said Thorpe.

Jacob nodded. "He knocked Aunty Ruth down. Only a Evil Villin would knock a lady down."

"We'll have to punish him again."

"Mmn." Jacob looked worried. "I don't 'spect he'll let us stay now."

"We can't anyway. He hurt Aunty Ruth. I heard her say so."

" 'Course," said Jacob doubtfully, "he *did* let her have the fish."

Thorpe chortled, "What was left."

"And Being got one of *them!*"

Coming in at the kitchen door, Grace glanced to the ceiling and said fondly, "Oh, they're back, thank goodness! Listen to the dear children. How good it is to hear them laugh so!"

CHAPTER VIII

ext morning Ruth walked to the chapel through a heavy ground mist that swirled about her and imparted a ghostliness to the trees looming on the hillside. The air was chill, but she was more chilled by her dread of facing Sir Brian, and of the reception he might accord her. Heavy-hearted, she realized that if Mr. Gordon's revelation of her duplicity (as much of it as he knew) resulted in her dismissal, she would grieve for more than the loss of her livelihood.

Quite a number of worshippers were attending services. Several people had paused to greet one another on the steps of the old building, some were probably from the villages and farms, but most were of the estate staff. Mr. Swinton, looking uncomfortable in his Sunday finery and wearing a wig that rendered him almost unrecognizable, touched his brow respectfully to Ruth and glanced about with a faintly disappointed air. Clearly, he'd hoped Grace would be here. It would be so nice if her faithful companion could indeed have come, but that was out of the question. The twins had been repentant but evasive when confronted with their disobedience in having gone outside in broad daylight yesterday. Ruth had demanded their word of honour never to do so again without permission, and they'd crossed their hearts solemnly, but Jacob had added, "Not 'less it's a 'mergency." And Thorpe, with an equally solemn nod, had agreed, "Not 'less that. There might be a accident." Jacob had contributed the possibility of a fire. Acknowledging the logic of such caveats, Ruth was plagued by the sense that they were up to something, and had warned Grace to keep a close eye on them.

As she went into the chapel she was offered some shy smiles and murmured "Good mornings." Mrs. Tate was playing the organ, one of the footmen, looking very drab minus his livery, pumping for her. Mr. Swinton guided Ruth to a pew, and when she rose from her knees and looked about she saw that Sir Brian and his son were already in the family pew at the front. They turned now and then to exchange murmured remarks with two fashionably attired couples seated behind them. Neighbours, perhaps.

There was an aura of serenity about the ancient little chapel, and the voices of the six rosy cheeked choirboys were so pure as to cause gooseflesh to break out on her skin. The service was charming, until the sermon commenced. The Reverend Mr. Aymer was preaching from the book of Leviticus, and had taken for his text "Do not deceive one another." He seemed to look straight at Ruth when he read this, and his subsequent exhortations were so pointed and so condemning that she felt scourged by guilt. She thought he would never stop his denunciation of "the deceitful among us" and, sure that other eyes were boring into her back, she was enormously relieved when the service came to an end.

Sir Brian and his party led the exodus. Mr. Aymer stood at the open door, looking ethereally handsome in his white surplice. He pressed Ruth's hand gently, saying that he trusted she had found his message uplifting, even as his sad smile told her he considered her a lost soul. She responded that she could not see how anyone could fail to be uplifted and, hurrying past, heard a low chuckle.

Gordon Chandler was beside her, unexpectedly dashing in a dull red coat that fit his broad shoulders to admiration, and with his eyes full of laughter. "Very proper sentiments, ma'am," he murmured.

She answered as softly, "I suppose *you* gave Mr. Aymer his topic."

"But, of course." He offered his arm. "Now, an you will step this way, our guests would have you speak to them about the work of restoration."

He led her to where Sir Brian and his friends were gathered about the fresco. Ruth whispered, "Have you told him about me?"

"Not yet. I must await the most—ah, advantageous moment."

She was not quite sure whether that indicated his usual concern for his sire, or whether he was trying to protect her. 'Twould be rather nice, she thought, if the latter was his object.

Sir Brian's guests were a stout and fiftyish Mr. and Mrs. Derby, and a younger and most elegant Sir Marvin Hadlett and his lady. They all were obviously curious that a female would be commissioned to undertake such work, their manner kind but slightly condescending. Ruth managed to answer their questions about the fresco and her methods, and politely evaded enquiries concerning her own background. She was grateful when Chandler intervened once or twice to ease a difficult moment, and more grateful when she was able at last to escape.

It was past one o'clock when she went outside. The mists had burned away, the air was warm, the sun bright, and Mr. Swinton was waiting. He walked beside her, offering awkwardly to escort her home. "There being no objection, ma'am."

She was amused by the prospect of being escorted on a journey of something over a hundred yards through charming and civilized grounds, but she restrained a smile and thanked the head gardener for his kindness. "When we reach the cottage," she said, "you must take a chair in the garden, and Miss Milford shall carry tea out to you."

He beamed, his blue eyes lighting up with delight. Unfortunately, that was a short-lived emotion. In a shady spot on the lawn, Enoch Tummet, neat if not elegant, was seated on one of the rustic chairs while Grace Milford poured him a glass of lemonade.

Tummet sprang to his feet at Ruth's approach. She performed the necessary introductions and asked, "Have you perhaps brought a message for me, Mr. Tummet?"

"From me guv'nor, marm," he answered, his eyes on Mr. Swinton, who had become very stiff but showed no sign of retreating. "Me temp'ry guv. Mr. August Falcon. Only me message aint' fer you, exackly. They're coming dahn fer the party. Sir Neville Falcon and all the rest of 'em." He turned away from Swinton, and his face contorted into a grotesque wink. "Thought you'd want to know."

'I am supposed to gather something from that remark,' thought Ruth. Before leaving Town she had sent a note round to Falcon House thanking August Falcon for the letter of recommendation he'd so kindly writ in her behalf. Grace had told her it had been delivered into Tummet's own hands, so he could not judge her to have been remiss on that score. Baffled, she said, "Party . . . ?"

"That'll be Sir Brian's birthday party," said Swinton. "Quite a occasion. Lots o' the Quality come. Though"—he fixed Tummet with a level stare—"Mr. *August* Falcon ain't never been invited."

"Ar. Well 'e *is* invited this year," said Tummet. "Being as Sir Brian Chandler's grateful to 'im"—his eyes slid to Ruth again—"on account o' a certain letter what certain folk knows of." And again came that horrendous wink.

His earlier wink must then have referred to Mr. Falcon's effort in her behalf, though why Tummet should find that a matter for such facial contortions was puzzling. Ruth turned to Grace and received so demure a look from that popular lady that she almost laughed. "I had invited Mr. Swinton to take a cup of tea," she said. "But I see you have prepared lemonade. Perhaps you would prefer that, now that the afternoon is become so warm, Mr. Swinton?"

"Anything prepared by the hands of Miss Milford will be gratefully accepted," he responded.

Miss Milford's lashes fluttered coquettishly.

"Me own words, exack," said Tummet.

Diverted as she was by these preliminary skirmishes, Ruth was somewhat uneasy as she excused herself and went into the cottage. It was apparent that her faithful handmaiden was of a more flirtatious nature than she had suspected, and that, however devoted, she had forgotten all about the twins. Ruth was relieved to find them in their bedroom chortling over a sketch of a monstrous creature they'd labelled "A Hidjus Deemon." It was really quite well done and did bear some resemblance to a wild boar, but when she praised their efforts they became so hilarious that she had to quiet them.

She went downstairs and enjoyed the cold lunch Grace had prepared. Her preoccupation with Tummet's peculiar behaviour was so frequently disturbed by Grace's giggles that it was eventually driven from her mind altogether. From what she could hear of the outside conversation, the male sallies were becoming ever louder and more pointed, and she was seriously considering putting a stop to the visitations when Tummet took himself off, and a few minutes later, looking rather grim, Swinton departed also.

Grace carried in the lemonade jug and the glasses. Her eyes were very bright and her cheeks flushed with the pleasure of having had two gentlemen bristling over her. Although she could sympathize with such feminine emotions, Ruth took her to task for having failed to keep an eye on the twins, and for quite forgetting to behave as though she was feeble minded. Ruth was more worried than angry, but Grace appeared to be quite crushed, and admitted she was wicked.

Since she soon added with a twinkle that it had made such a lovely change to be pursued once more, Ruth was not convinced of her repentance.

That her concerns were well founded was proven the following day. She was busily at work at about eleven o'clock when she sensed another presence and glanced around to find Gordon Chandler's brooding gaze upon her. Her "Good morning, sir," inspired only a grunt. Apprehensive, she asked, "Have you come to take me to your papa?"

He said harshly, "No. Nor to the executioner. Why do you wear your hair so?"

She was taken offstride. "Does the style displease Sir Brian?"

"It displeases me. And if you mean to remind me that 'tis my father who pays your wages, allow me to point out that he might not continue to do so were I to advise him of a certain discrepancy." He added ominously, "To say the least of it."

Ruth's grip on the bread tightened. "Perhaps you should tell me the—er, *most* of it."

"Would I *knew* the most of it! I begin to think I've come at only the top of the iceberg." He stamped up the steps and wrenched cloth and bread from her hand. "Go and sit down," he ordered roughly. "You look tired."

What a mass of contradictions the man was. She wandered to the nearest pew. "You mean hagged, I collect."

"An I meant hagged, I should have said hagged," he growled, commencing to scrub at the fresco.

"Oh, I've no doubt that you would. Still, I thank you for your concern."

"I have many concerns."

She thought, 'Yes, you do, poor man,' and broke a short silence to exclaim, "Not so rough, Mr. Chandler! We are not at war with the fresco!"

Moderating his efforts, he said dryly, "Perhaps not. But I collect there was a small war on your lawn yesterday afternoon."

"Goodness me! I'd not realized Swinton was so upset as to—er, lodge an information 'gainst us."

Chandler swung around and shook the rag at her, scattering crumbs. "No more he did. But he chanced to mention that August Falcon's ruffian of a valet was courting your cousin, and 'twas clear neither of her swains find the lady in the least dim-witted. I'd give much to know why you saw fit to paint her in so unflattering a light."

Ruth thought, 'Oh, Grace, you wretch! I *knew* this would happen!' And with the feeling that she struggled to escape an ever widening morass, she said, "I believe I did not use those words—er, exactly. But it requires no high intelligence in a lady to attract gentlemen, Mr. Chandler. Quite the reverse, in fact."

"Egad, but you've an odd notion of male preferences, ma'am! Some of us admire a lady with a well-informed mind." He glanced to the side as Mr. Aymer wandered in and, his eyes suddenly brilliant with laughter, he added *sotto voce*, "I cannot say as much for our worthy chaplain, however."

"Oh," she exclaimed in mock indignation. "Odious man!"

Chandler called, "Come on, Aymer! Lend Miss Allington your aid. I'm quite worn out assisting her!"

The chaplain came eagerly to take his turn, and Chandler disdained the steps and jumped down lightly.

"Sir Brian asks if you still mean to try for some game this afternoon," said Aymer, as he climbed to the platform. "Swinton is complaining about the depredations of rabbits again, and Chef would be glad of some for the kitchen."

"I've to ride into Dover this afternoon, but I'll hope to go out later." With a sly glance at Ruth, Chandler added, "Who knows? I may even bag a wild boar."

The chaplain begged Ruth not to be alarmed, and Chandler laughed and walked out with his long easy stride. Aymer said reassuringly, "I believe there have been no wild boars on the estate this fifty years and more. Mr. Gordon says the strangest things at times. Were he not so serious minded a gentleman one might suspect him of facetiousness."

Beginning to entertain the gravest doubts of Mr. Gordon's serious-mindedness, Ruth said, "I am sure you are an excellent judge of character, Mr. Aymer." She settled back comfortably to listen with half an ear to a learned discourse upon the evils of light-mindedness while she reflected upon how pleasant it was to see whimsicality banish the care from a certain pair of fine grey eyes.

Gordon Chandler's efforts to hire a new steward for the estate had met with little success so far, and the resultant additions to his own responsibilities were proving to be a heavy burden. He'd been sure his father would approve of the most recent applicant, but Sir Brian had liked Durwood, who'd had a greasy smile and a clever tongue. His own allegations that the man was dishonest had been met with doubts and arguments until, frustrated and impatient, he had insisted that the steward be replaced. Sir Brian's feelings had been ruffled, and although he knew he'd been justified, Chandler knew also that he had upset the old gentleman. It was not like Sir Brian, the kindest of men, to be petulant, but illness and the constant worry about Quentin had made his temper more uncertain than in past years. 'Knowing all that,' thought Chandler as he rode homeward through a veiled sunset, 'I should have handled it more tactfully.' And he sighed, aware that tact was not his strong point.

He glanced at the lowering clouds. Dusk would come early tonight. Discussions with the builder regarding the demolishing of the ancient lighthouse had kept him longer in Dover than he'd intended. It was another matter on which he differed with his father. Sir Brian was fond of the old structure and reluctant to have it pulled down. In their young days, he and Quentin had loved to play there. In later years it had served often as their meeting place where they could wrangle in private over political matters, although they'd known it was crumblingly unsafe and a potential death-trap. After he himself had found children of estate workers playing on the soaring steps that wound up the tower, he'd had the door padlocked, and had at last convinced Sir Brian that it must be razed. It was over a month since he'd given Durwood instructions to arrange for this to be done, and he'd been taken aback to learn this afternoon that the ex-steward had never even approached the contractor in the matter. It was typical of Durwood. Lord knows, he was glad to be rid of the man, but neither of the prospective stewards the registry office had found were satisfactory, one having been an obvious toad-eater, and the other lacking the experience and polish required to manage so large an estate.

He'd been up at dawn, and was tired when he rode into the stableyard, but he was determined to get in a little hunting before dinner. To that end, he avoided his father, changed clothes hastily and thoroughly upset his man by refusing the services of a loader.

"But, Mr. Gordon," protested Stoneygate, wringing his beautifully kept white hands in dismay. "You've no properly trained dog since your big spaniel—"

"I'll get along without one," Chandler interrupted, not caring to be reminded of dear old Stumble, who had fallen over his own feet since puppyhood and had been a loved and valued friend to the day of his death.

Poor Stoneygate stared his astonishment. "Perchance you could try the red hound called Traveller, sir. He is well named. Your keeper says he can run faster than any hound he ever saw."

"Very true, and always in the wrong direction. Thank you—no." Chandler walked over to his gun cabinet and selected a fine silver-mounted fowling piece. "Now stop fussing over me like an old hen, Stoney. I am quite strong enough to carry my own shot and powder, and I want no dog and *no loader*. And no arguments!"

The valet did no more than utter a few moans until his employer left. He watched from the window as Chandler set forth, game bag slung over his shoulder and hunting gun on his arm. He presented a fine figure of young manhood, with a trim physique and long muscular legs that would make any valet proud to dress him. "If only," Stoneygate told the damp evening air, "he was not so proud and stubborn. It is not fitting that he should have gone out without a loader, at the very least!"

Actually, Chandler had two reasons for refusing company. One of these was connected with the devious widow. He had been irked when she'd been annoyed in Brodie's Library. Where she'd come by the notion that someone was lurking about the woods, he had no notion, but—by God!—if there was anything to her suspicions he meant to get to the bottom of it! The memory of how pale and frightened she'd looked when she came out of the library still vexed him. He was sure she had held something back about that fellow who'd annoyed her on the Portsmouth Machine. It occurred to him that the same rakehell may have dared pursue her onto Lac Brillant land and the thought awoke such a wrath that he fairly burned to catch the miserable hound at his trespassing. Stalking briskly into the shadowy woods, he made the widow a mental promise that she would have no more cause for worry whilst she remained here. Not on that suit, at all events.

At the same instant, the object of his vow was very worried indeed, but for a quite different reason. The weather had become increasingly warm and close, with a hint of storm in the listless air. To work hard in such muggy conditions had been enervating, and she had come home eager to wash and change her dress. Grace had dinner ready and they had sat down to table earlier than usual. The boys had been restless and irritable, probably feeling the thundery tension in the air. The cottage was oppressively hot and at sunset Ruth had let them go out to play, having herself wandered about for a while in case the amorous head gardener might be nearby. The twins had now been gone for five and forty minutes. It was an unpleasant evening, and she had lit their bedchamber lamp a quarter-hour since; surely, they must have seen it. Plagued by a premonition of trouble, not all Grace's attempts to convince her they would return at any minute could calm her fears. She gave Grace strict instructions not to leave the cottage, and hurried into the woods.

It was dim amongst the trees and everything seemed very hushed and still. She did not dare call the boys, but several times she paused to listen in case she might hear their footsteps. The silence began to seem menacing as she moved deeper into the woods. The birds weren't singing and even the small wild creatures seemed to scuttle about on tiptoe.

She jumped when she heard a male voice at no great distance. The fear that it might be the whistling man made her nerves tighten, but stretching her ears, and with her eyes straining to pierce the dimness, she crept on.

The voice grew clearer. A soft grumbling. She realized then that she was hearing Gordon Chandler's deep tones. His words came to her sketchily at first.

". . . have told you repeatedly . . . don't want you seen at this stage of . . . had you any brain at all I'd have a better chance of driving it through your stupid head . . . damned lucky to be alive!"

He would only use such demeaning terms to a hireling for whom he had very little respect. Ruth's heart contracted painfully. Perhaps it *was* the whistling man. Perhaps he *had* been hired to watch her, and Chandler was irked because his henchman had been seen. She was very close now, and knew she ran a great risk of being seen, but strangely she wasn't frightened; just achingly disillusioned.

Edging around a tree trunk she looked into a small clearing, and she checked, and stood staring.

"No, damn you," said Chandler roughly. "Those tricks

will avail you nothing! I'm accustomed to dealing with toad-eating scoundrels, and—" He looked up then, and saw her.

He was sitting on a tree stump, his gun and game bag lying beside him. And the "toad-eating scoundrel" he chastised was a small and very thin mongrel that wriggled and leapt and butted its head in an ecstasy of joy against a lean and caressing hand.

For a moment the two humans stared at each other, equally shocked, equally motionless.

Then, Chandler drawled wryly, "Hercules, I fear we are found out."

For some reason a lump had come into Ruth's throat. She started forward and the dog cowered against Chandler's top-boot, regarding her in abject terror.

"Her-Hercules?" she managed unsteadily.

Chandler stood, scooping up the little animal and tucking it under his arm. "My—er, new hunting dog," he said, without much conviction.

Ruth reached out. Hercules sniffed her fingers apprehensively, then his ears went back and he began to wriggle, while behind Chandler's elbow a small tail wagged frenziedly.

Stroking the dog's head and conscious of a disproportionate relief, Ruth said, "So *this* is who you were talking to! Why, he is just a pup. Look at those big feet! What breed is he?"

"A Covent Garden Courser," he said blandly. "Very rare."

Laughing, she peered at his face. "I think you are making that up. Where did you get him?"

"I did nothing of the sort. He got me. Followed me here from the Market."

"Covent Garden? Good gracious me! What wonderful endurance for so small and starved a puppy."

"Yes. Er—well, he didn't exactly follow me. Not all the way. The truth is that I—sort of came upon him there, and he spun me such a tragedy tale that—"

"That you rescued him! Oh, how very kind. But—why keep him out here?"

He thrust Hercules into her arms while he took up his hunting gun. "If I introduced him to my father in his present condition, I'd likely be disowned."

"But surely you could at least take him to the stables?"

"So I thought, but my head groom is adamant. Fleas."

With a gasp Ruth returned Hercules to his owner. Chandler laughed, and accepting the dog asked, "Dare one enquire why you wander about the woods at this hour? What with whistling men and daemons lurking behind every tree, I'd have thought—"

Putting an end to his nonsense she said firmly, "I felt the need for a breath of air. 'Tis so warm tonight."

Even as she spoke, summer lightning flooded the clearing with a white glare. Hercules, who had just been put down, foiled Chandler's attempt to pick up his game bag by leaping into his arms with a little yelp of fright, and Ruth, who feared lightning, moved a step closer to him.

Amused, he said, "Well, I see I've to take you back to Swinton's cottage, Sir Shivershanks. You'll not object, I trust, do we see the lady home first?"

"No, but really, there is no need, Mr. Gordon. I am quite able to—" Ruth broke off with a gasp as thunder rolled distantly.

"Yes, I see how able you are. But even if you were, ma'am, 'tis not the height of wisdom to venture here after dark if you really have seen strangers lurking about. I've not been much plagued by poachers, but these are hard times and men driven by hunger are apt to lose their scruples."

The thought of the twins encountering such desperate individuals reinforced her resolve to forbid them to go out again unless she or Grace accompanied them. "I did not say I had *seen* anyone," she said.

"You just heard him?"

She crossed her fingers. "Mmm."

"Whistling."

"And always the same song," she said, recalling what the twins had told her.

"Ah. Then you heard him more than once." There was irritation in his voice now. "I'faith, but you beg for trouble, ma'am. You should have let me know of it at once."

"I did tell you! At least I started to."

"When? I don't recall— Oh! Is that what you meant when I brought you the fish? Good God! If you thought there were varmints about, why would you have continued to walk about the woods?"

"Er—well, at first I thought little of it. And then, since you obviously knew nought of it, I supposed it was one of the gardeners, or a groom out for a stroll, perhaps."

"Or a lover and his lass," he supplied ironically.

"Well, that is possible, of course. But I should not think a lover would be whistling." She added demurely, "Would you, sir?"

"Would I whistle at such a moment? You may believe I'm not so daft as to waste my opportunities, and—" Interrupted by another vivid flash and a closer grumble of thunder, he felt Ruth's hand slip onto the arm that held Hercules. "And in fact," he went on impulsively, "were you and I not betrothed to other people— Blast!"

They were coming out of the trees, and the light that glowed from many windows of the various buildings made it less dark in the gardens. Her heartbeat quickening, Ruth glanced up at him, and prompted, "Yes, Mr. Chandler?"

"Be dashed if I haven't left my confounded game bag! And I snabbled four fine conies for Chef. I'll have to go back. Here—" He thrust Hercules at her. "Keep him for a few minutes, will you?"

"But—"

"Oh, for Lord's sake! He likely has only one or two surviving fleas! I'll take him over to Swinton's when I get back."

"I wasn't thinking about fleas! Only—can the game bag not wait till morning?"

He said wonderingly, "An you are so kind as to worry for my safety, pray do not."

"I've no doubt you can guard yourself. Only . . ."

He patted her hand. "Thank you. But I do not like to kill pointlessly." Dimly, she saw the white gleam of his smile. He said, "You go on inside, Madame Restorer. I'll hurry back, and be glad of a cup of tea can you and Miss Milford spare one." And he was gone.

Hercules began to struggle and to yelp frantically. Troubled, Ruth carried him into the cottage and called to Grace, "Are the boys come home?"

Chandler blinked to the glare of the lightning and strode on. It was quite dark between flashes now, but he knew these woods as well as he knew his way about the rooms in the houses of Lac Brillant, and he went unerringly towards the spot where he had left the game bag. He was touched by the knowledge that the widow had been anxious about him. She may have stretched the truth a trifle when first she applied for her post, but after all, a woman alone . . . There was her soldier, of course. He frowned thoughtfully. One could but hope the major was not a pompous ass and would realize what a rare prize he'd captured. And Mrs. Allington, he had come to believe, *was* a rare prize. Not that he had any interest in her apart from her professional abilities, of course. He was a man soon to be wed, and would be a scoundrel and a fool to harbour a romantical inclination towards any other lady— least of all, one already spoken for. Still, the widow obviously possessed a kind heart. She had recoiled from the prospect of fleas—the reminder brought a grin to banish his frown—but she'd been quite taken with the little dog, a different reaction to that of Nadia when— Thunder boomed, cutting off that line of thought, and when the lightning flashed again he saw the game bag, lying where he had left it.

Rain began to patter down as he took up the bag. It felt odd, and with a deep dismay he realized it was moving. He despised the careless huntsman who neglected to make sure that his shot had resulted in a clean kill, and that he could have been guilty of causing needless suffering was unforgivable. Propping his gun carefully against the tree trunk, he wrenched open the bag, thrust his hand inside and drew it out with a startled "Ow!" His hand felt as though a dozen red hot splinters had driven into it. He dropped the bag instinctively, and caught a glimpse of a small shape scuttling across the clearing.

He stared after it. A *hedgehog?* How the devil could a hedgehog have wriggled its way into his game bag? He snatched up the bag. The conies were gone. Rage boiled through him. This was no daemon boar at work! This was a prankster! One of the village lads, doubtless! Well, by God! the young fiend would pay for his rascality!

He raced across the clearing, his language such as would have caused Lady Nadia to fall in a swoon. His hand stung like fire, but the deeper smart was to his pride for having twice been so taken in.

Even as he plunged into the opposite trees, he heard a sound that was at once cut short and that banished all thought of youthful pranks. Someone was whistling that old marching song called "Lillibulero." He caught a glimpse of dark figures, and thought, 'Four of the bastards!' as he skidded to a halt.

"Who's there?" he demanded.

Someone snarled, "It's the perishin' son!"

Another voice shouted, "Shab orf! Outta this! Quick, mates!"

Quite forgetting he had left his gun across the clearing and that the odds were four to one, Chandler charged.

The engagement was short, but very sharp. One of the intruders stayed well clear, but his companions answered the challenge zestfully. In perfect condition and no stranger to fisticuffs, Chandler sent one man reeling back, levelled another, and was himself sent sprawling. Dazed, he rolled to avoid a flying boot, grabbed it and with a heave brought its owner crashing down. He was on his feet again, the taste of blood in his mouth, but the dizziness fading fast. Another dim shape hurtled at him. He caught the gleam of steel as lightning flashed, but a cultured voice shouted commandingly, "No killing! We don't want him dead!" With his left arm thrown up to protect himself from the knife, Chandler rammed his right home, and heard an explosive "Ooof!" At the same instant, a tree seemed to fall on him. He was down again, struggling to get up, but hampered by a sick weakness. He got to his hands and knees. A boot drove at his ribs, slamming him onto his back. He heard mocking laughter. The lightning split into countless piercing shards, all flying at his head. A very long way away someone was whistling "Lillibulero." Pain took him, and wiped the night away . . .

Something icy cold was hitting his face. Whatever it was must be very sharp, because it hurt abominably. With a great effort he got one eye open. It was night. He was in the woods. Lying down, with raindrops striking his face. 'Ridiculous!' he thought. He tried to get up and stopped trying at once.

There came a shrill wail. "Sir! Oh, sir! Please don't go off again! I can't lift you!"

It was the outside of enough that this pestilent creature should shriek at him when his head had exploded. "Stop that!" he gasped. His voice sounded odd and distant, but the wails stopped.

The crack of thunder was close, shattering the brief silence and, it seemed, Chandler's head. A groan rose in his throat, but one didn't make such a sound where others could hear. He smothered it and, managing to force both eyes open, discerned a most odd figure crouching over him. Someone who had apparently been cut in half. But could still talk. This seemed curious. "How . . . ," he enquired, "d'you manage to be alive?"

"Thank goodness! I was 'fraid you'd died."

Chandler thought, 'It's a child, you stupid clod!' "I've not," he said. "But—I cannot seem to—to get up just now." He tried again, and this time his ribs joined with his head in sending him back into forgetfulness. It must have been a very temporary lapse, because the voice was coming to him again. "I'll help. Come on, sir. Try."

"Thank you," gasped Chandler, doing his best. "Oh, Gad! No use. Could you . . . d'you think, bring help?"

"I d-don't want to leave you." The voice sounded very young and scared. "They might—they might c-come back. They're bad. I knew they were bad the firs' time I heard them."

"When was . . . that?"

"A long time ago. Days 'n days. Weeks I 'spect. Please try an' get up."

"Are you," managed Chandler, "a boy?"

"Y-yes, sir. But I can help. I'm strong. You could l-lean on me."

"Thanks. But—I seem to be rather . . . tired. You'd help me most if you'd . . . you'd be so kind as to bring someone . . . with . . ."

He had intended to ask for brandy, but there was no need, because a flask materialized at his lips. He took a healthy swallow, and looked up again.

There were two figures this time. The boy, and a woman. The rain was still splashing onto his face. He said in a surer voice, "Don't tell my father."

"No. I knew you wouldn't want that. I'll send for Swinton."

"Wait, please. I'll be all right . . . in a minute or two." He realized that it was the widow, and with a sigh of relief muttered, "I hoped you'd come."

Ruth took the unsteady hand that reached out to her.

"Your head is hurt," she said gently. "I cannot see very well in the dark. Is there any other injury?"

The boy's voice, less tremulous now, said, "They kicked him in the side awful hard. I—I thought he was killed, Aunty Ruth."

"*Aunty Ruth . . . ?*" Chandler groaned. "Now, what—"

Biting her lip, Ruth said, "Never mind about that. If I prop you, can you sit up?"

It came to him that she was already propping him, for his head and shoulders were on her knees, and her arm was around him. He said weakly, "What's your name, boy?"

"Jacob, sir."

"Then take my hand, Jacob, and when your aunt . . . lifts, you pull. All right?"

"All right."

The first attempt was not a great success, but with the second Chandler was on his feet, clinging to Ruth as the woods revolved slowly around him. She made him rest for a minute or two while she steadied him on one side and Jacob propped him on the other. Then, they set off.

For Chandler, it was an interminable journey and not one he later cared to remember. Twice, he thought he was surely going to disgrace himself by casting up his accounts, but the dread of doing such a revolting thing in front of the widow gave him the strength to fight back the sickness and keep on. The cold rain and the brandy did much to restore him, and by the time they reached the cottage, although the pain had increased rather than diminished, his legs felt steadier and he could keep his head up.

Grace held the door wide and was peering into the night, a lamp in her hand. She uttered horrified little cries and fluttered about as between them they guided Chandler to a deep chair in the parlour.

He looked up at them blurrily. He supposed it was Miss Milford who brought a tray with water and bandages. Mrs. Allington, her gown lurid with his blood, was setting her shawl aside. The boy, Jacob, stared at him with huge frightened eyes, his face chalk white.

Chandler made an attempt to rally. "Must you always let me down, madam? Where's . . . my cup of tea?"

CHAPTER IX

ou should be laid down, Mr. Chandler." Ruth had washed the blood from his face, but she leaned nearer to the chair so as to dab gently at a crimson trickle that seeped from under the bandage about his dark head. "That is a very nasty gash, and I know you must be feeling dreadful."

He did feel dreadful. His head pounded so brutally that even his eyelashes hurt, and by the feel of his side a rib had been cracked at the very least. "If I lie down," he whispered, "I'll sleep."

"As you should. Oh, I wish you had told Grace to send word to the Watch, instead of insisting she say nothing to anyone save Dutch Coachman. What if she cannot find him?"

He'd insisted upon Dutch because that old friend was big enough to carry him if his legs gave out, and could be counted on not to throw the household into a panic. "Then you'll have to put up with me until she does find him. First, I must have some answers. Most—most importantly, where is my hound?"

She was won to a shaken chuckle and marvelled at the faint answering quirk to his pale lips. "We shut him upstairs for fear he would jump up on you when we brought you back."

"The boy?"

Ruth hesitated. Surely, now that he might have some small cause to be grateful to them, this would be the perfect moment to tell the truth about the twins? She gathered her courage and began nervously, "There is something . . . I er, must—"

Fighting against betraying the effect of a sharp wave of pain, Chandler made a heavy-handed attempt at humour and gasped out, "Speak up, ma'am. You've no cause for apprehension unless . . . unless, of course, there are more of your relatives lurking about the estate. That, I'll own, would be going . . . beyond the line of what my father would tolerate. *Is* Jacob your nephew?"

It was *not*, Ruth realized, the time for more confessions. "He is," she said. That was truth, at least. "Some friends brought him down to visit me. I was hoping you might let him stay for just a little while."

His eyes, which had closed, now opened and he peered at her frowningly. "When did you first hear that whistling maniac?"

"Maniac? Is that what you believe? But surely, a madman would not bring three other rogues with him. And if they were thieves or poachers, I cannot think it likely they would risk the death penalty by daring to attack a member of the Quality. If they knew who you were, of course."

"They knew. The leader howled I was . . . was not to be killed."

"Then, if they knew you, why ever—" She checked with a shocked gasp. "Oh! My heavens! You think they may have some connection with your brother!"

In point of fact, Chandler was finding it difficult to think at all. But there were matters he must clarify before he faced a minion of the law. And quite apart from the possible involvement of some of Quentin's Jacobite friends, Gideon

Rossiter's tale of the League of Jewelled Men lurked persistently at the back of his mind, however he tried to dismiss any possible connection as nonsense.

He evaded wearily, "What exactly did you hear?"

"As I told you. Just a man, whistling."

"When?"

"Er—I cannot recall. About a week after I came, I think."

"And you heard him more than once. How often? Every night?"

'Great heaven!' she thought, trying to remember what the boys had said.

"You do not know," he said, panting a little as he glared at her. "The truth is—you heard nothing! Own it!"

"Whatever do you mean? Why would I invent such a tale?"

"Because you've a—a very active imagination, Madam Widow, but I cannot feature you wandering alone in the woods at night."

"What are you concocting now? That I was in the woods at night—*with* someone? The whistling man, for instance?"

"Were you?"

"I think you are the one with the active imagination, Mr. Chandler! And a nasty one, besides!"

"There is nothing particularly nice about wallowing in—untruths," he pointed out acidly, then clutched at his side, wincing.

"You see!" Alarmed, she bent forward again to wipe his face with the damp rag. "Oh, if only you would lie quietly!"

"Speaking . . . speaking of lying. Which of you is doing so? Or is it both?"

She stared at him.

He made a febrile gesture of irritation. " 'Fore God, 'tis like drawing blood from a stone! *You* say your nephew just arrived. Whereas *he* told me he'd first heard the man weeks ago! I fancy the truth is that . . . he's been here . . . all the time!"

Ruth had suffered a severe shock when she'd found him in the woods, for at first she had thought him slain. Her nerves were still quivering, and her wits seemed to have deserted her. She faltered, "You cannot seriously believe that I could have kept a little boy hidden for weeks?"

"Yes I can! That's why you always have the curtains closed. And why you said your cousin Grace was simple—" He paused, closed his eyes, frowning, then went on haltingly, "—simple minded. I . . . doubt she's any more your cousin than Jacob is your nephew."

"Only see how you are hurting yourself, trying to trap me with all this rubbish. If you will rest now, in the morning I'll—"

"Have thought up another set of tales, no doubt! Jacob has your fair hair and delicate features. You'd as well give up spinning your farrago of . . . fibs. He is your son, isn't he?"

Momentarily taken by surprise, it then occurred to her that this might be a very promising development. If they believed Jacob was her own child, they'd be much more likely to let her keep him here. But it would also mean she must teach the boys to tell untruths, which Johnny would have disliked very much. Therefore, "An you doubt whatever I say, Mr. Chandler," she said, staring down at her hands, " 'twould be wasting my time to try and convince you."

"Or *en effet*, 'Ask me no questions'! An extreme unsatis-factory—"

At this point, to her great relief Ruth heard hurrying foot-steps, and she flew to open the front door.

Scattering raindrops, Grace came in, followed by Dutch Coachman, his rugged features strained and anxious.

"Oh, Mrs. A.," quavered Grace, closing her dripping um-brella. "Is he any better?"

"He might be, an I could but keep him quiet."

Horrified by Ruth's gruesomely stained garments and Chandler's battered appearance, the coachman dropped to one knee beside the victim. "Lor' but you're a proper sight, Mr. Gordon. How are ye, sir?"

Chandler summoned a tired smile. "A trifle knocked up, is all, Dutch. Nothing serious. Who knows about this?"

"Only me, sir, never fret. But Sir Brian will have to be told tonight. And we must have the Watch out. Miss Milford tells me there were four o' the murdering varmints."

"You can tell my father as soon as I'm a less gruesome sight."

"Aye. That'll be best, surely." The coachman stood. "If you'd let me fetch one of the grooms and a hurdle, we could carry you. It'd go easier on you, sir."

"No. With your help I shall do."

Ruth said, "Coachman, it will be so much better if he stays here tonight. We can make up a bed downstairs, and—"

"No," said Chandler mulishly. "I must—get home. Lend a hand, Dutch."

The coachman bent to slip an arm around him. "He's right, ma'am. We'd have Sir Brian in a proper taking!"

Irritated, she said, "Which might not be such a bad thing."

"I hear what ye're saying, Miss Allington." The big man gave her an approving nod. "But, 'twould never do. Ready if you are, sir."

Chandler struggled up gamely, and with the coachman's aid was soon on his feet, but wavering dizzily in the circle of his strong arm. He said in a fading voice, "My thanks, ma'am." His eyes narrowed. "Oh, Egad! I shall buy you a new gown . . ."

"Yes, but not *now*," she said, exasperated. "Go!"

He persisted stubbornly, "Dutch, I want a guard on this house tonight."

"We'll have one, sir. Never worrit. Now come ye along, and lean on me."

Grace held the door open and the two men made their erratic way into the rain.

Ruth sank down in the chair, her knees suddenly weak. Grace came and looked down at her with great, frightened eyes. "Poor Mrs. A. What a shock you've had! And whatever do it all mean? Why would anyone creep about the woods? Why would they hurt poor Mr. Gordon? And—oh, my Lor'! Now he knows about the twins!"

"Er, yes," said Ruth. And she thought, 'More—or less.'

Jacob and Thorpe were both fast asleep when Ruth looked in on them, but Hercules was so frantic to escape that Grace fashioned a lead from a piece of sheet and took the "Covent Garden Courser" back to Mr. Swinton's cottage. She returned with a wry face as Ruth was getting into bed and told her that Hercules had twisted out of his "lead" and disappeared.

It seemed to Ruth that no sooner had the curtains closed than Grace was pulling them back to admit full daylight. Much agitated, Grace said that it was eight o'clock, that there was a horrid wind blowing, and that Mrs. A. was wanted at the main house as soon as may be.

Ruth sat up in bed and gathered her thoughts. With slow reluctance she said, "Please tell Jacob to put on his blue habit and best shoes."

Grace gave a small scream.

Ruth nodded. "He must come with me."

"Oh, Lor'! But—but what about Thorpe?"

With a wry smile Ruth admitted, "Mr. Chandler does not know about Thorpe."

Wailing, Grace departed.

The morning was indeed windy, with clouds being hurried across the sky. Escorted by a footman and with Jacob's hand clasping her own tightly, Ruth asked, "How does Mr. Chandler go on?"

The footman shook his head and looked mournful.

"Passed a bad night, after the village constable left, ma'am. Very bad. Still, he's a game 'un is the young master. Bound and determined to get up s'morning, he was, but Dr. Keasden says no, and Sir Brian, he put his foot down. Now that we got more constables come, and more expected, Mr. Gordon will likely be glad enough to stay abed and out of their path."

They were at the front door when two carriages pulled up and disgorged several eager gentlemen who tried to crowd past the butler. Mr. Starret hurried Ruth and Jacob into the house, but advised the journalists at his most regal that the Reverend Mr. Aymer had a statement for the newspapers and that he could be found in the chapel.

Closing the door upon their outcries, Starret looked at Jacob curiously. "The young gentleman would very likely prefer to wait for you in the kitchen, Miss Allington."

"This is my nephew, Jacob," said Ruth. "He has information for Sir Brian."

Starret's eyebrows went up, but he led the way to the study without further comment.

Sir Brian was not accompanied by constables, as Ruth had feared, but sat alone, writing a letter. He stood at once and came around the desk to take her hand and press it fervently. "My dear lady," he said, with a curious glance at the child half hidden behind her skirts. "My son has told me of your courage in going to his aid. I am most deeply indebted to you."

Ruth said, "I see that Mr. Chandler has not told you about Jacob, sir. He saw the fight and came to fetch me."

Clearly bewildered, but ever the courtly gentleman, Sir Brian settled her into a chair before asking for explanations. Jacob refused to sit down, but stood close beside Ruth. He was very pale, his blue eyes wide and scared, and the bright morning light touching both the fair heads brought the dawn of suspicion to Sir Brian. "I see," he said, leaning back against his desk, "that Gordon had cause to ask that I speak with you privately before we meet the constables. This young fellow is er, very like you, ma'am. Might there be, perchance, a—relationship?"

Ruth gripped her hands together and drew a deep breath. "I must tell you first, sir, that I have not been quite truthful with you. My name is not Miss Allington. It is *Mrs.* Allington." She saw his dark brows twitch together, and said quickly, "I am a widow, sir. Jacob is my orphaned nephew."

"Indeed?" Sir Brian's face was rigid and austere. "Perchance you will be good enough to explain the reason for such duplicity, madam."

"It is that—that some people, sir, appear to regard a widow lady as of—er, questionable moral integrity. I was desperate to find employment, and I feared that if you knew the truth—"

"I would not hire you? I hope I am not so prejudiced! Or did you perhaps also fear to be judged as fair game? In either case, you did me an injustice, Miss— Mrs. Allington. Am I to infer that you *smuggled* your nephew here? That he has been hiding in your cottage from the first?"

He was by now flushed with anger, and Ruth knew her own face was red. She said miserably, "Yes, sir. I very soon realized I should have told you the truth, but—"

"You should, indeed! I *despise* falsehoods, ma'am! Especially one that casts such an aspersion on my character and that of my son!"

"I am—very sorry," said Ruth, hanging her head. "But—"

"We jus' wanted to keep together," interjected Jacob fiercely. He put a supportive hand on Ruth's shoulder. "My Aunty hasn't done nothing bad an' she's worked awful hard. Papa wouldn't like it. An' he wouldn't like you to talk to her like that. Sir," he added, belatedly scared by his own daring.

"Well, well." Sir Brian's scowl eased. "Quite the young champion, aren't you?" He pulled up a chair and sat down, returning his gaze to Ruth. "And regardless of those circumstances, I must not forget that you have rendered us a great service. Now come here, boy, and tell me exactly what happened. How came you to be in my woods after dark? The truth, if you please. Man to man."

Jacob edged forward uneasily. "It was the only time we could go out, sir. After the gardeners had finished work, an' no one would see us."

"Us . . . ?" probed Sir Brian in a deceptively gentle voice.

Jacob slanted a troubled glance at Ruth's tense face. "Me—an' Being."

"Being what?" asked Sir Brian.

"That's his name. My pet. Aunty said I couldn't have a proper one. Like a dog. Or even a cat. So when I found Being, I took care of him. He'd got a bad paw an' I think he would've slipped his wind if—"

"Jacob!" protested Ruth, as intrigued as Sir Brian by these revelations.

"I'm sorry, Aunty. But—he said 'man to man.'"

Sir Brian's lips quirked. "True. But a gentleman does not use cant terms in front of ladies. Be so good as to tell me what kind of—ah, creature is Being."

"He's a hedgehog, sir. Just a little one. An' he's no trouble."

"I see. So you take him for walks after dark?"

"Not in a reg'lar way, sir, 'cause he don't like to be put on a lead. But we heard Mr. Chandler. He was nasty to Aunty Ruth. An' when he knocked her down—"

"When he—*what?*" thundered Sir Brian, jerking bolt upright in his chair.

Jacob gulped and jumped back a pace.

Ruth said hurriedly, "He didn't really knock me down, Jacob. I tripped. Your son was cross, sir, because he'd found out I am a widow."

"Had he! What a great pity he did not see fit to inform me of that fact! But I am still confused. What has this to do with your going into the woods, Jacob?"

"We was goin' to punish Mr. Chandler." Memory brought a surge of joy and Jacob beamed, not even noticing

Sir Brian's astonished expression. "I took the rabbits out of his game bag an' popped Being in." He gave an involuntary chortle. "You should've seen his face when he put his hand inside! He yelled. Very loud. An' he swore something drefful an' comed after me, so I ran. An' then—" He paused, the mischief fading from his face.

Sir Brian, who had been trying not to grin, sobered also. "Go on, you young ruffian. Did he catch you? Gad, but he said naught of all this! No, don't be afraid. You sound to me like a fine fellow to so defend your aunt."

Taking courage from this, Jacob said in a lower voice, "That's when I heard the whistling man again. An' I hid, quick. But—I s'pose Mr. Chandler didn't hear them as soon as I did, 'cause he was makin' so much noise. When he did see them, he stopped running and asked, very fierce, what they was doin' on your lands. And then they all started to fight him." He drew himself up, his eyes blazing with excitement. "He didn't run away or anything, 'spite of there was so many! Oh, but he's a good fighter, sir! He popped one on the beak, and knocked another one down, and then *he* got knocked down but he snabbled one more, even when he wasn't up! Only—then they hit him from behind with a club. Like cowards an' sneaks! An' . . ." His voice trailed off and the scared look was back in his eyes.

Sir Brian said kindly, "Yes. Well, I think I know the rest. You were brave enough to go and fetch help. You did very well, young fella. Very well indeed, and I am so much in your debt for going to Mr. Chandler's rescue that I shall allow you to stay here with your Aunty Ruth for a day or two. Provided you don't get into mischief. Now, what d'you say to that?"

His eyes brightening, Jacob asked, "Does that mean I won't have to keep inside, sir?"

Sir Brian nodded.

"Oooh!" breathed Jacob. "How sp'endid!" He gripped his hands so hard that Ruth thought the frail bones would snap, and for an instant it seemed that Sir Brian was going to be hugged. But then the boy offered a jerky bow and said solemnly, "You're mos' kind. Thank you, sir."

"Bless my soul!" murmured Sir Brian.

Ruth said, "I promise faithfully that Jacob will cause you no trouble, sir."

"And no more disciplining of Mr. Chandler either, boy," said Sir Brian sternly. "I'll own he needs it at times, but that's for me to tend to."

"I think Jacob must apologize to your son," said Ruth. "How is he today, sir?"

"Oh, perfectly fit, I thank you. Solid steel is Gordon. Now, ma'am, the constables are waiting to hear your story, so if you will please to come this way . . ."

"What in the name of perdition is—*that?*" Sir Brian, who had gone to his son's apartments to apprise him of the latest developments, paused on the threshold of the small parlour, an expression of abhorrence on his face.

Wearing a dressing gown over his nightshirt, and seated in a chair before the open casement, Chandler lowered one hand to calm the little dog that cowered against his foot. "Hercules, Papa," he answered gravely. "I found him in Town."

"You'd have done better to leave him there!" Sir Brian closed the door and crossed to sit in the window-seat. "That's not a dog, it's a shiver! And not a fitting animal for a gentleman!"

Chandler sighed, put back his bandaged head, and closed his eyes.

Sir Brian looked at him anxiously. "Giving you pepper, is it lad?" he enquired in a gentler tone. "I shouldn't pinch at you when you're in queer stirrups. But *that*"—his kindling eye rested on Hercules again—"must—"

" 'Tis none so bad, sir," said Chandler, with a faint smile. "Seems to have put me off my stride a trifle. But I'll be up and about in no—" Here, attempting to rise, he swayed artistically and sank back again.

"For Lord's sake, stay there," cried his sire, alarmed. "You're properly wrung out, and small wonder. That's a devilish cut, and your side is a grisly mess. I wonder that fool Keasden let you out of your bed."

"To say truth, he didn't. But I don't care to languish like a schoolroom miss, only because I took a rap on the nob." From under his lashes he saw that he had successfully diverted Sir Brian's attention from his abominable pet, and he asked, "Have there been any new developments?"

"You may believe there have! I've set every available man to scour the grounds for the rogues who attacked you. Not a sign thus far, burn it! Mrs. Allington is— Why the deuce did you not tell me that she is a widow?"

"May I ask who did?"

"The lady herself. Just now. And the boy with her. Most damnable thing! You know I cannot abide untruths!"

"I'll admit I was most shocked. I had fully intended to tell you. But you knew I'd been set against your taking her on in the first place, and I was reluctant to seem to—er, gloat."

"The devil! Gloat about what? You fancy I made a mistake, eh? No such thing! She does her work well enough." Sir Brian's eyes darkened. "If it weren't for all her fabrications—"

"Just so. But we should not find it too difficult to replace her. I shall handle the interviews this time, and—"

"I think I did not say I had turned her off," put in Sir Brian testily. " 'Twould be a pretty thanks to the lady for having helped you. Not many women would've ventured into the woods at night, especially knowing there were murderous ruffians lurking about. And then to find you in the state you'd come to! Why, most females would have swooned on the spot and been worse than useless, for there's few of 'em can stomach the sight of blood." He frowned. "Still, I'll own I *cannot* abide deception."

Watching him from under his lashes, Chandler said with emphatic righteousness, "You are very right, sir. The fact that Mrs. Allington has some backbone don't excuse her disgraceful behaviour. She has deceived you on more than one count. I'd be willing to swear that repellant brat is hers. Surely, you have marked the likeness?"

"Well, I did, of course. D'ye think I'm blind? And as for deceiving me, if the boy is her own, one can scarce wonder she'd have gone to any lengths to keep him with her. Any mother worth her salt would do the same." He paused, and added musingly, "He's a quaint child . . ."

"Quaint! That's not the word I'd have used!"

Sir Brian grinned. "Aye. He told me how you swore when you found his hedgehog in your game bag."

"So it *was* his doing! Little hellion! Really, sir, you must not allow your obsession with that fresco to overwhelm your good judgment! The brat—"

"I am aware it has pleased you always to sneer at my fresco. The day may come when you laugh on t'other side of your face. However, 'the brat' did not seem so repulsive last evening when he came to your aid, I'll warrant. I do not scruple to tell you, Gordon, that you want for a proper sense of gratitude."

"And you, sir," said Chandler with his warm smile, "have the kindest heart in Christendom. I bow to your wisdom, and own myself at fault. The lady, whatever else, is a fine artist; the boy is courageous; and you are perfectly correct in that we stand indebted to them both." From the corner of his eye, he saw Stoneygate in the open door of the dressing room, shaking his head in amused rebuke. Ignoring his upright valet's high principles, he went on, "I shall raise no further objections to your allowing 'em to stay here till the fresco is finished, I give you my word."

"Hum," said Sir Brian, pleased to have bested his strong-willed son.

"Now, pray tell me, sir, what has our upright constable to say?"

"A lot of balderdash, as you might suppose. The big fellow who questioned you last evening came back this morning with an assistant who writ down everything. Not that Mrs. Allington could tell them much. The boy could not recognize anyone in the dark, but he heard one of 'em whistling some song or other. Much that has to say to anything."

" 'Lillibulero.' Yes, I heard it also."

"By God, but it makes my blood boil, to think of you being set upon in your own home! We must have more keepers about at night from now on. What the devil d'ye suppose the bastards were about?"

"Reconnoitering, I should think. With an eye to robbery. Is the constable finished with Mrs. Allington?"

"Yes. I sent her back to the cottage. She'll need to rest after such a shocking experience." Sir Brian added with faint amusement, "Aymer's escorting her."

Chandler looked at him curiously. "You cannot think he has a genuine interest in the lady?"

"Why not? Because you've caught yourself so beautiful a bride, you can see no other, but Mrs. Allington's a fine-looking young woman, and has been properly bred up, there's no doubting. Not every man can find a diamond of the first water like Lady Nadia, you know."

Chandler lowered his eyes to the softly snoring Hercules, and said nothing at all.

For several days Lac Brillant was a maelstrom of activity. The shocking news that a highly born gentleman had been attacked and nigh killed on his family estate was printed in every newspaper in the land, each account more lurid than the last. Bow Street Runners arrived from London, repeated all the questions asked by the local minions of the law, and departed looking ponderous, having succeeded only in irritating Chandler and infuriating the village constable and the law officers from Dover. Concerned relatives and friends came calling, their well-meant solicitude eventually proving to be so wearying that Chandler formed the habit of bolting from the house whenever the rumble of wheels was heard on the drivepath. Often, he would seek refuge in the chapel, and Ruth was able to gauge to a nicety how long it would be from the time she heard an approaching carriage or riders, until the fugitive would burst through the door and shut it tightly behind him.

She was counting the seconds while at work one overcast morning, and turned with a smile as he came, panting, to the platform. "Two minutes, precisely," she said, waving a piece of bread at him. "You must have been delayed."

"I was," he panted. "That fool—Aymer."

She clicked her tongue reprovingly. He had removed the tape from his head, and his dark hair was more loosely arranged than usual, probably to conceal where it had been cut away from the wound. She thought the less severe style charming, but said only, "For shame to speak so of a man of God. Mr. Aymer is far from a fool, sir."

"Aha!" He sprawled in the front pew, looking up at her. "So my father was right, as usual. Are we soon to hear an announcement?"

Ruth had gone back to work, but at this she spun around and said, startled, "You cannot be serious?"

He chuckled. "To say truth, I thought it hilarious."

"Indeed?" Perversely affronted, her chin tilted upward. "Do you think it a disgrace that he might find a—a hired worker attractive?"

"Say rather that I think it ludicrous for Aymer to turn his eyes in your direction. You would not suit, you know."

"How can *you* know whether or not we would suit? Faith, but I'd not realized Mr. Gordon Chandler is so expert in *affaires de coeur*."

He unwound his long length from the pew and wandered

to the foot of the platform steps. "He is far from that, Mrs. Ruth. But—"

"But one must keep to one's class, eh?" Flushed and angry, she said with scornful pride, "Mr. Nathaniel Aymer is socially above a poor widow! Well, I'll have you know, sir, that I am—" She retreated then, her heart giving a nervous little jump as he came up the steps. "I am every bit as well born as your precious chaplain! Nor," she added defiantly, "is he the only gentleman ever to have found me attractive!"

Very close to her now, he said quietly, "I know."

With the door closed not a sound penetrated the thick chapel walls. As though touched by some enchantment, Ruth was quite unable to tear her gaze from the grave grey eyes that looked so steadily into her own. Her heart began to thunder. She said a decidedly feeble, "Oh."

He took another step. "I think I have never properly thanked you for coming to help me."

"But indeed you have, sir. You sent me that beautiful gown." The box, from one of Dover's most exclusive modistes, had been delivered to the cottage two days ago, and had contained a delicately simple gown of blue silk to be worn over a white chemise with frilled sleeves. "You have most excellent taste, Mr. Gordon," she added with a twinkle.

"I must confess that Mrs. Tate was my aide-de-camp on that expedition. Although I can claim to have specified the colour, which I'd fancied would look very well on you. I wish you did not dislike it."

"How could I dislike it? Ah—you think I should have worn it. 'Tis much too fine to work in, you know. I shall save it for a special occasion."

"Then I must arrange a special occasion." There was a faint wistfulness to the smile that curved his mouth. "And very soon."

Caught in a trap from which she never wished to escape, Ruth experienced a brief sense of dreamy contentment. Then, Chandler's hands clenched hard, his head jerked upward, and, as if suddenly short of breath, he said, "It was small payment for your kindness, Mrs. Ruth. You are a very brave lady."

She felt dazed, but managed somehow to turn away and scrub blindly at the fresco. "Oh no," she said, struggling to control her foolish weakness. " 'Twas just more of my scheming. A fiendish plot to curry favour in Sir Brian's eyes."

"As I suspected." He gazed at the back of her head. A bright strand of hair had escaped the plait and was curling onto her snowy neck. He groped in his pocket. "But you are properly served for your fiendishness," he went on, lying glibly. "For there is a small beetle has become entangled in your hair."

"Ugh!"

Her hand flew up. He restrained it. "Keep still, intrepid one, and I shall remove the intruder. Bow your head a trifle."

She obeyed, shaken by an involuntary shiver when his fingers touched her neck lightly.

"There." Having completed his theft, he tossed the imaginary "offender" to the floor. "Now I have rescued you and evened the score. Do you acknowledge my valour?"

"Truly, you were superb." She stepped to the edge of the platform and peered at the floor. "Where is it? Was it very large?"

Chandler sneezed, and emerging from his handkerchief, declared, "Enormous." He folded his handkerchief meticulously over his small prize, and replaced it in his pocket. "Eighteen legs and sharp pincers to give you a good nip. There it goes, galloping under the pew. What, did you not see? Well certainly you could not fail to have heard the thunder of its hoofs."

She laughed. "And certainly, Sir Valour, you could not fail to see what is right under your nose."

His head whipped up and he stared at her.

"Only look," she said hurriedly, and stepped aside.

The restored area of the fresco was much larger now. The

surface was cracked and in places the paint was gone, but the scene was recognizable.

"Be dashed!" he exclaimed. " 'Tis our own estate! There's the old lighthouse! The top half anyway."

"Yes, so I thought. Only it was new when this was painted."

"In which case the fresco cannot be above three or four hundred years old!"

"My goodness! Was it in use that long ago?"

"Oh yes, and long before that. The Romans put up lights all around the coast, you know. I believe their name for 'em was 'pharos.' They almost all were wrecked by our charming English weather, but promptly put up again. We think our old tower was restored in the fourteenth century. It was more sturdy than its predecessors and would likely still be in service save that Cromwell's forces riddled it with shot when two of my ancestors hid there. The varmints did so much damage the tower became unsafe. That's why the new light was put up on the headland five miles to the north of us." He said enthusiastically, "Gad, but my father will be pleased to find the painting is part of Lac Brillant's history! What's this down here? Another house?"

"I cannot quite tell. I think the artist changed the shape of the rocks a little."

"The cliffs have changed, certainly. The sea is relentless, you know."

She sighed. "Very true."

"Now what have I said to make you sad? Was your husband lost at sea, Mrs. Ruth?"

Her thoughts had flown to Jonathan. She said brightly, "Did I look sad? I was only wondering what we will find when I have cleaned to the foot of the lighthouse."

"No, you weren't. Do you think that by now I cannot read your moods? Do you think I don't know that sometimes you are worried?" He gripped her hands and held them strongly. "You are not to worry for your future. Do you hear me? Devil take it! When is your confounded major coming home to take care of you?"

Scarcely knowing whether to laugh or cry, she said, "He is not confounded!"

"He is neglecting you shamefully! I've a damned good mind to trace the fellow down and see what he means by it!"

Desperate, she declared, "There is not the need, sir. He— he may be coming home very soon."

He released her hands but still watched her narrowly. "You've heard from him, then? How?"

She racked her brains. "Mr. Tummet brought me a letter. My fiancé wrote there was a chance he might get a leave. If it was granted he is already on his way home and will be here in—in the autumn."

"I see." Still watching her, he said, "Why will you not tell me his name? I know only that—"

"Good morning, Mr. Chandler."

In their preoccupation, neither of them had heard the door open.

Jacob stood smiling shyly up at them.

"Hello, young sir," said Chandler, returning the smile. "Come to see how your aunt goes on?"

"No, sir. Well, I have a'course, but Miss Tate sent me to tell you that Mr. Aymer is fetchin' your cousin, the Hon'rable Horace."

"He would!" Chandler looked at Ruth and gave a rueful grin. "I must escape the family prattlebox! Come, lad. You shall go with me to the Home Farm. Is that agreeable?"

Jacob gave a small leap of excitement, and Ruth watched fondly as, hand in hand, they fled.

At the stables the head groom was amused by Chandler's request for a nice quiet mount for Master Jacob. He pointed out with a grin that neither Mr. Gordon nor his brother had gone in much for "nice quiet mounts," and that Sir Brian's horses were all too large for a small boy.

"I c'n ride a real horse," declared Jacob with dignity.

"I am very sure you can," agreed Chandler. "Oakworth, we will take Carefree and Miss Nymph."

Oakworth, a nimble raw-boned man who had worked his way up from stableboy, looked dismayed, and protested, "But—that be Lady Nadia's mare, sir. I doubt her la'ship will—"

"Her ladyship will be glad to have the mare exercised. Make haste, man!"

Oakworth shouted orders, and very shortly the two horses were led out. Jacob was delighted with the pretty chestnut mare and, boosting him up, Chandler was relieved to see that the boy did not seem frightened, although he looked alarmingly small in the full-sized saddle.

They started off at an easy pace. Miss Nymph was well behaved and Chandler held Carefree in, much to her indignation. Overjoyed, Jacob concentrated on keeping his seat. Chandler slipped a hand into his pocket. His handkerchief was still tightly folded over its treasure. He smiled faintly, and his thoughts wandered to Ruth and the man who was likely even now on his way to claim her.

"Does your head still hurt, sir?"

Jacob was watching him anxiously.

"No, I thank you. As you see, I've taken off the last of the tape."

"Yes. Is that why your hair's not tidy?"

Chandler grinned. "Look a fright, do I?"

"Oh, no. You look younger. And not so cross."

'Gad!' thought Chandler. "Do you find me to be cross, Jacob?"

"Not always. Jus'—sometimes you look cross. Or—not so much cross, p'raps. More like you was thinkin' serious thoughts. Gran'papa made a picture once of a man what looked like that."

"Do you recall who was the gentleman?"

The smooth brow puckered. "He was a king, I 'member."

"Charles, perhaps?"

"No. Older ago than that. He had a funny table, or some-thin'."

"*Arthur?*" said Chandler, incredulous.

"That's the one! He wasn't so good looking as you. But his eyes was—sort of lonely. Like yours are sometimes."

Shocked, Chandler quickly turned the subject to games, but it developed that Jacob was far more interested in books than in sports, and Chandler was mildly surprised to learn that the boy was already a proficient reader. He was also devoted to animals, and wriggled with delight when Chandler said, "You will enjoy seeing the farm then. Lots of animals there."

"Oh, yes, sir! I shall have a farm some day. When I've got lots of prize money."

"Ah, you mean to go to sea, do you?"

The fair curls nodded. "It's in the family, y'know."

Chandler said he hadn't known, and waited hopefully, but nothing more was vouchsafed, and to worm information out of a child would be despicable.

They rode on through the rather dull morning, the boy full of eager anticipation, and Chandler lost in thought once more. He had, he was sure, seen a painting of King Arthur, the fabled monarch depicted as gazing at the distant figures of Guinevere and Sir Launcelot. It was likely not the same paint-ing, because he seemed to recall that the artist had been some giant of the world of art. If he could just remember the fel-low's name . . .

CHAPTER X

he sound of angry voices caused Mr. Aymer's steps to slow as he approached Sir Brian's study. One voice rose to a bellow. 'Poulsborough,' thought the clergyman, and stood aside as the door burst open and a very tall big-boned man with a very red face erupted into the hall.

"Damme, sir!" he roared, turning back into the room. "I see no reason for y'curst stubborn attitude! Durwood never objected!"

Gordon Chandler walked around the desk to face his fiery and departing visitor. "Which is one reason," he said coolly, "why Durwood is no longer my father's steward."

"What y'are, sir," raved the large Mr. Poulsborough, shaking his fist for emphasis, "is a dog in the manger. A damned dog in the manger! Y'don't use the cove y'self but once or twice a year. But y'r too damned mean-spirited t'let others benefit. No reason 'tall why m'captain has t'haul m'cargoes five extra miles overland, when he could unload—"

"Your captain," drawled Chandler, advancing to the door, "fouled our beach with his refuse, abandoned an over-worked donkey to expire in our wilderness area, and allowed his rascally crew to trample and destroy the plants and shrubs our gardeners had set out to prevent any more falling-away of the cliffs. Had my father taken my advice, Poulsborough, we'd have brought an action 'gainst you for restitution."

"Top-lofty," bellowed his irate neighbour. "That's y'r trouble, Chandler! Y'ain't *liked!* I'll talk to y'r sire, and—"

"Not whilst I can prevent it! Do you show your face here again, and we *will* bring an action 'gainst you! Good day."

Mr. Poulsborough snorted and swore and stamped down the hall, all but flattening Mr. Aymer against the wall, and imparting with a snarl that Gordon Chandler was a damnably hot-at-hand and uppity young pup, and that 'twas a great pity the poachers, or whatever they were, hadn't put a period to the bastard.

Shocked, Aymer called a blessing after the thunderous retreat and was more shocked when Poulsborough advised him exactly what to do with his "confounded blessing."

"I think you'll not save that sinner, Nathaniel." Returning to the chair behind the desk Chandler sat down and took up a letter directed to "Jos. Durwood, Esq." "My regrets that you were caught in the crossfire," he added, running his eyes down a lengthy and mis-spelled demand for payment for "five and twenty crates and barrels—LONG OVERDUE!" Becoming aware that the cleric had followed him inside, he asked absently, "Had you wished to speak to my father?"

The reverend gentleman settled himself into a chair. "No. To you, Mr. Gordon." He coughed behind his hand, as he did at the start of his sermons. "I have noticed, an I dare remark it, that since you were so viciously attacked, you do not seem quite— That is to say you look very tired. You have been working rather heavily of late—no?"

Chandler put down the letter and summoned a smile. "Heavily *and* late. The work must get done, and till my father settles on a steward . . ." He shrugged. "Thank you for your interest." He took up the letter again. "Was that all?"

Despite his efforts, there was a note of impatience in his

voice that was not lost upon Mr. Aymer. Poulsborough, he reflected, had been right to an extent: Gordon Chandler was considerably short on common courtesy and respect. He sighed. "No, as a matter of fact. 'Tis . . . about the boy."

Chandler's attention snapped from crates and barrels. "What about him?"

"I . . ." Aymer sighed again and said with his fine sense of drama, "Almost, I hesitate to mention it."

Unimpressed by the sonorously lowered voice, Chandler said curtly, "As you will. Then pray excuse me. I have much to do."

Aymer folded his hands. "However, it may indicate a serious problem, so—"

Suspecting what was troubling the chaplain, Chandler fixed him with a level stare. "What kind of problem? He's a grand little fellow and has quite captivated Sir Brian. I've not seen my father so light-hearted since—" He checked that remark.

"Since your poor brother was obliged to flee the country." Mr. Aymer shook his handsome head and sighed heavily. "A sad day for your father, Mr. Gordon. A sorry time for us all, and—"

Slamming down the letter, Chandler flared, "Oh, for Lord's sake, man! Say whatever is hiding behind your tongue and have done with it!"

A sad smile. A hesitantly uttered, "It is that . . . I begin to fear the child is . . . not quite— I mean— There seems a mental instability that—"

"A—what?" His eyes a blaze of wrath, Chandler leaned forward. "I feel sure you mean to explain that ugly implication!"

Alarmed, Aymer jerked upright in his chair. "I beg you will not be put about. Surely, you must have noticed? The boy is quite charming, I admit, but there is a major, even a sinister flaw in his character, for his personality shifts with each wind that blows."

Chandler's response was concise and to the point, but not calculated to please a clergyman, and Aymer drew back, spreading his white hands as if to ward off such vulgarity. "Mr. Gordon! Alas, I have caused you to lose your temper. Had I dreamed you felt so strongly in the matter . . ." Bright and unmistakeable now, there was malice in Aymer's blue eyes.

Battling the urge to demand that this man of God take himself elsewhere, Chandler gritted his teeth and managed a curt apology. "You may be sure I feel strongly. Jacob is not yet six years old. We can scarce expect him to behave with the decision of a grown man."

"We can expect that his preferences be consistent from day to day! Do you fancy, sir, that I would speak thus out of unkindness? Especially towards the nephew of so charming a lady?" Aymer said earnestly, "Let me give you an example. On Monday, I was pleased to find Jacob in the library. He was fascinated by a book of engravings, so I took him to my own quarters and showed him an illustrated text that I prize highly. He was enchanted. Truly enchanted. I asked him if he had any interest in becoming a man of the cloth, and pointed out that many gentlemen of my calling are fine scholars and write learned papers upon worthwhile subjects."

"Whereupon," said Chandler, amused, "he told you he meant to become a sailor."

"Just so. He said his father had been a captain for the East India Company."

"You asked him, I take it?"

There was scorn in the tone, and Aymer flushed and said huffily, "I see no reason why I should not have done so." Chandler looked at him steadily. Aymer was reminded that he never had cared for those cold grey eyes. So devoid of any feeling. He went on, "Jacob said he wished to follow in his father's footsteps, save that he would be a naval officer. Next day, he was coaxing Sir Brian to take him up to the top of the old lighthouse. As if your father could manage to climb those hundreds of steps!"

"No, but the boy would not comprehend that. If he wishes to climb to the top, I'll take him."

"So your father promised. The next instant the child was wanting to play ball! Thinking to spare Sir Brian, I suggested we go to the library instead. Jacob thanked me very prettily, but said he would be a moonling to want to read a book when he might play ball!"

"Well? I am sure my father was pleased to play with him."

"But—surely, you *must* see! 'Twas in direct opposition to what the boy had told me only the previous day! When I saw him later in the afternoon, I asked if he'd given any more thought to a career when he finishes school. He said"— Aymer looked shocked—"he said he would like to be a—*pirate!*"

Chandler laughed heartily. "So should I when I was that age! Lord, what an uproar to build over a trifle! He said he wanted to go to sea, did he not? Besides, the mind of a small boy is a capricious thing, at best."

Considerably ruffled, Aymer said with unusual acerbity, "Perhaps that would explain why he told me yesterday that he had bacon and eggs for breakfast, which is his favourite. And this morning he shuddered when I mentioned my own breakfast egg, and said that he cannot abide eating *unborn chicks!* I tell you, Mr. Gordon, that child has some deep-seated brain disorder and should be taken to a surgeon."

Chandler's eyes, which had returned to the letter, lifted again and meeting them, Aymer recoiled instinctively. In a very quiet voice, Chandler asked, "Are you perhaps implying that Jacob belongs in Bedlam?"

"No, no! I never meant— I did not— I would not—"

"I'm glad." Chandler took up Durwood's letter once more. "Have you broached the subject to Mrs. Allington?"

"Not yet." Furtively mopping his brow, Aymer thought that Gordon Chandler's temper had most definitely deteriorated of late. He said, "I rather hesitate to do so. She is making such progress on the fresco that it seems likely she will not be here for much longer. But—in the name of human kindness, I should perhaps offer her the benefit of my counsel."

Chandler feigned boredom. "You must do whatever you think best, of course, though in my opinion 'tis a matter for the lady and her family to deal with. I must ask however, that you do not worry my father with your—theories."

Variously shaken and indignant, Aymer left him and walked slowly down the hall. How could the man have failed to notice that one day Jacob was as if glued to his coat skirts, and the next could scarce bear to be parted from Sir Brian? Chandler was not a man of high intellectual achievement, of course, but one would think him capable of noticing the inconsistencies in the child. On the other hand, Chandler might be too caught up in anticipation of the arrival of dear Lady de Brette to pay attention to other matters. At least, he had kept away from the chapel these past few days, and buried himself in his work, which was, thought Mr. Aymer sternly, just as well.

Gordon Chandler was not the only busy individual on the estate. Ruth laboured long and hard at her task, making good progress but becoming so wan and pale that Sir Brian became concerned, and at length insisted she rest for a day or so. Grace was in full accord with this edict, and when Ruth reached the cottage that afternoon she was at once ordered to bed with the promise of a dinner tray to be carried to her.

"Worn yourself to a shade, you have," said Grace, bustling Ruth up the stairs. "Worked hard enough for two this week, and worried half the night away by the look of you. Though why you should worry so much now, when the boys can venture out in safety is more than I can come at!"

"It is because they can take turns going out that I worry so," said Ruth, sitting gratefully on the bed while Grace laid out her nightdress. " 'Tis wonderful to see them so happy. But I dread lest one of them gives the game away."

Grace knelt to take off Ruth's shoes. "How should they? They're alike as two peas in a pod and good as gold about taking turns for their 'Jacob Day,' as they call it. Besides, there's many times, Mrs. A., when I cannot tell whether I'm talking to Master Thorpe or Master Jacob."

"I know, and truly I am grateful they are so happy. But the thing is, they're very young and not accustomed to being— devious. If Jacob should forget to tell Thorpe something he should know, or if Thorpe chanced to contradict something Jacob had remarked to somebody—"

"I don't never do that, Aunty Ruth," declared Thorpe indignantly, knocking on the door as he opened it. "We're awful careful. They don't even guess." He giggled and took a bite out of the apple in his hand. "It's fun to 'tend to be Jake. We're not a bit alike really, y'know. I thought they'd find us out the first day. But they're proper sillies and don't see it."

Ruth moaned. "Heaven forgive me! 'Tis wicked to deceive people who have been so kind—so good to us!"

"Run along now, Master Thorpe." Grace had heard the tremor in Ruth's voice. She closed the door behind the boy and said soothingly, "You've done the best for us as you knows how, and we're harming none. Into bed with you. You shall enjoy a nice book and tomorrow you can sleep late and be a lazy-lady so you can start work fresh on Friday."

Aware that she really was over-tired, Ruth was soon gratefully tucked into bed. She ate a light meal and after the boys had joined her for evening prayers settled down with a book. Her many worries would not let her read, however, and when she drew the bed-curtains at half past eight o'clock the future looked so dark and grim that the pillow was soon wet with her tears.

Morning sunlight was flooding the room cheerfully when

she awoke. She washed in the cold water from her pitcher, and was brushing her hair when her eyes fell on the little clock on her chest of drawers. It was twelve minutes past six. "Good gracious!" she murmured. "Well, that's what you get, Mrs. A., when you go to bed so early!" She felt rested and refreshed, and ashamed of yesterday's surrender to melancholy. Crossing to the window she opened it wider and looked into the gardens.

It was a perfect morning, a few puffy clouds drifting in a cerulean sky and the air crisp and bracing. A perfect chance for an early walk, she decided, and was about to turn back into the room when she saw the shadow.

The breath seemed to freeze in her throat, and for a moment she was quite unable to move. It was exactly as Grace had described; a hunched, terrifying creature, with a long snout and a great mane about its shoulders. The shadow lay across the lawn in front of the cottage. She could not see the daemon, but her heart gave a lurch of terror as she caught a glimpse of Jacob's blue velvet coat in the far trees. She tried to scream a warning, but her voice was an almost inaudible croak. That fearful head swung towards the boy. Somehow regaining the use of her limbs, Ruth flew madly down the stairs, snatched up the poker from the parlour hearth, and was out of the door in a flash.

She was halfway across the lawn when she realized that the blue coat was not velvet but broadcloth, and that it was worn not by a child, but by a man.

For Gordon Chandler to spend the night tossing and turning through a futile rebellion against the machinations of Fate was a rare experience. It was all too clear that his sleeping heart slept no longer, and that this was no gentle awakening but a soul-shaking certainty that the perfect one was found. But the awakening had come too late, and had brought not joy, but anguish as relentless as it was pointless. At dawn he awoke from a fitful doze and took the old locket from his bedside table. He opened it and with one tender finger touched the silken gold strands he had appropriated with the aid of his pocket knife and that were now rather clumsily tied with a piece of string. He sighed. It was quite hopeless, and he was a very great fool. He was impatient with folly, especially his own, and be damned if he'd go back to bed and endure more hours of misery. He got up, cut himself shaving in icy water, took Carefree for a thundering gallop, and returned her to the stables. It being then still short of six o'clock, he decided not to astound the staff by appearing in the kitchen at such an hour, and wandered instead about the grounds. He had no intention of going anywhere near the blue cottage. Lost in thought, however, his feet betrayed him. He glanced up to find the cottage before him and a vision flying from the front door.

They both stopped, staring at each other.

Why she should have a poker in one hand he neither knew nor cared. Her hair was down and shimmered like a golden mantle about her shoulders, and the nightdress that billowed about her made her seem more of heaven than earth; an exquisite creature, all gold and white daintiness, her wide grey eyes fixed upon him, her lips a little parted.

Enchanted, he murmured, "How glorious is your hair . . ."

She watched him, standing there so tall and dark and unmoving, with a look on his strong face compounded of awe and delight.

Involuntarily, he reached out to her.

That she should appear surprised or offended did not occur to her. The husky quiver to his deep voice, the wistful tenderness in his eyes drew her irresistibly. She started to him, and not until she stretched out her hand and discovered the poker in it, did there come the shocking awareness that she was barefoot in the garden, clad only in her nightdress and with not so much as a wrapper for propriety. That did shock her, and with a startled gasp she turned away.

He snatched at her free hand. "No—please don't go."

"I must! I am—I am not *dressed!* Goodness! If someone should *see!*"

Smiling because it had not occurred to her that *he* had seen, he asked, "Do you mean to strike me with your poker?"

"Of course not! 'Twas—Oh! I'd forgot! The *daemon!* I saw its shadow, just as Grace did, and I thought you were Jacob, and—" Her frantic gaze found the shadow, clearer than ever. Her lower lip sagged, and she pointed wordlessly.

Chandler found the shadow. The sun was in the east, so the creature must be . . . His keen eyes searching, he laughed softly. "There is your daemon, my dauntless warrior."

Clinging to his hand, Ruth saw the creature he indicated, clinging precariously to a branch of the tree at the southeast corner of the cottage. "*Being!*" she gasped.

He said with a chuckle, "I never thought I would be grateful to Jacob's pestiferous pet."

With a sigh of relief, she attempted to disengage her hand.

He tightened his grip. "If I let you escape, will you promise to come down again?" She hesitated, and he coaxed, "Now, Mrs. Ruth, we are both safely—er, bespoken. Is it so very bad to ask that you spend only a little time talking to a lone and lorn gentleman?" She looked troubled, and releasing her hand he added lightly, "And perhaps bring along something to eat. I'm fairly starved and the kitchen a deserted wasteland."

"I might have guessed you had some dastardly motive in mind," she said laughingly, and ran back into the cottage.

Until the last flutter of her nightdress had vanished Chandler stood looking after her. He walked away then, to wait amongst the trees so that no prying eyes might see him and leap at once to a logical but quite mistaken conclusion. He watched the door, counting the seconds until it would open again, and ignoring the small inner voice that said this was unwise. He had a right, surely, to just one brief hour? He had slipped a little bit just now, but he would be cool and controlled so that she would never know; and it was so little to ask; so small a time to hoard in memory.

After a while, she came to him. She had plaited and coiled her hair, and put on a primrose yellow morning dress with modified hoops. It seemed to him that a shimmer of gold still surrounded her, and he stared briefly, then took the basket she carried.

They chatted comfortably as they walked side by side through the deserted gardens. Of the birthday party, and the guests, some of whom would start arriving this afternoon; of the scouring of the estate by keepers, grooms, farmhands, footmen, and gardeners, none of whom had found a trace of the whistling man and his bullies, nor the least clue to explain their presence. Ruth's eyes became troubled and, quick to see, Chandler turned the subject to the fresco and the progress that had been made. The moments flew and it seemed a very short time before the buildings were far behind them and they were going down the long gradual slope to the cliffs.

He made for the old lighthouse and they sat on the rocks in the brilliant morning and breakfasted on slices of cold pork, crusty buttered bread, and cheese. The gulls were already wheeling and calling; the sun grew warmer, and the faint haze on the air burned away. Except for the gulls it was very quiet and still, and they might have been miles from human habitation; alone in a world of peace and beauty.

Ruth folded the napkins and replaced plates, mugs and the water bottle in the basket. Leaning back against his rock, legs stretched out comfortably, Chandler watched the sunlight on her hair, the pretty movements of her hands, the shape of her lips.

"Tell me," he said, after a short silence, "about your husband. What sort of man was he?"

She smiled reminiscently. "He was a very dear person. Gentle and scholarly, and so kind."

It seemed an odd description of a husband. He turned his

head and looked thoughtfully across the blue waters of the Strait to where a schooner made its slow way to the Tidal Basin and two fishing boats were far out towards France. "Was it an arranged marriage?"

"Yes. Thomas was my papa's dearest friend." She saw his startled glance, and added, "You are thinking he must have been a good deal older than me. He was also the dearest and best of men. No wife could have known more—more unselfish kindness or—"

"Or a more passionate lover?"

Her face flushed scarlet. "Sir! You presume!"

"And have my answer, I think." He sat up straighter and asked intensely, "Mrs. Ruth, *did* you love him?"

"You have no right to ask such a question." She looked fixedly at the picnic basket. "But—yes. I loved him in many ways. And he was devoted and—"

"And kind. So you said. And how many years your senior?"

Stiffening, she said, "You know very well that you go beyond the line in asking such personal questions!"

"I can find out easily enough by making a few enquiries. Why should you be ashamed to tell me?"

"I am *not* ashamed!" But he might indeed make enquiries, which would never do, so she answered reluctantly, "When we married I was seventeen. Mr. Allington was—was six and fifty."

"Good God!"

She started up angrily, but Chandler grasped her wrist. "No, do not! I mean no disrespect. He was a good man, evidently. But—why on earth—" Warned by her stormy frown he went on quickly, "No. You are perfectly correct, and I have not the right to ask. Only—this morning with your hair down, you were so— Well, I mean you *are* so very lovely, and to marry a man more than forty years your senior seems— By God, I *will* say it! Was your father all about in his head? Oh, Lord! And off she goes again! *Peccavi!* Only— Fiend

seize it! Could you not have objected? Was your sire a tyrant?''

The variously penitent and indignant play of emotions
across his face had by this time reduced her to helpless laughter. Freeing her hand, she said, "I am very glad you know you
have not the right to ask, sir.''

He gave her a searching look, and said with a grin, "What
a clodpole you must think me. Truly, I do not mean to offend.
'Tis just, you are so young, and— It seems such a waste.
Unless—'' He closed his lips over the ill-considered words.

"Unless I married Mr. Allington for his money?'' Ruth's
eyes twinkled as his face reddened. "Perhaps that was in
Papa's mind, although I doubt it, for at that time we were
quite comfortably circumstanced. The thing was, you see, that
it was his wish. And I did not— That is to say, there was no
other gentleman in my life. But my papa was no more a tyrant,
sir, than—than is your own.''

"Which properly sends me to the rightabout,'' he acknowledged whimsically. "Unless you chance to believe my
father *is* a tyrant.''

Ruth avoided his eyes. "Sir Brian has been exceeding kind
to me—''

"But? By Jove! You *do* find him tyrannical!''

"No, no! I never would say such a thing!''

"Only think it.''

"You wretch! I do not! Only . . . Oh, I suppose, like most
older gentlemen he—er, likes his own way. I *have* wondered
sometimes how you— That is to say—''

He smiled. "You think I should resent the fact that he
cares more for my graceless brother than for me.''

Ruth gave a gasp and looked at him anxiously. "I am very
sure he is extreme fond of you, but it seems not quite fair. He
leans on you much more heavily than he is perhaps aware,
yet . . .''

He settled back again and drew up one knee, resting a hand
on it as he stared off towards France. "He does care for me,

you know. Just as much as Quentin, I dare to think. Only—in a different way. I remember him as he was before my mother died." He smiled nostalgically. "Theirs was a perfect match. Mama was the very prettiest creature; a happy, laughing, joyous sprite of a lady. All tenderness and grace and caring. I was nine when she died, and Quentin six. We all had adored her. We all were shattered. My father seemed overnight to become an old man; crushed and without hope. Quentin always was sensitive and tender-hearted. He was utterly bewildered by Mama's death. He couldn't comprehend the finality of it, and would search about the houses, calling for her, long after we had thought he understood. When he did understand . . . well, he lost all power to speak."

"Oh, poor little boy," said Ruth, touched.

"For two years he was the shadow of a child, shrinking, frightened, silent. He would follow me about, and if I got too far away he would run to cling to my coat in terror." Chandler began absently to gather a small pile of pebbles. "Papa was so kind and understanding. How many men, I wonder, would simply have placed us both in the care of some female relative, or engaged a tutor? Not he! He talked to us, played with us, and took us everywhere. I was kept at home for a few years, and being a typically selfish young animal I resented it and longed to go away to school like the other boys I knew. I aired my grievances to Sir Brian one day, and I remember how gravely he listened. He said that Quentin was of a different temperament to him and me. And that we must never let down our family, especially if one person is damaged in any way. Quentin had been damaged, he said and, just now especially, he stood very much in need of us both."

Watching him, Ruth said quietly, "I take it your brother did regain his speech."

He laughed. "Yes, confound him! And became a proper rapscallion. All wildness and daring. My Lord, how I had to race to keep up with his starts, much less prevent 'em!"

"But, perhaps because he was at first so helpless, and

because you both guarded him, you gave him extra of your love. And your papa feels lost now and to an extent no longer needed."

He did not at once respond, and then said slowly, "I hope I've not made him feel unwanted. Do you fancy him a Jeremiah? He's not. 'Tis mostly that these last few years he has been ill, and worried for the Rabble, and——"

"The—what?"

"Rabble." His grin was slanted at her. "My harum-scarum brother."

"Is that what you name him?" Amused, she said, "Poor fellow! And how does he call you?"

"Sir Knight. Only because I shall inherit the title, and he is sadly lacking in respect."

'And because you always come to his rescue,' she thought. "I take it," she said, "that you were unable to keep up with his last—er, start."

"True." The smile left his eyes. "Almost we buried the idiot. Only by the grace of God and the help of some very good friends is he safely in France. Jupiter! 'Twas a close run thing. A terrible strain on my father." Caught up in memory, he shook his head, his expression very stern. Ruth was silent. After a minute he went on, "The discovery of the fresco has given him a fine new interest, thank heaven. And now, since Jacob came, he seems ever more cheerful and light-hearted. So much like his old self." He smiled at her, "Another thing for which I have to thank you."

Her guilty conscience felt a little eased, and she said warmly, "I could not be more pleased. Jacob needs the guidance of a gentleman, and has become most fond of your papa. And of you, sir. I vow, 'tis a puzzle to know which of you he'll run to when he's released from his studies."

They had arrived at the topic Chandler had hoped to broach, and he said carefully, "Is a fine boy, and I enjoy him quite as much as does my father. Though, I'll own he puzzles me at times."

Apprehensive, Ruth asked, "How so?"

"He is either the youngest diplomat alive, or of a most—er, mercurial disposition."

With a rather unconvincing laugh she said that Jacob was likely nervous. "For I cannot convey to you the depth of my gratitude at being allowed to keep him with me, and I've fairly dinned into his brain that he is not to offend either you, or Sir Brian."

Her tight-gripped hands told him that she was scared. "Oh, he won't do that," he said easily. "My father fairly dotes on him. The young rascal has convinced him he's another Quentin—all high-couraged, panting for risk and adventure, and begging for tales of derring-do. Whereas with me he's a born scholar, a'thirst for knowledge, especially about the sea. Which is, I suppose natural enough since his papa captained an East Indiaman, and— Egad, ma'am! Are you ill?"

Ruth stammered that she was just shocked to hear that her nephew was capable of such toad-eating airs. "I shall see to it the little rogue does not bother you again!"

"You will do no such thing! Do you want my father to have me put in the stocks? Jacob is no bother. Say rather that he is a complicated child and we all shall be most sorry when . . . when you leave us." The tone of his voice had changed; he lifted his head and looked at her, then averted his gaze hurriedly.

But she had seen that dreadful look again. The wistful caress that seemed to enfold her heart. And the knowledge that she still deceived him became unbearable, so that she stammered, "Mr. Gordon, there—there is something I *must* tell you."

"You are not done with your work already?" He said almost desperately, "No, you cannot be finished before— I mean, you must stay for the party, at least. It is such a little while."

'Such a little while . . .' And after all, in another week or two she would have gone out of his life forever. Surely, 'twould be foolish to spoil these last few precious days? She stifled the voice of common sense and said with determined gaiety, "Oh, I think we shall not leave you just yet, sir. I only hope Sir Brian will not be too disappointed. I had expected to have the first cleaning completed in time for his party, and 'tis not done. Though I made quite some progress this week."

"By working much too hard, so I'm told! I think we never asked that you become a slave to that curst painting!"

The protective note in his voice warmed her heart. She said, "Curiosity drove me. Speaking of which, can we go inside the lighthouse?"

"No. We have to keep it locked now. It has been unsafe for years, and there is always the fear small children may get inside. The steps are very steep and there's a sheer drop where the stair railing has fallen away."

"How high is it, do you know?"

"A hundred feet or more I'd guess, from the dome over the roof to the ground. All the undergrowth about it has made it appear rather forlorn now, do not you think?"

"Yes, poor old thing. In fact, I had meant to ask you when the changes were made, and why."

"Changes?"

"Ah, but you've not seen the fresco for a few days. I have uncovered more of the lighthouse and it was evidently much taller when 'twas painted, and I think must have been in another location. Is it possible that the lighthouse in the fresco was an earlier version? You said it had been rebuilt several times."

He shaded his eyes and peered up the length of the tower. "I very much doubt that. To the best of my knowledge—" Lowering his gaze, he interrupted himself and in a blending of resentment and surprise said, "Be dashed!" and sprang to his feet. "You're early abroad!"

August Falcon strolled towards them. He wore riding dress, and although Ruth still could not like the cynical boredom of his smile, she could not deny that the man was breath-takingly handsome.

Falcon, always quick to sense another's moods, had at once noted the brief flash of annoyance in Chandler's eyes. "Poor form to pay a morning call at such an hour, is that what you mean," he drawled, amused.

"Not at all." Chandler shook his hand. "I believe you are acquainted with Mr. August Falcon, Mrs. Allington?"

"I am certainly much obliged to him," said Ruth, dropping a curtsy.

Falcon looked blank, but bowed with lazy grace.

Chandler said, "My father and I are also obliged to the gentleman."

Mystified, Falcon looked from one to the other. "Always glad to be of service," he lied. "Is all this obligation why I am invited?"

Chandler thought that very likely, and said evasively, "I'm sure Sir Brian will be pleased you are able to accept. Never say you rode from Town?"

"Why? 'Tis not become obscene to ride, I believe. Am I to be offered sustenance?"

Ruth delved into the basket. "Alas, sir, there is only a heel of bread, and the cheese looks rather shiny."

Falcon lowered his elegance to a suitable rock and dazzling her with a smile declared that he was "addicted to shiny cheese." Accepting a plate and a somewhat crumpled napkin, he inspected the latter fastidiously before spreading it across his knees.

"Mrs. Allington has done wonders with my father's fresco," advised Chandler.

"But how charming." Falcon sampled the cheese. "We reached Dover last evening. 'Twas too late to demand your hospitality, so we racked up at the Ship. My sister follows, with Miss Rossiter."

Startled, Chandler said, "Not unescorted, surely?"

"I'faith, I almost wish they were!" Falcon scowled. "That

dimwit, Morris, rides escort. I'd not have come on ahead, save that I want a private word with you."

Ruth stood. "Then I shall take my leave, gentlemen. No, pray do not get up, Mr. Falcon." She reached for the basket, but Chandler stood and swung it out of reach.

"I'll bring it back," he said. "You will be all right?"

Her eyes quizzed him. "Now that we have unmasked the daemon, I believe I shall survive a stroll through the park, sir."

He grinned, but his expression changed as he watched her graceful walk. He recalled his guest then, and turned to meet a speculative stare. Irritated because he knew he was colouring up, he sat down and demanded, "Well?"

"I don't know. Is it?"

"If you mean her task—she has done splendidly."

"Did I mean her task, I wonder? I had thought I referred to your air of—"

"My apologies if I appeared somewhat—er, taken aback," Chandler intervened hurriedly. "I had not expected to see you."

"Oh, that was quite obvious, my dear fellow. Shall I change the subject if I remark that your betrothed will arrive tomorrow?"

"Damn your eyes, Falcon!"

Falcon sighed. "I am come on an invitational—though I was coming without one. Still, I am met with shiny cheese and a crust of less than fresh bread, and now my eyes are impugned. Alas, but polite customs are dying in Britain."

Chandler leaned back against his rock. "Had you but whispered a plea Chef would have offered you a proper breakfast. Since you have chosen instead to spoil the picnic I enjoyed with your protégée, you had best—"

"With my—what?"

"Yes, the word was ill chosen, perhaps. However, 'twas your letter that—"

"Aha! We arrive at the reason I came. *What* letter?"

"The letter you writ to my father, of course, recommending Mrs. Allington to restore the fresco that—"

"Hell and the devil! Are you run mad? I writ no letter. I scarce know the woman by sight, much less— To restore— what?"

"Our fresco. We discovered it in the chapel when— But never mind all that. If you did not write the letter, who in blazes did?"

Falcon finished his meagre breakfast and rose to his feet. "I should very much like to know. Have you this entrancing missive?"

"I saw it on my father's desk only yesterday. Come. We'd best get to the bottom of this."

A quarter of an hour later, Falcon looked up from the notorious letter and said savagely, "How a'plague could you be such a fool as to fancy this disgusting collection of mangled grammar and primitive scrawl originated at my hand?"

Dreading the answer, Chandler asked heavily, "Is a forgery, then? Do you—er, recognize the writing?"

"I can scarce recognize what is not! I do know the unmitigated villain and unprincipled scoundrel who perpetrated this monstrosity and had the colossal gall to append my name to it! Zounds, but I'll force him to that duel, if I have to bind him and cut him into gobbets to do it!"

Brightening, Chandler said, "You think Morris forged it? But why on earth should he?"

"Because they knew I would have none of it!" Falcon crumpled the letter and hurled it into the fireplace, then ran to snatch it up and try to smooth it out again.

"They . . . ?" ventured Chandler, beginning to grin.

"Aye. Him and his conniving accomplice, Gwendolyn Rossiter. They tried to prevail upon me to assist your widow in St. James' Park one day, only because she'd become involved in an imbroglio with the Buttershaw dragon."

"You're an uncouth devil," murmured Chandler.

"Yes. I thank you."

"I heard her ladyship had dropped the handkerchief in your direction."

Bristling, Falcon declared, "That female may drop every tablecloth, sheet, and curtain in Christendom for all I— Devil take it! Find it amusing, do you? Wait till I get my hands on that damned slippery forger! I promise you *he'll* not be amused!"

CHAPTER XI

race and the twins were busied with the morning lessons when Ruth reached the cottage. She went straight to her bedchamber and sat in the window-seat, staring unseeingly at the weeping willow tree. She had spoken truly when she'd told Gordon Chandler that she had loved her husband. Thomas Allington had won her affection by his unfailing kindness, his gentle ways, his unselfish and generous devotion. But her heart had never leapt to the sound of his voice; her breath had never quickened if his hand chanced to brush against hers; never had his gaze held the wistful tenderness that she had glimpsed once or twice in a pair of steadfast grey eyes and that, however swiftly veiled, caused her to feel weak and shaken.

'Ruth . . . how glorious is your hair . . .'

The memory of those awed words brought a lump into her throat. 'Resolution!' she thought. He was betrothed. Even if that so special light in his eyes shone for her alone. Even if he had never given his heart to the beautiful Lady Nadia de Brette. The marriage had been contracted when they both were children, and the announcement had been published in the newspapers. No gentleman could in honour draw back from such a contract. Besides, Sir Brian obviously adored the lady who would soon become his daughter-in-law, and nothing would induce Gordon to wound his father.

"Resolution!" murmured Ruth hopelessly.

'You are so very lovely . . .'

Sighing, she stood and moved to sit at her vanity table and scan her reflection. 'I really am not very lovely,' she thought. But he had seen her with her hair down—and in her nightdress! Had *he* really judged her to be lovely?

'It seems such a waste . . .'

Sadly, she thought, 'It is indeed,' and knew she must abide by her decision to see as little of Gordon Chandler as possible.

An hour later Thorpe, whose "Jacob Day" it was, galloped from the cottage, passing a lackey who brought a request that Mrs. Allington favour Sir Brian with her company at luncheon. With a perverse leap of the heart, and a sigh for Resolution, Ruth changed her gown, tidied her hair, and walked up to the main house.

The hall was a bustle of servants conveying a small mountain of valises, bandboxes, and portmanteux up the stairs. The butler explained that Sir Brian's cousin, Mrs. Bertha Witterall, had come down from Rochester to act as his hostess and was even now being settled into her suite. Mr. Gordon had taken some guests to West House, which contained, in addition to the magnificent ground-floor ballroom, a kitchen, dining room, and several ante rooms, while on the first floor were guest suites and quarters for their servants. The unmarried gentlemen would stay there, and single ladies and married couples would be accommodated in the main house.

"Master Jacob," Starret told Ruth with a smile, "is in the kitchen with Mrs. Tate."

Thorpe was perched on a stool in a quiet corner of the busy kitchen, eating a muffin and chattering with the housekeeper. "Chef's gone over to West House, Aunty," he advised, wiping butter from his chin, "else I wouldn't be here."

"Disturbing Mrs. Tate," said Ruth severely.

The housekeeper turned a laughing countenance. "No, never scold him, ma'am. 'Pon my soul, 'tis like having Master Gordon and his brother young again, and laughter back in the house."

"Has you seen Miss Falcon yet, Aunty Ruth?" Thorpe's eyes were round. "I 'spect a princess would look like that. Grandpapa would've liked to paint her, y'know. And a lieutenant came. 'Least, they said he was a lieutenant, but he's wearing ordin'ry dress an' he doesn't look fierce like a soldier." His eyes sparkled. "Mr. Falcon's the fierce one, an' chased him off."

Ruth looked questioningly at the housekeeper.

Mrs. Tate shrugged. "Mr. August Falcon and Lieutenant Morris do not cry friends." She turned from the boy and lowered her voice. "A wicked temper has Mr. August, for all his good looks. And heaven help the gentleman who crosses him. People say, 'tis what comes of being half-foreign. He's always fighting someone, and never loses."

Ruth said as softly, "Good gracious! He'll not fight here, I hope. Surely, Sir Brian would put a stop to it?"

"You may be sure he would, ma'am. Especially with Lady de Brette arriving at any instant." The housekeeper's lips tightened. "He'd allow nothing to upset that one! Or her brother!"

There was a grimness in the brown eyes. One gathered that Mrs. Tate had no high opinion of my lady or her brother. Intrigued, Ruth said experimentally, "Mr. Aymer says that Lady de Brette is the most beautiful woman in London Town."

"Does he, indeed. Well, if you want my opinion, Mrs. Allington, the most beautiful woman in London Town already arrived. With *her* brother."

She meant Miss Falcon, of course. Ruth asked, "Is Lady de Brette's brother as dangerous as Mr. Falcon?"

The housekeeper gave a secretive smile. "They should be here soon, ma'am. You will be able to judge for yourself."

Despite her curiosity, Ruth found herself singularly reluctant to meet the great beauty, and leaving "Jacob" with instructions to do exactly as Mrs. Tate told him, she retreated to the chapel.

Opening the door, she stepped into chaos. A sturdily built gentleman appearing to be in his mid-twenties gave a whoop as he vaulted one of the pews. Mr. August Falcon sprinted along the centre aisle in hot pursuit, and Gordon Chandler stood watching them, clearly torn between exasperation and amusement.

The fugitive's inexpertly powdered hair showed traces of the light red shade called sandy. Dodging around the end of the pew as Falcon started along it, he turned a pleasant featured countenance, notable only for a pair of green eyes and freckles. "No, really, August," he called laughingly, "how can you be so resentful only because I tried to give a bad dog a good name?"

"*Dog*, is it?" snarled Falcon, then disappeared from sight, apparently having tripped. "You're a confounded forger, sir!" He heaved himself up again, as flushed as his quarry, and with his once neatly tied-back hair rumpled. "An you've any honour at all, Morris, you'll meet me—to defend it!"

"But the poor little widow was in distress," protested Morris. "Surely the milk of human kindness ain't so sour in your veins that—"

"There is *no* milk in my veins, you accursed villain! And furthermore—"

"And furthermore," put in Chandler, moving forward purposefully, "I really cannot permit that you desecrate our family chapel with Morris' blood, Falcon. The letter that was sent in your name was a blessing to us—all, and I am grateful, no matter who wrote it, but—"

"Well you owe *me* no gratitude, blast you!" snapped Falcon.

Morris caught sight of Ruth and said sharply, "Guard your tongue, man! There's a lady present."

Chandler jerked around, his irked gaze softening as he saw Ruth.

"I thought you might wish me to explain my work to your friends, Mr. Chandler. But if—" She broke off with a shocked gasp as Falcon lunged at Morris and fastened his hands about the lieutenant's throat.

"Stop that at once!" Angered, Chandler started forward.

A slight young lady, whom Ruth recognized as having been with Mr. Falcon on that fateful day in St. James' Park, limped rapidly along the aisle. She carried the handbell that Mr. Swinton was delegated to ring for various services and she rested a detaining hand on Chandler's arm and advanced upon the combatants. Swinging the bell up, she rang it vigorously beside Falcon's ear. It was an old bell, well cast, and remarkably powerful.

Falcon uttered a howl, clapping his hands over his ears, and shrank away. Equally afflicted, Morris sat down, panting. Chandler and Ruth exchanged mirthful glances.

The young lady put down the bell and turned, holding out her hand. "How do you do," she said, smiling warmly. "You must be Mrs. Allington. I am Gwendolyn Rossiter. I do apologize for my friends, but gentlemen are very silly at times, do you not agree?"

Her eyes alight with laughter, Ruth agreed.

August Falcon did not share these sentiments, however, and between moans he voiced an impassioned denunciation of unprincipled forgers, and cruel bellringers. Despite his grumbling it seemed to Ruth that his real wrath had spent itself. She returned her attention to Miss Rossiter and was surprised to see anxiety in the girl's eyes as Falcon made his way slowly from the pew.

Chandler came up, with the lieutenant beside him. "Allow me to present Lieutenant James Morris, ma'am. Jamie, this charming lady is Mrs. Allington."

Ruth dropped a curtsy. "How do you do? I rather gather, sir, that 'tis you I must thank for intervening in my behalf. I am indeed grateful that you should have gone to so much trouble."

Morris blushed and took her hand as though it were made of the sheerest glass. "Very glad to—to have been of service," he mumbled shyly.

Her voice sharp, Miss Rossiter asked, "Have you hurt yourself, Falcon?"

"Much you would care if I had," he responded bitterly. " 'Tis not enough I am met with stale bread and shiny cheese! 'Tis not enough I fell over Chandler's stupid hassock and sustained severe injuries! You must deafen me for no more reason than that I was trying to—"

"To do away with poor Jamie," Miss Rossiter interrupted. "You have reaped a just reward for your savagery. But you had best let me look at your foot."

Chandler said, "Jove, are you really hurt, Falcon? I'm very sorry if—"

"Why should you think I am hurt?" interrupted Falcon rudely. "I only limp like this to keep certain people company."

Ruth was taken aback by such an unkind remark. Miss Rossiter however, seeming not at all put out, said an emphatic, "Pish! If you were really hurt you'd not utter a word. Now, sit down, do."

"Yes, please do, sir," urged Ruth. "If you have twisted your ankle, you cannot walk on it."

Falcon said with a grand gesture, "There is nothing a man of decision cannot do, Mrs. Allington, does he really put his mind to it."

Morris, who had followed this exchange with interest, said, "I'd like to see you put your mind to making an empty flour sack stand upright."

They all laughed. All except Falcon, who snatched up the handbell and hurled it at Morris.

The bell missed, its target having jumped aside.

The Reverend Mr. Aymer, entering with Miss Katrina Falcon and Sir Brian, was less fortunate.

Luncheon was a merry meal. Poor Mr. Aymer appeared to have recovered from the shock of being, as Morris put it, "belled in the breadbasket," and he had accepted Falcon's apology, the abject nature of which was somewhat dimmed by a following remark that it was a great pity the bell had not tolled for the proper party.

Chandler was amused by Miss Rossiter's candour, and pleased by the swift repartee between the guests, which so often drew a chuckle from his father, although Mrs. Witterall only stared uncomprehendingly. Cousin Bertha was not his favourite relation. Small of stature, with beady brown eyes, quick jerky movements, and a high-pitched voice, her pointed nose and chin had caused the irreverent Quentin to dub her "Birdwit." She was actually a quick-witted lady, especially with regard to her own interests, and lost no opportunity to ingratiate herself with Sir Brian. Gordon could have forgiven her such behaviour, had it stemmed from gratitude for the allowance his father made her. He considered her gratitude doubtful, however, and her innate snobbishness and ability to find fault with those she did not need made it impossible for him to do more than be polite to her and count the minutes until her departure. Mrs. Witterall was aware of his antipathy, and because she believed that very soon now he would inherit the title and estates, she tried to say nothing that might offend him. It was a great strain at all times, and she soon realized that this particular visit would tax her powers of restraint to the limit.

Ruth was very soon made aware of the fact that she did not meet with Mrs. Witterall's approval. Sir Brian introduced her to the lady, and after a raised eyebrow stare clearly expressing disbelief that such a person should be invited to take luncheon with family and guests, Mrs. Witterall said, "I think I did not quite understand, dear sir. Is this the *artist* you have hired to work on your fresco?"

"Yes, indeed," said Chandler heartily. "My father was fortunate to find so talented a lady, and is most pleased with the progress she has made. You must come and see the work, cousin." And before Mrs. Witterall could contribute what he guessed would be a remark calculated to depress the artist's "pretensions," he turned to his father and went on, "I fancy the ladies will want to go for a walk after luncheon, sir. Falcon and Morris and I had thought to get up a game of rounders. Can we persuade you to join us? We're counting on you, and I have already promised Jacob you shall captain our side."

Mrs. Witterall looked aghast, but Sir Brian said eagerly, "Have you, by Jove? Then I must not disappoint the young rascal."

"I only hope you may not overtax your strength, dear sir," sighed his cousin, her mournful expression leaving little doubt of his imminent demise. "As for me, I have travelled quite far enough today and have no desire to go outside again. You shall have to go without us, dear Miss Rossiter, for Mrs. Allington will be anxious to return to her work."

Chandler said lightly, "The lady would not dare! She has laboured so hard this past week, that my father has given strict orders she must have a short holiday."

"How very kind you are, Sir Brian," purred Mrs. Witterall. "I am sure your servants must count themselves extreme fortunate to work here. Now do pray tell, Gordon, when is your so dear lady to arrive?"

Amused, Falcon leaned to Gwendolyn Rossiter, and murmured, "And that takes the trick, eh, ma'am?"

Far from amused, she answered, "Confucius said 'the mean man is always full of distress.' I fancy that would apply to females, also."

As usual, her reference to the other side of his heritage

irritated him. He grunted, "Do you ever read anything but Chinese philosophy?"

"Oh, yes," she said demurely. "I find Chinese art and history equally fascinating. Did you know that . . ."

Mrs. Witterall called, "Now I wonder whatever you two charming people can be talking about that leads you to look so grim?"

Falcon said brusquely, "The Chinese water torture, ma'am. I am most eager to put it to the test!"

"Do not heed him," said Katrina, laughing. "Sir Brian would not permit such savageries on his estate, I am very sure, for there is only beauty here. Speaking of which, I have not yet viewed your fresco, sir. Will you permit that Mrs. Allington show it to me?"

Sir Brian said expansively, "My dear, I am only delighted by your interest."

Mrs. Witterall, who considered it appalling that one must be subjected to sitting at the same table with half-castes, pursed her lips and fixed her affronted gaze upon the windows. There was, she thought, no end to nonsensicality in this house.

Ruth's impressions were very different, and when they left the chapel she was only too glad to join the two young ladies on their walk. The coldness in August Falcon's dark blue eyes, the cynical curve of his lips, his often acid remarks, were not qualities shared by his sister, who Ruth found delightful, the more so because she seemed to possess a most affectionate nature, and was not in the least conceited over her beauty. As for Miss Rossiter, the crippled girl's unaffected outspokenness and merry nature made Ruth feel as comfortable with her as though they had been lifelong friends.

The afternoon was becoming rather sultry, a few clouds building on the eastern horizon, and the breeze scarcely stirring the air. Even so, Ruth thoroughly enjoyed their walk, and during the hour that passed she learned a good deal about her companions. It appeared that there was more to the quarrel between Lieutenant Morris and August Falcon than the matter of the forged letter. Having accidentally shot Falcon during an attempted stagecoach robbery, Morris had compounded the felony by tumbling deep into love with the beautiful Katrina, a development that her volatile brother deplored.

"Is nothing new, however," explained Gwendolyn. "August refuses every gentleman who offers. None of them suit him." She added darkly, "Or ever will, I doubt!"

"Good gracious," murmured Ruth turning to Miss Falcon. "I do not mean to pry, ma'am, but—"

"Katrina," the girl corrected. "And if you wonder how many gentlemen have offered for me. Not so many as Gwen would have you believe."

"Pho!" snorted Gwendolyn. "Trina chooses to call twenty and more proposals of marriage 'Not so many!' Would I had received so few!"

"And—were all these gentlemen truly ineligible?" asked Ruth.

Katrina smiled. "Some were. The problem is that I am of mixed blood as you must know, and therefore am considered beyond the pale by most of the *ton.*"

"But Katrina is an heiress," put in Gwendolyn. "So August chooses to believe all her suitors are fortune hunters. Nothing could be farther from the truth!"

"Oh, no, you must not judge him so harshly," protested Katrina in her gentle way. "My brother seeks but to protect me, as well you know."

Gwendolyn scowled. "I know that Jamie Morris is no fortune hunter. And I know he is a good man who loves you devotedly. Yet August is determined to force him into that stupid duel, and Lord knows what the end may be!"

Katrina looked troubled and turned the conversation to Ruth and her work and her nephew. Ruth answered with caution, but she sensed that their interest in her was genuine, and she was deeply moved when they insisted that now they were friends she must let them help her.

"You shall visit us when you finish your work here," said Gwendolyn. "My papa and my brothers are exceeding well acquainted about Town, and between us all, we will find a perfect situation for you."

"Better we should find her a perfect husband," said Katrina, her eyes mischievous.

Gwendolyn clapped her hands. "What a splendid notion! Only let us have your requirements, Ruth, and we will— Oh! Unless you are already bespoken, of course."

Laughing, Ruth said, "No, but—" And then she remembered her "major," and said in confusion, "Well, that is to say— I am—er, rather—er, betrothed."

They stared at her. She felt her face burn, and stumbled her way through an involved explanation concerning the major she had not seen for "some years" and from whom she never heard.

Gwendolyn said in her forthright way, "Good gracious! Do you fear he is dead?"

Belatedly recalling the letter Tummet was supposed to have delivered, Ruth wished the major had never been "born," and was obliged to make unkind allegations about "the dreadful state of the mails" plus the merciless demands of her fiancé's military duties. She was sure they were not convinced, and, guilt-ridden by all the fibs she'd told, contrived to turn their attention to the old lighthouse and its changed appearance in the fresco.

When they approached the house, the game of rounders was well under way, footmen and grooms having evidently been commandeered to augment the teams. Chandler, egged on by ear-splitting howls from a small crowd of apparently insane males, was sprinting at amazing speed around an irregular circle marked by hay bales, while Mr. Swinton, also a fine runner, tore after a flying ball.

Entering into the spirit at once, Gwendolyn and Katrina called encouragement. Ruth was also caught up in the general excitement, and when Chandler shot past the last post just ahead of the ball Swinton hurled at him, she squealed enthusiastically and jumped up and down clapping her hands.

Panting, Chandler turned to grin at her triumphantly. He had shed his coat, and she smiled back at him, admiring the breadth of his shoulders, and his long, powerful legs. Recovering from that lapse, she saw Katrina watching her with a rather odd expression. Embarrassed, flustered, quite sure she had betrayed herself, Ruth stammered, "It—er, was splendid, no?"

"Yes," agreed Katrina quietly. "He was."

Gwendolyn exclaimed, "Only look, here comes Lady de Brette. Oh, what a delicious gown!"

Chandler had already seen the approach of his bride-to-be, and he hurried to shrug into his coat before going to welcome her.

Turning quickly, Ruth stood rigid, frozen with shock.

The lady who came gracefully across the grass on the arm of a most elegant gentleman wore an off-white Watteau gown trimmed with light blue velvet. She was tall and shapely, with great eyes of a velvety brown, and brown curls charmingly arranged in the new shorter style. Every bit as beautiful as rumour said, she was also the lady who had come to Lingways to purchase the desk and the various other items of furniture; and who had been so very rude and unkind. With an anguished pang, Ruth thought, 'No! Oh, no! She will not make him happy!'

Chandler bowed over the white hand extended to him, then dropped a kiss on the brow of his bride-to-be. "Welcome, welcome," he said. "How lovely you look, ma'am."

"You are hot and dirty," said my lady, poutingly disappointed. "And you have guests arrived before us."

"Yes." He shook hands with her brother and uttered a rank falsehood.

"Very good to see you again, de Brette. Come and meet our friends." He led Nadia to the nearest of these. "May I present Mrs. Allington, our resident artist?"

Ruth curtsied.

Lady Nadia's gaze flickered over her with neither interest nor recognition, and came to rest on August Falcon.

Lord Vincent de Brette was a rather angular man, a decade older and of lesser stature than his regal sister, but with well-cut features and a fine pair of dark eyes. He put up his quizzing glass, and said, "Good God!"

Chandler looked at him sharply.

Ruth held her breath.

" 'Tis the Mandarin!" lisped Lord Vincent all too audibly.

"Oh no!" said Lady Nadia, very much aware of that fact. "Chandler, you surely have not invited the Falcons?"

A muscle rippled in Chandler's jaw. He said quietly, "My dear, I think you must not have heard. This is—"

"Yes, yes. The artist person. How do you do, Mrs.— er . . . Now, *surely*, Gordon . . . ?"

Ruth stepped back, but Chandler caught her wrist. "Mrs. Allington," he said, an edge to his voice, "allow me to present Lord Vincent de Brette."

Flushed, Ruth curtsied again.

De Brette waved his quizzing glass airily, and, his amused gaze still on Falcon, said, "Charmed, ma'am."

Indignant, but relieved that she had not been recognized, Ruth slipped away.

"And be dashed if it ain't that fellow Morse who dangles after Miss Falcon," his lordship continued. "And— Oh, egad! The Rossiter chit! Gadzooks, Chandler! *What* a collection of oddities you have assembled for our—ah, entertainment!"

Chandler pulled his eyes from Ruth's retreating figure, and drawled, "No, do you think so? I trust our other guests don't share your opinion." De Brette looked at him, and he went on, "But I doubt they will remark upon it. They're well-bred people."

Lord Vincent tittered, and rapped his glass lightly on his sister's arm. "Listen to this, m'dear. I believe we stand rebuked!"

Tearing her fascinated gaze from Falcon's aloof face, my lady encountered so steely a look in Chandler's eyes that she felt a tingle of alarm. She was accustomed to adulation, and had attributed his occasional coolness to the fact that his was not a demonstrative nature. True, he had balked now and then at attending some social function or other, or had refused to bow to her cajolery regarding his reluctance to stay in Town, or her desire to invite certain of her friends to Lac Brillant. Not having much cared about such issues, she had shrugged and thought only that she had not bothered to put forth her best efforts. It had never occurred to her that he might prove difficult to handle. She had him, of course, but this glimpse of steel titillated her, and besides, it was never wise to take chances.

Therefore, she rested her hand on Chandler's arm and summoning her most enchanting smile, said, "Just as we deserve. Faith, but you are very right to rebuke us, dear sir, for we were being rude. Come now, Lord Vincent, we must be kind to my dear Chandler's guests."

She was properly polite to Gwendolyn Rossiter, and echoed her brother's remark that Miss Katrina Falcon was quite cruelly lovely. She smiled upon Morris, and August Falcon was permitted to kiss her hand while her great eyes flirted with him over her fan.

"And now, Lieutenant," said Chandler, "I think you are the only person not acquainted with my future—"

Morris was still seething over Lord Vincent's unfortunate earlier remarks. With a hauteur that astounded Falcon and delighted Katrina, he said, "Assuredly, I am. You ain't a man I'm likely to forget, Fowles."

To have been mistaken for Sir Gilbert Fowles, one of London's most mincing and dandified macaronis, brought a flush to Lord Vincent's pale cheeks. Chandler's mouth twitched, August Falcon chuckled, Katrina's eyes glinted with laughter, and Gwendolyn made no attempt to restrain a broad smile.

"I'd heard you was a funny fellow," snapped his lordship.

"Oh, I don't know," drawled Falcon. "Sometimes he's quite shrewd."

Lady Nadia was deeply fond of her brother. She was also as attracted by Falcon's remarkable looks as she was revolted by his mixed blood. She gave a nervous ripple of laughter and her fan fluttered. "La, sir, but you are naughty to tease my brother so. Ah, here is my dear papa-in-law!"

Delighted to greet his favourite, Sir Brian kissed her hand, bowed to her brother, whom he privately considered an unfortunate encumbrance, and quite missed the tense air about the group. My lady took his arm and enquired with an assumption of interest how the work of restoration progressed. Pleased, he said that she must "come and see."

Chandler made his excuses to his team, Dutch Coachman took his place, and the game resumed as the small party began to wander towards the chapel.

Thorpe, in his role of Jacob, galloped to them, Hercules gamboling at his heels.

"You are sufficiently muddy for three boys," said Sir Brian, amused, "but I think I cannot present—"

He was interrupted by Lady Nadia's squeal as Hercules, finding his god among those present, hurled himself at Chandler.

"Keep it away!" she cried angrily, drawing her skirts close about her. "Oh, 'tis just like that horrid mongrel that attacked me in Covent Garden!"

Chandler scooped up Hercules and tried to avoid having his face washed.

With an irritated glance at his son, Sir Brian said, "My regrets that the animal annoys you, Nadia. It has no business here."

"Is my fault, sir," said Thorpe uneasily. "I must have left the gate open. I'll take him back to Mr. Swinton's house."

"That's a good little boy," said Lady Nadia. "Give him a penny, Vincent."

Relinquishing Hercules into Thorpe's ready arms, Chandler stiffened. "You mistake it, ma'am. Jacob is not a servant here."

"No, no." Sir Brian patted my lady's dainty hand and nodded to the boy. "Be off with you, rascal. And convey my apologies to your cousin for sending you home in such disarray."

Thorpe grinned, and hurried off, the complaining Hercules tucked under his arm.

Curious, Lady Nadia asked, "Do you say he came with one of your guests?"

"He is Mrs. Allington's nephew," said Chandler. "And a fine young man—"

"*Mrs. Allington?*" interrupted de Brette, amazed. "Your hired artist—or whatever she is?"

Chandler fixed him with a steady stare.

"Do you say the woman has brought her cousin *and* her nephew with her?" asked my lady. "If ever I heard of such a thing! I wonder you permit my poor papa-in-law to be so imposed upon, Chandler."

"No, never scold him, my dear," said Sir Brian. " 'Tis thanks to Jacob that Gordon was found after those scoundrels attacked him, and—"

"And only see how you all have turned my poor intellect!" My lady stopped abruptly and, transferring both hands to Chandler's arm, cried, "We were gone down to Torquay to visit my dearest godmama and—la! When I read of it in the newspaper 'twas already days old. I was fairly frantic—was I not Vincent?"

"Inconsolable, dear soul," confirmed de Brette with his affected lisp. "No living with her, Chandler. Must leave Torquay on the instant, said she. For a day or two I quite feared she would fall into a decline, for she fancied you to be on your deathbed, dear boy. Is why we raced here, hell for leather as one might say, if you'll forgive me, my lady."

Chandler said, "My regrets that you were distressed,

Nadia." And thought it remarkable that his "frantic" betrothed had not run to him with anxiety when first she saw him, rather than complaining that he was "hot and dirty."

"Of course I was distressed," she declared, her lovely eyes aswim with tears. "Never have I been so relieved as to see you hale and hearty. And what must you do but bewilder me with all the talk of mongrels and boys and—and your artist person. As if it were not all stuff compared to your dear life! Tell me truly, I beg you! *Are* you well? Are those dreadful ruffians caught and hanged? Who were they?" And turning in desperation to Sir Brian, she transferred one hand to his, and asked, "Does Quentin know of it? Oh, 'tis so *ghastly!*"

Sir Brian did his best to reassure her and to explain matters, so that by the time they arrived at the chapel my lady had recovered her composure.

"So this is your famous discovery." Lord Vincent peered at the fresco through his quizzing glass. "Interesting."

" 'Twould be more so an we could see the whole," observed Lady Nadia. "Your woman has been here long enough that one might think it should have been completed."

" 'Tis very tiring work, ma'am," said Chandler, a flash in his eyes.

Lord Vincent looked at him thoughtfully.

"I can vouch for that, dear lady," said Sir Brian. "I have taken a turn at it, as has Gordon, and even Nathaniel Aymer. I doubt I could spend as many hours at it as does Mrs. Allington."

My lady nodded. "Which does but confirm my belief that it is no task for a female."

"It must be fascinating work, even so," murmured her brother, "to have won the lady so many willing helpers."

"I'll not deny 'tis intriguing to watch the colours creep back through the grime," admitted Sir Brian. "Come up and have a closer look."

Lady Nadia declined, but Lord Vincent climbed the steps to the platform.

"What material does she use to clean the surface?" asked my lady.

Lord Vincent said, " 'Pears to be . . . Blister me! 'Tis dry bread, m'dear!"

My lady shook her head. "She would do better to moisten it."

With an indulgent smile Sir Brian said that he was assured Mrs. Allington knew what she was about.

My lady was irked. She had gone to the trouble of requiring an indigent cousin to investigate the subject of art restorations and advise her, whereby she flattered herself that she could sound quite knowledgeable. She did not comment, but she was gratified a few minutes later when Sir Brian said, "Ah, here is our artist come back. Lady de Brette has a question for you, Mrs. Allington."

Ruth had not realized they were in here, and had started to back away, but now she waited, taking care to stand with the brightness from the windows behind her.

Lady Nadia said, "I fail to understand why you do not use moistened bread, Mrs. Allington. Surely, your method requires twice as much time."

"Moistened bread can be used on some surfaces, ma'am," Ruth answered. "But one has to be careful, and—"

My lady made a gesture of impatience. "You would do even better did you employ Greek wine, rather than water. Surely you are aware that the great Mazola used such means in restoring part of the Sistine Chapel?"

" 'Tis true that Signor Mazzuoli used such wine," said Ruth, pronouncing the great man's name correctly, but without emphasis. "However, recent examination has shown that method to cause considerable deterioration and allow dirt to become—"

She was again interrupted as Lord Vincent exclaimed, "Jupiter! Never say you claim to be more knowledgeable than such a master, Mrs. Allington?"

Ruth flushed, but her attempt to respond was cut off by

Lady Nadia, who remarked scornfully that it was a great pity, because the painting was now so sadly cracked. " 'Twill require much repainting and glue-varnishing in order to repair the damage that has been done here!"

Sir Brian looked at his fresco in dismay.

Chandler, who had also been reading on the subject, put in, "I am very sure that the damage was done long years ago, Nadia. We have Mrs. Allington to thank in that although the work may need some repainting, it will not be dulled or permanently darkened, as might have been the case with a less proficient method."

Lord Vincent chuckled softly. "And that sends you to the ropes, m'dear!" He noted his sister's tight lips and angry flush and, all too aware of her dislike of any form of opposition, went on, "I am sure Lady de Brette will be the first to own that her opinions are based more upon interest than a deep knowledge of the matter. Which Chandler appears to have er, . . . developed. Confess, my dear."

Nadia's glinting eyes met his bland ones. She read a warning there, and glancing at Chandler saw again the inflexible look that had earlier disturbed her. With commendable speed, she summoned her tinkling laugh. "Alas," she said with a pretty moue. "I tried so to impress my dear papa-in-law, and have failed miserably." Turning her smile on Ruth, she said, "Dear Mrs. Allington you will forgive an I discomposed you? I did but—" She broke off, her eyes narrowing. "Have we met somewhere? I seem to know you."

Ruth lowered her eyes. "I scarce think I move in your circles, my lady. Might you have seen me in a London bazaar or lending library?"

There was no denying, thought my lady, that this drab creature most definitely did not move in her own exalted circles. She nodded, gave her hand to Gordon, and asked plaintively if she might be offered a cup of tea, in spite of her attempt at fraud. That made Sir Brian laugh, and they all left the chapel.

Chandler hung back to close the door.

Ruth had climbed to the platform, but she turned to glance at him.

He gave her a slow smile and winked encouragingly, winning an answering smile.

Seemingly engrossed by an elaborate rose bed, Lord Vincent missed no least detail of this small exchange.

By late afternoon more overnight guests had arrived. These included Mr. Neville Falcon, a short plump gentleman with a cherubic countenance, an atrocious taste in dress, and a penchant for scandalous behaviour. He arrived with a tall and voluptuous "bird of paradise" on his arm and seemed far less embarrassed at being caught by his son and daughter with such a lady than he was surprised at finding his children present at the gathering.

They sat down thirty to table and passed a most enjoyable two hours. Sir Brian was in high spirits, only the absence of his younger son casting a shadow on this beginning to his birthday festivities. To have such spectacular beauties as Lady Nadia de Brette and Miss Katrina Falcon present added lustre to the occasion. Katrina was so well liked that her mixed birth was overlooked, although few at that table would have included her in their own parties. Her unpredictable brother was no less caustic than usual, but the ladies could scarce keep their eyes from him, and the gentlemen were much too aware of his deadly reputation to risk cutting him too obviously.

Lady Nadia was ravishing in a great-skirted rococo-style gown of off-white faille with a looped-back overskirt of deep pink satin and exquisite embroidery of the same shade on the bodice and fashioned in deep swoops above the hemline of the gown. Full of fun and vivacity, she charmed all the gentlemen, but directed her main effort towards August Falcon. During the impromptu dance that followed dinner it pleased that gentleman to encourage her coy glances, and when he claimed her for a partner she flirted with him so daringly as to bring a sardonic gleam to his cold blue eyes, a troubled look to Sir Brian, and a rather set smile to the lips of Lord Vincent.

When his sister was restored to him, his lordship took her aside and spoke softly to her. My lady at once sought out her fiancé, who was chatting with Gwendolyn Rossiter, nor did she leave his side again until he handed a candle to her some three hours later and wished her a good night. She smiled up at him, then lifted her face invitingly. Surprised, he bent to kiss her and she reached up to caress his cheek and murmur softly, "Thank you, dear Gordon, for a very happy evening."

"I hope we shall enjoy many happy evenings," he responded, then watched with a faint enigmatic smile as she drifted up the stairs, her great pannier skirts swaying provocatively.

"You know, my boy, she does not mean anything by it," murmured Sir Brian, coming up to scan his profile uneasily. "She's like a playful kitten, is all."

Mystified, Chandler asked, "In what way, sir?"

"Why, her trifling attentions to young Falcon. I think she sought only to be kind. 'Tis seldom enough the fellow is invited into Society."

"Oh. Yes, I feel sure you are right, Papa."

Sir Brian went away, wishing he'd said nothing. It was clear that his son, betrothed to the loveliest of the eligible ladies in the room, had not even noticed her rather naughty flirting. Shaking his head slightly, he wondered if he would ever understand the boy.

He felt rather too wide awake to at once seek his bed, but he was not of a mind to join Neville Falcon and those gentlemen who had settled down to cards. Instead, he wandered out to his beloved gardens. The moon was bright when it emerged from the clouds, dusting silver onto flower beds and walks; the sultry air was heavy with the scents of honeysuckle and jasmine, and the stream chattered its unending gossip. Seating himself on a favourite bench in front of West House, Sir Brian sighed deeply and allowed peace and beauty to envelop him and ease his rather jangled nerves.

CHAPTER XII

olite of you to have walked us home," said Morris, disposing himself on a sofa. "Could've found it ourselves, y'know."

Gordon Chandler closed the door of the blue and gold ante room in West House and crossed to a side table where were decanters and glasses. "A man who's about to become a benedick must polish his skill as a host," he said, pouring port wine. "I am merely practicing."

"More likely, you feared I might murder Morris en route here," said Falcon, accepting a glass and settling himself on a gold chaise.

"One strives to protect one's guests," Chandler said with a smile. "For instance, I noticed you only danced once."

Morris held his breath. He had suspected that Chandler had a motive for accompanying them here.

Falcon said coolly, "Yes. With your betrothed. She is a beautiful woman."

"I gathered you found her so. But I think you were unwise."

"Because I succumbed to temptation? Does that offend you?"

"I hope you may not pay the price."

Falcon's eyes narrowed. Always ready for a challenge, he waited tensely.

"You still limp slightly." Chandler raised his glass and his companions joined him in a silent toast. "I wish you will let my physician have a look at that foot."

"There is not the need," said Falcon. "When one ventures into rurality one must be prepared for disasters. Especially with Sir Gudgeon among those present."

Morris liked Chandler and, relieved, he said affably, " 'Tis a jolly beautiful rurality. Always wanted to see it."

"Then I am pleased you were able to come." Chandler glanced from one to the other. "Are you going to tell me now *why* you came?"

His brooding gaze on Morris, Falcon said, "I came to find out what you meant about my having writ you that stupid letter."

"And *I* came because Rossiter asked me to find out about this attack on you," said Morris. "D'you really think 'twas poachers?"

"Poachers!" Falcon gave a snort of derision. "Bird-brain!"

"Not always, dear boy," said Morris. "Rabbits some-times, y'know."

Falcon muttered under his breath.

" 'Twas a rum business," said Chandler thoughtfully.

"One can but hope not," said Morris.

Incredulous, Chandler exclaimed, "You're not serious? Smuggling? What, right under our noses?"

Falcon drawled, "The imitation valet with whom I am presently afflicted tells me that your steward left—er, some-thing to be desired."

Frowning, Chandler nodded. "What he did not leave was a number of crates and barrels." Both men looked at him curiously. He elaborated, "I found an unpaid bill among the many Durwood should have attended to. 'Twas for a dozen crates and as many barrels. I've had my people scouring the buildings and grounds, but be damned if I can discover any trace either of them, or of whatever they were intended to hold."

"Likely shipped already," said Falcon. "Your steward could have been storing supplies to sell and line his own purse."

Morris looked solemn. "Or perchance he simply looked the other way. 'The cuckoo finds a snug home without ever lifting a claw to build—'" He gave an alarmed yelp and dodged the cushion that was hurled at him.

"One of these fine days," snarled Falcon, "I'll raise a claw and cut off your damned stupid homilies forever!"

Frowning, Chandler said slowly, "Do you say that my steward was in cahoots with Free Traders? And that I was attacked because I stumbled onto some of the rogues lurking about?"

"Is a possibility." Falcon shrugged. "You've a large estate and a secluded cove with an old lighthouse to act as marker. Ideal for rum runners."

With a shade too much nonchalance, Morris enquired, "Any other nocturnal visitors?"

"Lord, I hope not!" Curious, Chandler asked, "Such as?"

Morris glanced at Falcon and said reluctantly, "Ross wondered . . . well, y'know, the newspapers were full of accounts of the attack on you. To read some of 'em one might fancy you to have languished at death's door. It—er, must have frightened your lady out of her wits."

Chandler said without expression, "So she told me. But Lady Nadia has no need to be a 'nocturnal visitor.'"

Falcon pointed out, "News has been known to reach France, you know."

"And Ross is wondering what my madcap brother may do if he hears those tales?" Chandler acknowledged, "He judges Quentin aright, but— Good God! Does he think those bastards are bounty hunters waiting for my brother to land here?"

Morris shook his head, "No use asking me, old boy. Ross can out-think me any day of the week."

"Young Jacob could out-think you any day of the week," observed Falcon cuttingly. "Still, it could be damned nasty, Chandler. Your brother's a wanted fugitive. Were he taken on your lands . . ."

Morris said gravely, "The charge would be high treason!"

"For which we all would pay with our heads." Chandler nodded. "Damned nasty, indeed. Fortunately, however, my father posted off a letter to Quentin at once, assuring him I was little damaged."

"Jolly good," said Morris.

"Always supposing he got the letter," qualified Falcon.

"Pay him no heed," said Morris soothingly. " 'Tis his greatest joy to pop a spider in the sherbet."

Chandler laughed, bade them good night, and left them.

Crossing to open the French doors Morris leaned against the jamb and watched Chandler's brisk stride.

"I'm for bed," announced Falcon, setting his glass aside. He took a step, swore, and muttered, "If, that is, I can negotiate the stairs."

"Hmm . . . ," murmured Morris.

Falcon limped to his side. "I hear a rusty creaking emanating from your brain box. Could this denote anything of interest, I wonder? Or are you just ruminating with the rest of the cattle?"

"I like Gordie," said Morris. "Thought at first he held himself too much up. Don't. He's a good man. Kind of fella would stick through thick and thin. A bit like good old Ross, y'know. Or Furlong. Or—"

"Ye Gods! Are we to have a list of every gentleman in London save my unhappy self?"

Morris turned to him. "Are you unhappy, August? Gwendolyn said you was, but—"

Gritting his teeth, Falcon snarled, "You unmitigated clod! Had you a point to make about Chandler?"

"Oh. Yes. Well, I can't but feel sorry for him, y'know. 'All that glitters—' No, do not go berserk. I only meant . . . well, I wondered why he would have chose such a—a—"

"Shrew?" Falcon chuckled. "I think your 'good man' lacks experience in the petticoat line. And if the de Brette is a shrew, she's a lovely one. Besides, from what I hear, 'twas his sire's choosing, not his own."

"Arranged, eh? Pity. No way out of it, I suppose. If he wanted a way out, I mean."

"I'd find a way. He won't, for in honour he cannot. There are advantages, my good block, to being a social outcast."

Morris sighed, and reached to pull the door shut. "True. I don't envy him. And as for that simpering wart he'll gain as brother-in-law . . ." He made a face and secured the lock.

Alone in the silent garden, Sir Brian stared blankly after the disappearing figure of his son. He had almost hailed Gordon when he'd left West House. Only the fact that he was disinclined for more talk had restrained him. He wished now that he'd done so. He came to his feet and began to follow the path that wound towards the main building.

Whatever else, those two young fools were gentlemen, and would never have voiced such sentiments had they known they were overheard. He took a deep breath. They were jealous, that's what it was. Nadia de Brette was a darling; a lady of rare beauty, impeccable lineage, a comfortable fortune, and with a voice like one of God's holy angels. A damned fine catch for any man, and the perfect mate for Gordon. If he hadn't liked it, he should have spoken up! It was true he *had* balked a little when it had become necessary to point out that 'twas past time to publish the betrothal. He'd said he had no deep feelings for the lady. But when asked whether he disliked her or whether he cared for any other lady, the answers to both questions had been negative.

Sir Brian's steps slowed and he frowned uneasily. He remembered that he had been provoked when Gordon had said in a clumsy sort of way that he'd hoped to wed a lady he could really love. Such stuff! When he himself had stood at the altar with Marie they'd met only twice in their lives—and then with chaperones attendant! He'd been scared. So had she. But they had been contracted in their cradles and would not have dreamed of opposing the wishes of their parents. Lord knows, they'd been happy. He sighed nostalgically. Love had come *after* marriage. A love that continued to this day, God rest her sweet soul. He'd said as much to Gordon, and it had only brought about the mulish set of the jaw that he knew too well. That had really made him angry, and he'd pointed out that it was disgraceful and not the part of an honourable gentleman to draw back, especially since Nadia had loved him for years, and had refused all others knowing they were as good as betrothed. That had turned the trick. He could still recall how white and stunned Gordon had looked. To give the boy his due, there'd been no more show of reluctance after that, and he had behaved as a well-bred man should.

Sir Brian walked on, eager now to get to his bed. But he could not outdistance the knowledge that his heir would go to almost any lengths to please him. Or at least to avoid upsetting him. And he had become extreme upset during that particular confrontation. Still, it was all water under the bridge now, and everything would go well, he was sure. Gordon would live to thank him for choosing so unexceptionable a lady for his bride. Besides, the boy had never looked at another lady—not in a matrimonial way. Although . . . once or twice of late, he'd thought . . . He scowled. Nadia was right, by God! Mrs. Allington had been here entirely too long. She must finish by the end of this month and take herself off. His stride faltered. 'Twould mean taking Jacob too . . . Still, it would not do. The widow must go! And soon.

Ruth worked hard next day, determined to shut out her troubles. She heard carriages arriving with the guests, and a growing hum of merry chatter interspersed with laughter. Later, there was music when the minstrels came and wandered among the brilliant company, their songs adding to the festivities. Mr. Aymer sought her out in early afternoon, and asked if he could bring her some of the jellies or delicacies, but she noted he did not bring an invitation that she join the throng. She was saddened, yet relieved, for if Lady Nadia recognized her and mentioned Lingways someone was sure to know of it, and she would be unmasked as sister to the notorious Captain Jonathan Armitage. Gordon would know she had told him yet another lie—or at least withheld the truth. And if it was revealed that she had twin nephews and that Thorpe was here also . . . She shuddered.

The birthday cake was to be cut at four o'clock. It was a gigantic confection, requiring two footmen to carry it into the gardens, and according to tradition every worker on the estate was to be given a piece and a glass of punch and would join the guests in a toast to their master.

Ruth's prayer to be forgotten was doomed. She sensed Gordon's presence and stood very still, without turning to him.

He said quietly, "You must come. It is tradition, you see."

"No."

"My dear—you must. Everyone knows the custom. Already Miss Rossiter and Katrina Falcon have been asking for you. Everyone else is there."

Desperate, she faced him. He was formally clad in a coat of blue velvet richly embroidered with silver lace at the front openings and on the deep cuffs of the sleeves. A great dark sapphire winked in the laces at his throat, and a sapphire ring was on his bronzed hand. She thought he looked magnificent but rather weary. "Sir Brian did not ask me to attend," she said.

"He sent me to fetch you."

"Gordon—I *cannot!* This old dress! And you know Mrs. Witterall thinks—"

"Do you suppose I care what she thinks?" His eyes slipped past her. "Gad! You've done a lot." With two long strides he had mounted the steps.

Ruth said eagerly, "Oh, yes. I'm so glad you can see it now. Look here. The shape of the cliff is different, no?"

"Yes," he leaned nearer, one hand on her shoulder. "You are quite right, by Jupiter! I'd—"

"So here you are!" Lord Vincent smiled up at them as they jerked to face him like two guilty children. "Your sire grows impatient, Chandler. Perchance you should admire the—er, painting . . . at another time."

The grounds had been transformed for the party. Little tables and chairs were everywhere, a marquee covered the area where were long tables heavy-laden with good food. The guests, like so many brightly hued butterflies, hovered about those tables, waiting for Sir Brian to blow out the six candles—one for each decade, he said—and from the mighty Mr. Starret to the lowliest gardener's boy, the household, garden, and stable staff gathered to offer their shy good wishes to the master.

Ruth stayed as far back as she could. Her heart contracted painfully when she saw that Lady Nadia was also far to one side, August Falcon's handsome head bent close to her ear, her eyes full of mirth as she peeped at him over her fan.

A cheer went up as Sir Brian blew out the candles. Gordon clapped him on the back. Chef, a portly French genius, condescended to help as Mrs. Tate and the kitchen staff began to cut and dispense slices busily. Soon, footmen and maids were bustling about with trays of the birthday cake. Champagne flowed freely, the guests drifted to various tables, and Ruth was seized upon by Katrina and Gwendolyn. Her protests were ignored and she was hurried to a small side table. Chandler carried over a tray of plates for them all, one of which, together with a glass of champagne, he put determinedly before Ruth. He went off to find his fiancée then, and Falcon wandered up to sit beside Katrina.

Ruth saw Chandler seat Lady Nadia at a nearby table and hand her a plate of the birthday cake. A vision of dainty beauty, all pink silk and lace, my lady held up a glass of champagne, laughing, and fluttering her long lashes at him.

And in that same moment, Ruth saw Thorpe playing camp or football with the gardener's boy. The gardener's boy was bigger than Thorpe, and more proficient at the game. His kick sent the ball hurtling high into the air past the smaller boy. Looking upward, Thorpe tore after it exuberantly. With a gasp of horror, Ruth stood. And as though Fate had decreed it, of all the laps, or all the plates on which the ball might have landed, it eluded Thorpe's clutch and thudded into the laden plate of my Lady de Brette, sending champagne and icing to shower her liberally, and awakening an instinctive laugh from the onlookers that swiftly died away.

My lady could bear some small embarrassments quite well. To be made to look ridiculous she could *not* bear. With a shriek she sprang to her feet. "Oh! You horrid, *horrid!* You *evil* little monster! How *dare* you!"

Trembling, poor Thorpe stammered, "T-truly, I am very—"

"*Look* what you have done!" screeched my lady, her face at that moment far from beautiful.

Chandler took out his handkerchief and removed a piece of icing from her chin. " 'Twas an accident, my dear," he said quietly. "I think—"

"It was *deliberate!*" She snatched his handkerchief and wiped gingerly at her cheek, her shrill voice keening through the spreading silence. "That vicious brat thought to revenge himself on me because I despise his ugly mongrel!"

Chandler scooped up the football and turned to the frightened child. "Take this, Jacob, and—"

"Yes! *Take* it!" Lost in fury, Lady Nadia snatched the ball and hurled it into the boy's face.

Ruth ran to take the weeping child in her arms.

Before she could speak, Chandler said in a voice of ice, "You forget yourself, madam! Jacob was trying to catch the ball, merely."

"Pon my soul!" she raged. "You see me abused and insulted and you take the side of this trollop and her brat, who—"

"I think you have said quite enough." He made an imperative gesture, and the minstrels who had been watching with hanging jaws, began to play hurriedly.

Lady Nadia's temper had quite overpowered her; she was much too angry now to realize the spectacle she was making of herself; too angry to see her brother bearing down upon her; too angry for anything but her need for revenge. Turning on Ruth, she shrilled, "You may think—" And she stopped, for a strong arm had clamped about her waist; a steely voice said in her ear, "Have done! You are behaving like any fishwife!"

Dizzied with rage, she gasped, *"Fish—"*

"Be—quiet!" Chandler hissed. "I'll remind you that this is a birthday party, madam. Your tantrum is upsetting my father!"

That iron arm was urging her inexorably toward the house. Everyone was staring—including her brother, a glint in his eyes she did not at all care for.

My lady burst into tears and went where she was led.

The weather, which had been threatening for several days, started to deteriorate that evening. Far past midnight, Ruth could hear music from the ballroom interspersed with gusts of wind and the tossing of branches. She'd gone early to bed, for it had taken some time for her to quiet Thorpe's distress, and her own rioting emotions had left her feeling drained and tired. She had been sure she would fall asleep at once, but the recollection of the boy's repentance haunted her.

"I got you into trouble in St. James' Park, Aunty," he had sobbed. "Now I did it again! I'm . . . I'm a wicked boy, like that lady said."

Seething, Ruth had assured him she loved him dearly, and knew very well he hadn't intended to upset Lady de Brette. " 'Tis very true you should not have been playing football so near to the guests," she'd said gently. "But you made your apologies, just as you should."

Grace had said apprehensively that they would be turned off for sure now, but when Ruth had returned to work on the fresco, only the Reverend Mr. Aymer had come to see her, and he had appeared more disturbed by Lady Nadia's behaviour than by "Jacob's" prank. "I cannot feel that you will be held to blame, ma'am," he'd said. "For despite his partiality for the lady, Sir Brian is a fair-minded man and such a display of temper was distasteful in the extreme."

A violent gust howled around the house, sending the bed-curtains flying and rattling the open casement. Ruth got up and crossed to kneel in the window-seat. Light blazed through the tossing branches from the windows of the ballroom. He would be in there. Dancing, no doubt, with his beautiful bride-to-be . . . Holding her close through some measures of the dance . . . Smiling down at her with those magnificent darkly lashed grey eyes. And doomed to marry a creature who was as selfish and spiteful as she was lovely. Ruth sighed miserably.

Her suppositions were incorrect, however, for at that instant the arms holding Lady Nadia were not those of Gordon Chandler. The eyes that smiled down at her were midnight blue with a trace of the Orient in their shape. Nor were they in the ballroom, but stood instead in a secluded ante room, locked in each others' arms, the music and laughter muted by the most improperly closed door.

My lady's gasped out and insincere protests that August was "really very naughty" were cut off as his lips once more closed hard over her own. Her response was no less passionate, her soft body pressing against him eagerly.

It was the flicker of the candles that alerted Falcon, so that he looked up from his willing captive.

"Oh, dear me," he murmured with a mocking and unrepentant grin. "And does mine host mean *faire des embarras?*"

With a muffled squeak of shock, Lady Nadia whipped around.

Chandler stood watching from the open doorway. "Make a fuss?" he said coldly. "Not at the moment. Be so good as to leave us."

Falcon looked from Chandler's grim face, to the beauty's flushed one. "I forced myself upon the lady," he lied.

Chandler said, "Force yourself to close the door behind you."

With a sigh, Falcon bowed to Lady Nadia. "He has the right, m'dear, but I shall wait within call. An he strikes you, scream, and I will charge to your rescue."

Ravishingly lovely in a ball gown of silvery green set with spangles that glittered in the light of the candles, Nadia watched Chandler with dilating eyes.

The door clicked shut. "You must be aware, madam," said Chandler, still in that voice of ice, "that for a single lady to be alone in a closed room with a gentleman who is not her betrothed is conduct past forgiving."

Her heart was thundering, for she knew that what he said was perfectly true, and that such an indiscretion would never be countenanced by the *ton*. She could have screamed with frustration. How could she have been so stupid as to risk all at this stage of the game? That accursed Falcon with his bewitching eyes and incredible looks! He had lured her on. 'Twas his fault—not hers!

Trying for nonchalance she said airily, "La, sir, what a piece of work you make of it. A harmless flirtation merely."

"I do not judge that passionate embrace to have been 'a harmless flirtation.' Rather, I am forced to assume either that your morals are sadly at fault, or that you have mistaken your heart."

"He lured me here!" Afraid that she might have ruined herself, her voice took on the shrillness that had been all too evident in the afternoon. "Falcon is an accomplished roué and—"

"And you have scarce been able to keep your eyes from him since first you came. I am not the only person to have remarked it. No doubt you think me sadly old-fashioned. Perhaps I am. But I have no least desire to marry a lady who is in love with another man."

Her eyes opened very wide. Incredulous, she said, "I? In love with the *Mandarin?*" She gave a trill of mirth. "You cannot be serious! He is a half-breed!"

"Yet, considering him beneath your touch, you still went to a private room and allowed him to make love to you? Pretty behaviour, 'pon my word!"

She became very red in the face, and, enraged by his hauteur as much as by her own folly, she hissed, "If you think to call off our betrothal, Chandler, I warn you—"

"No, ma'am. I will allow you to be the one to draw back."

"Well, I will not! Our betrothal has been published and I have every intention to become your wife. Besides, Sir Brian would not let you do so ungentlemanly a thing as to draw back!"

"You should have been more discreet, Nadia. Several people saw you come in here with Falcon. Including my father."

Speechless, she glared at him.

He said in a milder tone, "Come now, never look so dismayed. If truth be told you have no love for me, I doubt you even like me. And very obviously we share few interests. Our marriage could only be a disaster. You have many admirers who will be eager to step into my shoes." He put out his hand. "Let us part friends, for old times' sake."

Her head had lowered. Now, ignoring his hand, she looked up at him, her eyes glittering, her face white and twisted with fury. "You are perfectly right," she said in a low half-whisper that shook with wrath. "I have no love for you. I do love though. Oh, not the Mandarin. Another gentleman—who chances to have a wife." She saw disgust come into his eyes, and laughed scornfully. "Never pretend to be shocked. You know perfectly well that most of today's marriages—between people of our class at least—are for convenience only! We live in a modern age, and people are no longer bound by such fusty things as betrothals and wedding bands."

"Then how fortunate it is that we have come to a parting of the ways. Because, you see, I shall expect my wife to be bound by just such—er, 'fusty things.' "

The chill determination in his face told her she could not change his mind, and in her fury she raged, "La, what a high flight, were it genuine! But 'tis a lie! The truth of the matter is that my brother was right. You are enamoured of that dowdy slut of a widow!" She ran back as a deadly look narrowed his eyes. His hands clenched, but then he turned to the door. "Well, you'll not get her, I promise you that!" she shrilled. "*I* will be chatelaine of Lac Brillant! And you and your doxy—"

Chandler closed the door and walked down the hall more shaken than he would have cared to admit.

Falcon rose from a chair near the ballroom and waited for him to come up. "Well?" he drawled. "Pistols at dawn? You'll have to wait till I've fought Morris, I'm afraid. But that should be soon enough."

Chandler looked at him steadily. "The lady said you lured her."

"Did she, though. Hmmn. Let me see . . ." Falcon rubbed his quizzing glass along the bridge of his nose. "Did I follow the Code by which *you* live, at this point I would gallantly shield her reputation by replying that she spoke truly. I, however, am the ultimate cad. I do not give a fig for your Code, and will tell you with despicable candour that it—er, really didn't take much luring." He added hopefully, "Are you shattered?"

Chandler's slow smile dawned. "Do you know what I think?"

"Morris is the only man whose mind I can read. And that is only because 'tis empty."

"I think you did it deliberately."

Falcon looked bored. "Why should I? To be of assistance, perhaps? I assist no one—especially in so devious a way. My nature is too simple and uncomplicated for that."

With a shout of laughter, Chandler said, "Egad! What a rasper!"

Falcon's glance shifted. "Speaking of which, your—er, almost brother-in-law just scuttled to support his sister. How are you with pistols?"

"Not as good as Quentin, but not contemptible, I think. Why? Do you think his lordship may call me out?"

"Might. I'd second you, but I cannot endure the sound of gunfire." Falcon shivered realistically. "Quite oversets my poor nerves."

Grinning broadly, Chandler walked past, feeling that the weight of the world had been lifted from his shoulders and that his life began tonight. He knew he should go back to the ballroom, but he was overwhelmed by the need to share his happiness. He must be near her, at least. His step light, his heart lighter, he slipped out by the dining room French doors and hurried into the blustery night.

He came to the front of the cottage while Ruth was still kneeling in the window-seat. She was startled when she saw someone approaching the low wall that edged the cottage lawn. For a scared moment she thought it was the whistling man again, but then she recognized the athletic stride, the proud set of the head, and joy possessed her. Snatching up her dressing gown and thrusting her feet into her satin slippers, she ran swift and silently down the stairs.

The moment she opened the front door the wind snatched at her. Perhaps it was the wildness of the night that blew away all restraint. Perhaps her thoughts had been so much with him that nothing could have stayed her. She ran to him, the wind blowing her hair until it eluded the broad riband that tied it back, and streamed out behind her.

Chandler halted, and held out his arms, and she flew into them, as simply, as naturally, as though their vows had been exchanged, their troth long since plighted.

He hugged her to him in a bliss too deep for words, and knew with his eyes closed, and his cheek against her silken hair that this was the love he had hungered for all his days; this was the perfect one, the beloved and only woman for him.

Clinging to him, joying in his strength and the sure knowledge that he returned her love, Ruth forgot that he was betrothed, and that she still had not told him the entire truth about herself. Conscious only that she had given him her heart, she lifted her face.

And kissing her, Chandler discovered that his was not a cold nature after all; that passion had waited only for the right lady, and that Ruth's yielding body and soft responsive mouth seemed to ignite his very soul.

A gust staggered them, awaking them from that ecstatic embrace. Breathless, he said, "I must get you out of this wind." He led her around to the side of the house, where they were somewhat sheltered. And with his arm still tight around her, he ran one finger around her lips and said huskily, "You must fancy me a proper rogue."

"Whereas I," she murmured, gazing lovingly up at him, "seem to make a habit of running to you in my nightrail. I wonder what *you* must think of *me!*"

He kissed the end of her nose, "I wish that I had the right to tell you exactly what I think of you."

Those words poured the cold light of reality upon Ruth's

joy, and, shivering, she shrank close against him. Straightening then, she made a belated attempt to be sensible, "Where were you going when I—so shamefully flung myself at you?"

He smiled tenderly. "Do you ask if I came this way deliberately? The answer is that I often do so. I wonder you have not seen me gazing up at your window like any moonstruck halfling."

Her hand flew up to cradle his cheek and so, of course, he captured it, and kissed the soft palm until she began to tremble again and pulled it free.

With an effort, he let her slip from his arm. "I came to tell you that you are not to be worried," he said, more or less truthfully. "My father attaches no blame to you, my dear."

She drew a steadying breath. "I am not to be sent packing, then?"

"God forbid! I could not bear it!"

"Gordon," she said faintly, "you should not say such things."

He concentrated upon the soft silken rope of fair hair that he wrapped around his hand. "I know. Forgive. I have not the right. But—" And suddenly very nervous, he stammered, "But—Ruth if—if I were free, might you have . . . ? I mean— Could you— Do you think you might, under such circumstances, perhaps, have the least interest in a—a rather dull dog of a fellow, who cares more for the country than for Town, and is not a bit the bold and dashing type you ladies so admire?"

With a tender smile she unwound her hair from his hand, and holding that strong hand between both her own, she said softly, "I rather doubt it, sir, for I have not the acquaintance of such a person. But—under those circumstances, if a far from dull gentleman, who loves the country as do I, and is *very* bold and beyond words dashing—if such a man were to ask me that question—"

She was not allowed to finish her sentence, and when he at last released her, she was so weak and trembling that she fled into the house, leaving him standing there in the wind-swept darkness dazed with delight.

"I warned you to control that nasty temper of yours," said Lord Vincent angrily. "A fine spectacle you made of yourself, and now there will be a scandal, and I despise scandals! Why the deuce do you want Chandler anyway? He's a damned sight too high in the instep for my liking. And certainly, you've an adequate fortune of your own."

Rounding on him, Lady Nadia raged, "I don't want an *adequate* fortune, you fool! I want a *great* fortune! And I don't want *him*, I want Lac Brillant! And I mean to have it! 'Tis one of the most beautiful estates in all England, and situated so near to Dover 'twould draw all our friends when they come and go from Paris or Rome. The parties we could have here when the Season is over and London a dead bore! I would become the most envied hostess in the land. And with his fortune and my own, I could afford to connect the three blocks and make a veritable palace here! Do you think I've put up with Chandler's off-hand ways and the old man's puritanical notions all this time only to fail now?"

He grunted and said with a marked lack of sympathy, " 'Tis a pity you did not think of all that before you slithered back here with Falcon. You both draw the eye and deuce take it, you drew many tonight! Yes, I know—you wanted him, and you think that always you can take whatever you want, do whatever you want, and that you can bend any man to your will because you're beautiful. Well, you'll not bend Gordon Chandler! You've lost him, my girl!"

"He is an arrogant, overbearing—yokel!" She snatched up a vase and would have hurled it at the door had de Brette not wrested it from her. Through her teeth she hissed, "His stupid head is full of the most antiquated notions imaginable! Were you a loyal brother you would be after him with a pistol in your hand!" His lordship's only response being a derisive snort, she began to pace up and down, wringing her hands. "I wish you might have *heard* how he insulted me! Much love he has for me, to treat me in so abominable a way!"

"You brought it on yourself, dear heart. Besides, did I not say he was smitten with the Allington woman?"

Her eyes narrowed. "Yes. I accused him of it, and I believe you are right. My God! Who would *dream* the fool would lust after that cheap, worthless baggage? Is *she* the Toast of London? Has *she* received dozens of offers from the pick of the *ton*? She is a nothing!"

"I disagree," said de Brette with a slow smile. "Mrs. Allington has a luscious shape, and a graceful way with her. And did she wear decent gowns and dress her hair in a less severe style, she could be a beauty."

Incredulous, she said, "You must be addled! She is a dowd! A cheap slut! Yet did you mark how she stood there in the garden this afternoon? Holding that revolting brat, and looking down her nose at me for all the world as if she was of the Quality! The impudence of the creature! I declare she put me in mind of . . ." Her words trailed off. Her eyes became very round and her lower lip sagged. For a long moment she stood there, gazing into space so that her brother became alarmed and asked if she was ill.

Ignoring his question, Lady Nadia half whispered. "It *cannot* be! Surely she was not so destitute as to . . . She changed her appearance, of course, and how should I dream—" With a sudden squeal of excitement she spun around, clapping her hands. "It is! It is! Oh, how rich! How delicious!" Her eyes brilliant with laughter she said, "Vincent, you will not believe I could have been so *blind!* It must be properly staged of course. And the question is"—she paused, resting one pink fingertip on her pouting lips—"which cast of characters would be most effective?"

At a loss, de Brette asked, "What on earth has inspired such transports? What do you mean to do, wicked jade?"

Her laugh trilled out. "Sing, my dearest. And when I have properly captivated them into forgiving my—indiscretions, why then . . . oh, *how* I shall teach Mr. High and Mighty Chandler to rue the day he called me a fishwife!"

CHAPTER XIII

he ballroom was quiet when Chandler slipped back into West House. The guests stood in groups about the floor or were seated at the sides, whispering together and watching Lady Nadia, who was conferring with the musicians. Chandler started to back away, but a deeper hush fell, the music started, and he was bound by the dictates of good manners to remain. While the introduction was played Nadia faced them all, a faint sad smile on her ruddy full-lipped mouth. She had chosen Dido's beautiful song of farewell from Purcell's *Dido and Aeneas*, and her rich soprano voice rippled out pure and true and thrilling in its poignancy.

Chandler watched her. She looked almost regal with the candlelight gleaming on her soft curls and drawing sparkles from the spangles scattered about the great skirts of her ball gown. Truly an exquisite beauty. And he marvelled that she could look so angelic, yet be so selfish; that the heartbreak sung with such tender feeling that it sent shivers down his spine could be rendered by one who seemed to have no heart at all. When she finished there was a breathless silence, then the enthralled crowd burst into thunderous applause.

Many in the audience had been moved to tears, and Sir Brian's eyes were suspiciously bright when he came up to grip his son's arm and say huskily, "Isn't she magnificent? Rather naughty, I grant you. But—by God, she can sing! What a great gift, eh, my boy?"

Chandler's response was cut short as the applause died away and the music began once more. This time, Nadia sang one of Mr. Arne's songs, "Blow, Blow, Thou Winter Wind," and when she reached the line "Thou art not so unkind as love remembered not," she stretched out her rounded arms, her great dark eyes fixed pleadingly on Chandler, so that many envious smiles were turned to him. He gritted his teeth. She might as well have begged his forgiveness before them all! Angered by such tactics, he drifted back and back until at last he could quietly slip away.

Half an hour later, he was at the door chatting with some guests who had to leave early when a footman hurried to him with a message that brought a black scowl to his face.

He crossed the gardens to the main house, stamped along the hall, and flung open the door to his father's study. Lord Vincent and his sister sat with chairs close together, conversing earnestly.

"What the deuce is all this nonsense?" demanded Chandler.

My lady sprang to her feet. "I did not send for you! I told the footman to summon a constable."

"Instead of which, he came to me as he very properly should have done. Why the— Why do you want a constable?"

She had known very well that the footman would go to him, but she strove to look wounded. "If you must know, in spite of the way I have been treated, I am trying to protect my dear Sir Brian. I have discovered that a thief is hiding here right under your so moral nose."

Chandler closed the door. "I think it far more likely,

ma'am, that you mean to serve me out for having severed our connection."

De Brette said, "If my dearest sister is grieved by your cruelty, as she has every right to be, it has nothing to say to the point. I trust you have sent for the constable." He stood. "If you have not—I shall."

Leaning back against the door, Chandler said, "You will do nothing of the sort until I know what this is—"

A knock sounded. He jerked upright and whipped the door open.

Her eyes huge with fright, her comely face very pale, Grace Milford stood on the threshold. "Oh, sir," she said, breathless. "I come so fast as I could get dressed. The footman said 'twas a matter o'life and death. Is it poor—" She saw Lady de Brette then, and stopped with a yelp of fright.

"Aha!" exclaimed my lady triumphantly. "You recognize me, I see! Wretched creature! Where is your thieving mistress?"

Chandler had been watching Grace, but at these words he jerked his head around to direct a frowning stare at his ex-fiancée.

Pale with terror, Grace mumbled, "What a—a *awful* thing to say! My mistress is no more a thief than—"

My lady smiled. "We will see what the constable has to say after I bring charges 'gainst her!"

Chandler lifted his hand in a haughtily commanding gesture that made my lady yearn to scratch him. His premonition of disaster deepened by Grace Milford's obvious terror, he said, "I feel sure you mean to explain your remarks, Lady de Brette."

"You may believe I do!" The beauty stepped closer to Grace. "I *knew* I had seen your mistress somewhere before, but she was so cunning as to have changed her appearance, and how should one believe a lady of Quality would sink to do menial work? Had I laid eyes upon you, I would have had her! You will remember my telling you, Chandler, of how I was cheated when I sought to purchase a desk and some other furniture? Well, 'twas your precious artist who so wickedly choused me out of one hundred pounds!''

Her voice breathless and quavering, Grace argued, ''You were far from cheated, my lady! The pieces you selected were worth four times what you offered!''

''I did not *offer*! I *paid*, you conscienceless wretch! And when my servants went to collect my purchases there was a bailiff in possession who would not give them what I'd bought. The pair of you had run off with my money, well knowing the furniture Mrs. Allington sold me no longer belonged to her!''

Chandler felt the blood drain from his face, and heard as from a distance that shrill voice rant on. ''Your mistress knew perfectly well her furnishings had all been confiscated for debt! 'Tis why the conniving thing gave me a false name! She said she was Mrs. Lingways!''

''No!'' Grace wrung her hands but faltered bravely, ''That is—is not true, milady. The *estate* is called Lingways. You gave Mrs. Allington no chance to—''

''Gave her no *chance*?'' Contemptuous, Lady Nadia exclaimed, '' 'Pon rep, how you lie, woman! She had *every* chance, for she kept me there forever, looking through all the sorry stuff she had the gall to offer me, while *you* were so brazen as to try to make her raise her already exorbitant prices. I told you of it, Chandler, so do not pretend you don't remember. I had planned to give the desk to your papa for his birthday. 'Tis what made it all the more distressing, for I know he would have liked it prodigiously.''

Struggling to gather his wits, he said, ''But that must have been another purchase, surely? For you would not have selected his gift from goods you judged to be 'a sorry lot'?''

She flushed, but said defiantly, ''I do not propose to discuss the case with you! Vincent—find out whether the constable has been summoned!''

Her brother marched forward resolutely, but again Chandler blocked the door, the glint in his eyes, the jut of his chin causing Lord Vincent to hesitate.

Chandler said, "I will not have my father upset by more of your histrionics until I have heard the other side of this story."

"I have given you no histrionics, sir, but a faithful accounting of what transpired," declared Lady Nadia angrily. "Why should we listen to the lies of a thief?"

"There may be another explanation than theft, ma'am. Besides which, we chance to live in Britain, where a person accused of a crime has a right to be heard."

"Yes, indeed," drawled Lord Vincent. "Heard by a judge—which you are not. And in a court of law—which this is not! After which thieves are hanged or transported. As such creatures deserve."

He was quite correct. Suddenly, Chandler could see that terrible yard at Newgate Prison where people of morbid curiosity went to see convicted felons hanged. The theft of so large a sum as one hundred pounds was most definitely a capital crime, and to envision Ruth's gold and white daintiness being dragged to those hideous steps caused him to break into a cold sweat. Somehow, he controlled his terror and asked, "Miss Milford, can you explain this?"

She attempted to answer, but her voice broke and she burst into tears. "My dear Mrs. A. did not know, sir!" she said between sobs. "Truly—she did not *know!* So hard her life has been since her poor brother died . . . And—and always she has managed somehow to . . . to keep us together. We knowed the estate was to be sold for debt, which like to broke her heart. But many of the furnishings were her own . . . handed down from her mama. She sold some, so as to pay the . . . servants and—and settle some debts." Through a haze of tears she pleaded, "Sir—may I be struck down if I lie! We thought that only the *property* was to be sold. We never *dreamed—*"

"Never dreamed, indeed!" scoffed Lady Nadia. "Is that why you ran so fast, and so far? Is that why you went to such lengths to confuse anyone trying to discover your where-abouts that my agents could find no trace of you? What rub-bish!''

Grace sobbed louder and her voice was muffled as she sank her head into her hands. "That was my doing, milady. I found out the truth when I went into Shoe-Shoeburyness to pay off the grocer. And I couldn't bear to . . . tell Mrs. A., when she'd already give the servants their back pay and they'd gone. She couldn't of . . . got the money back, y'see. So I made her hurry, saying we'd miss the coach. 'Twas all *my* doing, Mr. Gordon! But''—she raised a ravaged, tear-stained face—"Mrs. A. didn't know, sir. She *still* doesn't know! I *swear*—''

"What a farradiddle!'' said Lady Nadia, impatient. "Save your swearing for the court, woman! Much good it may do you or your wicked mistress!''

In desperation, Grace sank to her knees. "Ma'am—do not! I *beg* of you. I've no money, but—I'll work for you. For the rest of—of my days, I'll work to pay you back!''

" 'Twould take more days than you have to repay one hundred guineas!''

Chandler was very still and very white. Watching him, De Brette drawled slyly, "Perchance Mrs. Allington would also be willing to work off her debt, m'dear.''

Chandler turned such a murderous glare on him that, involuntarily, he stepped back a pace.

My lady said, "Thank you for nothing, brother. I had sooner have a woman of the streets in my service than take in a thief!''

Grace shrank lower, a shaking hand pressed to her lips. They were lost, then. At the very least the boys would be put in a workhouse. At worst, they would go with her and her beloved mistress into the dreaded Newgate Prison. And if Mrs. A. was hanged . . . or transported . . . "Oh, God!'' she moaned. "Oh, my dear Lord, help us!''

Chandler met Lady Nadia's smug smile, and knew that his glimpse of heaven had been very brief.

The morning dawned with a bluster of wind and rain. Low-hanging clouds had a yellowish tinge that caused Enoch Tummet to purse his lips. "Bad weather coming," he muttered, brushing his employer's thick black hair. "It were like this the one and only time I set me trotters on a boat. Cor! Couldn't get me on one never agin. Not if you paid me!"

"I would pay a good deal to get you on one," said Falcon. "Pull it back tighter, you block!" He rolled his eyes at the ceiling and advised it that he was surrounded by clods, adding, as the door to his bedchamber opened, "And here's living proof of it! Are you acquainted with any sea captains, Morris? I need one to take this imitation valet off my hands."

Tummet met the lieutenant's eyes and winked brashly. "Got outta bed on the wrong side, 'e done." And he added under his breath "as usual!"

Morris grinned and replied that the only sea captain of his acquaintance was his sire. "Ain't been to sea for years now, of course," he added. "Curst glad of it, what with all this wrecking that's going on. Two more East Indiamen lost. Dreadful!"

Falcon opened his jewel case and selected a great emerald ring. "They're very ready to blame wreckers," he said indifferently. "More likely poor navigation is the culprit. People of low intelligence delight to add drama to commonplace events."

Morris was unconvinced. "D'ye call it commonplace when there have been at least a score of ships wrecked this past year or so? You'll recollect poor Johnny Armitage going down with most of his crew off the Cornish coast, and since then—"

"*Poor* Johnny Armitage? The rogue was drunk in his cabin when he should've been on—" Falcon checked, frowning. "Now—why, I wonder, does the name Armitage ring a bell with me . . . ?"

" 'Never send to know for whom the bell tolls,' " said Morris solemnly. He whooped, and made a run for the door, with Falcon in limping but rapid pursuit, and the rest of his quotation echoing after him, "—it tolls . . . for thee!"

Tummet went over to listen for the sounds of bloody murder and, hearing only laughter and fast disappearing footsteps, closed the door. "Good thing the lieutenant set 'im orf, Tummet," he told himself thoughtfully. "That were a close call!"

Falcon abandoned his bloodthirsty chase when the two men plunged into the stableyard and the wind sent dust and haystalks whirling into his face. His pained yowl brought Chandler hurrying to him. "Something in your eye, Falcon?"

"Never mind about him," panted Morris. "You look a proper candidate for the undertaker, Gordie. I thought you'd shot the cat last night, but I'd not realized you were that bosky. Paying the price, are you?"

Chandler's smile was rueful. " 'Fraid so. My father's brandy should be handled with caution." A sudden gust caused him to stagger, but he said, "I am at your disposal, gentlemen, if you'd care for a game of cards, or billiards. For some reason nobody seems to want to sail in this wind, but—"

"God forbid!" Falcon extracted a haystalk from one eye. "Actually, I was about to look for my sire. 'Twould be advisable, I think, were I to offer him my escort to Sussex."

Mr. Neville Falcon and his ladyfriend had been in excessively high spirits at the ball, and remembering some of their antics Chandler's lips quirked. "He said you might be of that opinion. Wherefore, he and his lady drove out an hour since."

Falcon swore.

Morris said, "I must get back to Town also. I thank you for a very nice party, Gordie." And he added experimentally, "Jove, but your—ah, lady can sing!"

"Thank you. She can, indeed."

Falcon's sly grin faded as he saw Chandler's enigmatic expression. Curious, he drawled, "Are we to expect an announcement of some kind, soon?"

"Do you mean, have we set the date?" Chandler said blandly, "Yes. Lady Nadia would like a summer wedding, so we've settled on the twenty-fifth of August."

"Have you, by Jove," said Morris, disappointed.

"Idiot," said Falcon.

"Your pardon?" Chandler's voice was cool, but his eyes spoke a warning.

"I was talking to Morris," drawled Falcon. "Oh, Gad! It's coming on to rain. We'd best collect our ladies and be on our way."

They started across the yard all together. Morris asked, "You've not found any trace of the missing crates and barrels, eh, Gordie?"

"I wish to God we had! I'd give a deal to know what that whistling maniac was about!"

As one man Falcon and Morris halted and turned to him. Morris said, *"Whistling . . . ?"*

"What kind of whistling?" demanded Falcon. "Not an ancient marching song by any chance?"

Mystified, Chandler said, "Yes, as a matter of fact. 'Tis called 'Lillibulero,' and—"

"You unconscionable blockhead," snarled Falcon. "Why the deuce could you not have told us that before?" And not waiting for Chandler's astonished response, he went on, "Then they're after Lac Brillant! Ye gods! We've wasted a deal of time! Rossiter must know of this at once."

"Know of what?" asked Chandler. *"Who* is after— Jupiter! Do you mean your League of Golden Men—or whatever 'tis called?"

"Jewelled Men," corrected Morris. "If you're right, August, one of us should stay here—no?"

"No. Chandler has an adequate staff. We've to get the ladies safe home and find Gideon. If the League thinks we're here because we've rumbled their scheme—" Falcon hesitated. "I'll leave my man, Tummet. If aught should go amiss, Chandler, send him to us."

"But why do you think this League is after Lac Brillant?" persisted Chandler. "Only because some rascally Free Trader chanced to whistle an old song? That's not much to go on."

Morris said, "A man who was in the habit of whistling 'Lillibulero' was one of those who broke my head and came within a whisper of sending Tio Glendenning and his family to the block."

Chandler frowned. "He'd have a devilish task to send me to the executioner! My hare-brained brother is safe in France; I've had no dealings with Bonnie Charlie and his Cause; my father's past is *sans reproche*; and I'm perfectly sure that neither my betrothed nor Lord Vincent would knowingly come within a mile of a Jacobite sympathizer! There is nothing can be used 'gainst us!"

The rain was getting heavier. Falcon said, "I'd not count on that, were I in your shoes. There's no telling what webs they may have already spun round you."

Morris nodded and looked solemn. "Guard yourself, dear boy. These varmints have no mercy."

"Morris is a dimwit," advised Falcon tersely. "But once in a great while he stumbles over the truth. Guard yourself!"

Ruth glanced up as the wind sent leaves pattering against the chapel windows. She had awoken in the night to the sound of a gate slamming somewhere, and by morning it had become very clear that they were in for some bad weather. The guests still remaining at Lac Brillant were obviously anxious to get home. She had heard carriages rumbling down the drivepath several times since Katrina and Gwendolyn had come to say their good-byes at eleven o'clock. She had embraced them, warmed by the knowledge that she'd made two new friends.

Gwendolyn had seemed to be troubled, but had renewed her invitation that they all visit her in Town, and had written down her direction, and insisted on a promise to send word when the fresco was nearing completion.

As sorry as she was to see them go, nothing could depress Ruth's spirits this morning. Even Grace's melancholy gloom (the result, she said, of a horrid nightmare), had failed to dim her happiness. Last evening her own dearest dream had come true, and the man she loved with all her heart had made it clear that he returned her affections. Actually, she had sensed for some time that he had a *tendre* for her. His eyes had told her that, even though as an honourable gentleman he had been powerless to speak. Last night, he had spoken. Well—as good as. And for him to have done so meant beyond doubting that he had found a way for them. Perhaps he had asked Lady Nadia to draw back from their betrothal. The woman was eaten up with pride, and would likely recoil from marriage to a man who loved somebody else. How heavenly, if eventually there could be a marriage planned between Mrs. Ruth Allington and Mr. Gordon Chandler . . .

She realized that she had stopped working and was smiling at the fresco, and at once resumed her task, humming happily, her mind full of joyous speculation. When Gordon came, as he would certainly do very soon now, she would tell him about the twins, and confess that she had been Miss Ruth Armitage, sister of the infamous Captain Jonathan Armitage. He would likely be shocked—at first. But he loved her, and she would be forgiven. Sir Brian would probably not approve of her as a prospective daughter-in-law, especially since he so greatly admired Lady de Brette. But surely he would come to understand? And he already loved Jacob, little knowing that his affection went to two boys rather than one.

She began to sing softly as she envisioned a golden future at this beautiful estate; a future with the man she loved beside her, and the boys happy and secure at last. And she thought of her father and dear Johnny, and of how delighted they would be to know she was to marry so fine a gentleman as Gordon Chandler.

Lost in such rapturous imaginings she had not paid much heed to her work, but the emergence of a most unexpected colour brought her full attention to the fresco. Red? What on earth was that shade doing at the foot of the lighthouse? Intrigued, she began to concentrate on the area and it was not until another hour had slipped away that the pangs of hunger caused her to pause once more. It must be past one o'clock, and that was odd, for she had expected Sir Brian to come and see how much progress she had made, and the Reverend Mr. Aymer invariably dropped in to chat with her before noon. With guests to be entertained Gordon must be busy. He would come as soon as he could slip away, if only for a moment, but— Troubled, she glanced to the door, and as always her pulses quickened at the sight of him.

He stood watching her, and her initial joy gave way to alarm. She ran quickly down the steps. "Oh, my dear! Whatever is it?"

He stared at the hand she extended, and backed away uneasily. The glance he slanted at her was guilt-ridden. He said with uncharacteristic diffidence, "I wish I knew. My father tells me that my—er, conduct last evening was little short of disgraceful. I've a vague recollection of visiting you at your cottage, though if I did indeed, it must have been very late."

Ruth felt cold suddenly. "Yes. Of course you came."

A tremblingly embarrassed smile, and he asked, "Do I owe you an apology, ma'am? I must own I was—very drunk."

'Very . . . drunk . . . ?' Fear was smothering her happiness. But she was mistaking his meaning—that was all. He could not be saying what he seemed to be saying. Surely, he had not been "very drunk" when he had crushed her to him and kissed her with such dear passion? Surely he had not been "very drunk" when he had stammered his way through his enquiry as to whether she might have "the least interest in a rather dull dog of a fellow." Clinging to hope, her voice trembled when she said, "It does not offend a lady to know she is loved."

He groaned and threw a hand over his eyes. "Oh—egad! Then my conduct was *indeed* disgraceful! I beg you will accept my most humble apology. Lady de Brette and I set the date for our wedding last evening, and—and I collect I was—ah, celebrating too unrestrainedly. 'Tis unforgivable, I own, but—I *do* ask your forgiveness for—whatever nonsense I may have uttered."

He had half-turned from her during this disgraceful admission, and stood with his head downbent. Gazing at his dejected figure, those awful words seemed to echo and re-echo in Ruth's mind. ". . . Set the date for our wedding . . . Whatever nonsense . . . nonsense . . ." Her thoughts would not seem to move past the terrible fact of his duplicity. He had implied that he loved her. He had kissed her, and all but declared himself. She thought achingly, 'All but . . .' And it was true that with his white face and those dark smudges under his eyes, he looked quite ill. Johnny, the dearest and best of brothers, had sometimes looked like this after a riotous evening with his friends. Was that all last night had meant? Nothing more than that strong spirits had weakened his resolve and caused him to say the things he had for so long fought against saying? Despairing, she could see again the tender light in his eyes, hear the husky voice declaring that he often stood gazing up at her window "like any moonstruck halfling."

She said slowly, "No, Gordon. You do not have my forgiveness."

His head came up. He turned to her with a wary look.

She went on, "There is nothing to forgive. Why you would try to have me despise you, I cannot know. But you will not succeed. You were not, as my brother would have said, 'above par' when you came to me last night." He started to speak, but she went on, "Oh, you may well have taken too much wine later, but that does not change what you said then. And it will not change . . . my heart."

For a moment he stood very straight and still, his eyes fixed on her face. Then he said harshly, "Nor will it change the fact that I am to be married next month. I'll not deny I am attracted to you. I seldom drink to excess and when I do so, brandy has a way of making all my problems appear of small account." His smile mirthless, he added, "An unfortunate illusion because with the dawn comes the light of reason, and reason says that I cannot draw back from my betrothal without scandal and dishonour. Even were I willing to tread that path, my father would never approve my union with a lady who—forgive if I am blunt—who seems to find it difficult to refrain from telling falsehoods."

It was as if she had been struck and she could not at once respond.

He went on deliberately, "I must admit I was shocked by your callous disregard of the feelings of your major." His eyes narrowed. "Or is he another of your fabrications?"

Ruth found that her lips were trembling. She whispered, "Yes."

"I see. I rather suspected it. May I know why he was created?"

Shrinking from the contempt in his voice, she answered, "You thought I had set my cap for Sir Brian."

He nodded slowly. "Yes. Well, I must tell you that my father desires that you finish your work by the end of the month, if possible. If not, he will—he will find another artist."

So she was to be turned off, after all. And only last night when she had asked if she was to be sent packing, he had said "God forbid! I could not bear it!" She felt as if she was drowning in tears, but managed with an effort to say that she quite understood.

Chandler grunted and stalked away, remarking over his shoulder that it would be better for all concerned if they did not meet again. At the door he glanced back. "So I will say good-bye, Mrs. Ruth. And—wish you well."

He did not wait for her response, but walked outside, not seeing the bending treetops and flying clouds; not feeling the buffets of the wind or the occasional flurries of rain. He felt nothing but the crushing weight of his despair, and saw only a slight young lady with a white anguished face and great eyes that glittered with unshed tears.

CHAPTER XIV

he thing is," said Chandler, propping up Hercules' right ear and settling his own back more
comfortably against the tree trunk, "I was pretty
fairly caught, at all events. My beautiful affianced
has no intention of relinquishing her claim—not to me, my
friend, but to Lac Brillant. The marriage *was* contracted, the
announcement *was* published. She gave me grounds to draw
back in honour, but—at what cost! No, I cannot have that, can
I? And I cannot allow a very lovely lady to waste her dear life
in useless regret. You see that, do you not?"

Hercules wriggled, cocked his head, and gave a gruff little bark. The ear slipped from Chandler's grasp and
promptly bent in half again. Righting it, Chandler sighed.
"You're likely right. She would not have been so hurt if I
had told her the whole. But she would have . . . I mean, she
might have kept on . . . loving me. She might have refused
some fine gentleman—" His eyes became bleak and his grip
tightened, so that Hercules whined.

"Sorry, old fellow." Repentant, Chandler stroked the
dog, and was rewarded with a lick and some frenzied tail
wagging.

The rain had stopped in the wee hours of the night, but the wind still blustered about on this grey morning, at times rising into gusts that whipped the treetops of the Home Wood and sent wet leaves and twigs and droplets showering down on the man and the small dog who conversed at the foot of the gnarled old beech tree. Oblivious of such minor discomforts, Chandler retrieved the ear and again attempted to make it stand up so as to match its fellow.

"We were right about the major," he muttered. "One of her fibs—rascal that she is . . ." Here, his voice trailed into silence and his eyes became so wistful that Hercules, sensing something was amiss, leapt up and butted his nondescript head against the god's chin, anxious to be of comfort.

"Thank you," said Chandler. "And you're right again. We must put our heads together. There *will* be a major—or a captain perhaps, sooner or later. She's so very lovely . . . isn't she? No—I'm all right, I don't need my chin washed. Very well, I'll stop being a fool . . . Let us, then, take the—er, dismal view and assume there will be no major for a time, at least. She must have—*they* must have a roof over their heads. We shall have to see to it, eh? Something legally registered in her name, that no one can take away from her. And an income, my Hercules. We must arrange an income. What do you suggest?"

Deciding that this was a frivolous question, Hercules crouched down panting, then barked vigorously.

"But why should Lady de Brette object?" argued Chandler. " 'Tis none of her affair. Our business arrangement does not entitle her to—" He broke off, his face becoming very red. "Oh, hello, Oakworth. What the deuce are you doing out here?"

"Begging your pardon, sir," said the head groom, his wind-tossed hair conspiring with his eye patch to make him look even more villainous than usual. "Mr. Tummet said as you'd come this way, and I didn't mean to worrit you, Mr.

Gordon. But if I could just have a word." He peered around curiously.

"Is something amiss? What are you looking for?"

"Why, I heard you talking, sir, and I thought—"

"Oh. Well, never mind that." Oakworth, who seldom wore a hat while at work, was wringing one between his bony hands. Wondering if some crisis had arisen in the man's family, Chandler asked, "Something I can do for you, Bill?"

Oakworth's face took on an even more hunted look. He wet dry lips and said haltingly, "I were hoping, sir. Meaning no disrespect, but—well, I thought maybe you could put in a good word for me. With Sir Brian."

"I'm sure you know what you're talking about. I do not. Is my father displeased with you?" Chandler's eyes hardened. "If 'tis a matter of Blue Ruin again—"

"No, sir! It ain't! I've swore off gin altogether, sir. Account o' me bowels cannot abide it. No, Mr. Gordon. It's about that there boy—Jacob. And Miss Nymph. And now, Sir Brian—" Oakworth's voice cracked and Chandler was appalled to see tears come into his eyes. "He's gone and turned me off, sir! And without even a good reference. Sir—I been here all me days . . . *Please* . . ."

"Of course I dismissed the man!" Sir Brian frowned across his desk. "I'll not tolerate impertinence in my servants, Gordon. Particularly when that impertinence is turned upon Lady Nadia. For Oakworth to have allowed the child to appropriate the mare, and then try to lie his way out of it was downright disgraceful!"

"Your pardon, sir. Jacob had my permission. In point of fact, Oakworth was reluctant when I ordered him to saddle up Miss Nymph for the boy."

Sir Brian stared. "*You* did? But Nadia said— Why on earth did Oakworth not explain?"

"When he attempted to do so, he was accused of insolence. The mare needed exercise and Jacob was eager to ride with me. I saw no harm in it."

Troubled, Sir Brian muttered, "No, of course. But . . . from what Nadia said, I thought . . ." He looked up at his tall son. The grey eyes met his own as steadily as ever, but of late they held a lacklustre look and a suggestion of a deep weariness. There were lines in the strong face, besides, that made the boy look older than his years. "Dash it all," he said. "You've been working too hard, Gordie."

"Oh, I think not, sir. Lots to be done, you know. And with this confoundedly unending gale—"

"Never mind about the gale. Sit down for a minute. I've wanted to have a word with you." But after Gordon had obediently settled himself into a chair beside the desk, there was a brief silence before Sir Brian said slowly, "Cousin Bertha left this morning. I fancy that will not grieve you."

"The lady has never been unkind to me, sir. Although, she is a meddler." With a shrewd glance at his father's face, Chandler added, "What has she been saying to trouble you?"

"That you are unhappy in your betrothal. And that you have interests in another direction." He saw Gordon's hand grip spasmodically at the arm of the chair, and his heart sank. "Ah. It is truth, then."

A brief pause, then Chandler said expressionlessly, " 'Tis the custom for marriages to be arranged, after all. And these days, one seeks elsewhere for the—ah, tender emotion."

Sir Brian watched him. The smile did not reach the veiled grey eyes, and the knuckles of the hand on the chair arm were white. Shock and guilt rushed in upon him. He drew a hand distractedly across his forehead, then said in a frantic rush of words, "My dear boy, I know you think— That is— 'Fore God, all I have *ever* wanted is happiness for *both* my sons! Your brother's wife is a delightful creature, and I thought— Well, Nadia is so very beautiful, and I had hoped— But I am not blind, you know! At least, I may have been in the past, but

I had never before been shown that side of the woman. I could scarce believe my eyes! I was quite taken in, I suppose. And now—this business with poor Oakworth . . . It begins to look . . ." He gulped, "Oh, dammitall, Gordie! What have I forced you into? *Whatever* can we do?"

Chandler sprang up. The smile reached his eyes now, and he moved quickly to grip the hand his father stretched out to him. "Do not be in a taking, sir," he said firmly. "I think Nadia's beauty has caused her to be a little spoilt, perhaps. She has many good qualities. Certainly, she is fond of you. At all events, there is nothing to be done at this late date, and likely we shall live together happily enough if I—" Interrupted by the thunderous boom of the wind rushing around the side of the house, he exclaimed, "The devil! I must go and have a word with Swinton. I'm afraid we're in for a proper gale, and I'm not easy about the loft roof over the stables."

With an affectionate grip of his father's shoulder he was off and striding rapidly down the hall. He felt warmed by the real caring that had been revealed to him, and amused by the awareness that Sir Brian witheld a display of affection until he believed it was needed. His own self-sufficiency may have inhibited such a display until now, when he had evidently been judged vulnerable.

He looked far from vulnerable when he found his betrothed and her omnipresent brother taking coffee in the morning room and reading *The Spectator*. Nadia was clad in a primrose yellow *robe battante* edged with swansdown, a matching riband was threaded through her curls, and she looked so lovely that for an instant Chandler stared at her as one might gaze at a work of art. Giving himself a mental shake, he said curtly, "A word with you, madam."

The Spectator jerked. She put it aside and turned briefly alarmed eyes to him.

"Understand me," he went on. "We may have an arrangement—"

"One you dare not try to wriggle out of," purred Lord

Vincent. "We have your signature on the marriage contract."

Chandler gave him a disgusted look. "I have already instructed our chaplain to have the banns called." He paced closer. "I will not go back on my given word, however disgracefully it was obtained, but—"

"I mislike your tone, sir," declared his lordship, standing and putting up his quizzing glass.

Chandler marched to open the door. "Out."

"Do not dare speak to my brother so," said Lady Nadia indignantly.

"You may walk out of this door, De Brette, or be thrown through it. Make up your mind. You have to the count of three."

"You tread on very thin ice, I remind you," said his lordship, forgetting to lisp and with rage glaring from his dark eyes.

"One . . ."

"Oh, very well, Vincent," said my lady. "He'll not dare abuse me."

De Brette hesitated until the count of "two." The look in Chandler's hard eyes convinced him then, and he sauntered out.

My lady rose and demanded haughtily, "Well? What have we to discuss?"

"Nothing, ma'am." Closing the door, Chandler walked over to face her. "I am not come to discuss, but to state. In exchange for one hundred pounds and your signed receipt for that sum in full payment of a debt owed you by—another lady, I have agreed to make you my wife. You should understand however, that I have no intention of living 'under the cat's foot,' nor—"

"Oh! How *dare* you?"

"—nor of having my people bullied and intimidated by your shrewish tantrums."

With a squeal of wrath she flew at him, hands clawed.

He caught her wrists, but she was strong, and one sharp

nail raked his cheek. "Cat, indeed," he grated, and shook her hard. "What you need, my fancy feline, is a damned good spanking!"

Never in her pampered life had my lady been shaken. Dizzied with fury, she spat out, "*Brute!* I can still destroy her! Much good that note would do you if I told any prospective employers about her infamous brother!"

Chandler frowned, and she tore free and, cherishing her wrist, went on spitefully, "What? Did not your strumpet tell—" With a squeak she darted behind the sofa. "One more step, and I shall scream the house down!"

He halted, eyeing her with grim distaste. He looked strong and dangerous, and her heartbeat quickened. Truly, she had never realized how very good looking he was. And, Lud, but it had been thrilling to be handled so roughly. She said in a softer voice, "But I shall keep my word, Gordon, and not betray her secrets, unless you are—very cruel to me."

He foresaw a life of blackmail, and said with contempt, "Much anyone would care about her brother."

"No? Not even if he was Captain Jonathan Armitage? You've a short memory! 'Twas the talk of . . .'" And she stopped, his astounded expression causing her to exclaim, "Why, you really did not know! That sly little jade! I had thought that was how she obtained the position, by bragging of her almighty papa!"

His eyes blank with shock, Chandler recollected what Jacob had said about the painting of King Arthur, and he remembered now who had created that famous work of art. Greville Armitage! So his lovely Ruth was the daughter of that genius . . . And the sister of *Jonathan* Armitage!

Lady Nadia took a tentative step from behind the sofa. "I will be good, dear Gordon. Truly, you will not have to be ashamed of your bride."

He scarcely heard the words, nor saw her wistful little smile. 'Yet another fib,' he thought. 'Or at the least, a truth concealed. My God! How many more?'

These two days had been anguish for Ruth, her heartache so intense that she could scarcely endure it. But she fought tears, determined to hide her grief from the twins. She had issued strict orders that they were no longer to approach the other buildings, and that whichever was "Jacob" for that particular day must venture only into the garden or the woods. Their protests were milder than she had expected, partly because Thorpe was now thoroughly afraid of Lady Nadia and had no wish to encounter her wrath for a third time. Grace was steeped in gloom, and wept at the slightest provocation. Ruth's attempts to discover what distressed her were met only with tears and sighs, this lachrymose behaviour doing nothing to lighten her own burdens.

She was isolated now when she worked in the chapel. Neither Gordon nor Sir Brian ever came in while she was there, even her clerical admirer only glancing in occasionally to offer a sad smile and a shake of the head that conveyed his sorrow for her sinful nature. The only person to visit her was Mrs. Tate, who would bring her a cup of tea and a biscuit sometimes. If the housekeeper was aware of the reasons behind Ruth's dismissal she gave no sign of it, but would chat pleasantly of "Jacob" and how much she missed having him about the house.

"Sir Brian misses him as well," she said on this stormy afternoon. "And Mr. Gordon." She sighed. "Such a pity it is."

Ruth managed a composed voice as she asked how the wedding plans progressed.

Mrs. Tate looked irked and said shortly that she supposed things were being set in train. "Which is surprising, considering that Lady Nadia behaved so *disgracefully* at the ball. Still, the banns will be called for the first time on Sunday. I fancy my lady would be in Town, busying herself with bride clothes and plans, save that she is afraid to travel in this dreadful weather."

If anything the weather had worsened when Tummet appeared in late afternoon to walk Ruth back to the cottage.

"It was kind of you to come for me," she said, holding her skirts against the boisterous wind and avoiding the whipping branches of a holly bush. "Are you to stay here long, Tummet?"

Falcon's unpolished valet allowed as how he was to "keep a eye on things" until his "temp'ry guv" sent for him.

Ruth tried to appear cheerful. "Do you enjoy the country?"

"That I does not, marm!" He took her arm as they were staggered by a gust that robbed them of breath. "Terrible place, the country. Give me the Big Smoke, any day. Nice and quiet and peaceful. No cacklers crowing fit to wake the dead every morning. No owls asking questions all night. No perishing crickets! Cor, I 'ates crickets! Never was in the country till me bailiffing took me outta London."

Ruth wondered absently what a "baley fing" was, then said, "Oh! you mean you were a bailiff?"

"Ar. Watch that there branch, marm. Lumme! What a blow!"

"Did you mind being a bailiff? I'd think it must be very sad work."

"There you got it right, mate. Sad is just what it is. Specially fer a cove what's got lotsa hen-fer-rent." He saw her puzzled look and imparted, "Sorry, marm. I lapses, me guv says. Rhyming cant. Hen-fer-rent, meaning in other words, sentiment."

Ruth laughed, then paused to detach her shawl from a low yew tree.

"Worse part," went on Tummet, "was the childers. Useter cry something awful when I 'ad ter do a execution." He gave Ruth a dig with his elbow, and a sly wink. "Good thing I knowed about 'em, though. Eh, marm? Only just got you and Miss Grace outta that there bobbery in, as you might say, the nick o' time."

"Poor Grace," said Ruth, wishing that if Gordon would not come and see the discovery she had made, she might at least have a word with him. "I wish I knew what is making her so terribly unhappy." She waited hopefully, but Tummet contributed only a shake of the head, and having freed her shawl she started off again, then asked abruptly, "What did you mean? What—er, bobbery did we escape in the nick of time?"

He took her arm again. "Why—that there bailiff. Didn't Miss Grace tellya as one was on 'is way? If 'ed come and caught you selling them bits of furniture . . . Cor! Bobbery and no mistake! And when I see that Lady de Bretty at this 'ere very estate! Cor, again! Good thing you'd changed yer curly locks and the way you dress. Not meaning no disspeck, but I'd not put it above that one to 'ave yer clapped inter Newgate and a rope ready fer that pretty neck o'yourn if—" He checked as Ruth halted and stood staring at him. "Ain't said nothing I shouldn't oughta, 'ave I, Mrs. A?"

Ruth said faintly, "Mr. Tummet, would you please step around to the side of the cottage with me, where we may be out of the wind for a minute or two?"

"The gravy's lumpy, Miss Grace," observed Jacob, peering critically into the pan.

Grace sniffed, and started to stir again. "Never mind," she said hoarsely. "I'll strain it. Now go upstairs and brush your hair, dear. Aunty will be home any minute." She sighed heavily. "Unless she works late again."

The child made for the stairs. "She'd oughta be early. She'd oughta blow all the way 'cross the gardens. P'raps she did." He started up the stairs adding dreamily, "P'raps she's blowed all the way to London, an' is floatin' round St. Paul's . . ."

Grace muttered to the gravy, "Be best if she had. Be best if—"

The front door burst open. Leaves and twigs blew in; an old copy of *The Spectator* whirled from the parlour table and dispersed itself about the kitchen. Then Ruth managed to shut the door and followed the scattered pages.

"What a dreadful wind," said Grace, setting the pan of gravy aside. They say 'tis causing havoc on the seas, and there's no knowing how many ships—" She had bent to take up a page, and Ruth's shoe stepped onto it. Looking up enquiringly, Grace gave a gasp. Mrs. A's hair was windblown and untidy and there was a leaf over one ear, but on her flushed face was an expression that banished all thought of gales and storm-tossed ships. An expression that caused Grace to straighten up, then draw back uneasily.

"How *could* you?" demanded Ruth, her voice low but ringing with anger. "No! Never look bewildered and pretend you don't know what I mean. Your friend Tummet has just let the cat out of the bag. I know the whole dreadful story, and I want to know—*why?* Why did you not tell me I was committing a crime in selling those things to Lady de Brette? Why did you trick me into leaving early—rushing away like—"

"Oh, *don't*, Mrs. A," wailed Grace, dropping the long-handled spoon and snatching her apron to her tearful eyes. "I didn't—trick you. Not to say—*trick!* I were only trying to help as—as best I knowed! Oh, that horrid Enoch Tummet! Wait till I—"

Ruth advanced on her purposefully. "Never mind about Tummet! How could you think you were *helping* me by making me run away? Do you not realize that you've made me appear a criminal?"

"Oh . . . Mrs. A!" Grace raised a pleading, tearful face, and sank onto the kitchen chair. "I bin . . . breaking me poor heart, not knowing what to do. I thought—"

"Stop that silly blubbering at once! Tell me, if you please, why you failed to warn me of what I had done. I was unaware I was breaking the law. *You* knew it! Yet you said nothing!"

"But I *didn't* know, Mrs. A! God's truth, I didn't know till Tummet met me in—"

"Yes, I know he met you. And I know he warned you. What I cannot understand is why a'God's name you did not then tell *me!* Had you lost your reason? Did you really think I was so dishonest, so unprincipled as to take that wretched woman's money knowing she could not claim her purchases?"

"But, Miss Ruth—dear Mrs. A.—what else was there to *do?* You'd give all the money away, almost. How could you have paid her back? They'd have put you in gaol sure as sure! All I could think was that the bailiff would likely come walking in at—at any second . . . Oh, my *Lor'!* I didn't care nothing about her nasty ladyship. If her servants had come quick, she'd have got her goods and no one the wiser. But—oh, dear ma'am . . ." Grace seized Ruth's hand and pressed it to her wet cheek. "Don't talk to me like you hates me. I—I only done what I thought was best."

Ruth jerked her hand free and said furiously, "*Best?* My heavens! If I go to the authorities now, do you think they'll believe I hadn't known the furnishings were no longer my own? I *ran*—because of you! I have branded myself no better than a—a common felon! If Lady Nadia recognizes me, and why she has not done so I cannot guess, I can be taken away in chains! I can be put into Newgate Prison and—and charged with conspiring to defraud that horrid woman!" Suddenly faced by the full implications of that terrible prospect, Ruth whitened. "If I am hanged, or—or transported—what will happen to the children? Have you thought of that?"

"But it won't never *happen*," said Grace frantically. "Mrs. A, you're not—"

"I *am!* I am *guilty* in the eyes of the law! People have been hanged for stealing a loaf of bread! Transported for picking an apple from someone's orchard! I cheated an earl's daughter out of *one hundred pounds!*" Ruth pushed back her hair distractedly. "Those two dear little boys will be put in the workhouse, or—or on the Parish! And should they survive, God help them, they'll be marked for life! Their father a drunkard who allowed his ship to founder and his crew to perish! Their aunt a felon—a common thief!" Her voice broke, and she bowed her face into her hands.

Grace jumped up and threw her arms about her beloved mistress. "No, Mrs. A. Never even think such things! Mr. Gordon won't let them! He put a stop to it! He—" She stopped as she felt Ruth stiffen.

Lifting her head, Ruth half-whispered, "Gordon—*knew?*"

She looked so white, her eyes wide with shock. Frightened, Grace whimpered, "Y-yes, ma'am. They come for me in the middle of the night. After that ball, it was. And Lady de Brette was there, and saying—oh, the most dreadful things! But Mr. Gordon made her listen to what I said. And he *promised*, Mrs. A. He told me—"

But with a muffled cry, Ruth was gone, running to the front door and out into the storm, desperate to be alone; to hide her grief and her shame. The man she loved had found out that she was not only a liar, but a thief! Indifferent to the flailing of branches, the convulsive dance of shrubs and ferns, even the billowing of her own skirts, she wandered blindly.

"The night of the ball," Grace had said. That then, explained everything. That was why he had turned against her. Why he had been so cold and said such hurtful things. Oh, how he must despise her! She sat on a tree stump and wept heartbrokenly until at last her sobs faded into spasmodic hiccups. She wiped her eyes and leaned there, listless amid the uproar, gazing blindly at the mad gyrations of a nearby sapling.

At worst, she thought dully, she was a thief. At best she had behaved disgracefully. The words seemed to find an echo somewhere. Someone else had behaved disgracefully. Who? Oh, yes. Mrs. Tate had said Lady Nadia behaved disgracefully at the ball. In fact, the housekeeper had seemed disappointed because the banns were to be called. She didn't like Gordon's affianced, of course, but had she hoped . . . ? Ruth sniffed, and blew her nose. If Lady Nadia had disgraced herself it must have been long before Grace had been summoned, for she'd said they had come for her in the middle of the night. What could the beauty have done? She had very obviously been fascinated by August Falcon, and he, rake that he was, had as clearly led her on. A new and fascinating idea dawned. Could my lady have been so indiscreet as to give Gordon an excuse for terminating their betrothal? Her pulses began to race. Was *that* why he had come to the cottage? Had he fancied himself free? It would explain why he had dared to kiss her with such sweet passion, and why he had so tentatively, so charmingly, asked how she might feel if he "had the right" to address her.

She pressed both hands to her temples. It was silly to hope. To build a drama with no basis in fact. She must not get so excited, but must assemble her facts sensibly, as Papa had taught her to do. Very well, then—firstly: Gordon had certainly not been "very drunk" that night. Secondly: Much later that same night, Grace had been summoned to the main house, and Lady Nadia had said "dreadful things." Thirdly: The next day, Gordon had been so changed. He'd looked drawn and haggard, and she'd thought . . .

She gripped her hands tightly. Never mind what she'd thought. 'Count again!' Fourthly: Grace said, Mr. Gordon had "put a stop to it." How? Lady Nadia had clearly taken a deep dislike to her, and she was a ruthless woman; she would delight in bringing charges against someone she fancied had cheated her. What possible weapon could Gordon have used to make her drop those charges? Unless . . . If my lady had determined to be mistress of Lac Brillant and the dream was denied her. Would she fight to protect her interests?

"Yes!" whispered Ruth. "She would indeed! And with whatever weapon was at hand!"

The next thought was appalling. It would be infamous!

Surely even Lady Nadia would not stoop to what was no less than blackmail? But yet, it all fit together so neatly. It would be typical of Gordon, who seemed to make a habit of protecting others, to sacrifice his own happiness to save her.

But still, 'twas all conjecture. If only she could know for sure. Grace had said, "Mr. Gordon promised . . ." She must go back. She must find out at once what it was he had promised!

She began to run, but the wind fought her, and she had to hold her shawl with one hand and her skirts with the other. She had no recollection of coming into the woods, and why she had done so she would never know. But at last she caught a glimpse of the gabled roof. Grace would tell her—

She halted, her anxieties dissolving into a deep tenderness. He was there again. Standing just within the trees, watching the cottage even as he'd said, hands loosely clasped behind him. He did love her, then. How inexpressibly gallant, that he had been willing not only to pay such a price to keep her from shame and perhaps death, but had tried to conceal his sacrifice. And how was she to save him from such dear chivalry? If she confessed her guilt to the authorities, not only would she pay the penalty, but the twins' innocent lives would be wrecked also. If she did not confess, she condemned the man she adored to life with a selfish, spiteful woman, who could bring him only unhappiness.

She was overcome by a need for the comfort of his arms; a need to tell him of her love and gratitude, and to try with his help to find a way out of this frightful dilemma. With a stifled sob she ran forward and, blinking away tears, touched his arm.

He all but sprang into the air and turned, crouching, one hand darting for the pocket of his coat.

Ruth's heart seemed to stop beating. Only the fact that she'd been so distraught and her eyes dimmed had led her to make so terrible a mistake. She gazed not into the clean-cut features of her love, but into a smooth pink and white face and heavy-lidded grey eyes. The countenance that had haunted her on the stagecoach and in Mr. Brodie's Lending Library in Dover. The for once unsmiling face of the man she knew as "the smiling man."

An instant they stared at each other, both momentarily stunned. Then, Ruth gave a choking cry, picked up her skirts, and ran faster than she had ever run in her life, abandoning the Code of Correct Behaviour, which decreed that a Lady of Quality should never, under any circumstances, be so vulgar as to walk in a hurried fashion, much less hold up her skirts and gallop like any hoyden.

Her one thought was to find Gordon and tell him that the smiling man was here again.

CHAPTER XV

residing over the teapot in the withdrawing room Lady Nadia refilled Sir Brian's cup and offered it with a glowing smile. He murmured his thanks, but there was no answering smile, and his eyes were grave. She thought uneasily that he had withdrawn the affection that had always been so easy to awaken, and she wondered how much he knew. She had worn the pale green silk *robe battante* with the rosebud trim that she knew he particularly admired. Much good it had done her. He was politely icy. Still, she was safe now. There was nothing he could do, even if Chandler had told him of their bargain. Likely he would not have done so however, for the old man would worry, which Chandler would not at all like.

She started to pour another cup for her brother, but a gust slammed against the windows and her hand jolted, the tea spilling over.

"Easy, m'dear," said Lord Vincent, accepting the cup and saucer. "This house has withstood many such storms I fancy, eh, Chandler?"

"Very many. You are quite safe, my lady."

"Well I wish I was safely in London," she said, fear making her forget her vow to be tactful. "We should have left this morning, Vincent, as you said. I wish I had listened to you."

"So do I, sweet. But you seldom do."

"I fancy the roads are still safe," murmured Sir Brian. "Should you wish to leave, my dear, we will send some of our people to escort you."

"Perhaps, by the morning, sir, the wind will—"

She was interrupted by alarmed voices and running footsteps in the hall. The door burst open and Ruth Allington rushed in, out of breath, windblown, obviously distressed.

At once Chandler sprang to his feet. Ruth flew to him, and he took her outstretched hands into his strong clasp. "What is it?"

"How dare you burst in here like this?" exclaimed Lady Nadia angrily.

Looking only at Gordon, Ruth panted, "He—he is here! That man from . . . the library! He was watching the house!"

"Devil he was!" Ignoring his betrothed, Chandler put Ruth aside and started to the door, but the butler was already entering. Starret looked dismayed and offered a salver. Chandler took up the card. "Sir," he said, turning to his father with a frown, "are you acquainted with a Mr. Burton Farrier?"

Lord Vincent, who had watched this scene with faint amusement, sobered abruptly, and his cup clattered onto the saucer. "The Terrier?" he gasped. "My God! What mischief have you been about, Chandler?"

Lady Nadia threw him a sharp look.

Sir Brian said, "I seem to have heard the name . . ."

"I would rather think you had." Lord Vincent elaborated, "He's a glorified bounty hunter. Works with military intelligence, they say, and has the reputation of never having failed once he's set onto someone's trail."

"You are too kind, my lord." Farrier waved Starret aside and strolled into the room. He had smoothed his wig and aside from being slightly flushed gave no sign of having just run at speed across the gardens. He bowed low and gracefully to Lady Nadia, and again to the gentlemen.

With an irked glance at Starret, Chandler said, "I think you were not invited to enter, sir."

"But does my presence alarm you, Mr. Chandler?" Farrier smiled kindly. "I am but a humble government servant and unless you have a troubled conscience you've nothing to fear."

"We entertain guests." Sir Brian had risen and regarded the newcomer with distaste. "If you wish to see me you must make an appointment with—"

"The King's officers are not required to make appointments when dealing with matters of High Treason," purred Farrier.

Predictably, his words created consternation. Lady Nadia's white hand flew to her throat, Ruth gave a shocked gasp, Lord Vincent positively goggled at the "King's officer," and Sir Brian, suddenly very pale, groped at the chair behind him for support.

Chandler said softly, "I wonder does his Majesty know you are one of his officers. Or that you force your way into the home of a titled gentleman on some trumped-up pretext and do your best to frighten ladies."

For just an instant, Farrier's smile disappeared.

Lord Vincent said, "I can waste no more time." He turned to his sister. "M'dear, an you are ready to leave, we should start at once."

With a notable lack of argumentation Lady Nadia stood.

Farrier raised a languid hand. "I must ask that you remain, my lord. I will but keep you long enough to make a brief enquiry."

"About what?" Lady Nadia spoke with regal hauteur, but her fingers plucked nervously at her fan.

"About nothing we care to hear," snapped Chandler. "Starret, show this upstart out!"

The butler bit his lip, but started forward obediently.

Farrier said, "Would you prefer I call in the troop I have posted at your gates?"

Sure that there was no troop, Chandler smiled. "By all means."

My lady's eyes grew wide with fright.

Again, Farrier's sly smile wavered, and his eyes darted a glare of intense dislike at Chandler. "I wonder why you should be so very hostile, sir?"

Uneasy, Lord Vincent said, "Perhaps we should hear what the fellow has to say. If 'tis indeed a matter of High Treason it would not do to hinder any investigation."

Farrier bowed. "Very wise, my lord."

With an imperative gesture Sir Brian silenced his son's attempt to comment. "What is it you wish to know? Be brief, if you please. I do not care for my guests to be inconvenienced."

His smile restored, Farrier said, "But of course, sir. 'Tis in the matter of this very serious outbreak of shipping losses."

Chandler suppressed a sigh of relief. He had feared this little wart was after Quentin again. He did not dare look at his father, knowing Sir Brian had shared his apprehensions and guessing that, although Farrier did not seem to be watching him, those cunning eyes missed nothing.

"My superiors," Farrier went on, "suspect there are wreckers at work along this coast. Many of the cargoes were lost to the sea, of course, but salvage attempts have revealed a surprising discrepancy between goods believed to have been washed up on shore, and those actually reclaimed."

"Your superiors must suspect there is a veritable army of wreckers at work," said Chandler ironically. "From what we've heard there have been ships gone down all around our shores from Dover to the Scots Border, and from the Mersey to Cornwall!"

De Brette shook his head. " 'Tis bad enough to think of such tragedies occurring due to wind and weather, but that human beings could be so heartless as to have engineered them . . . ! Dreadful! Many of those lost were women and children, I believe. Especially on the East Indiamen."

"Your compassion does you credit, my lord," purred Farrier. "May I assume you will not object to cooperating?"

De Brette looked startled. "Cooperating, you say? How?"

"Why, my lord, you are . . . here, after all."

Chandler's brows twitched into a dark frown. "What the deuce d'you mean by that remark?"

"Only that the *Empress of Calcutta* was—er, went down off your cove earlier in the year, I believe."

Taking a stride towards that gentle grin, Chandler grated, "Do you dare to imply—"

"But my dear sir." Farrier's hands waved gracefully. "I imply nothing. I merely attempt to discover if you, or your guests, have noted anything—er, untoward, shall we say. Or have found any trace of the goods that were, alas, never recovered."

Chandler roared, "Why you festering little wart!" and sprang at Farrier who, nothing if not fast on his feet, darted behind his chair.

"Stay back!" His voice shrill now, and his smile quite gone, Farrier declared, "There are sufficient counts 'gainst you already!"

"What counts?" demanded Sir Brian angrily.

"He's bluffing, sir," cried Chandler. "Do you not see that he only—"

"Be still! Answer me, Farrier! *What* counts?"

Farrier's right hand slid into his pocket. His smile shaken but restored, he replied, "Your youngest son is a known traitor—an enemy of this country. He—"

"My brother lives in France, confound you!" snarled Chandler. "And he is far less an enemy of England than are slippery toads of your ilk!"

"Then 'tis as I thought! You are in sympathy with his revolutionary beliefs!"

With a growl of rage Chandler again started forward.

"Stay back! I warn you!" Farrier snatched a small pistol from his pocket and aimed it steadily.

Lady Nadia screamed.

Lord Vincent sprang to her support.

Terrified, Ruth watched from the corner to which she had retreated.

Sir Brian's voice cracked through the tense room. "How *dare* you bring a weapon into my home! Put it up at once! Put it up, I say!"

"Not until you restrain your son!"

"Gordon," rasped Sir Brian, "I'll remind you there are ladies present! Let the creature be!"

Between his teeth Chandler said, "He should be put out like any other rubbish, sir. Only let me deal—"

"You heard me! Over here, if you please!"

Seething, Chandler went to his father's side.

De Brette said, "Your superiors will hear from me, Farrier! Such conduct is unforgivable! You have alarmed Lady de Brette! I wonder the dear soul did not swoon to see a deadly weapon brandished under her nose. Furthermore, your charges are absurd. Sir Brian is well known to have condemned his younger son's loyalty to the Stuart Cause. Gordon Chandler did all in his power to dissuade him. If that is all you can produce 'gainst them—"

"There is a great deal more, my lord. 'Tis far from my wish to have upset her ladyship, but the facts remain. Your neighbour, Mr. Poulsborough, states that you are extreme secretive about anyone venturing near your cove. One cannot but wonder what you seek to conceal. Furthermore, Mr. Gordon Chandler was only recently alleged to have been badly injured by poachers. Yet your former steward has told us that Mr. Chandler had clandestine meetings in the woods at night with several ugly-looking customers. It was, in fact, after the steward had become suspicious of these meetings and attempted to discover what was afoot, that he was dismissed on a charge of incompetence."

"That is a bare-faced lie!" raged Chandler. "Durwood was a larcenous, lazy—"

Sir Brian cut off that accusation with a gesture and interpolated, "What have you deduced from these spiteful allegations by an unpleasant neighbour and an untrustworthy steward? Who do you suppose the men in my woods to have been? And why would they have harmed my son was he in league with them in some sort of skullduggery?"

Farrier shrugged. "We will have the answers when they are safely under lock and key. There are many possible reasons. A falling out among—er, conspirators, mayhap."

"Do not wrap your accusations in clean linen," Chandler said harshly. "You mean—*thieves!* Perhaps you can also advise me of the details of our conspiracy. The invasion of a Jacobite force from France, led by my brother, perchance? A little Free Trading? Or are we your fictional wreckers?"

Farrier's eyes widened. "My dear sir, those are *your* words. Not mine. Mark this, however. On the night the *Empress of Calcutta* went aground off this coast, the new lighthouse to the north of here was dark. Someone, we believe, had tampered with the fire. Now I put it to you, Sir Brian, that if the same—er, someone had lit the logs atop *your* old tower, a ship's captain struggling through heavy seas, might well be lured—"

"I'll lure you!" Unable to contain himself any longer, Chandler fairly leapt forward.

Farrier's pistol swung up, but he was too late. With one swipe of his fist Chandler sent the pistol hurtling across the room. Farrier emitted a strangled squawk and clawed at the iron hands that were throttling him. Sir Brian swore and ran to restrain his son. De Brette made an attempt to assist. Before they could stop him, Chandler had shaken Farrier savagely, and flung him aside. "You all heard him," he panted. "With neither warrant nor proof, this fanatic invaded our home, alarmed our guests, spoke slander and libel 'gainst us, and aimed a deadly weapon at me! I'd be well justified to shoot him out of hand!"

Picking himself up from his knees, clutching at his throat, and all but incoherent with wrath, Farrier wheezed, "Vicious . . . *lunatic!* You have attacked a government officer! A s-servant of the Crown! Did you think us so stupid as . . . to fancy it merest coincidence that *she*"—he pointed a trembling finger at Ruth—"should be under your roof? The sister of a man responsible for . . . for wrecking another great ship!"

Chandler heard his father's shocked gasp and, not daring to glance at him, said mockingly, "A man must be a dedicated wrecker indeed to be willing to go down with his ship!"

"How d'you know Armitage drowned?" shrilled Farrier. "His body was never recovered. He's likely alive somewhere, living off his ill-gotten gains. Do not count on doing the same, I warn you! We know you're all tarred with the same—" He broke off and made a staggering run for the door as Chandler wrenched free and sprang for him. "You'll pay for this outrage," he gulped chokingly, his voice fading down the hall. "You'll rue the day . . . !"

Sir Brian, who had been staring at Ruth in horror, followed him, but turned a grim look on Gordon and commanded, "Stay here! You've done enough damage!"

"Vincent," gasped Lady Nadia, "I wish to go back to Town. Now!"

Chandler said, "I regret that you were subjected to such a scene, ma'am, but you must not travel in this weather. That revolting bounty hunter has no shred of evidence 'gainst us, I promise you."

She turned on him in a blaze of rage. "Are you mad? Do you know how many men the horrid creature has sent to the scaffold?"

"I tell you he has no proof! De Brette, listen to that wind. You *cannot* venture the roads tonight!"

De Brette frowned. "I think 'twould be a greater hazard to

remain in your company than to travel as far as Dover, at least. Were I in your shoes, Chandler, I'd make demned sure you've people ready to swear your lighthouse was indeed dark the night of the wreck!" He glanced at Ruth. "And that you stay clear of anyone with the *slightest* involvement in the filthy business."

"As I mean to do!" Lady Nadia hurried to the door. Glancing back, she said, "Our betrothal is at an end, Chandler! I was willing to endure a lot to become your bride, but I've no least desire to be a traitor's widow!" She tore some papers from her reticule and flung them onto the floor. "I've no more need of these. My brother will send the notice to the newspapers as soon as we reach Town. As for you"—she glanced with contempt at Ruth—"he is free—if you're fool enough to want him!"

With a flutter of skirts and a click of her high Spanish heels, she was gone, her brother nodding curtly as he walked out after her.

Chandler picked up the papers and put them on the desk. Turning to Ruth, he asked gently, "My dear, are you very frightened?"

She was very frightened indeed. "Will you please ask Dutch Coachman to take us to Dover? I must—I must leave at once."

"Yes, of course." He moved to stand before her, and said with a rueful smile, "But I wish you will believe that I am not—*we* are not wreckers."

She put out her hand, and he took it eagerly and held it in both his own. "I know you are not," she said. "And I know what you did, to try and protect me. Oh, my dear—my *very* dear!"

He bent his head and pressed a kiss on her fingers. "How did you find me out? Was I not convincing? I tried to be, but—Lord! I pray I never again have to essay such a part. 'Twas"—his voice trembled—"the very devil!"

"It was the most gallant tribute any lady could wish." She

reached up to caress his thick hair tenderly. "You played your part to perfection, my love. I—quite thought my heart would break. No—let me finish! Tummet said something that set me to thinking, and gradually I pieced it all together. I should never have been such a stupid as to believe that a gentleman as fine, as honourable as you, could have been so—" The light in his eyes was weakening her resolve and she turned quickly away, biting her lip, then said threadily, "I . . . *must* leave, Gordon!"

He stifled a sigh. "Yes. I'll send word down to Dutch. But I shall walk you back to the cottage."

Smiling through sudden tears, she asked, "Do you not want to know why I am leaving you?"

"Because of Farrier, of course. And rightly so. Indeed, I would have insisted you go away."

"I am Greville Armitage's daughter."

"Yes, love. Was it because of your brother that you concealed that particular fact?"

She blinked and her eyes fell. "Dearest one, I dared not—"

"Small wonder you did not dare!" Sir Brian came in, his face grim. "You were perfectly correct, madam, in thinking that I would not allow the sister of a disgraced murdering drunkard to so much as set foot on—"

Chandler interrupted sharply, "Sir, whatever Armitage may have done, Ruth is not to be—"

"Blamed? Must I not blame her for yet *another* lie? 'Fore God, she's proficient at it! She has neatly forged another link for your friend Farrier's chain about us. Rest assured his superiors will call it a conspiracy! No! Do not defend her to me, sir! Are you too besotted with the woman to see what peril she poses for—" He reeled suddenly, and leaned against the desk, a hand to his chest.

Chandler was at his side in an instant, one arm about his shoulders. "Father! Sit down here. All this nonsense has been too much for you. Ruth, will you please ring for—"

But glancing up he saw that Ruth had gone.

The cottage shuddered to a howling gust of wind and the curtains billowed inward. Tightening the strap around the portmanteau, Grace wailed, "But, Mrs. A., we cannot journey tonight. Hark to that! Is a *gale*, no less!"

" 'Ullo? 'Ullo? Anybody 'ome?"

The eyes of the two women met. Ruth muttered, "Tummet!"

His hair dishevelled and his coat unbuttoned, Jacob galloped into the room. "I found him, Aunty. I found him for you!"

"Bless you, my darling. Now help Miss Grace. She has already packed your clothes, but you must gather whatever else you wish to take."

The small face was a study in dismay. "Packed? Oh, Aunty, we're not goin' *away?*"

"Yes, I'm afraid we are, dear." She patted his shoulder and hurried to the door. "Be quick, if you please. We've to leave at once. I'll tell you about it later. Go now!"

With lagging feet and tragic face, he crossed to the other bedchamber, and Ruth ran down the stairs.

Enoch Tummet stood in the hall, hat in hand and curiosity on his rugged countenance. "I see yer valises 'ere, marm. 'Opping the twig, is you?"

Assuming that "hopping the twig" meant going away, she nodded and said urgently, "Mr. Tummet, is your master really a friend to Mr. Chandler? Or, if Mr. August Falcon is not, might Lieutenant Morris be?"

"They both is, marm. Though me guv wouldn't never admit as 'e was a friend to no one. What's to do?"

"Have you ever heard of a man called Burton Farrier?" She had no need to wait for a reply, his shocked expression was enough. "He was here," she said. "He has brought some most terrible charges 'gainst Sir Brian and his son. I am afraid—"

He interrupted briskly, "Say no more, Mrs. A! Me guv was afeared o' this very thing. I'm orf. You tell Mr. Gordon as me *real* guv—Cap'n Gideon Rossiter, that is—will be dahn 'ere 'fore the roach can run!"

She thanked him, struggled to close the front door against the blast that swept in when he opened it, and went up to the twins' bedchamber again.

Jacob was solemnly forcing a wooden ship into his valise. He looked up at her, sad-eyed. "Mr. Gordon carved it for me. Herc'les chewed it a bit, but . . . Oh, Aunty! *Must* we go? I like him. Lots."

Hugging him, Ruth said in an unsteady voice, "I'm afraid we have no choice, dearest. Where's Thorpe?"

He looked around blankly. "He was here . . ."

Once more someone was pounding on the front door. Her heart convulsed. Dutch Coachman? Already? When she opened the door however, a lackey stood there, clutching a flapping cloak about his finery. He handed her a folded paper, then hurried off again not waiting for an answer.

Unfolding the note, she read:

My only love—

I know you will be worrying for my father. He is resting now, and I pray he is merely over-excited, but I cannot leave him for a while.

Meanwhile, I have told Dutch to take you all to the Ship in Dover, where you must pass the night. Tomorrow, go to the Rossiter's house on Snow Hill. I've handed Dutch a letter for Gideon, and funds to provide for you. When we are clear of this nonsense I shall come for you.

Pay no attention to Farrier's rantings. He cannot

harm us. I mean to make sure that nothing ever comes between us again.

God bless you, my darling. I adore you.

Chandler

It was some minutes before Ruth was sufficiently composed to go back upstairs.

When she went into the boys' room there was still no sign of Thorpe. Nor was Jacob to be found.

With one hand on the mantel, Chandler stared into the empty hearth and listened to the rain beating in wind-driven flurries against the windows. The thought of Ruth travelling through this chaotic night was worrying. If he could only go with her. If Keasden came in time and pronounced his father in no danger, he *would* go! That fool of a groom should be back from Dover by now, surely? He glanced at the clock. Almost nine. If Farrier meant to—

The door opened. Starret said, "Your pardon, Mr. Gordon."

"Is the groom back?"

"He couldn't get through, sir. There are trees across the lane. He says the doctor's coach wouldn't be able to get by."

"Damnation! Then tell Swinton to take some men and clear the way. Keasden must come out and see Sir Brian, and it is essential that Mrs. Allington reach Dover tonight."

Starret bowed and went off again.

Chandler drove his fist against the mantel. Ruth *must* not be here if that wart Farrier came slithering back. The precious lady had known enough of trouble. And speaking of trouble, he had best get up to the top of the old lighthouse and make very sure there were no logs or any trace of a recent fire.

He ran up the stairs to his father's bedchamber. Ludley,

the elderly valet who had served Sir Brian for forty years, put a cautioning hand to his lips and tiptoed across the room to meet him.

"He's asleep, sir. His colour's much better now. I think he was just over-wrought. You know how he gets, Mr. Gordon. Is Dr. Keasden coming?"

"Soon, I hope. There are trees down, but our fellows are clearing the road now."

Bending over the bed, Chandler was relieved to find his father's distinguished features calm and composed, the breathing regular. He nodded to the valet and went to his own suite to get his cloak. Fortunately, Stoneygate was not there to register a protest as he certainly would have done. Chandler smiled faintly as he swung the cloak about his shoulders and pulled the oilskin cover over his tricorne. If dear old Stoney dreamed that his destination was the top of the lighthouse, he'd properly go into the boughs. Lord knows, it was fool-hardy to enter the crumbling old tower tonight, but he dare not wait till morning. That accursed Farrier might have troopers out here at any minute, and it was quite possible Durwood or the whistling man—or both—had indeed been responsible for the shipwreck.

He settled the hat onto his head as he ran down the stairs, and was almost to the lower hall when he heard the crash. The entire house seemed to shake. He thought, 'That was more than a tree!'

Starret was already opening the front door. Joining him, and staggered by the inrush of wind and rain, Chandler said, "What the devil was that?"

"It seemed to come from the stables, sir!"

Chandler ran, but erratically. The night was black as pitch, the rain coming down like a solid wall, and when the wind got behind it he had all he could do to stand up straight. He thought, 'God help any ships out there tonight,' and then a horse galloped straight at him. Only by flinging himself desperately to the side did he avoid being trampled. The panicked animal thundered past. Wet and muddied, Chandler fought his way to his feet and ran on.

He reached the stables and chaos. The gale had torn off part of the loft roof and the rest had collapsed, trapping horses and three grooms who had been trying to calm the frightened beasts. Two more grooms and a stableboy were tearing at the great pile of rubble with their bare hands. A lantern, swinging on a beam that was still standing, lent a bizarre and shifting light to the scene. With screaming neighs of terror, its eyes rolling, a horse, buried from the shoulders down, was lunging frenziedly to break free.

Chandler could find no sign of Oakworth. He slapped one of the rescuers on the back and his shouted enquiry was met by the information that Oakworth was under the wreckage.

"Have you heard him?"

"Yessir! They're hurt, all on 'em. But they're alive yet. The horses is fair crazed, though. One's killed."

Chandler sent the stableboy scrambling to the house with an order that every available man should come at once. And he knew there wouldn't be many. The gardeners and most of the menservants had gone to help clear the lane.

Joining the effort, he tore desperately at tiles and splintered beams. A great roof timber was bared, and he found a sturdy post that they used as a lever. It took their combined efforts, but at last the timber was rolled aside. The trapped horse plunged out and went limping off at an uneven canter. The rescuers toiled on, but no reinforcements arrived. The rain poured down on them in an unrelenting deluge, punctuated by the howling wind, the crashes of falling tree limbs, and an occasional deeper sound that told of an entire tree toppled.

They freed two more horses, and then a groom. Chandler lost track of time. He was soaked to the skin, his back ached, and his hands felt raw. On top of all else, his feet were icy cold. He blinked downward. Water was swirling around his ankles. He took down the lantern and walked a short distance up the hill, peering into the ravening darkness. By the flickering lamplight he saw white ripples, and with a gasp realized that the stream was over its banks, the usually gentle waters surging down the slope. If the main branch of the river also overflowed there would soon be a torrent of mud coming this way, and the buried men would drown before they could get them out.

He raced back to join his grooms. Another interminable period of desperate effort ended in the uncovering of Oakworth, conscious and tearfully grateful. Chandler was helping to lift him out when Starret tapped him on the shoulder. "I'll take care of him, sir." The butler handed Chandler a small package. "One of the farmhands brought this for you. Says a gentleman gave it to him and it is of vital urgency."

Chandler shoved the package in his coat pocket. "Take his arm. Gently, man! I think it's broke. Up you come, poor fellow."

The head groom was a dead weight in their arms, but he gasped that they must get the lad out, for he'd a smashed leg and was in a bad way. " 'Fraid . . . your mare, sir."

Chandler flinched. "Carefree? Is she killed?"

"She ain't trying to get up . . . like the other two."

They all reeled to a mighty gust and Chandler shouted, "Carry him over to the tack room. Not so much water there! We've to get the others out before the flood beats us!"

They strove on, battling wind and rain as well as the tangled debris while the water crept ever higher around them. But at last the other grooms and the stableboy were found and dug out, mercifully all living. Miss Nymph was freed, and hobbled off favouring one front leg. A bay was dead, but to Chandler's relief Carefree had held her head above the flood. She rallied when he called her name, and began to kick and thrash about, and when they were able to free her they had to leap for their lives to avoid her frantic bolt.

The injured were carried off to the main house. Chandler hesitated, torn between going on to the lighthouse, or attempting to divert the stream so as to protect the chapel. They might, he thought, be able to haul some of the fallen trees to act as a breakwater.

He became aware that his hand was throbbing. A large splinter had driven deep into the side of his palm. He wrenched it out, swore, and groped for his handkerchief to stop the bleeding. His fingers closed around an unfamiliar shape and he took out the package Starret had brought.

Stoneygate loomed up, carrying a lantern and looking half drowned. "Sir," he bellowed. "Atkinson just rode in from the Home Farm. A tree's down on the barn, and they can't get the cows out. Water's rising fast over there. And a chimney fell through the ceiling of Mr. Quentin's bedchamber. Caused a lot of damage and left a big hole and the rain's pouring in!"

"Is my father all right?"

"Yes. We haven't told him about this, or the farm, sir."

Chandler howled, "Don't! Take as many men to the farm as are able to go. I'll need Swinton and two others to stay and help with that broken chimney." He had wrapped the handkerchief about his hand. "Tie this for me, will you?" Stoneygate obliged, and Chandler asked, "Has Dutch taken Mrs. Allington and her party to Dover?"

The valet's answer was wiped away by a screaming gust, and the two men clung together. Breathless, Stoneygate repeated, "He cannot . . . sir. There's a troop of . . . dragoons across the drive. They won't let anyone leave the estate."

Chandler stared at him blindly. Troopers! And he hadn't gone up to the tower yet! Damn Farrier! "Very well. Get to the farm. I'll go and swear at the military."

Stoneygate grinned and reeled off, his lantern soon swallowed up by the darkness.

Clenching his fist angrily, Chandler found that he still held the small box. The butler had said it was urgent. He went back to the lantern that miraculously was still shedding its bobbing circle of light. When he unwound the outer wrapper it was whipped from his hand. He dashed rain from his eyes and peered at the box. It looked battered, as if it had come a long way. He opened it carefully, grabbed the enclosed folded paper before the wind got it, and held it to the light. The message was printed: USUAL PLACE. TONIGHT. Baffled, he took out another crumpled piece of paper and unwrapped it. Something gleamed in his hand. His heart seemed to stop. He held a ring: a uniquely crafted golden dragon with rubies for eyes. Quentin's dragon ring!

For a moment he felt frozen. "You . . . madman!" he whispered. "You stupid, damned . . . looby!" He tossed the box aside and slipped the ring into his pocket, then started down the hill. The "usual place" meant the old light, of course. It had often been their meeting place. How the devil his brother had made land in this fierce storm was beyond comprehension and, Lord knows, he couldn't have picked a worse moment to pay a call. At any time it would be risking his life, for anyone wanted for High Treason could be summarily executed by any loyal citizen, unless caught by the military, in which case a far worse death would be meted out. But here he was, home again, with dragoons patrolling the drive and that repulsive and relentless Farrier sniffing about, fairly slavering for the chance to add more lives to his ghastly toll.

Chandler began to run, slipping on sodden grasses and skidding through wet mud that clung to his boots. The rain drove into his face, the gusts battered him as if bent on preventing the progress of this puny human creature. He flung up one arm as a vague mass hurtled at him, but the flying branch sent him sprawling. He dragged himself up again, driven by the need for haste and the gnawing fear that Farrier would get there first. He *must* be in time to warn Quentin! He must beat the troopers to—

He came to a jolting halt and stood panting, his eyes fixed disbelievingly on the vague outline of the lighthouse, while fear closed like an icy shroud about him. He thought, 'Oh, my dear God!' For from the top of that ancient and long-abandoned tower rose blazing tongues of flame that sent their silent warning far out to sea. The wreckers were at their devilish work again! He strained his eyes toward France and there came another horror, for it seemed that he had caught a glimpse of another light. A feeble gleam far out on the storm-tossed seas. A gleam that rocked and heaved then disappeared, only to blink forth again. There was a ship out there! And her captain would fancy himself five miles northeast and steer southwesterly where should be deeper water; instead of which he was drifting ever closer to the treacherous banks, and the rocks off Chandler Cove!

The light would bring the dragoons. And Farrier. And Quentin was down there, somewhere. Lord, what a mess!

He began to run again, reckless now, in a mad dash to reach the cliffs and his brother, and put that damnable fire out before it lured another great ship to destruction and death.

CHAPTER XVI

he long struggle to dig out the victims at the stables had taxed Chandler's strength more than he
realized, and when at last the race to the cove
ended and the tall tower loomed up before him,
he half-fell against the door and leaned there for a minute,
fighting for the breaths that seared his lungs.

There had been no sign of Quentin as yet, but his brother
must be here somewhere. He dared not call, for fear that
others might also be nearby. The door was unlocked. So
Quentin was here. Or—someone was!

He swung the door open and then could not hold it, the
gale tearing it from his grasp and slamming it against the outer
wall. He had to fight to close it behind him. The round lower
chamber was lit by a faint glow from high in the tower. Whoever was up there might have heard the door crash open. He
crouched, waiting for a shout, or an attack, and wishing he
had a pistol or was wearing his swordbelt. He heard only the
fierce voices of the storm. If someone was still here, he might
be on the roof, feeding more logs onto the fire.

Not for a month or two had he been in this room. There
had been a clutter of old and no longer used furniture then,

which he'd told Durwood to have cleared away. The steward appeared to have neglected his orders, as usual. But as Chandler began to creep through the gloom he realized that the dark shapes he discerned were not discards but neatly piled stores. He thought, 'What the devil . . . ?' and testing one of the boxes discovered it to be heavy. It dawned on him then, that these must be the missing boxes and crates Durwood had ordered but not paid for. There were bales, too. There was printing on the boxes, but by this light he was unable to distinguish the words. A direction, no doubt. Some little private matter of business between their rascally ex-steward and—whom? Whatever the answer, it must wait. For the moment his main task was to find Quentin and put that confounded fire out!

Every nerve alert, he made his way to the foot of the rough stair that wound around the walls. The march of years and the relentless hand of the elements had taken a heavy toll on this old tower. The steps had crumbled away in places, only occasional sections of the hand-rail remained, and there were long stretches with nothing between the edge of the stair and a long drop to the stone floor. He went up carefully, with his right hand on the outer wall, feeling the tower shudder to the gusts. The rain beat through cracks to leave the surface wet and slippery. When he was about forty feet up, his boot turned on an unseen chunk of masonry and he clutched the rail. It came away in his fingers. Off balance, he teetered at the edge desperately and gave a gasp of relief when he was able to lurch to the support of the wall. He breathed a swift but grateful prayer, but he kept the iron piece of hand-rail, just in case whoever awaited him was not his brother.

There were two rooms at the top of the tower; the lower for supplies and storage, the upper where the keeper had lived. The brazier on the roof was enclosed by heavy mullioned window-walls, large sections of which had been destroyed by gunfire and harsh weather. The dome above the brazier, which was a combination of rain-shield and large chimney, was mostly intact but this wind would drive rain through the broken panes, which would not make it easy to keep the fire ablaze.

It was a hundred feet to the first room; a hundred feet that seemed to contain a thousand steps. Up he climbed, and ever up, while the gale sent gust after gust pounding at the tower and howling through the cracks. From above came occasional piercing shrieks, which he knew to be made by the air rushing through the broken panes. Impatient, he pushed himself relentlessly, refusing to slow when his legs ached and his breath came hard and painfully.

He tightened his grip on his impromptu club, prepared for combat. Here came the floor, at last. Cautiously, he lifted his head above it. The room was lit by a candle in a wall sconce fitted with a hurricane shade. There were no furnishings, nor any sight or sound of life. A brief pause to catch his breath, then he climbed on.

The glow from the upper room was brighter. A lull stilled the mighty voice of the wind, and through that brief oasis of quiet came evidence of a human presence. A man was whistling. And the tune he whistled was that old marching song called "Lillibulero."

Chandler's hand tightened on his club. Falcon had been right, then. This varmint was in league with Durwood, and had been lurking about the estate filling and storing those crates belowstairs. Readying them for collection! By God, but there would be an accounting tonight!

He had reached the top of the steps. His eyes raked the room. It was a stark chamber, but not so stark as he remembered. There was a large crate in the centre, used as a table evidently, whereon was set a basket apparently containing food, and a candelabrum with two lighted candles. There was also a half-empty bottle of what looked to be gin. On the far side of the room was a long pile of logs, and between logs and "table" was the ladder that led to the roof and the signal fire. A burly man was gathering an armful of logs. Chandler felt a surge of relief because it was not the lithe figure of his brother, but relief was supplanted by rage as the man straightened and glanced his way.

Durwood!

"You treacherous hound!" Weariness forgotten, Chandler raced across the room.

With a shout of alarm the ex-steward dropped the logs and made a grab for his pocket and the pistol that resided there, but Chandler was upon him. In his wrath he had forgotten his club, and it fell unheeded as he drove a sizzling right at Durwood's lantern jaw. The steward reeled back, snatched up a log, and hurled it. Chandler swayed aside. The log flew past and sent the candelabrum crashing to the floor. The candles went out and the room was illuminated only by the flickering glow from the open trapdoor to the roof.

Chandler sprang in to ram home a left, but then was staggered by Durwood's muscular fist.

"Perishing . . . fool," gasped the steward. "We've been waiting—"

Chandler closed again and drove home a solid uppercut that shut off the vindictive words and sent Durwood slumping to the floor.

Panting, Chandler wiped blood from a split lip. Durwood had said "we've been waiting!" And Durwood wasn't the whistling man. He'd heard that rogue talking in the woods, and it had been a cultured voice. He leapt for the steward and wrenched the pistol from his pocket.

"Do—not!"

The shout cut through a great gust that made the tower sway.

Chandler's gaze shot to the ladder.

The man backing down sideways held the rungs with one hand. With the other he aimed a pistol. He was slight, with a thin intelligent face framed by windblown powdered hair. It was a face from his school days and, astonished, he exclaimed, "Poinier!"

The man on the ladder smiled mirthlessly. "You've a good memory, old boy. Step back."

Chandler said, "You're no traitor! At school you were—"

"At school I was an idealistic young fool." Henry Poinier held the pistol aimed steadily at Chandler's heart, and there was a grim set to his mouth that spoke of unwavering purpose.

Accepting that this acquaintance of his youth was indeed a smuggler, or worse, Chandler moved back. "You've maggots in your head," he said scornfully. "If your friends follow this light they'll never reach land safely, and your cargo—"

"Not mine, Gordon." Poinier stepped down and faced Chandler squarely. "Yours. And a second wreck that will be credited to your account. Another nail in the coffin, I'm afraid."

Chandler's hands clenched into tight fists. "So you're part of this unholy League of Jewelled Men, are you? Lord, what has happened to you? Does it not weigh with you that there may be women on that ship?"

"It does. Children too, unfortunately, for she's an East Indiaman out of Ceylon."

"An East Indiaman would be more like to drop anchor at Southampton."

"Ah, but destinations can be changed, and this vessel was—ah, diverted, you see. Ostensibly"—again the faint, cynical smile—"by the weather."

"Then your League is responsible for all the wrecks! You've agents who sabotage the charts or buy the officers, is that it? And you give not a tinker's damn for the lives of passengers and crew! My God! How can you be so pitiless? How many ships have you destroyed? How many innocent lives sacrificed to your greed and—"

"You would have a difficult time proving that, Chandler."

The voice came from behind him, and he whipped around to face Burton Farrier, wet and windblown, but with his eternal grin wider than usual, and his pale eyes glowing with triumph. "As hard a time," he went on, "as you will have trying to prove that the goods downstairs are not those you stole when you wrecked the *Empress of Calcutta!* But you look shocked. Did you not see her name stencilled on the crates? Every one was part of the cargo of that unhappy vessel—or so it will appear. My troopers are going to discover that undeniable proof of your crimes when they come. And I shall have caught you in the act of building the fire to draw another ship to her doom."

Shaken, Chandler said defiantly, "No one will believe it. As if I'd be so stupid as to set the fire. It can be seen for miles and would bring the law down upon us before—"

"Do not take me for a fool, sir. The light can be seen for many miles, true. But many miles out to *sea.* Your estate is vast and there are hills inland and to the west also that block the light. It was for that very reason it was not rebuilt when—" Farrier stopped speaking as another gust hurled against the tower, causing it to sway and creak alarmingly. "Good God! Poinier, call Durwood down. He must go and signal my troop."

"He's already down." Poinier gave a disdainful gesture, and Farrier stepped around the table and scowled at the steward's sprawled form. Poinier added grudgingly, "Chandler always was handy with his fives."

"Much good it will do him. Is the fellow dead?"

"He's been heavy with the bottle and Chandler hit hard."

"Drunken imbecile! Well, since you allowed it, you will have to take his place. I left a burning brand in the bracket at the foot of the steps. Take it with you and wave it when you reach the first pathway. The troop will come at once."

"If the wind doesn't blow it out."

"Then *you* shall have to run and fetch them! And don't be too long about it. Your last assignment was not a great success and you've used up your quota of failure."

Poinier said sullenly, "My cousin Trethaway died in that curst fiasco. And despite all the Squire's cunning, Glendenning escaped the axe. Your own success rate slipped badly there, eh, dear friend?"

While the two rogues were preoccupied with their quarrel Chandler had edged closer to the log pile. Now, moving with stealthy caution, he reached for his fallen club. He had almost grasped it when Durwood rolled over, snatched it up and howled, "Hey!"

"Another move and I shoot!" screeched Farrier. "I'd just as soon finish you now, Chandler!"

To defy that steady pistol would be suicidal. Reluctantly, Chandler straightened.

Farrier said, "You see what happens! Curse you for an argumentative fool, Poinier! Go!"

"Why the devil did you not just bring the dragoons with you?"

"Because I had to be sure Chandler was found *here* of course! He could have gone off to the farm with the rest of the men, or sent someone else here."

"What, after he saw that ring? Hah! He and his brother are thick as thieves!"

Chandler stiffened, wondering how these varmints had got their hands on Quentin's ring.

"Why d'you think we went to so much trouble to get it, idiot?" Farrier almost screamed with rage, "Damn your eyes! *Will* you go?"

"No, I will not! Send Durwood. He's got sufficient brains for that task."

"He's half drunk and liable to fall down the stairs."

Durwood had hauled himself clumsily to his feet. "I ain't too drunk . . . to even . . . score," he said thickly. He back-handed Chandler in a savage swipe that knocked him off his feet.

For a dazed minute the room was a whirl of flickering light and echoingly distant voices. When his head cleared, Poinier had gone and Farrier was shouting at Durwood. He lay very still, trying to organize his sluggish thoughts. If Poinier had gone after the troopers there was very little time left. The plotters were evidently not disposed to wait until the ship ran onto the rocks, though how they hoped to retrieve their precious cargo after the troopers came was a puzzle. Perhaps they would be satisfied with having incriminated the Chandlers as wreckers. Perhaps the cargo would be written off as fair exchange for the opportunity to acquire Lac Brillant after it was confiscated and sold. But—

A boot rammed into his side. He had to grit his teeth to choke back an involuntary cry, but managed to smother the sound, and allowed himself to roll loosely. A shadow fell across him.

Durwood growled, "He's fair and far out. When I knock 'em down, they stay down, and I owe this top-lofty Buck more'n that."

Chandler nerved himself to withstand another kick.

Farrier said curtly, "That's enough! He may be down, but he's a gentleman and fought bravely. If you feel so spry you can go up and throw some more logs on the fire, and see if the ship's on the rocks yet."

"You think you can manage him if he comes round?"

"He may be handy with his fists, but fists cannot outrun a pistol ball. Do as you're told."

Chandler heard Durwood's resentful grunt as he gathered some logs. Then came the squeak of the treads of the ladder. This would be his best chance, while he had only Farrier to deal with. He opened his eyes a crack. He lay between the "table," and the steps. There was something on the floor near him; an object he could not at first distinguish. He realized then that it was the candelabrum. Farrier had either not been willing to take the time to pick it up, or had not seen it, for the flickering glow from the fire above them threw areas of the room into deep shadow.

He could not locate "the King's officer," and of necessity moved his head slightly.

At once the purring voice said, "Well, well. Our valiant

patriot is returning. Wake up, Chandler. You'd not want to miss meeting your brother."

Chandler rolled onto his back. Farrier was sitting on the piled logs. In a very faint voice, he said, "You're bluffing. Quentin's not . . . within miles."

"Very true. But the ring brought you just where we wanted you. A good plan, eh?"

So they'd found another dragon ring. Thank God! His hand inched toward the candelabrum. Still in that faint voice, he murmured, "Not one devised by . . . a man of your . . . level of intelligence, I think." His fingertips touched the coldness of brass.

"Never underestimate my level of intelligence, Chandler. Many better men than you have paid with their heads for—"

Chandler had gripped the heavy candelabrum. He sat up and, hurling it with all his strength, shouted, "Then this is for *them*, you slimy head-hunter!"

Farrier jerked his pistol up, but the heavy candelabrum whizzing at his face startled him, deflecting his aim. Still, he fired, the shot thudding into the table.

Chandler had sprung to his feet and with a shove sent the roof ladder crashing down. No coward, Farrier seized his pistol by the barrel and flailed it club-like as Chandler rushed him. Chandler blocked the blow with his left arm, and smashed his right fist into Farrier's middle. As he straightened out the bounty hunter with a well-placed left to the jaw, he had the impression that someone had run across the room. Farrier went down hard. Durwood had certainly heard all that! Chandler whipped around. Durwood was leaning down through the roof aperture sure enough, but his pistol was aimed at the steps. From the corner of his eye, Chandler saw who was coming. "No! Don't!" he shouted. But Durwood's finger was tightening on the trigger. Desperate, Chandler threw himself between that deadly muzzle and the person coming up the steps.

The ball that would have caught that most unexpected new

arrival in the head, struck Chandler like a gigantic hammer. This time, the blackness was immediate, and absolute.

Ruth hunched her shoulders against the screaming force of the gale and stumbled breathlessly onto the relative protection of the cottage porch. The boys would be home by now, surely? She had searched and searched, screaming their names, no longer caring who heard, but to no avail. Almost, she had been killed in the woods, for she had leaned wearily against a big elm, heard an ear-splitting creak above her, and had run madly as a dark mass came crashing down. The tips of a branch had raked her skirts, telling her how narrowly she had escaped and increasing her dread that the twins may have gone to their favourite retreat for a last visit and been struck by one of the many trees that had fallen.

She opened the front door, managed to close it, and ran into the kitchen. Her calls were answered only by the outer uproar. Distracted, she lit a candle and hurried upstairs just in case someone might have returned and was sleeping. The rooms were empty. A pane of glass had shattered in her own bedchamber, and the curtains billowed into the room. Shielding her candle flame she was appalled by the sight of her reflection in the mirror. Her hair had come down and straggled in soaked tangles beside her tired face. 'As if it matters,' she thought, and hurrying back into the hall gave a cry of relief as there came a crash and a bluster of wind from downstairs. The front door had been opened.

"Mrs. A.? Are you come home?"

"Yes! Yes!" She ran down the stairs.

Grace was almost as wet and muddy as Ruth. She had just come from the main house, and she shook her head dismally. "They're not there, dear Mrs. A. I went to all three buildings. Never look so scared, though. They're safe somewhere—I knows it!"

Ruth asked worriedly, "Have you heard anything of Mr. Gordon?"

"I heard he done wonders down at the stables, getting out the men what was trapped when the whole lot was blown down. Mr. Swinton and Mr. Starret are nailing boards up in one of the bedchambers where a chimney come right through the roof. Some of the men went to clear the road, and the rest are helping at the Home Farm. Perhaps Mr. Gordon's with them."

"Yes. What about Sir Brian? Is he all right?"

"Up and about, he is. Giving orders right and left, and keeping folks' spirits up. They've got their hands full at the main house. One of the maids was cut by flying glass, and the scullery boy was knocked down the cellar steps when someone opened the back door and the wind caught him. A tree came down by East House and broke some windows, but . . . Oh, Mrs. A.! Did *ever* you see such a awful storm? Like the end of the world! I only hope . . ."

They stared at each other.

Distraught, Ruth cried, "*Wherever* can they be? Do you think they've run away? Jacob was dreadfully upset when I told him we must leave."

Grace thought it was exactly what the twins might have done. She said sadly, "Master Thorpe told me that Sir Brian had said he should go for a sail one day, and Mr. Gordon had promised Jacob he'd take him up to the top of the old lighthouse. Both the lads was wild to go up there. But, surely, in this storm they'd not have gone all that way?"

"Oh, I pray not! Yet, if they thought it was their last chance, they might."

Grace nodded. "They took Being. Did you notice his cage was gone? Mayhap that's it! The little thing ran off, and they're looking for him."

"But they've been gone for hours, and it is so dreadful outside." Ruth bit her lip, then said resolutely, "I'll go down towards the cove, just in case they *have* tried to get into the lighthouse. Please find Sir Brian and ask if he can spare anyone to help us search."

She stopped only long enough to wrap a dry cloak and hood about her, and then hurried out into the storm once more.

For a moment Jacob was too petrified with terror to move. The smoke drifted from the muzzle of Durwood's pistol, then was whipped away by the wind that shrieked from the open trapdoor in the roof.

Durwood growled ferociously, "Danged brat! Who the devil are you?"

Jacob's eyes were still glued to Chandler. He had fallen on his back and lay with both arms wide-tossed. Out of breath from climbing all those steps, Jacob gasped, "You've hurted him . . . bad!"

"He's a wrecker. He'd be hanged anyway. Now you go on. Get out!"

"But—but he's bleeding. If we don't help him, he'll die!"

"What're you doing up here, boy? Come to see the fire he made on the roof, did you?"

Jacob knelt beside Chandler and stared in horrified fascination at the slowly widening stain on the white cravat. He began to feel sick, but gulped, "Please, sir. Help him."

Perhaps that small frightened face galled Durwood. He snarled savagely, "You'd best run, my lad, if you know what's good for you, else I might throw you off the top!"

Jacob looked across the crate "table" at the big man with the red face and angry frown. 'Papa,' he thought, trying not to shake so, 'was a brave gentleman. An' I must be one, as well.' He waited out a bellow of wind, then said through chattering teeth, "You're . . . a bad man."

"Well that's done it, that has! Now I'm *going* to throw you down the stairs." Durwood took a menacing step closer to the child.

"You couldn't." Jacob drew a shuddering breath. "Afore you could touch me, I'd of jumped behind you."

Durwood picked up the gin bottle and said with a grin, "That'd be a good jump, that would. I'd like to see it. Do it now."

"If I was a real boy I 'spect I couldn't. But I'm not a real boy. An' I don't need to jump. I c'n change myself from here to there. Look! There I am!"

Durwood uptilted the gin bottle. When he lowered it, the boy was gone. A screech sounded behind him. With a gasp he jerked his head around. There was the boy, beyond the wood pile!

"Here!" gasped Durwood, setting the bottle down hastily and fixing Thorpe with a bleary-eyed stare. "How the hell d' you do that?"

"I'm a b'ginning wizard. I c'n do lotsa things. Mean things, if I like. I c'n go back over there so quick you'd never see me go."

Durwood rubbed his eyes. "No, you can't. You're a lying brat is what you are."

Thorpe put his arms straight out at the sides, waved them up and down, and sank while uttering a screeching howl.

The sound broke through Chandler's dulled consciousness. He opened his eyes, and stared blurrily at the wall and two words chalked there in large letters: *Châtiment deux!*

Durwood was also having difficulties with his vision, the result of too many samples from the gin bottle. It seemed to him that the boy melted. Incredulous, he took a cautious step toward the wood pile. A louder screech rang out behind him, and he jerked around to find the horrid brat leering at him from beyond the crate. Once, he had known a man who'd come under the evil eye of a witch, whereof he had been trapped in a burning house, and died. Beginning to be afraid, he backed away, peering at Jacob apprehensively. Then he wet

his lips and lurched forward again. "Y-you can't make a f-fool
'f me," he declared unsteadily, and took up his pistol. "I'll
brain you. Then we'll see how quick y'can move!"

To Chandler, puzzled on several counts, this conversation
was ever more curious. He supposed he must be dreaming,
and tried to get up. The immediate and excruciating stab of
pain high in his chest took his breath away, but restored
memory with a rush. What was going on in this room was
beyond him, but he had no business lounging about while that
accursed fire still blazed on the roof. His right arm made it
clear that it was best left alone, but he strove doggedly to get
the other elbow under him.

He saw Jacob then, crouching down beside him. He also
saw Jacob pop up across the room. He shut his eyes hard, then
looked again.

Jacob over there. Jacob crouching here.

He was either in the grip of delirium, or there were indeed
more things in heaven and earth than are dreamt of . . . But
yet—Jacob was not actually disappearing as he claimed to do.
He merely popped up when the other— The *other!* 'Oh, my
Lord!' he thought. 'There's another one!'

At once everything fell into place. This was why "Jacob"
had shown such strange personality shifts. This was why the
boy loathed eggs one day, and loved 'em the next! Twins! His
naughty love had hidden not one, but *two* nephews! And
whether one, or two, they were only small boys. And here was
he, half knocked out of time, one arm useless, and a drunken
murderer to deal with!

Jacob had popped up again, but the scared eyes glanced to
Chandler and relief dawned in them. "Oh, sir!" he said softly.
"Whatever shall I do?"

Chandler fought his way to the point that he could lean his
back against the crate and thus free his left arm. "Try to kick
that bar over to me," he whispered. "And—and keep him
talking . . . if you can."

Jacob's foot groped out toward the fallen piece of stair

railing as he cried shrilly. "You better stop, or I'll turn you into a hedgehog!"

Durwood had swung around again and at this he paused, irresolute. "I don't b'lieve you!"

"I'll make myself into one, an' show you!"

"See!" screamed Thorpe, as Jacob ducked.

Durwood turned but saw no boy this time. Instead, a hedgehog wandered about on the logs. It was the last straw. With a hoarse cry of terror, he staggered back.

Gripping his makeshift club, Chandler dragged himself to his knees.

Durwood's gaitered legs passed the crate. Chandler shoved the stair railing between them. With a startled yell, Durwood tripped, but fought to regain his balance. Chandler lurched to his feet and shoved hard, and the steward reeled back and disappeared through the aperture beside the steps. They heard his shocked cry, abruptly cut off.

The room rippled before Chandler's eyes. He reached out blindly.

Jacob sprang to support him. "Lean on me, sir!"

"An' me!" cried Thorpe, coming up on the other side.

"Don't—touch my arm!" gasped Chandler.

Thorpe looked frightened, then gripped the top of Chandler's breeches.

Between them, they manoeuvred to the steps and peered downward. Durwood lay in a huddled heap on the floor of the storage room.

In a quivering voice Jacob asked, "Is he—"

"I don't know," said Chandler. "Are you Jacob, or . . . ?"

"Yessir. That's Thorpe. He's my twin."

Chandler peered at the two blurred faces. "Rascals," he said thickly and sagged against the wall.

Thorpe gave a squeal of fright.

Jacob stammered, "We b-better tie up your hurt, sir!"

The wound was bleeding, but only sluggishly. Probably, thought Chandler, because the ball was still in him. To expect the twins to tear up shirts, then struggle to tie so difficult a bandage and to tie it tight enough to be of use would be asking a great deal of two little boys. And would likely be just a waste of time. If he moved fast, he might be able to hold out long enough to accomplish his purpose. The boys helped him back to the crate, and he sat on it and took two healthy swallows from the bottle. He wasn't fond of gin, and it made him cough, which was racking, but he began to feel less faint. He looked at the two so similar, so scared young faces, and managed a grin.

"A fine time you've had . . . with us, haven't you? Well, now you're going to have to help me, twins. I've got to get up on the roof. The fire has to be put out, or . . . or another ship will go down."

They looked at each other doubtfully, but agreed to go up with him.

He knew what the wind would be like up there, and with the glass walls broken away in spots, and the flames blowing about . . . And they were so small. At least Farrier still lay where he had fallen. Obliging of the beastly fellow. Chandler said, "No. Thank you, but I want you to . . . to find something to tie up that bad man over there. Get his arms behind him if you can, and tie his thumbs together. Use the riband from his hair."

"There's some rope over by the logs," said Thorpe.

"Good! Use that for his feet. Tie your knots tight as you can. Then, go down and do the same to the other man." They looked frightened, and he said, "You've been very brave. Do your best, then run and bring help. You understand?"

They nodded obediently. Chandler took another pull at the bottle, restrained a cough, and felt stronger.

The boys helped him to get the ladder propped up again. His knees were shaky, and the slightest movement of his head sent such a lance of pain through his shoulder that he thought the shot must have broken his collar-bone. But he'd manage. He must manage. He looked down at the twins. "Be as quick as you can," he said and added with a quivering smile, "Good luck, you scamps!"

He climbed the ladder one rung at a time, hanging on with his left hand, swearing in anguish with every step. When he reached the top, the wind sent his hair streaming, and heat scorched at his face. The logs were piled high in the great brazier. Flames and sparks shot at him when he clambered up, and he retreated until his back touched what was left of the glass walls. Looking about, he located an iron stand containing a heavy pair of tongs and a poker. If he could get the logs out of the brazier and shove them through a hole in the wall . . . He managed to pick up the tongs, but his attempt to use his right hand to grip the poker was useless, and the pain made him feel sick and so dizzy that he abandoned the effort. He'd have to contrive with one hand.

He advanced on the brazier determinedly. The top log was fairly easy, for it was balanced on the others, and above the iron cage. He got the tongs under it, and on the second try it rolled onto the floor. He made his way around the edge of the roof, but the gale caught him, almost knocking him into the flames. He fought to keep upright, then barely avoided tumbling through a yawning hole in the window-wall where the glass was gone from top to bottom. It was a good thing the boys hadn't come up, he thought. But this was where he could dispose of the logs. It was tricky, but at last he'd rolled the blazing log to the hole and with a lucky break in the wind, was able to send it plunging down.

"Look out below," he muttered foolishly, and then peered into the night, straining his eyes seaward. Gradually, he was able to distinguish the lights of the ship. Closer inshore this time. God send they would realize that this was the wrong light, but it was taking so long to put the confounded fire out. Hurry! Hurry!

The next two logs were much more difficult. The tongs were hot now, and his hand was scorched. When he went back for log number four, the wind shifted and he had to again retreat from licking tongues of flame. He advanced once more and gave a feeble cheer when the fourth log was despatched. But there were still four left, and they were big fellows, and it was damnably hard to maneouvre them over the edge of the brazier. It seemed to take forever to get number five upright. The smoke blew into his eyes momentarily blinding him and he blinked tears away, waiting till the wind slackened. With his next effort the accursed log fell flat once more and he groaned in frustration. If *only* he could move his right arm!

Rain sheeted through the break in the wall, drenching him. It was welcome, but infuriating to think that with all that water only a few feet above he could not get it in here to put out this stupid fire. It seemed so unfair that when they wanted the fire to burn in the book room, it so often persisted in going out . . . He was getting terribly tired, and Lord above, but his shoulder hurt like fury. He said sternly, "Buck up, Gordie! You've only just been hit, don't be a weakling. Old Quentin rode for days—wasn't it days?—with a musket ball through him!" If Quentin could do it . . . Aha! He'd worked the confounded log upright again. Now if he could just get round to the other side of the brazier . . . but the beastly object was . . . dodging about so . . .

Horrified, he found that he was on his knees. "Get up, you idiot!" But he couldn't get up. He couldn't even lift the tongs any more. Only four more logs, but they were burning merrily . . . sending out a fine light. Just four more . . . and he was weak as any kitten. He'd failed . . . Failed his father, and all those poor folk on the . . .

Hands were pulling at him. He peered dazedly into a mud-streaked face with wet hair plastered about it, and two great eyes, tearful, tired, yet full of joy.

"Ruth!" he gasped. "But . . ."

"I'm here, my darling. How wonderfully well you have done! And—oh! your poor arm!"

"Logs," he mumbled weakly. "Ruth, I—I can't—"

She blinked tears away, but held the gin bottle to his lips. "Drink up, lushy one!"

He did. And she had come to him! Her dear arm was about him, and the love in her eyes made it all worthwhile and so heartened him that he was able to get up.

Between them, they conquered the last four logs. Ruth threw down the poker, flung her arms about Chandler's unsteady figure, and they both cheered.

Afterwards, he was never quite sure whether he climbed down the ladder, or fell down it, but somehow they were all the way to the foot of the tower, and Jacob and Thorpe, shouting with excitement, were rushing to hug them.

But in that moment of victory, came crushing defeat, for Chandler's dimming eyes lit on the piled boxes and crates. "Oh, my God!" he groaned. "I'd forgot all this!"

Supporting him as best she could, Ruth asked, "Whatever is it?"

"Smuggled goods from . . . from the last wreck. Durwood left it all here to incriminate us when the dragoons come!"

"Oh, heavens! We must hide it!"

He sighed helplessly. He was much too weak now to lift even one of those heavy crates. Nor could Ruth and two small boys hope to move it all, even if there was anywhere to hide it. Poinier would arrive at any second with Farrier's dragoons. It was remarkable, in fact, that they hadn't come before this.

His heart contracted as the outer door crashed open.

Through the maelstrom of wind and rain came a voice raised in anger. "I'll tell you what, Chandler, you've an odd way of thanking your friends for services rendered! Your blasted flaming log damn near brained me!"

A very wet August Falcon stamped inside, shaking water from his tricorne. Following, in a soaking wet uniform came a dragoon . . . only it was Jamie Morris!

"What . . . the deuce . . . ?" said Chandler faintly.

Morris battled the door shut, whereupon it slammed open

again, and Sir Brian came in, accompanied by the Reverend Mr. Aymer carrying a lantern.

Sir Brian peered around the dim room. "Is that you, Gordon? What the devil's going on here? Are you responsible for that damnable fire on the—"

"He is responsible for putting it out," interrupted Ruth, irked.

"Tossed burning logs down onto people's heads," grumbled Falcon.

"This—this room is full of smuggled goods, sir," said Chandler through stiffly uncooperative lips. " 'Fraid I wasn't able to—"

"Full of—*what?*" roared Sir Brian.

"Cargo, stolen from the *Empress of Calcutta*," said Ruth. "It was brought here by your horrid steward, who nigh killed Gordon."

Sir Brian said in a changed voice, "Gordie? Are you all right, boy?"

"Just . . . a trifle damaged," muttered Chandler, wanting very much to lie down.

"He is not 'a trifle damaged,' " Ruth contradicted. "He has been shot and has been bleeding for hours!"

Sir Brian ran forward. "Good God!"

"Jupiter!" gasped Morris. "Either I am gone demented—"

"About time you admitted it," said Falcon.

"—or there are *two Jacobs!*" finished Morris.

Four startled pairs of eyes turned to the twins.

"Has it occurred to anyone that these goods can put your heads at risk?" enquired Aymer in an unprecedentedly crisp voice. "With the estate crawling with dragoons, I'd think it logical to tuck it all away somewhere."

Sir Brian, one arm about his drooping son, said bitterly, "Logical, but impossible, alas. Where the devil could we hide it in time?"

"I know where," said Ruth.

Chandler sighed, and lay down.

one?" said Chandler, bewildered. "All of 'em?"

"Neither mourned nor forgotten," said Sir Brian grimly.

"The troopers won't be forgot," put in Morris. "They were a great help out at your Home Farm, old boy."

Falcon said dryly, "Which you may live to regret, you block."

They had all gathered in the sunny bedchamber on this bright morning and positioned themselves on or near the bed where Chandler lay propped up with pillows, his right shoulder heavily bandaged and the arm strapped to his side. Ruth's chair was drawn very close against the bed so that she might hold his hand. Sir Brian sat on the side of the bed, Morris was perched on the end, Falcon leaned against the clothes press, and Jacob and Thorpe sat cross-legged on the floor with Hercules between them, panting happily from one to the other, but keeping a watchful eye on his god.

"Why should I regret it?" asked Chandler, flinching slightly as he forgot and turned his head.

"Not you," said Falcon. "Morris. The birdwit was in

uniform and they had no choice but to follow orders he had no legal right to give."

Chandler stared at Morris in helpless confusion.

"Never fret, dear boy," said Morris. " 'Tis simplicity itself. Unhappily, it took us two days to get back to Town, and I suddenly recollected that m'third sister was getting married at St. George's. They all want to be married in Hanover Square nowadays, y'know. I'd promised to attend in uniform, so I had to rush to my flat and change clothes while Falcon went off to tell Rossiter how matters stood here."

Falcon took up the tale. "I wasn't able to tell Ross, unfortunately. He was gone frippering down to Promontory Point to see about buying his papa's estate back from Rudi Bracksby. I was on my way home when I caught a glimpse of a very slippery customer named Poinier. We know he's a member of"—he checked, looked at Sir Brian, and reworded—"of an ugly set, and he was going into a house—" Another pause, his glance this time turning to Ruth. "Well, never mind all that. I sent a boy running to St. George's with a note for Morris, and—"

"And I joined him as soon as I could get away," put in Morris. "When Poinier left the house, we followed him. Thought for sure the fellow would just go to his lodgings, but instead his coach turned onto London Bridge. He was travelling the Dover Road when we lost him in that abominable hurricane."

"We came here," resumed Falcon, "just on the off-chance this might be his destination. We were much delayed, of course. Frankly, I doubted we'd ever get through, for the roads were in a most ghastly mess. We had to walk the last mile, and when we reached your gates there was a troop of dragoons hanging about and generally making themselves useless. And then, who should come running up but our lost quarry."

Chandler said, "That must have been when Poinier had been sent down to fetch the dragoons to catch me with all my guilty loot. How ever did you manage to keep him from doing so?"

"I?" Falcon drawled, "But my dear fellow, I'd not dream of interfering with any order dear Farrier had sent forth."

Morris gave a snort of mirth. "This Poinier fellow started ranting and raving about traitors atop the old lighthouse, and said the troopers were to go with him at once. I knew he was a bad man, and it was likely he had some murky meanness in hand, so I marched over." He grinned. "Falcon yelled Poinier's name together with a few home truths, and Poinier ran like a rabbit."

"He really did work up to a fair rate of speed, didn't he?" said Falcon, amused. "In spite of that foul wind."

"Your head gardener came begging for help at the Home Farm," said Morris, "so I ordered the troopers to go over there. The sergeant was a trifle reluctant, but I outranked him of course, and off they went."

Chandler said, "I wondered why Poinier never came back. What became of him?"

Falcon looked pious. "Who can say?"

"*You* can say," declared Morris. "If ever I saw such a fellow! You know perfectly well you ran him into the stream."

"I did nothing of the sort! I merely wanted to ask him a few civilized questions, and he preferred to have a swim. Most odd fellow."

They all laughed, and Hercules barked and wagged his tail companionably.

Morris said, "We had no wish to be judged unpatriotic, so we decided to investigate this 'traitor at the lighthouse' business."

"And encountered a baptism of fire," grumbled Falcon.

Chandler moved restlessly. "Yes, but last night you said—"

"That was two nights ago," interrupted Sir Brian. "You slept the clock round, my boy."

"Two—days?" said Chandler, astounded. "And you're still here, Falcon?"

"Not by choice, I assure you."

"What you are is rude," Morris informed him. "Just the same, Gordie, we really should be getting back to Town. If that tempest struck London as hard as it struck here, Rossiter's house on Snow Hill is likely in Hampstead Heath now. And I worry for Miss Katrina, stuck out there in the wilds of Great Ormond Street."

Falcon looked thunderous, and Sir Brian intervened to explain that the roads were still blocked in all directions. "There's not been a single Portsmouth Machine get through from Town for almost three days now, and riders are carrying the mails. What with trees down and mud everywhere, travel is well nigh impossible."

Ruth, who had been watching Chandler's face, inserted gently, "I think you are tired now. We will leave you in peace."

"No!" He clung to her hand as she tried to withdraw it. "You cannot go yet. I want to know what happened to Farrier, and Durwood, and all that illicit cargo. And how it is I am not in chains and en route to the Tower."

Sir Brian smiled. "I think we must humour the poor fellow, my dear. Of course, we don't know with any certainty, Gordon, but we believe that your unpleasant acquaintances must not have been able to retrieve sufficient containers from the wreck of the *Empress of Calcutta* in February. So Durwood ordered some made, filled them with goods, and marked them in such a way that they'd appear to be part of the original cargo. Then, they had to wait for bad weather, which they certainly got this week."

" 'Twas a neat ploy," said Falcon. "Had those boxes been found I'd not give much for your chances of convincing anyone they were not just what they seemed to be—wreckers' loot."

Chandler said, "Yes, well I know all that. But how on

earth did you get rid of all the beastly stuff? Or did the troopers never come at all?"

"Oh, they came," said Sir Brian. "The fire on the tower had been reported. But luckily, by the time they reached us, all our ill-gotten gains were out of sight."

"But—*where*, sir? There was no hiding place, I think."

"So I thought, also. What I'd forgot was that even in the olden times lighthouses had of necessity to have very deep cellars to prevent the wind bowling them over. Ours is so old and so primitive, I thought the foundations we could see only went down a few feet. But—well, I'll let our lovely lady explain."

Ruth said eagerly, "When I finished cleaning the fresco to the foot of the lighthouse, I found it was most definitely taller than it now appears to be, and that there was in fact another doorway a floor below the main one. I wanted so to tell you of my discovery, Gordon. But then that horrid Mr. Farrier came and drove all else from my mind. I suppose that down through the centuries there were floods, perhaps such as we have just experienced, and gradually the mud built up around the base of the tower and weeds and shrubs grew, and because it was no longer used, in time people forgot there had ever been cellar rooms. At all events, the lower door was red originally, and is clearly shown in the painting. That patch of blue you uncovered is a lady's gown. She is standing by the door."

Sir Brian broke in, "When Mrs. Ruth told us of it, we hunted about. We couldn't discover the outer door, of course; it must be buried deep. But we did find a trapdoor leading down into the cellar, and with two more cellars below! You may believe we all went to work, and between us, the illicit cargo was packed away just in time."

Jacob said proudly, "Me an' Thorpe helped!"

Sir Brian smiled at the boys. "You did, indeed!"

"What happened when the troopers came?" asked Gordon.

Morris said, "We told 'em Durwood had set the fire and shot you down when you tried to stop him." He glanced from Ruth to the twins and said with delicacy, "Truth, after all. And he won't argue the point."

"Broke his neck," remarked Falcon, less tactfully.

Morris groaned disgustedly. " 'Let go of a grindstone, and it'll keep turning for a minute'!"

Chandler overrode Falcon's impassioned response. "But what about Farrier? Has he brought charges 'gainst us?"

Ruth chuckled.

Sir Brian said, "Your friends pretended to help him, instead of which they got so much gin down his throat that he was lushy drunk when the troopers arrived. I rather suspect he is disgraced, and his testimony will be regarded as questionable. Especially without the proofs he needed." He stood. "And that's all you'll get today, Gordie. Mrs. Ruth is right, you look very tired. Come along you two young rascals. We've much work to do at the stables."

The twins sprang up, Hercules gamboling excitedly about all three.

"An' out at the Home Farm, sir?" asked Thorpe hopefully.

Sir Brian ruffled his curls and winked at Ruth. "Most decidedly out at the farm."

He went over and shook hands with Falcon and Morris. "I am all too aware of how much I owe you, gentlemen. We have had a very narrow escape, and your part in it will never be forgotten. I hope you will make Lac Brillant your home whenever you feel inclined for a change of air."

Morris turned brick red and mumbled incoherently.

Falcon bowed, but said nothing.

Hercules followed the twins, then darted to the bed and sprang to lie at the god's feet.

Sir Brian turned back. "I'm damned proud of you, Gordie. But you've twice put the fear of God into me! Please do not become over-tired. I doubt I could stand another fright."

A faint tinge of colour brightened Chandler's wan face. He smiled speechlessly. Sir Brian nodded and closed the door.

"Phew!" gasped Morris, then recoiled as Ruth ran to hug him.

"Thank you! Thank you! You have been so good." Amused by his shy blush, she stepped back. "There. I have done embarrassing you. But when you see Miss Rossiter, will you please tell her we shall visit her just as soon as we return to London?"

Chandler said, "Oh, we'll see Miss Rossiter before that, I fancy."

Ruth turned and looked at him wonderingly.

Falcon said, "Do not interrupt, Chandler. 'Tis my turn."

With a little gurgle of laughter Ruth gave him his hug, but he pressed a kiss upon her cheek. "I'm quite safe," he declared airily. "He's too levelled to attack me."

"Do not be too sanguine on that point," argued Chandler. "Keasden says my collar-bone is cracked, not broken, and I'll be able to deal with you in jig time."

"Do not get his hopes too high," warned Morris. "The silly fellow will be arranging a meeting!"

"Speaking of which," said Falcon. "We've a meeting to arrange in Town. I hope!" He nodded meaningfully to Chandler, and followed Morris.

Ruth went back to the side of the bed. Chandler reached out, and she put her cool hand into his warm one. "I thought as much," she said. "You have done entirely too much chattering, sir, and—"

He tugged imperiously, and she sat down. "No, Gordon— really you must rest."

"What I must do is know about that ship. Is she safe?"

"Oh, yes. Entirely thanks to you, my dear. And now, go to sleep!"

"No," he said drowsily. And slept.

The afternoon was mild, but the windows were closed, and it was very quiet in Chandler's private parlour, each of those assembled there seemingly lost in contemplation.

Sir Owen Furlong, a tall man in the early thirties, light of hair and complexion, turned his pleasant blue eyes to Chandler who, clad in shirt and breeches, shared the sofa with him. "Are you sure you're well enough to be out of bed, Gordie? Three days is awfully soon, I'd think, and that shoulder must be a deuced nuisance."

"Thank you, but I'm quite comfortable," lied Chandler.

Morris, wearing civilian dress, looked up from *The Spectator* and said with a grin, "He likely wouldn't feel it if it did trouble him, Owen. He is conscious only of a certain lovely widow."

"Here they come!" Falcon sprang from his chair and turned to the door.

Chandler said, "I hope they've been successful."

Standing also, Morris remarked, " 'Hope is a good breakfast, but a bad supper.' "

"Why in the name of sanity I put myself within earshot of your gibberish—" Falcon broke off as the door opened.

Unannounced, Gideon Rossiter and Horatio Glendenning came in. Lord Horatio, heir to the Earl of Bowers-Malden, was a well-built, pleasant-featured young man with a smile seldom far from his green eyes. It was far from them today, and Chandler took one look at his set expression, and his heart sank. He asked, "Would you be so kind, Owen?"

Furlong went to the side table and poured two glasses of cognac, which he carried to the new arrivals.

Rossiter and Glendenning pulled chairs closer and sat down wearily.

Chandler said, "I take it you were unable to see the King."

Lord Horatio Glendenning nodded his auburn head.

"Our audience was cancelled," he said. "No explanation given. My sire's influence will carry us only so far, I'm afraid."

Rossiter stretched out his long legs, and sighed. "We were blocked at every turn. Couldn't get near Horace Walpole, either. The best we could manage was to see Lord Anson, which—"

"Admiral Lord Anson?" Furlong said hopefully, "He's a jolly good man and with his naval background must have been impressed by our conclusions, eh, Tio?"

Glendenning gave a derogatory grunt, and took another mouthful of cognac.

"He'd been given a dossier on all of us," said Rossiter. "My father's questionable business dealings; Tio's suspected Jacobite associations; a charge of wrecking that was not entirely disproved by the Chandlers, plus their unfortunate association with Johnny Armitage's sister! Egad! We're a disreputable crew! I wonder we were not clapped up on the spot!"

"*Not—entirely—disproved?*" sputtered Chandler. "Had it not been for the efforts of this 'disreputable crew' that ship would be on the bottom today!"

Glendenning shrugged. "So we tried to tell him. Much good it did."

"I am not permitted Anson's acquaintance, but I think he is no fool," said Falcon. "Were you able to at least tell him of our suspicions?"

"We tried." Rossiter looked glum. "Between us, we jawed the old boy's ear off for half an hour."

"He just stared at us," said Glendenning. "Then, he asked if we realized how little proof we had of our allegations, and how reprehensible it is to suppose that fine gentlemen such as the Earl of Collington, Rudolph Bracksby, or General Underhill would be involved in some kind of treasonable plotting."

Falcon murmured, "I am striving not to say 'I told you so.' Did you see fit to mention dear Terrier Farrier's part in all this?"

"We mentioned it." Rossiter said with disgust, "Farrier is still held in high regard. Which is more than we are!"

"They've nothing 'gainst me. Or Furlong," said Morris. "Perhaps we should—"

"Oh, have they not!" Glendenning said, "Furlong is believed to have aided and abetted Kit Aynsworth when he helped his Jacobite brother-in-law get clear of the dragoons. And as for you, Jamie, you associate with the rest of us unsavoury individuals. Tarred with the same brush, old fellow."

"In which case I am the only one of unimpeachable reputation amongst you all," said Falcon, amused. "How droll. There is something to be said for neither aiding, abetting, nor crying friends with any man."

Morris said, "You don't have time. Too busy shooting people."

Rossiter interposed angrily, "Have done, for God's sake! This is no time for petty squabbles."

"What *is* it time for?" demanded Falcon, at once bristling. "We do little more than defend our own. We should carry the fight to the Squire and his merry band of bastards! At least," he added hastily, " 'tis what I would do, had I any real interest in the business."

Morris opened his mouth, caught Rossiter's eye, and shut it again.

Chandler said curtly, "Fish, or cut line, Falcon!"

Falcon's lips drooped disdainfully. "By all means, since you require my superior understanding."

Rossiter clapped a hand over Morris' mouth.

Affecting not to notice, Falcon went on, "We know that the League of Jewelled Men has six members, of whom the leader is called the Squire. We know that the Earl of Collington was—perhaps still is—a member; that Rudolph Bracksby is very probably a member; and this fellow Poinier is either a member of the League or one of their agents. We can say with a fair degree of certainty that both General Underhill and his man Farrier are in the plot. And—I think we may have come across another member."

They all sat straighter.

Glendenning said eagerly, "Jove! Have I missed something?"

"It has always seemed odd to me," drawled Falcon, "that I should have been inveigled into foisting Jonathan Armitage's sister onto the Chandlers."

"What the devil do you mean by that?" demanded Chandler, flushing angrily.

Morris argued, "*You* did nothing, August. *I* writ the letter. Not you."

"You writ it in my name." Falcon ignored Chandler, who had come to his feet and was glaring down at him. "At the instigation of a lady who has never been known to lift a finger for anyone, much less for a scandalous widow she scarce knows. Ross, will you control this maniac? I can't hit him with his arm in a sling!"

"Hold up, Gordie," said Rossiter, his voice sharp. "Falcon has a point. Mrs. Allington is a delight, but you must own her brother's supposed connection with wreckers."

Chandler scowled, but lowered himself cautiously to the sofa again. "Do you say it was a deliberate scheme to bring more suspicion down upon us?"

"Damme, if I hadn't forgot it!" interrupted Morris excitedly. "When Falcon spotted that block Poinier in Town, he was at Lady Buttershaw's house!"

Furlong's jaw dropped, then he put back his handsome head and gave a shout of laughter. "*Clara Buttershaw?* Oh, you jest! She's one of the most odious females I ever met, but— Come, you're not serious?"

Equally astonished, Glendenning said, "A *woman?* A member of that murderous league?"

Falcon said, "A woman may be just as murderous as any man. Consider Lucretia Borgia, or Delilah, or Lady Macbeth—"

" 'Off with his head!' " quoted Morris ghoulishly.

"That's *Richard III*, not *Macbeth*, you dolt," sneered Falcon. "Do you never get anything right?"

"I think *you* may have got something right," said Chandler. "Ruth told me that Lady Buttershaw raged at her when first they met in the park, but that she became quite pleasant when she discovered Ruth's identity."

"Do you know," said Morris with a thoughtful frown, "it struck me at the time that Lady Buttershaw made no least attempt to avoid Jacob—or Thorpe, whichever one it was— when the child ran into her. Might it have been a plot from the beginning, and the collision a means to scrape up an acquaintance?"

"If so, they weave their webs far in advance," muttered Chandler.

"Farther back than that incident, I think," said Rossiter. "Did you not say, Gordie, that your brother's dragon ring is what drew you to the lighthouse that night?"

"I thought it was his, yes. But as it turns out, it was too small. More the size for a lady's hand. In all the uproar of the storm, I failed to notice that fact, unfortunately."

"Dragon ring . . ." Falcon rubbed his quizzing glass on the bridge of his nose. "Wasn't there some business in the newspapers a month or so ago about a dragon ring?"

Rossiter said, "Exactly so. A ring of just such description was among the objects stolen during a robbery at Boudreaux House. A servant girl was murdered."

They all stared at him.

"Good Lord," exclaimed Chandler. "They don't draw the line at much, do they?"

"Nothing, I'd say," muttered Furlong. "And we still don't know what the curst varmints are about."

Rossiter said, "When you saw them over the wall at Larchwoods, Gordie, you said they seemed to be playing charades. Was it a military-type game?"

Chandler started to shake his head and thought better of

it. "More as if they were reciting, and being instructed on how to stand and gesture; as if they rehearsed a play perhaps."

After a silent moment, Glendenning said, "Could that be it? Might they plan a large entertainment to which many prominent gentlemen are invited, and then—another Guy Fawkes gunpowder plot?"

"If that is so," said Morris, "how does the shipping business come into it? And why do they gather up all these fine estates?"

Falcon stood and began to wander about. "Perhaps they wreck the ships to gain funds to finance their schemes. And the estates are used to store their stolen cargoes."

"But the estates aren't all near the coast," Rossiter pointed out. "Damme! I wish we might have questioned the Terrier! He knows the answers, I'll warrant!"

"He'd be a hard man to break," said Furlong. "And has not sufficient love for us to volunteer the information."

"*Love* for us?" Chandler gave a derisive snort. "His object appears to be punishment. Did I tell you he'd chalked up a message on the wall of the tower? *Châtiment deux!*"

The others exchanged grim looks.

Morris said, "Your personal *billet doux* from the Squire. Tio got the first chastisement. Well, if nothing else, we've frustrated their schemes for revenge."

"Thus far we have," qualified Rossiter. "Certainly, Gordie's message confirms the fact that the League was at work here. And that they wanted Lac Brillant."

"An arrogant lot," muttered Falcon. "One cannot but wonder who they've selected for *Châtiment trois.*"

Rossiter said bracingly, "Perchance *we* can administer the next *châtiment.* We learn a little more with each encounter. Now we can add Lady Buttershaw to our list. With luck, next time we shall carry the fight to *their* borders."

Morris sprang up and raised his glass. "To Lady Luck!"

They all stood and drank the toast with enthusiasm. Even the "disinterested" August Falcon.

Ruth entered the room very quietly. Gordon had put his head back against the sofa and appeared to be sleeping. She crept closer, scanning his face anxiously. Without opening his eyes, he reached out suddenly and caught her hand.

She said gently, "You are very naughty to have got up. You look properly worn out and must go back to bed before Doctor Keasden comes."

He smiled up at her, then an awed expression came into his eyes.

She wore the gown he had bought for her. The great skirts were a swirl of blue silk, the stomacher laced over the snowy bodice of the chemise and the full white sleeves frilled and embroidered with blue. Her hair was swept up and dressed in ringlets that shone pale gold. He thought her angelically lovely and thought also that he was glad August Falcon had never seen her like this. For a moment he could not command his voice, but his eyes were eloquent and Ruth blushed.

Recovering his wits, he tugged at her hand until she relented and sat beside him.

"So at last I am to be humoured, eh?"

She said demurely, "I cannot think what you mean, Mr. Gordon."

"You can, indeed. *That* is how you should wear your hair!"

The dimple peeped bewitchingly beside her mouth. " 'Tis quite out of the present style and must be cut, sir."

"The devil with the present style! I'll strangle any barber who dares take a pair of scissors to it!"

She put her hand over his lips. "Hush. You are supposed to be quiet and if you leap about so, you will wrench your shoulder."

He reclaimed her hand and with a great effort refrained

from kissing it. "I think," he said airily, "I've not seen that gown before. Have I?"

"You know very well you've not. 'Tis the one you gave me."

"Oh? Well, it looks—er, very nice. But will not help my concentration, I fear."

"Is that what you were doing? I thought you were asleep."

"No. Just trying to put it all together."

"Did you?"

"Not all. 'Tis the most foolish thing, I know, but I cannot quite seem to recall what happened when my father came to the tower. I think Nathaniel was with him—no?"

"Yes. And, oh Gordie, Mr. Aymer was wonderful! He became quite another person. Very brisk and authoritative, and worked like a Trojan, though he must certainly have realized he would have been arrested had the troopers come."

"I must thank him. Has he remained so assertive?"

"No. The next morning he was as quietly pious as ever. Still, I think he thoroughly enjoyed his moment of peril. And I admire him for it."

"Well do not be admiring him too much!"

She gave him an arch look. "Why?"

"You are in no state to be coy, madam. You have still to account for another fib. *Twin* nephews!"

Her smile rueful, she said, "And almost I lost one. Jacob told us how you threw yourself in front of him! My dear . . ."—she stroked the hair back from his forehead—"you saved his life."

"A fine reward I got!" He again recaptured her hand. "When I saw Thorpe hop up behind that pile of logs—gad! I wonder I did not suffer a seizure!"

"I can only thank God you were not killed!"

Through a silent moment two pairs of eyes met and said a great deal. Chandler pressed her hand to his lips, then asked, "What of your faithful Grace? Will she wed Tummet, do you suppose?"

Ruth hesitated. "Not in the immediate future, I think. She is the most dreadful flirt, Gordie. But—bless her heart, is such a dear soul, and so joyful now that I've forgiven her for—for trying to save me from being thrown into Newgate."

"Hmn. For the moment I will not comment upon your marked tendency to—er, illegal pursuits, although I'm sure you know you must pay the price." Briefly, his eyes twinkled at her, then he went on blandly, "How has my father reacted to the fact that you've insinuated two brats into his household?"

She said gratefully, "Oh, 'tis beyond words wonderful to see him! He looks younger, and so happy, and told me only this morning that 'twas as if the years had rolled back and he had his two sons about him again!"

"Just as I thought," he said indignantly. "Now they'll steal all his affection away, and he will likely disown Quentin and me in favour of those two rapscallions! How do you propose to rectify the matter, madam?"

Moving carefully, so as not to jog the injured shoulder, she kissed him. It was not the gentle caress she intended, for his good arm whipped about her, and she was breathless when he allowed her to draw back. "What—what would you think I should do?" she asked hopefully.

"Another of those would do. Just to be going along with."

She gave him a prim look. "You were not, sir, referring to kisses."

"Indeed? Then to what did I refer, most saucy widow?"

She lowered her eyes, but pressed his hand to her suddenly hot cheek. "You know very well."

"Do I?" He tried to pull her to him, only to gasp and lie back.

"There! Your wicked advances have made you hurt yourself!" She leaned to him anxiously, whereupon of course, she was seized and kissed again.

"I suppose," he sighed, drowsily content and with his arm

still around her, "you thought my plans had to do with winning my sire's esteem by providing him with a grandchild."

She stroked his pale cheek lovingly. "Is that what you mean to do?"

"Don't see how I can. I've no wife."

"You might . . . find one."

He yawned, his eyelids drooping. "Not likely. Nadia . . . threw me over, y'know."

Frowning, Ruth drew back one of his eyelids and fixed him with a stern look. "Gordon . . . Chandler!"

He blinked at her. "Yes, ma'am?"

"Never look so innocent. You're not *that* tired!"

"But I am, m'dear. Much too worn and wan to endure this merciless interrogation."

"Beast! What *are* your plans?"

His slow smile dawned, and the adoration in his eyes took her breath away. Then he drew her closer and dropped a kiss on her temple.

After a blissful moment, she ventured, "Gordon . . . ?"

He chuckled, and murmured happily, "Ask me no questions . . ."